RUTABAGA
THE ADVENTURE CHEF

2

Feasts of Fury

ERIC COLOSSAL

AMULET BOOKS
NEW YORK

Cataloging-in-Publication Data has been applied for and may be obtained from the Library of Congress.

Library of Congress Control Number: 2015949580

Hardcover ISBN: 978-1-4197-1658-4
Paperback ISBN: 978-1-4197-1659-1

Text and illustrations copyright © 2016 Eric Colossal
Additional coloring by David McGuire

Printed and bound in China
10 9 8 7 6 5 4 3

Amulet Books are available at special discounts when purchased in quantity for premiums and promotions as well as fundraising or educational use. Special editions can also be created to specification. For details, contact specialsales@abramsbooks.com or the address below.

ABRAMS The Art of Books
195 Broadway, New York, NY 10007
abramsbooks.com

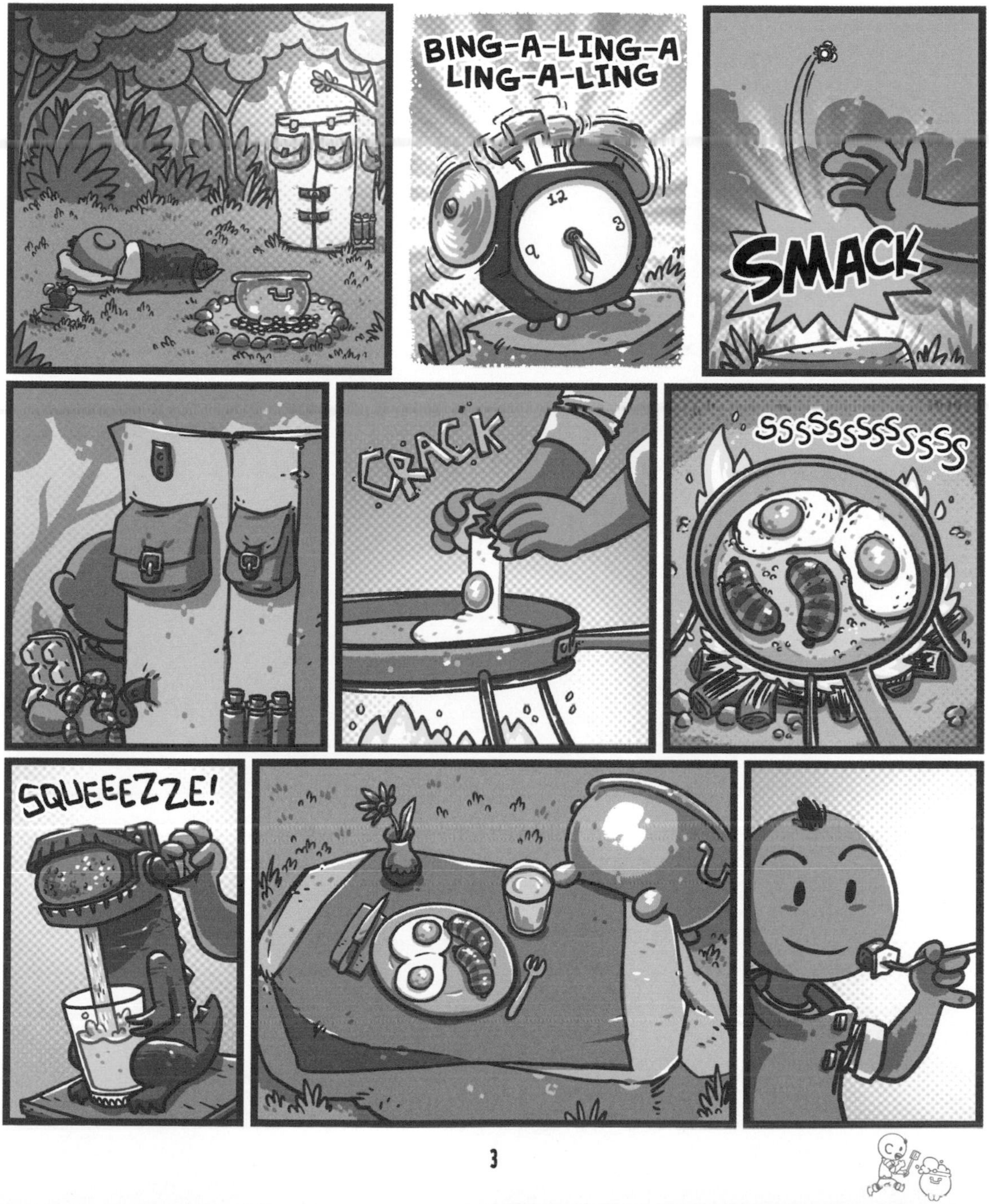
BING-A-LING-A
LING-A-LING
SMACK
CRACK
SSSSSSSSSSSSSS
SQUEEEZZE!

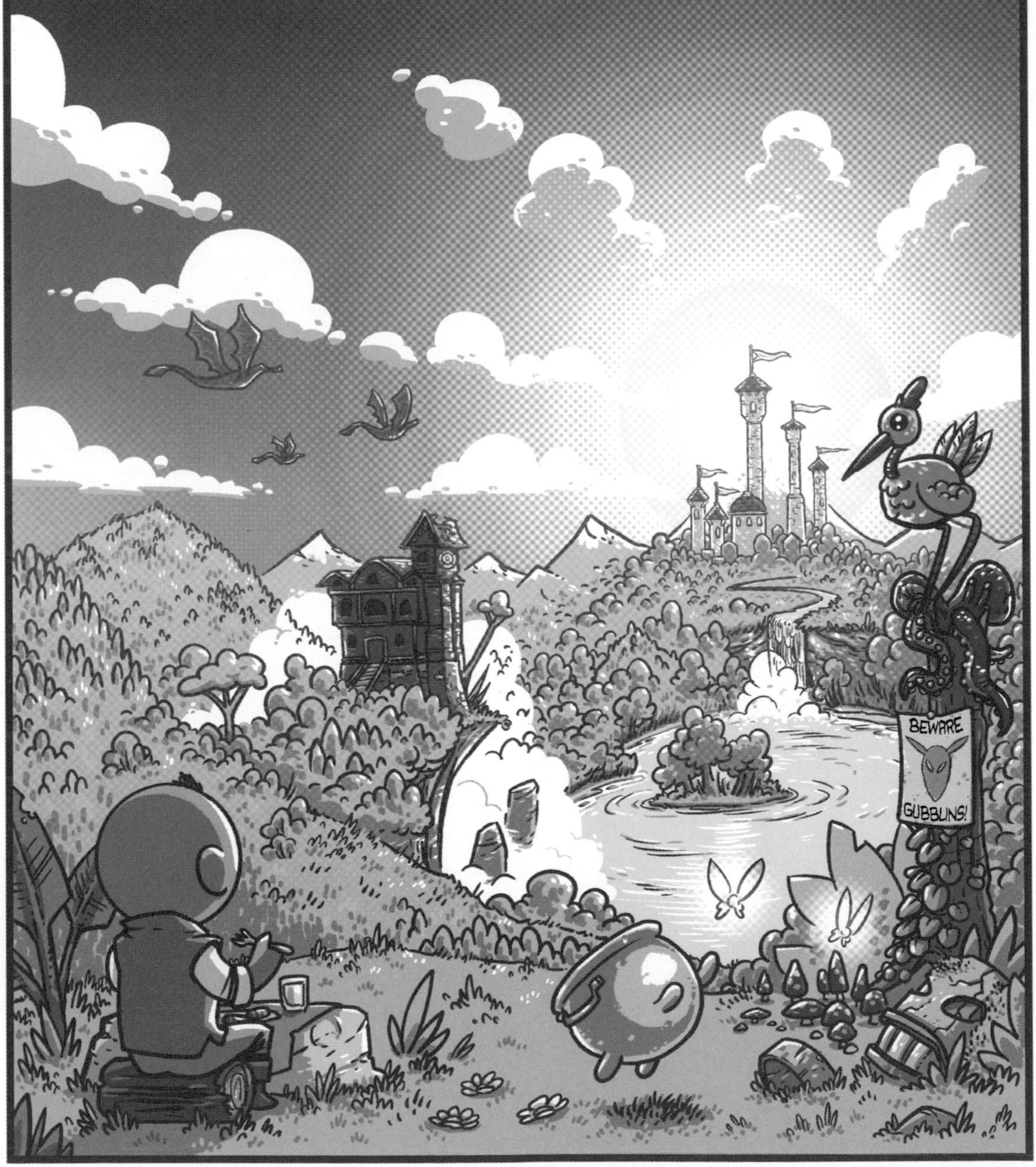

BEWARE
GUBBLINS!

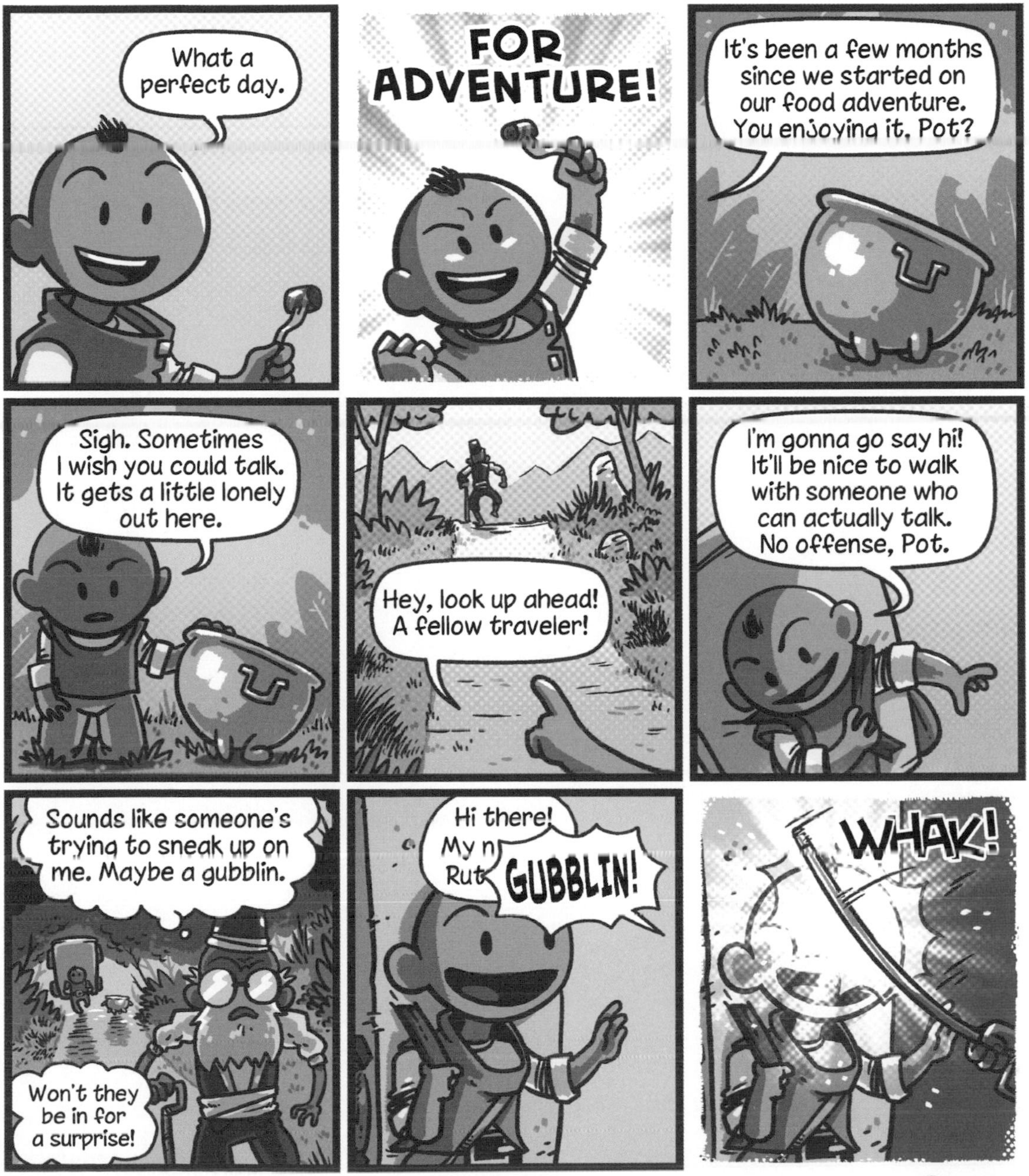
What a perfect day.
FOR ADVENTURE!
It's been a few months since we started on our food adventure. You enjoying it, Pot?
Sigh. Sometimes I wish you could talk. It gets a little lonely out here.
Hey, look up ahead! A fellow traveler!
I'm gonna go say hi! It'll be nice to walk with someone who can actually talk. No offense, Pot.
Sounds like someone's trying to sneak up on me. Maybe a gubblin.
Won't they be in for a surprise!
Hi there! My n Rut
GUBBLIN!
WHAK!

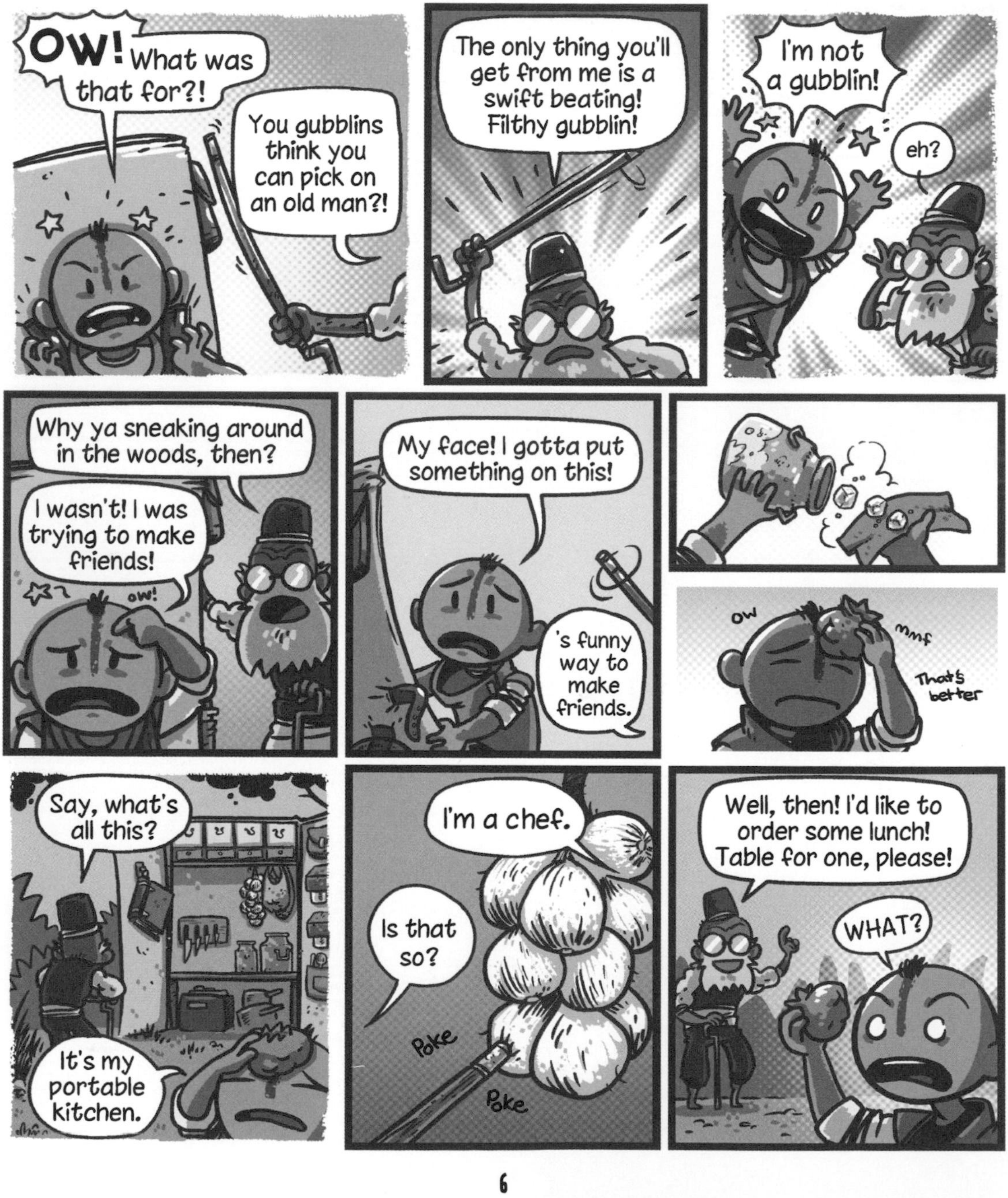
OW! What was that for?!
You gubblins think you can pick on an old man?!
The only thing you'll get from me is a swift beating! Filthy gubblin!
I'm not a gubblin!
eh?
Why ya sneaking around in the woods, then?
I wasn't! I was trying to make friends!
ow!
My face! I gotta put something on this!
's funny way to make friends.
OW
mmf
That's better
Say, what's all this?
It's my portable kitchen.
I'm a chef.
Is that so?
Poke
Poke
Well, then! I'd like to order some lunch! Table for one, please!
WHAT?

Not like that! I'm an Adventure Chef! I travel around looking for new ingredients to cook with.

As an apology for startling you, I'll gladly make you some lunch.

What do you say?

Golly, that'd be great, sonny!

Let's Get COOKING!

Whoa! Calm down there!

SLICE!

1. Cut a nice crusty roll in half.

2. Add lettuce and rolls of lunch meat.

3. Cut cheese into triangles and place on roll. Add a tomato.

4. Spear 2 olives and crinkle-cut carrots with toothpicks.

You have made a . . .

SANDWICH MONSTER

RAR!

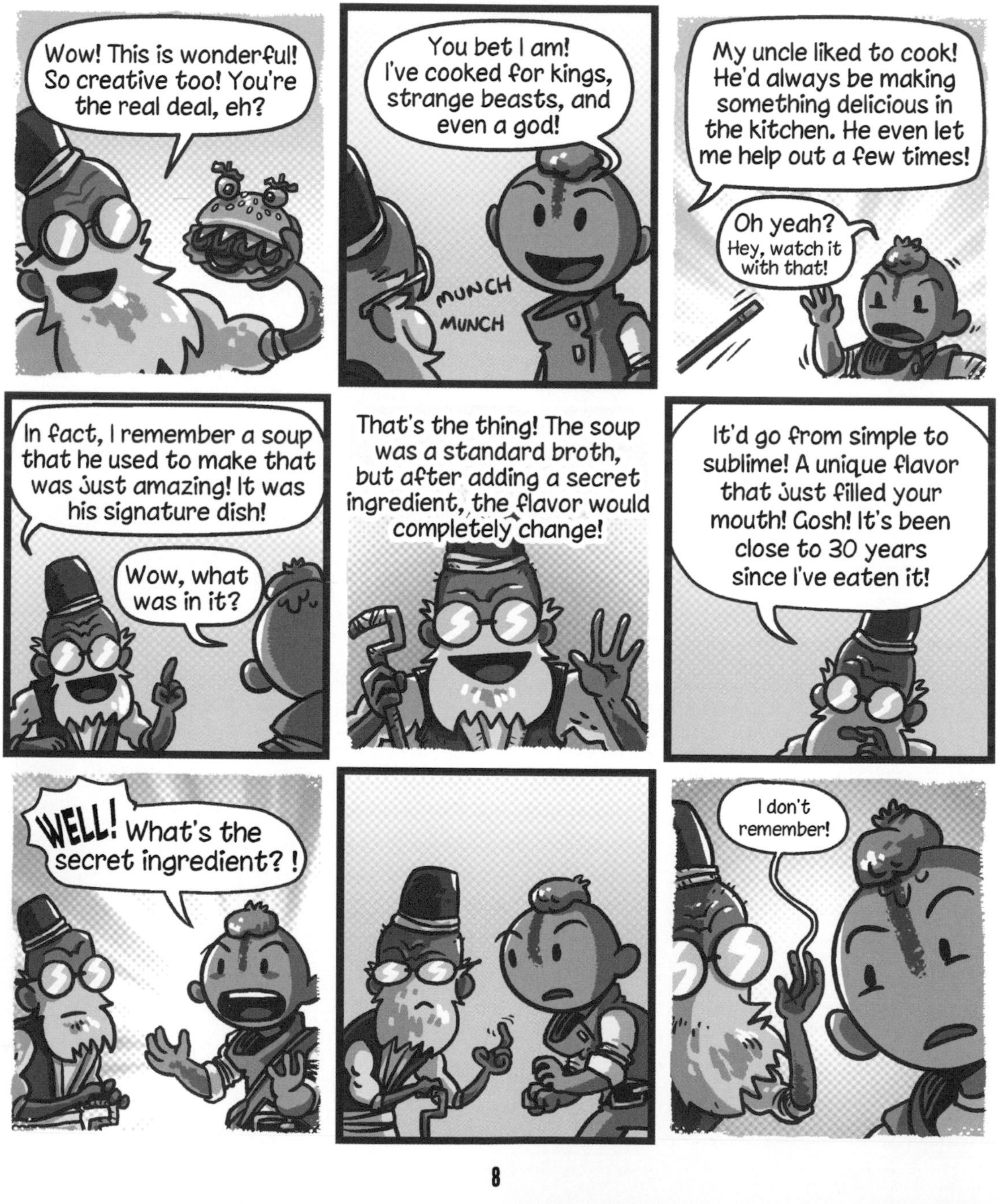
Wow! This is wonderful! So creative too! You're the real deal, eh?
You bet I am! I've cooked for kings, strange beasts, and even a god!
MUNCH MUNCH
My uncle liked to cook! He'd always be making something delicious in the kitchen. He even let me help out a few times!
Oh yeah? Hey, watch it with that!
In fact, I remember a soup that he used to make that was just amazing! It was his signature dish!
Wow, what was in it?
That's the thing! The soup was a standard broth, but after adding a secret ingredient, the flavor would completely change!
It'd go from simple to sublime! A unique flavor that just filled your mouth! Gosh! It's been close to 30 years since I've eaten it!
WELL! What's the secret ingredient?!
I don't remember!

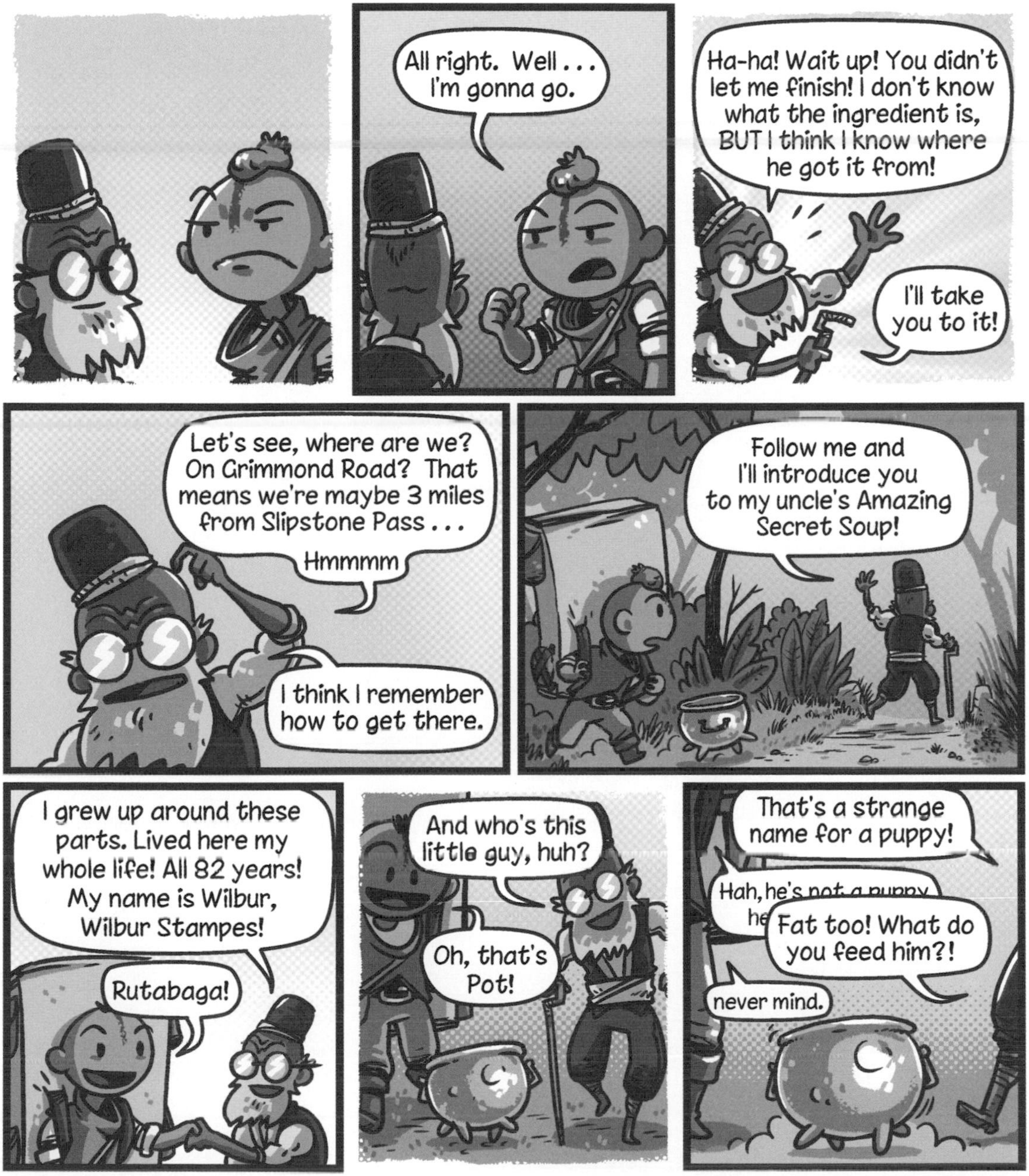
All right. Well . . . I'm gonna go.
Ha-ha! Wait up! You didn't let me finish! I don't know what the ingredient is, BUT I think I know where he got it from!
I'll take you to it!
Let's see, where are we? On Grimmond Road? That means we're maybe 3 miles from Slipstone Pass . . .
Hmmmm
I think I remember how to get there.
Follow me and I'll introduce you to my uncle's Amazing Secret Soup!
I grew up around these parts. Lived here my whole life! All 82 years! My name is Wilbur, Wilbur Stampes!
Rutabaga!
And who's this little guy, huh?
Oh, that's Pot!
That's a strange name for a puppy!
Hah, he's
Fat too! What do you feed him?!
never mind.

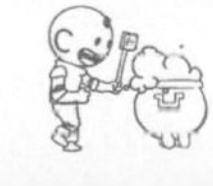

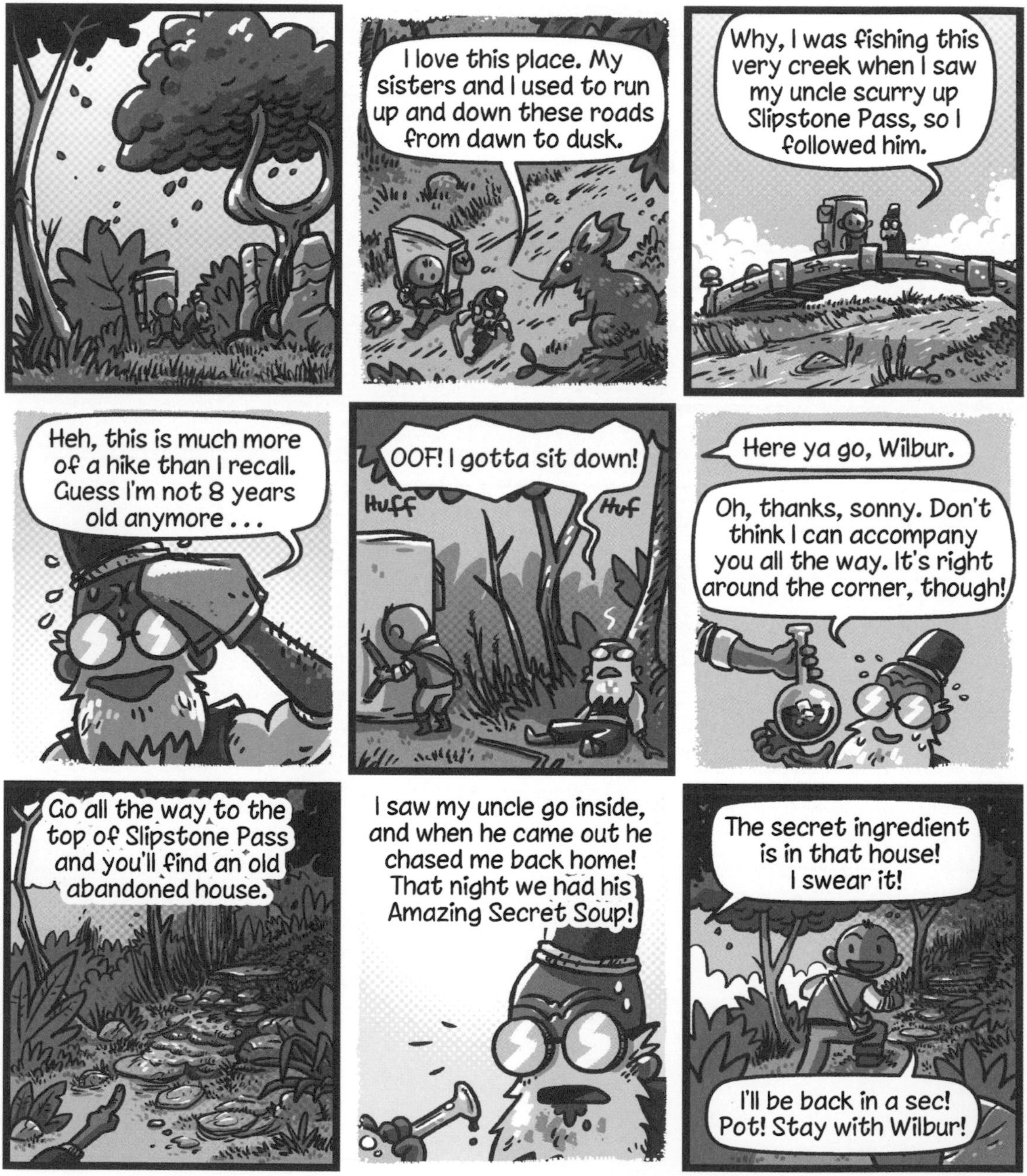
I love this place. My sisters and I used to run up and down these roads from dawn to dusk.
Why, I was fishing this very creek when I saw my uncle scurry up Slipstone Pass, so I followed him.
Heh, this is much more of a hike than I recall. Guess I'm not 8 years old anymore . . .
OOF! I gotta sit down!
Huff
Huf
Here ya go, Wilbur.
Oh, thanks, sonny. Don't think I can accompany you all the way. It's right around the corner, though!
Go all the way to the top of Slipstone Pass and you'll find an old abandoned house.
I saw my uncle go inside, and when he came out he chased me back home! That night we had his Amazing Secret Soup!
The secret ingredient is in that house! I swear it!
I'll be back in a sec! Pot! Stay with Wilbur!

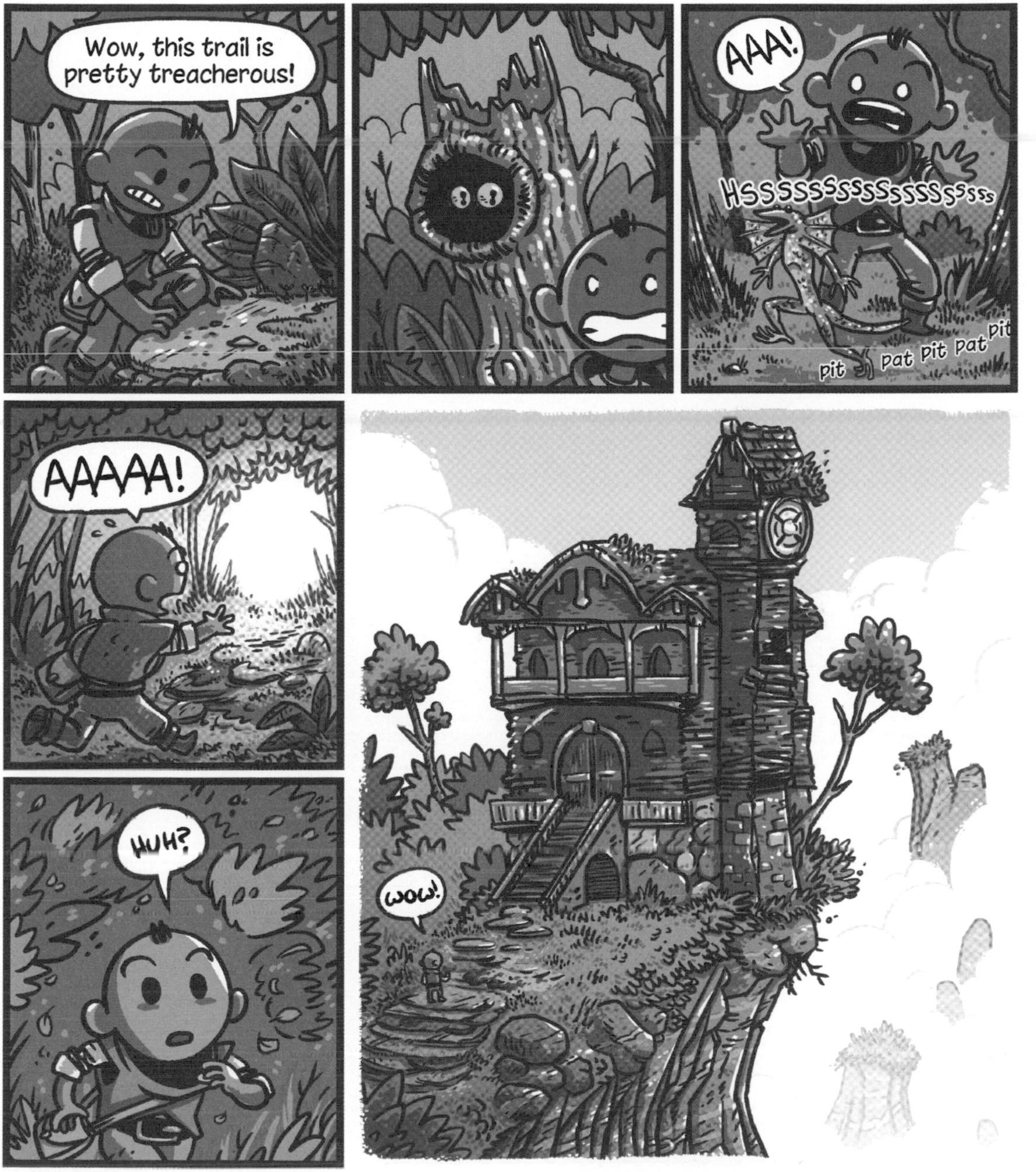
Wow, this trail is pretty treacherous!
AAA!
HSSSSSSSSSSSSSSSSSSss
pit pat pit pat pit
AAAAA!
HUH?
WOW!

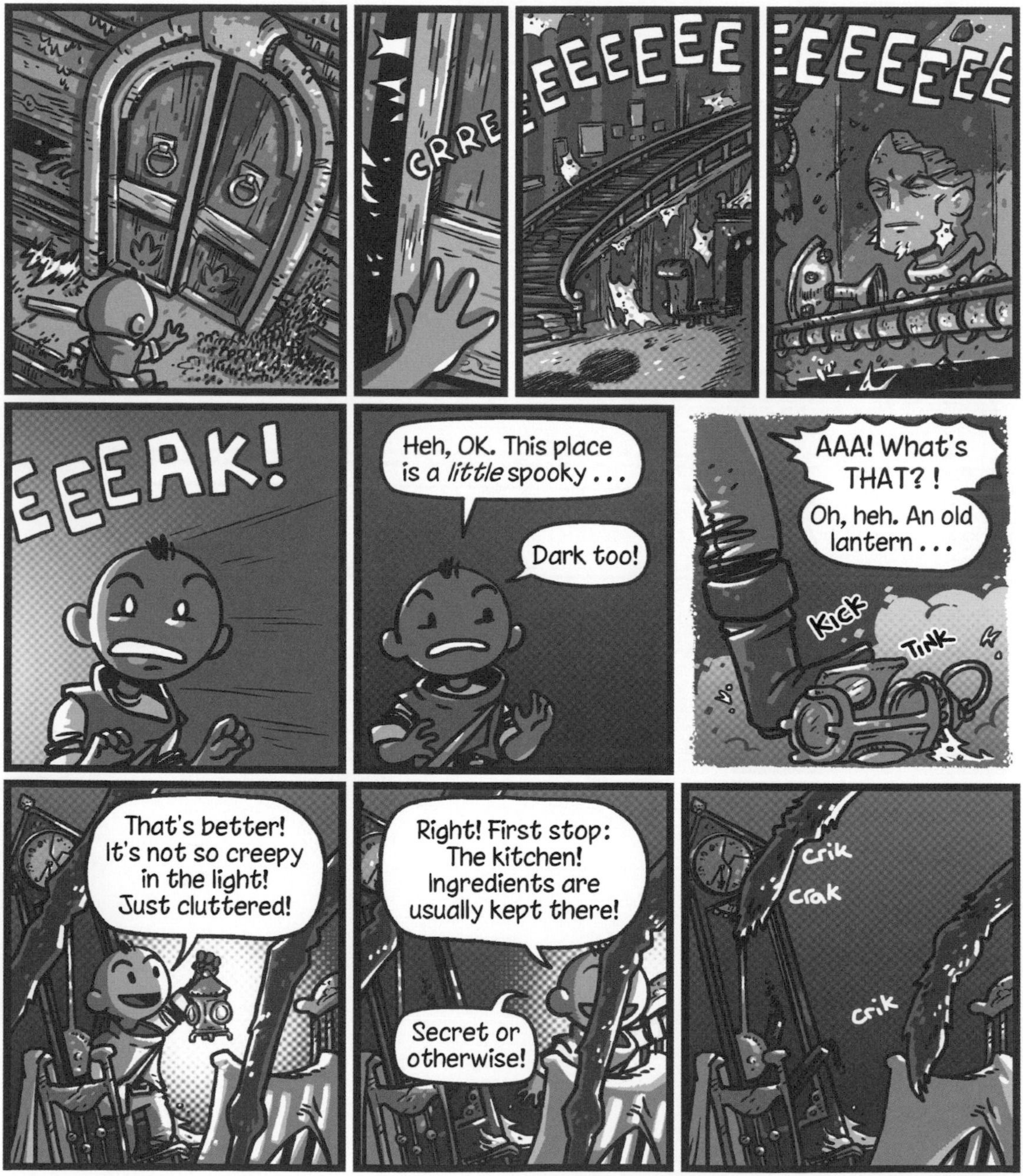
CRRE
EEEEEEE
EEEEEEE
EEEAK!
Heh, OK. This place is a *little* spooky . . .
Dark too!
AAA! What's THAT? !
Oh, heh. An old lantern . . .
KICK
TINK
That's better! It's not so creepy in the light! Just cluttered!
Right! First stop: The kitchen! Ingredients are usually kept there!
Secret or otherwise!
crik
crak
crik

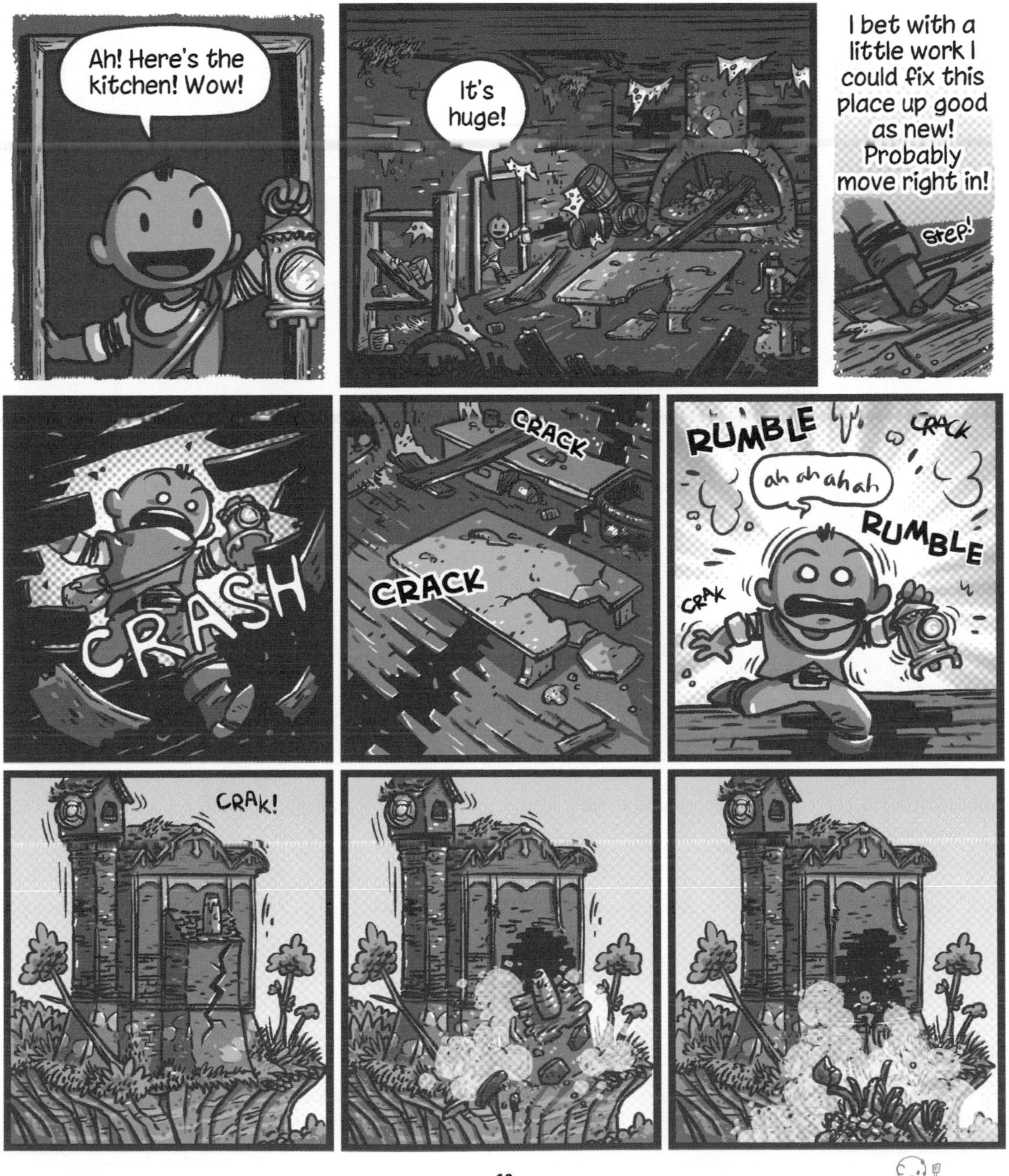
Ah! Here's the kitchen! Wow!
It's huge!
I bet with a little work I could fix this place up good as new! Probably move right in!
STEP!
CRASH
CRACK
CRACK
RUMBLE
CRACK
ah ah ah ah
RUMBLE
CRAK
CRAK!

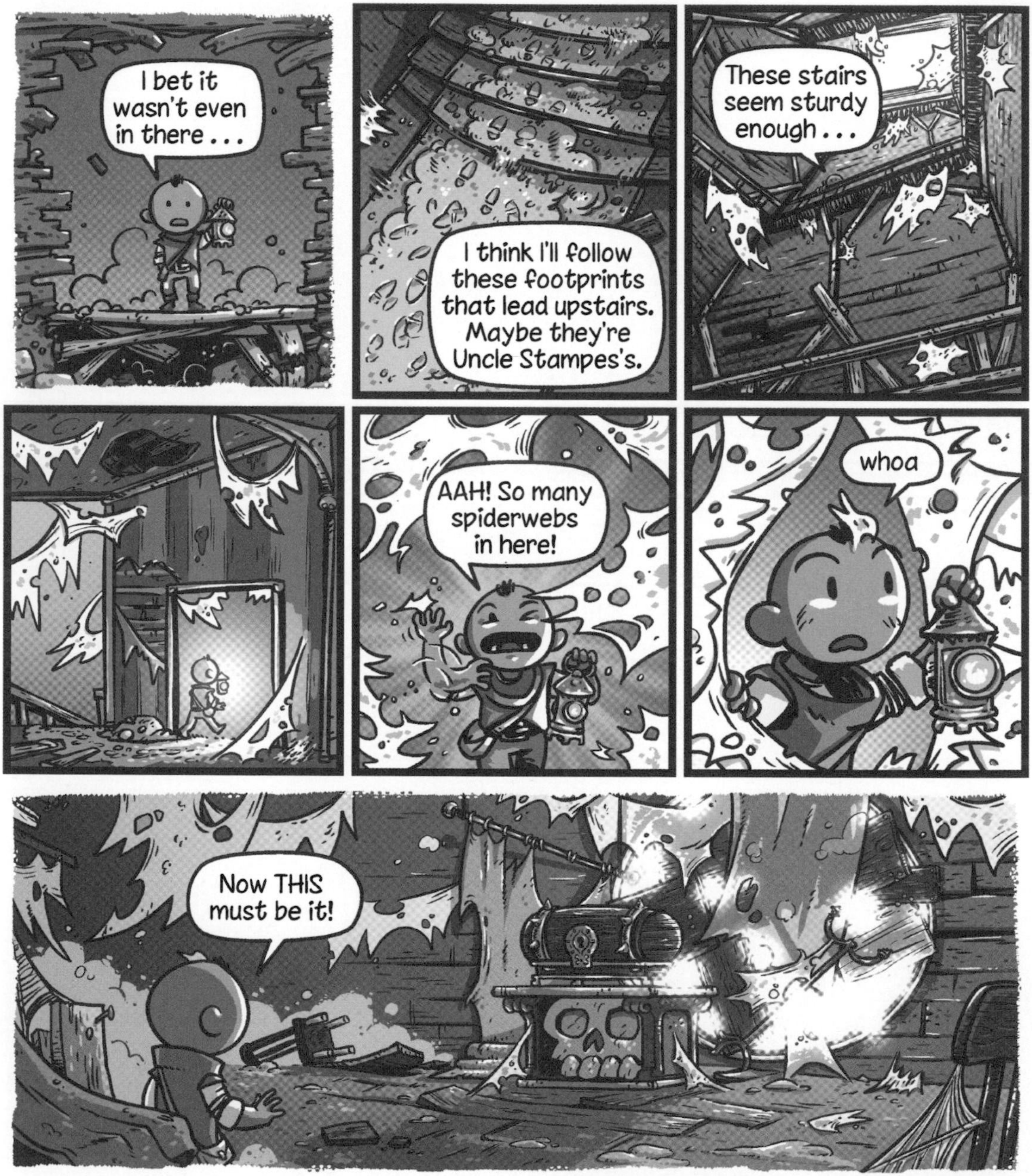
I bet it wasn't even in there . . .
I think I'll follow these footprints that lead upstairs. Maybe they're Uncle Stampes's.
These stairs seem sturdy enough . . .
AAH! So many spiderwebs in here!
whoa
Now THIS must be it!

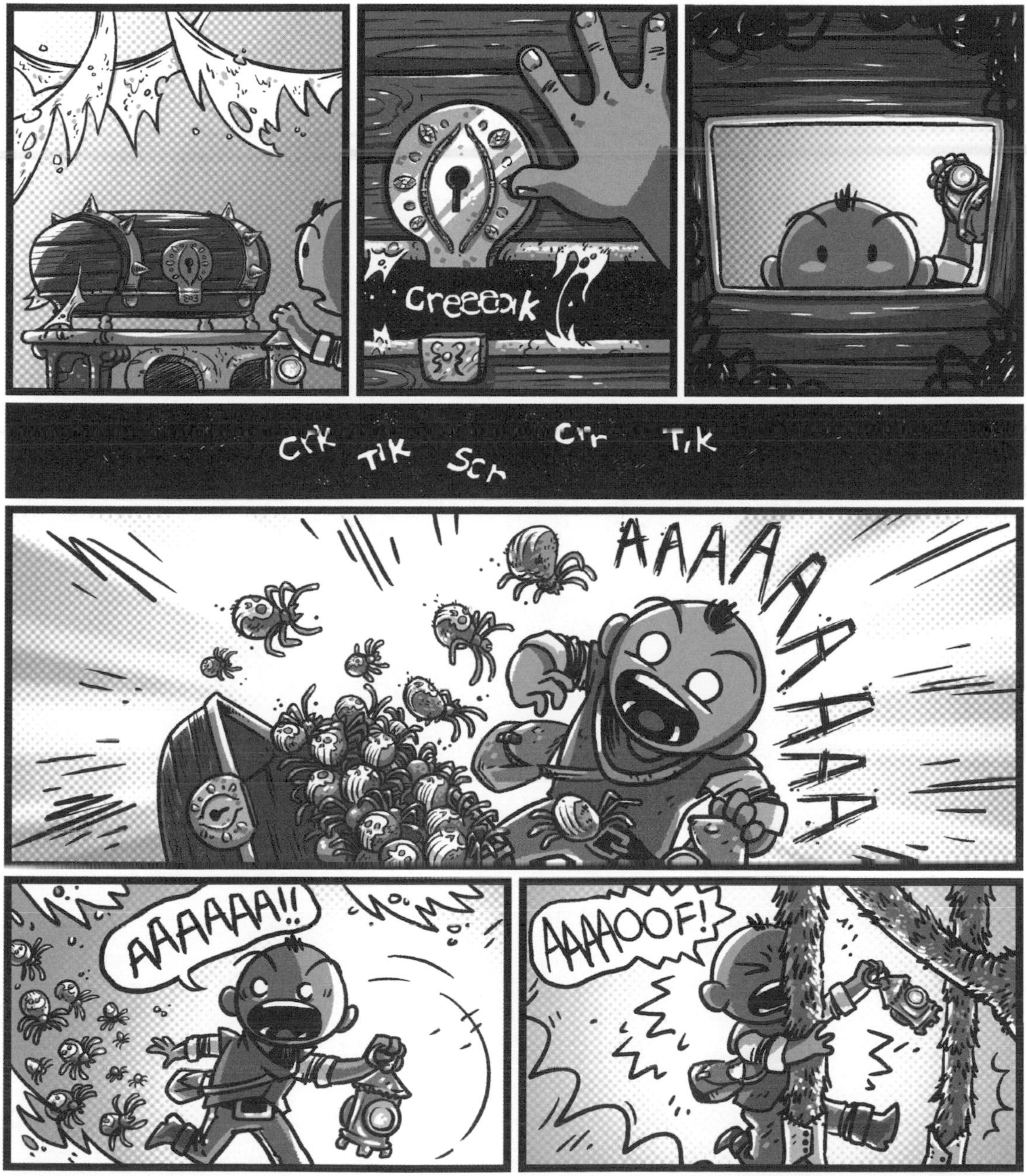
Creeeak
Crk
Tik
Scr
Crr
Tik
AAAAAAAAAA
AAAAAA!!
AAAAOOF!

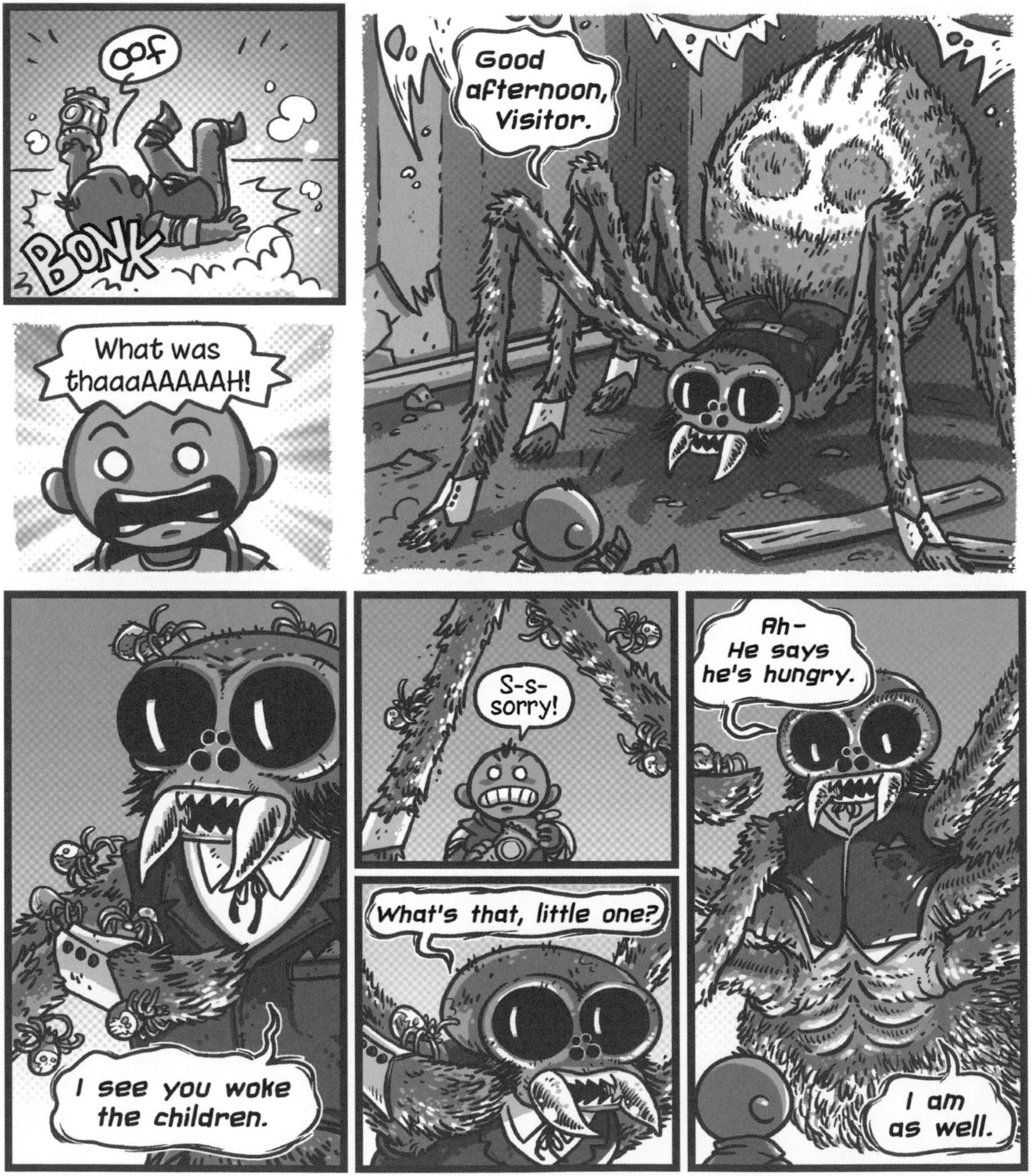
OOF
BONK
What was thaaaAAAAAH!
Good afternoon, Visitor.
I see you woke the children.
S-s-sorry!
What's that, little one?
Ah- He says he's hungry.
I am as well.

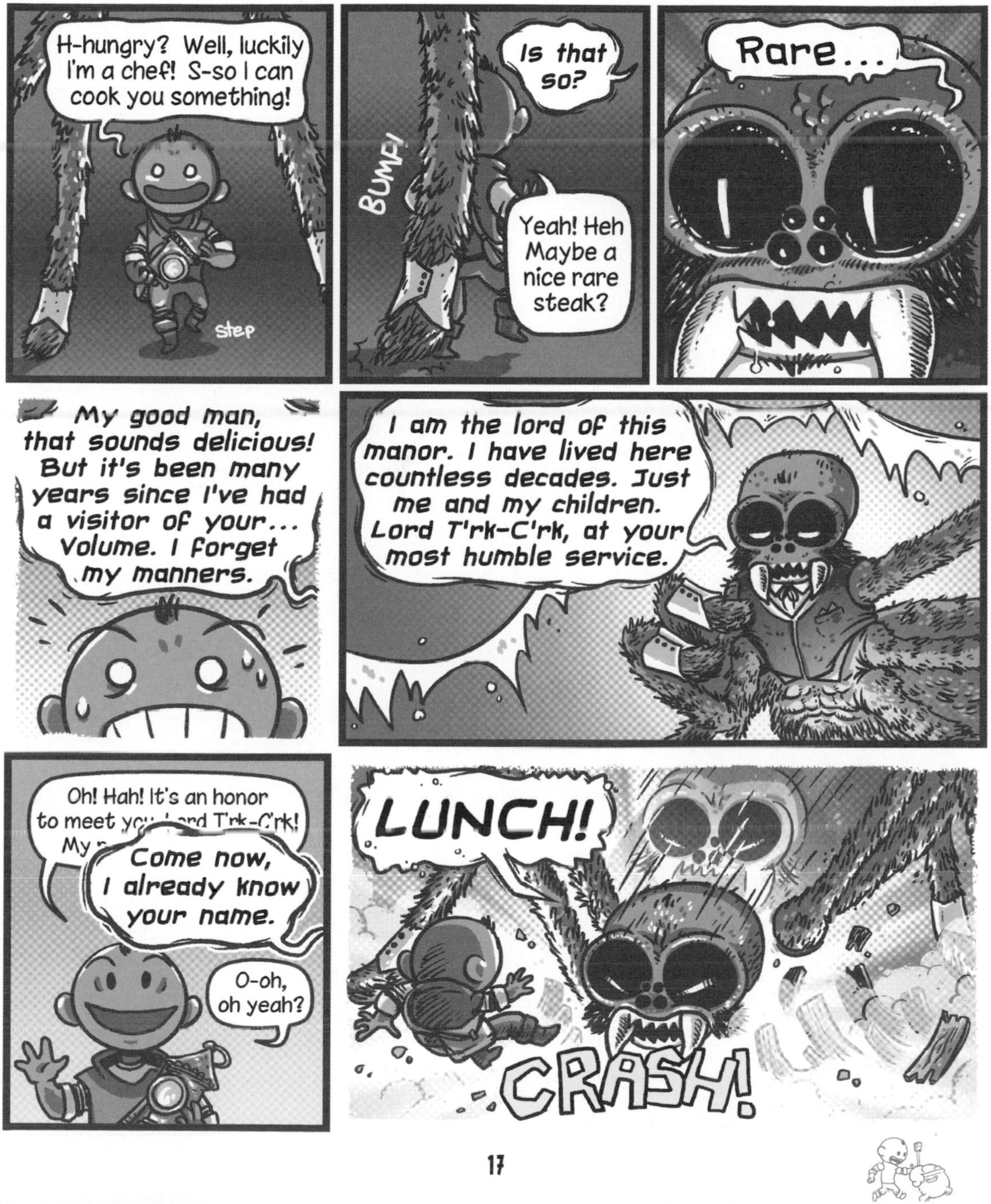

H-hungry? Well, luckily I'm a chef! S-so I can cook you something!
step
Is that so?
BUMF!
Yeah! Heh Maybe a nice rare steak?
Rare...
My good man, that sounds delicious! But it's been many years since I've had a visitor of your... Volume. I forget my manners.
I am the lord of this manor. I have lived here countless decades. Just me and my children. Lord T'rk-C'rk, at your most humble service.
Oh! Hah! It's an honor to meet yo T'rk-C'rk! My
Come now, I already know your name.
O-oh, oh yeah?
LUNCH!
CRASH!

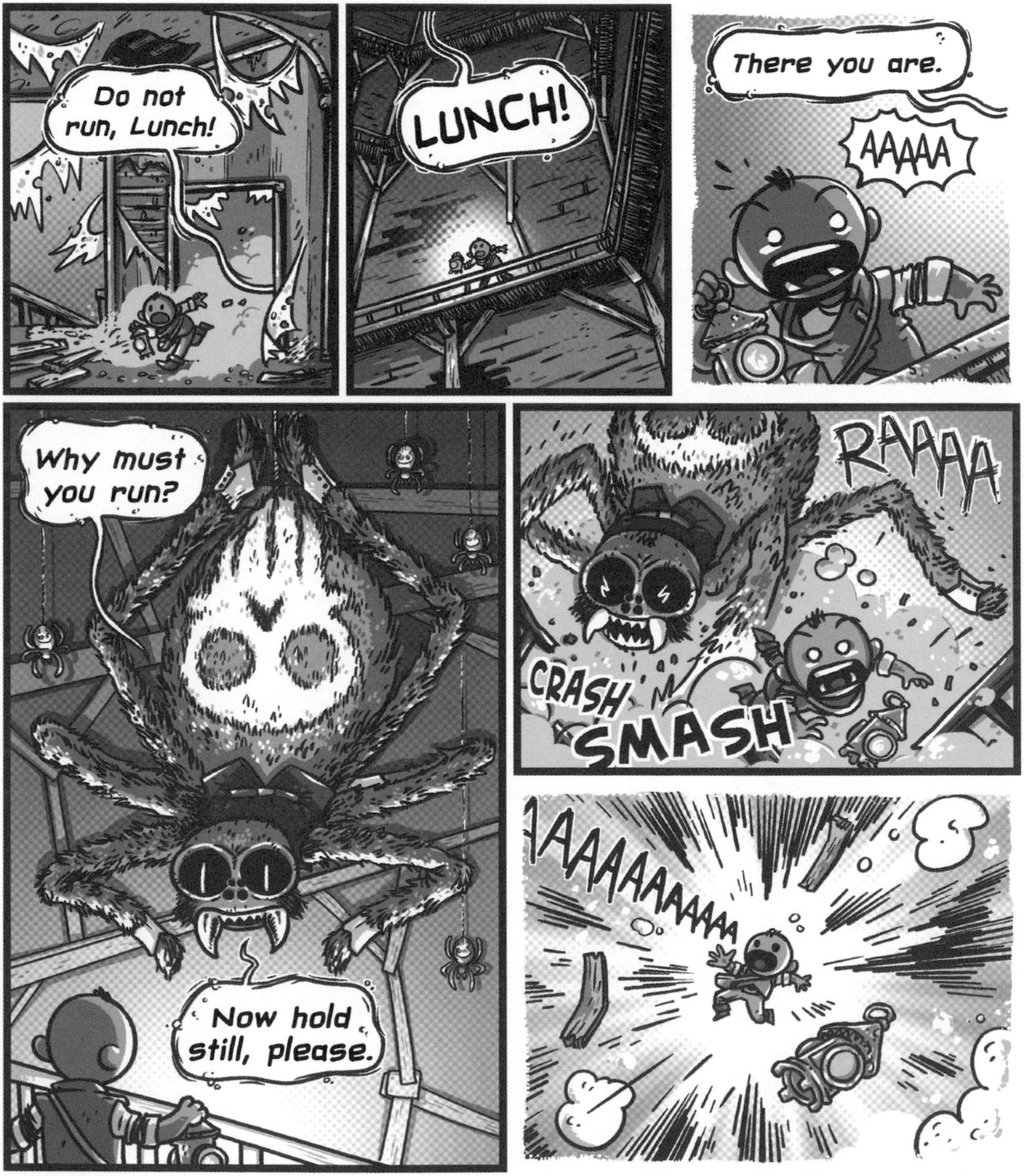
Do not run, Lunch!
LUNCH!
There you are.
AAAAA
Why must you run?
Now hold still, please.
RAAAA
CRASH
SMASH
AAAAAAAAAAAA

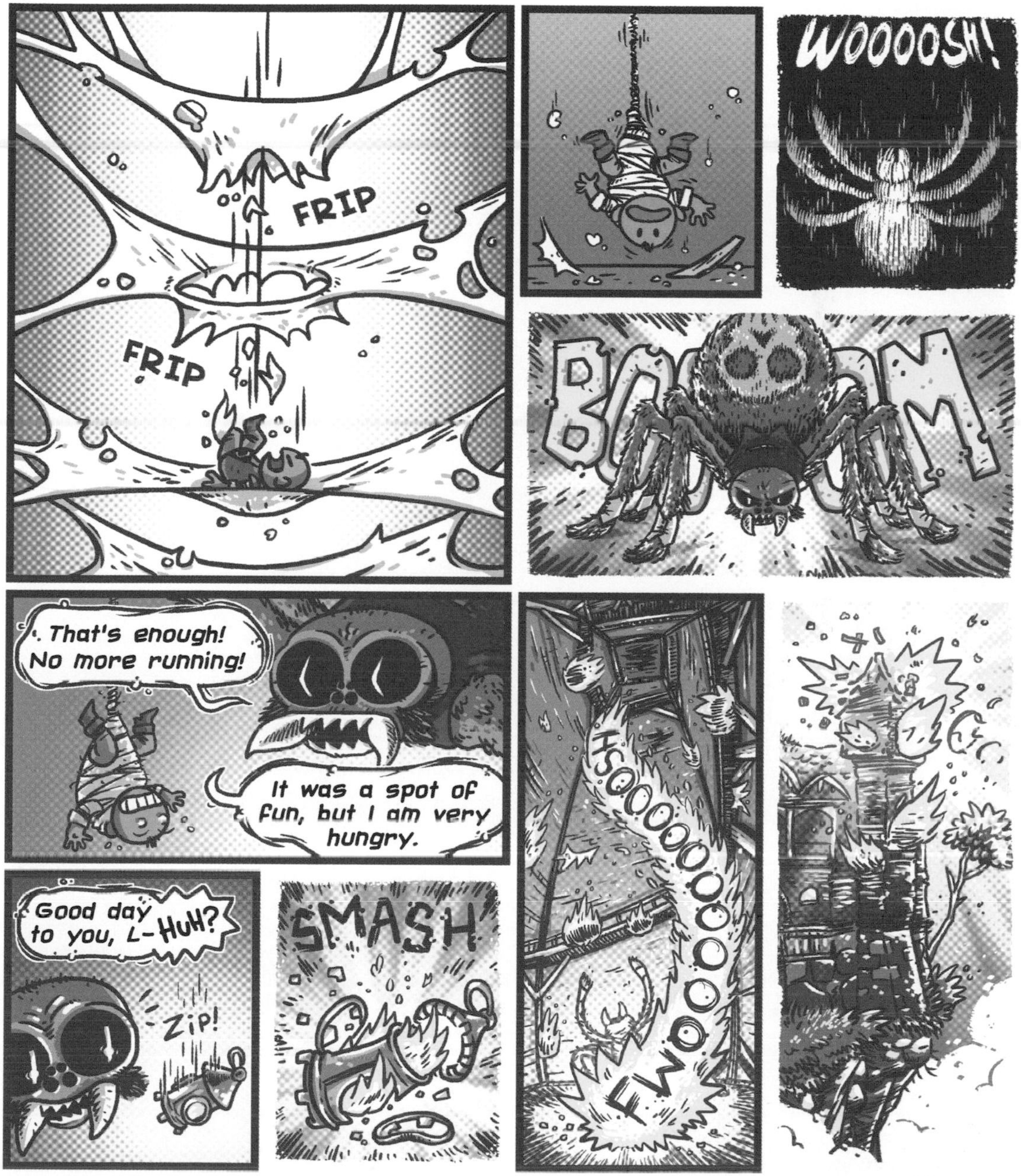
FRIP
FRIP
WOOOOSH!
BOOOOM
That's enough! No more running!
It was a spot of fun, but I am very hungry.
Good day to you, L-HUH?
ZIP!
SMASH
FWOOOOOOOOSH

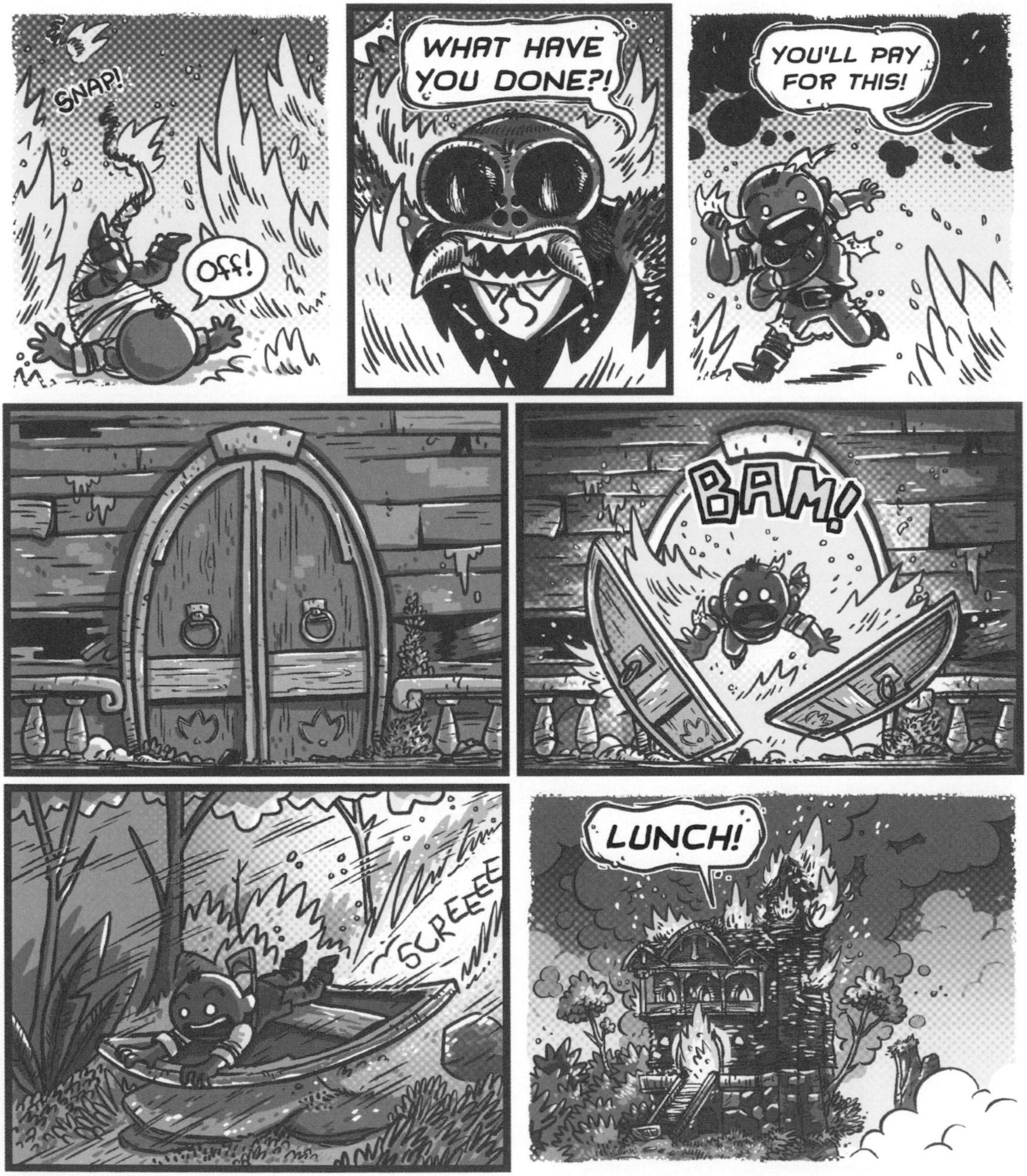
SNAP!
Off!
WHAT HAVE YOU DONE?!
YOU'LL PAY FOR THIS!
BAM!
SCREEEE
LUNCH!

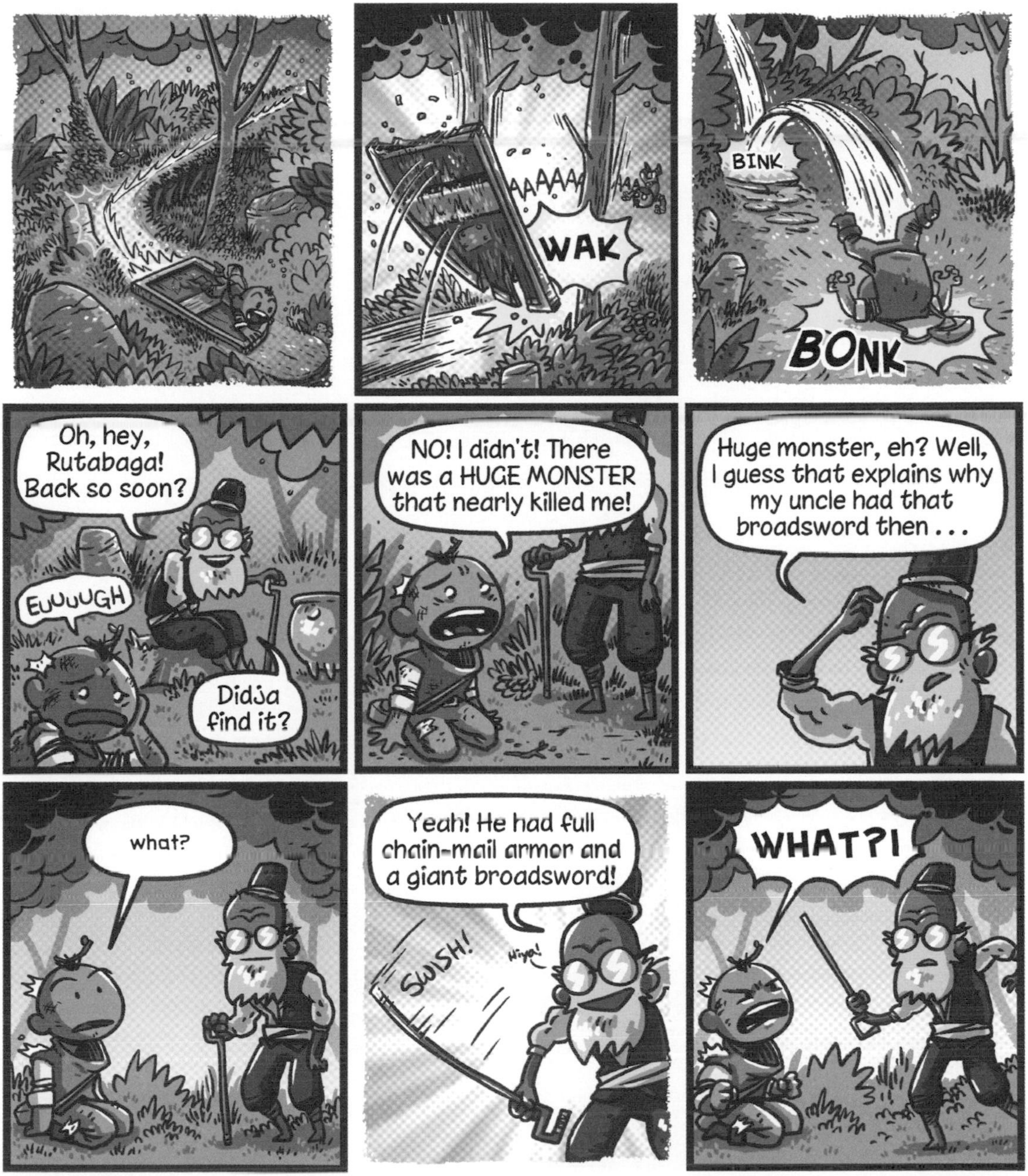

AAAAAAA
WAK
BINK
BONK
Oh, hey, Rutabaga! Back so soon?
EUUUUGH
Didja find it?
NO! I didn't! There was a HUGE MONSTER that nearly killed me!
Huge monster, eh? Well, I guess that explains why my uncle had that broadsword then . . .
what?
Yeah! He had full chain-mail armor and a giant broadsword!
SWISH!
Hiya!
WHAT?!

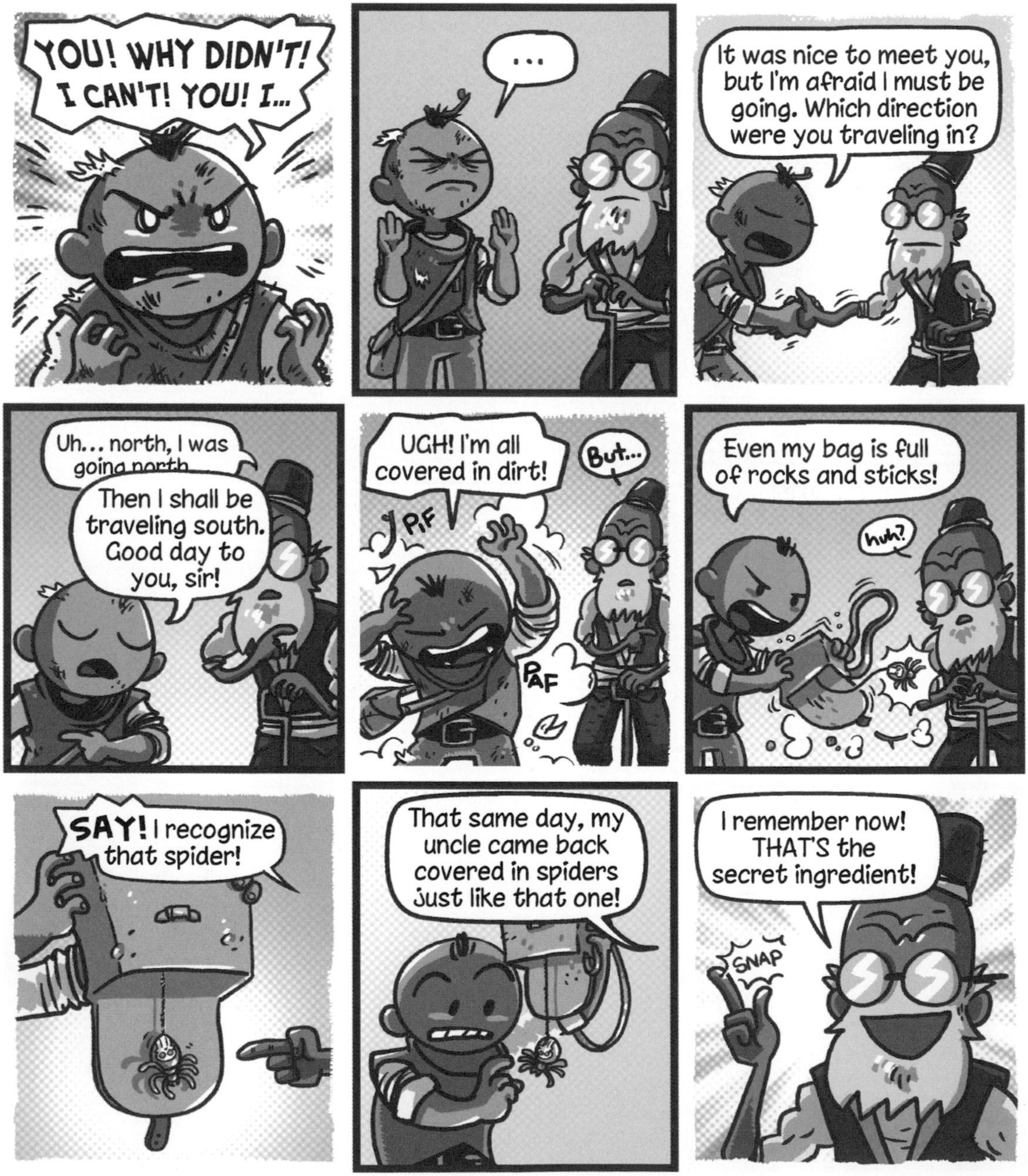
YOU! WHY DIDN'T! I CAN'T! YOU! I...
...
It was nice to meet you, but I'm afraid I must be going. Which direction were you traveling in?
Uh... north, I was going north...
Then I shall be traveling south. Good day to you, sir!
UGH! I'm all covered in dirt!
But...
PIF
PAF
Even my bag is full of rocks and sticks!
huh?
SAY! I recognize that spider!
That same day, my uncle came back covered in spiders just like that one!
I remember now! THAT'S the secret ingredient!
SNAP

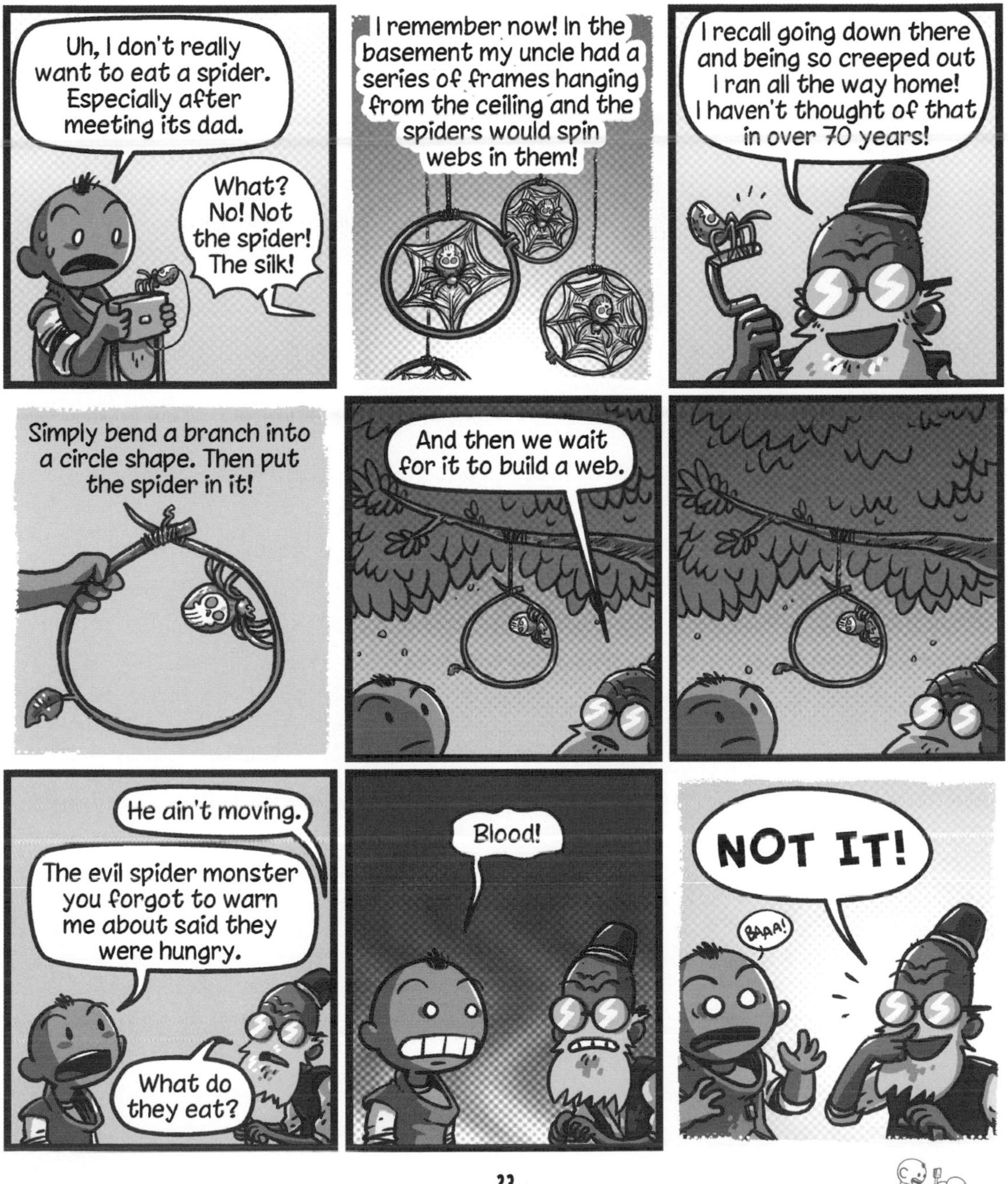
Uh, I don't really want to eat a spider. Especially after meeting its dad.
What? No! Not the spider! The silk!
I remember now! In the basement my uncle had a series of frames hanging from the ceiling and the spiders would spin webs in them!
I recall going down there and being so creeped out I ran all the way home! I haven't thought of that in over 70 years!
Simply bend a branch into a circle shape. Then put the spider in it!
And then we wait for it to build a web.
He ain't moving.
The evil spider monster you forgot to warn me about said they were hungry.
What do they eat?
Blood!
NOT IT!
BAAA!

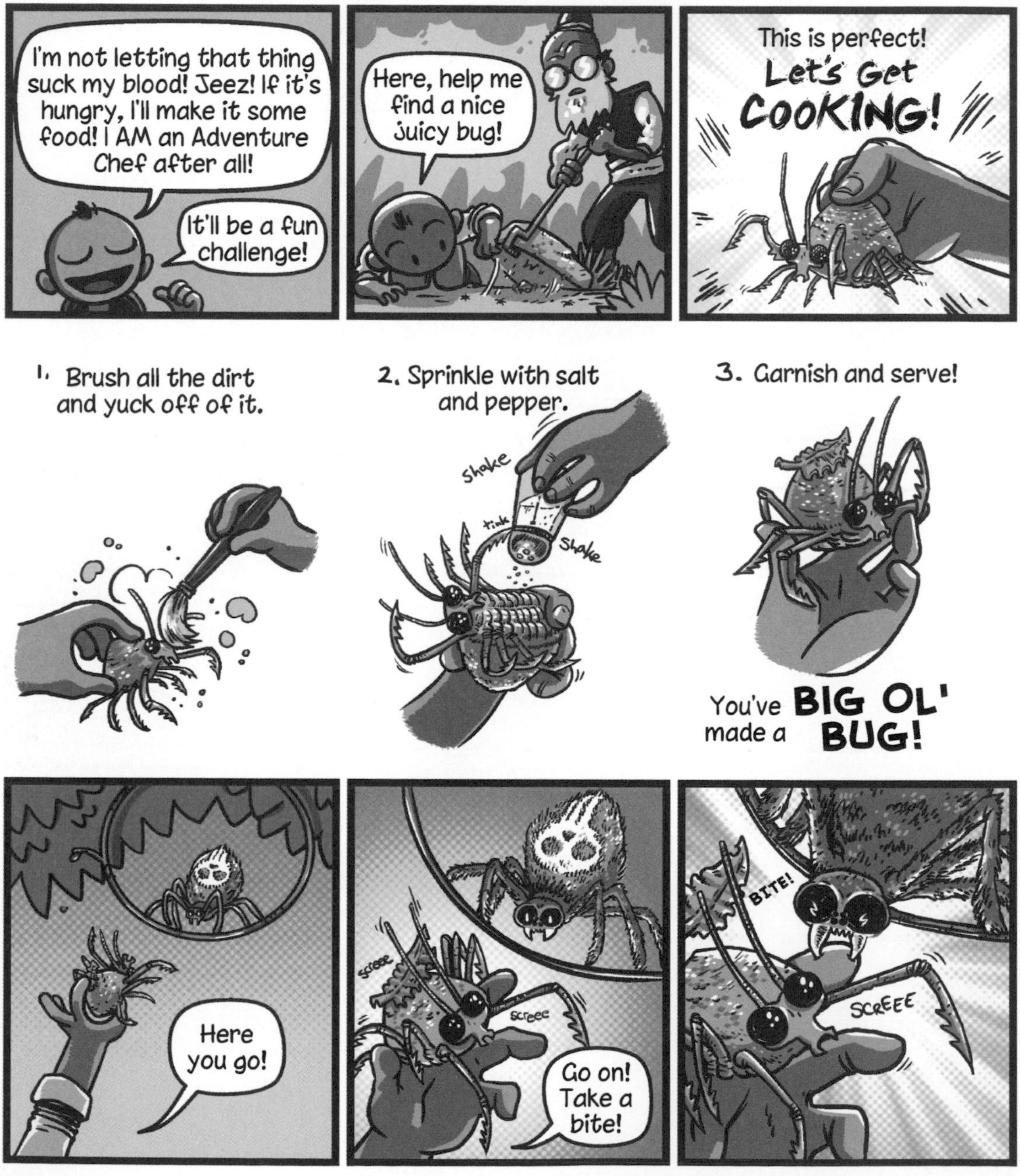
I'm not letting that thing suck my blood! Jeez! If it's hungry, I'll make it some food! I AM an Adventure Chef after all!
It'll be a fun challenge!
Here, help me find a nice juicy bug!
This is perfect!
Let's Get COOKING!
1. Brush all the dirt and yuck off of it.
2. Sprinkle with salt and pepper.
Shake
tink
Shake
3. Garnish and serve!
You've made a BIG OL' BUG!
Here you go!
Go on! Take a bite!
BITE!
SCREEE

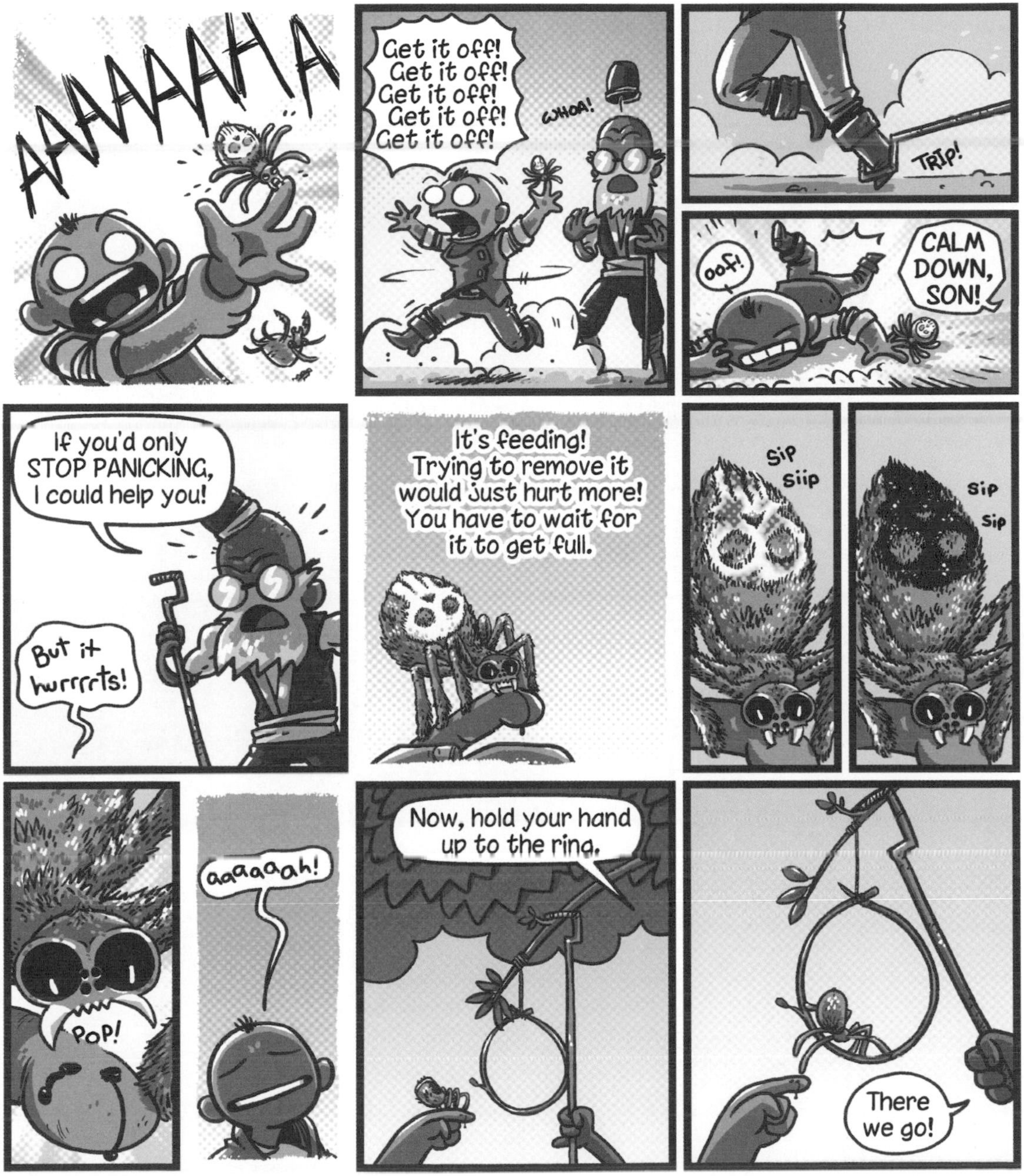
AAAAAAHA
Get it off! Get it off! Get it off! Get it off! Get it off!
WHOA!
TRIP!
oof!
CALM DOWN, SON!
If you'd only STOP PANICKING, I could help you!
But it hurrrrts!
It's feeding! Trying to remove it would just hurt more! You have to wait for it to get full.
Sip
Siip
Sip
Sip
POP!
aaaaaah!
Now, hold your hand up to the ring.
There we go!

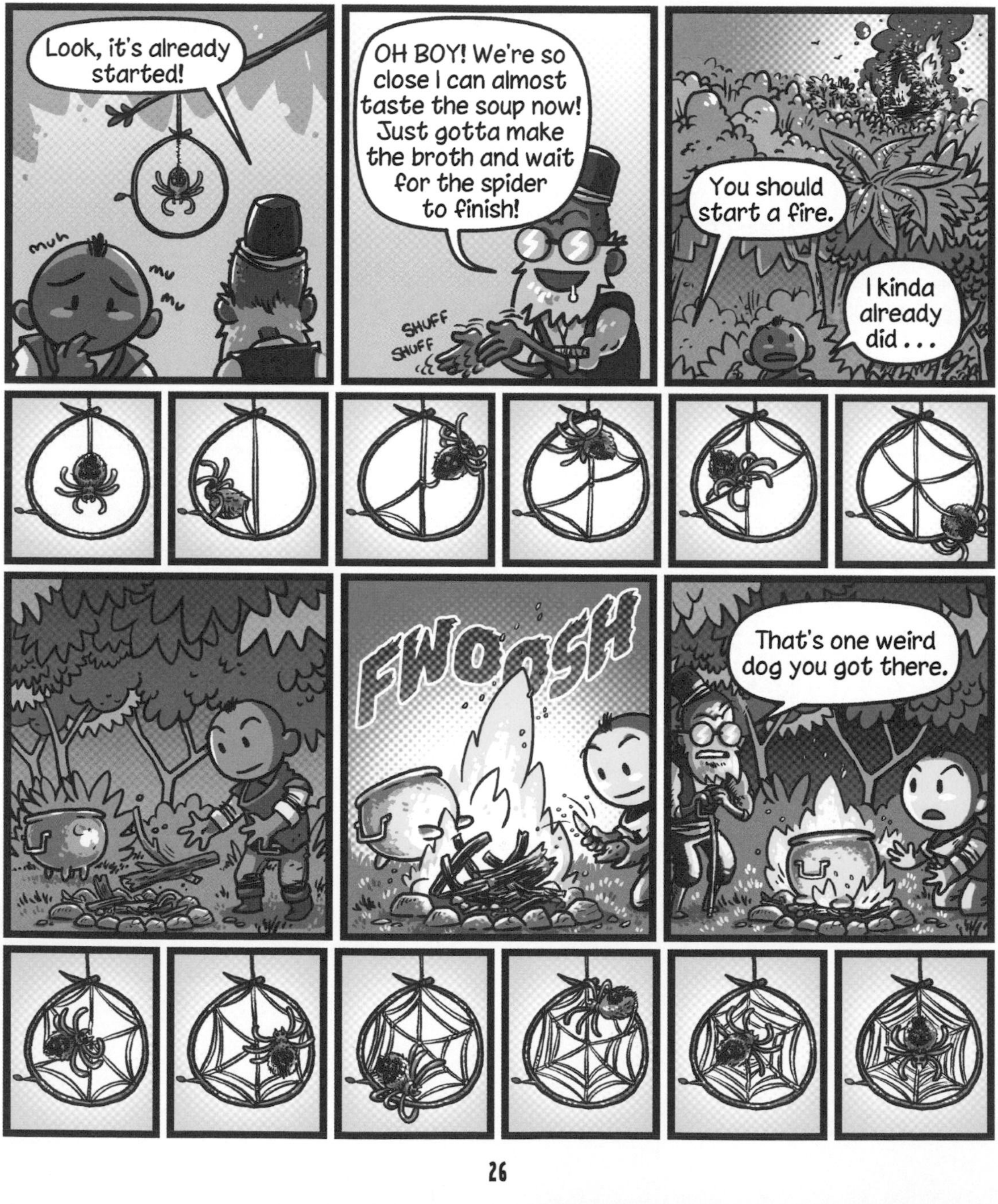
Look, it's already started!
muh
mu
mu
OH BOY! We're so close I can almost taste the soup now! Just gotta make the broth and wait for the spider to finish!
SHUFF
SHUFF
You should start a fire.
I kinda already did . . .
FWOOSH
That's one weird dog you got there.

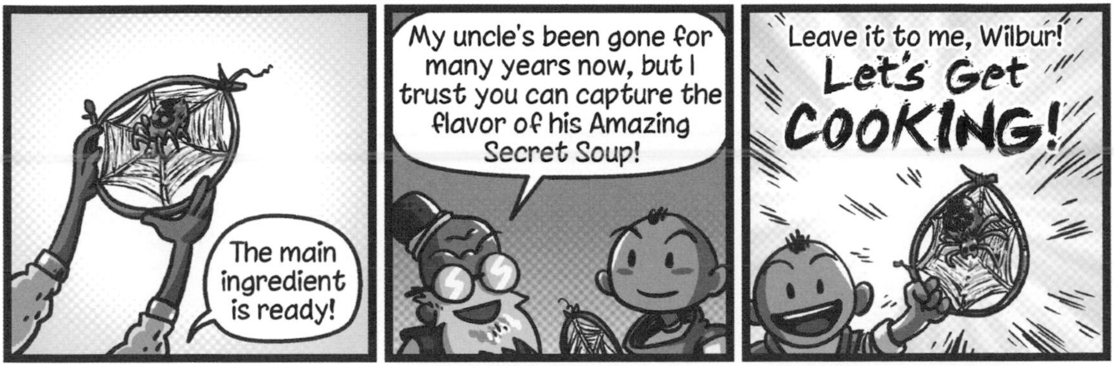
The main ingredient is ready!
My uncle's been gone for many years now, but I trust you can capture the flavor of his Amazing Secret Soup!
Leave it to me, Wilbur! Let's Get COOKING!

1.

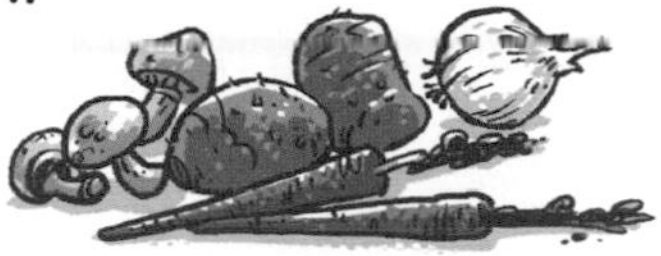

Let's make a simple vegetable soup.

2.

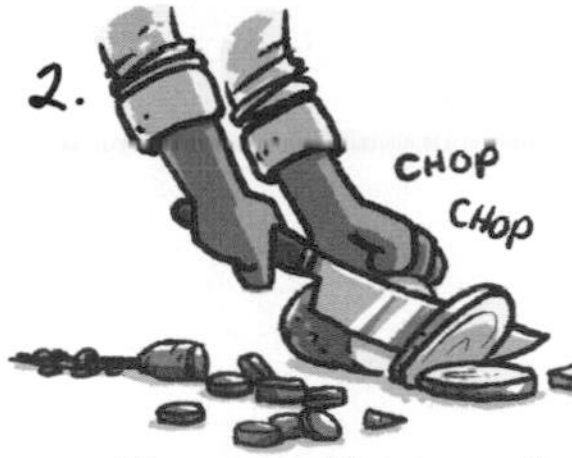
CHOP
CHOP

Chop up the veggies!

3.

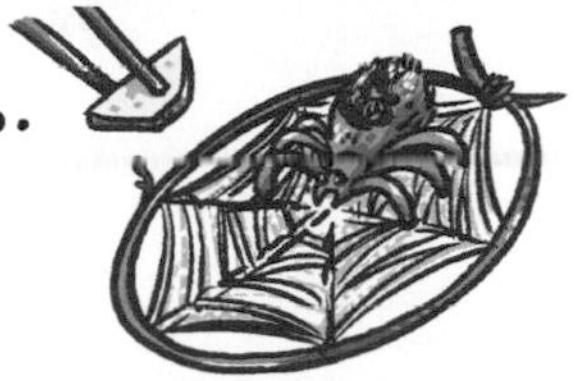

With a pair of pickup sticks, gently place them on the spiderweb.

4.

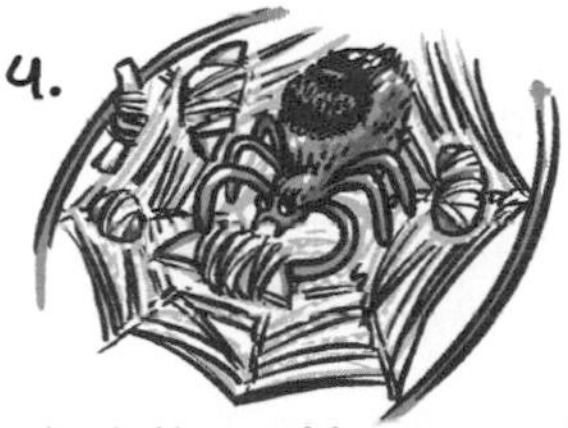

Let the spider mummify the vegetables.

5.

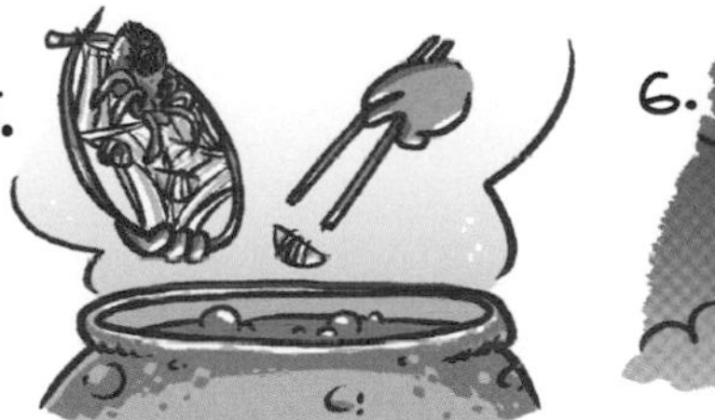

Carefully remove them from the web and add them to the broth!

6.

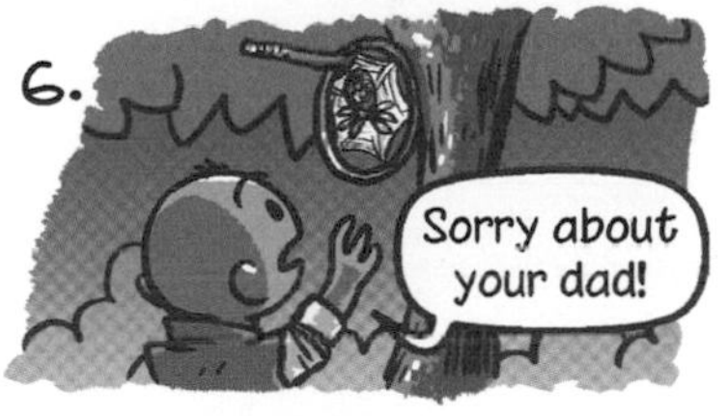
Sorry about your dad!

Cook for 15 - 25 minutes and release the spider safely back into the wild.

You have made

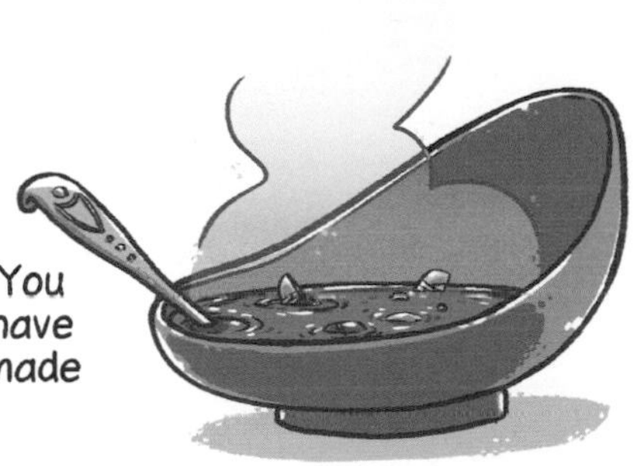

UNCLE STAMPES'S

AMAZING SPIDER SOUP!

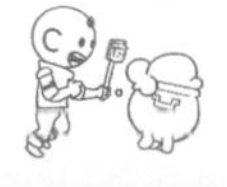

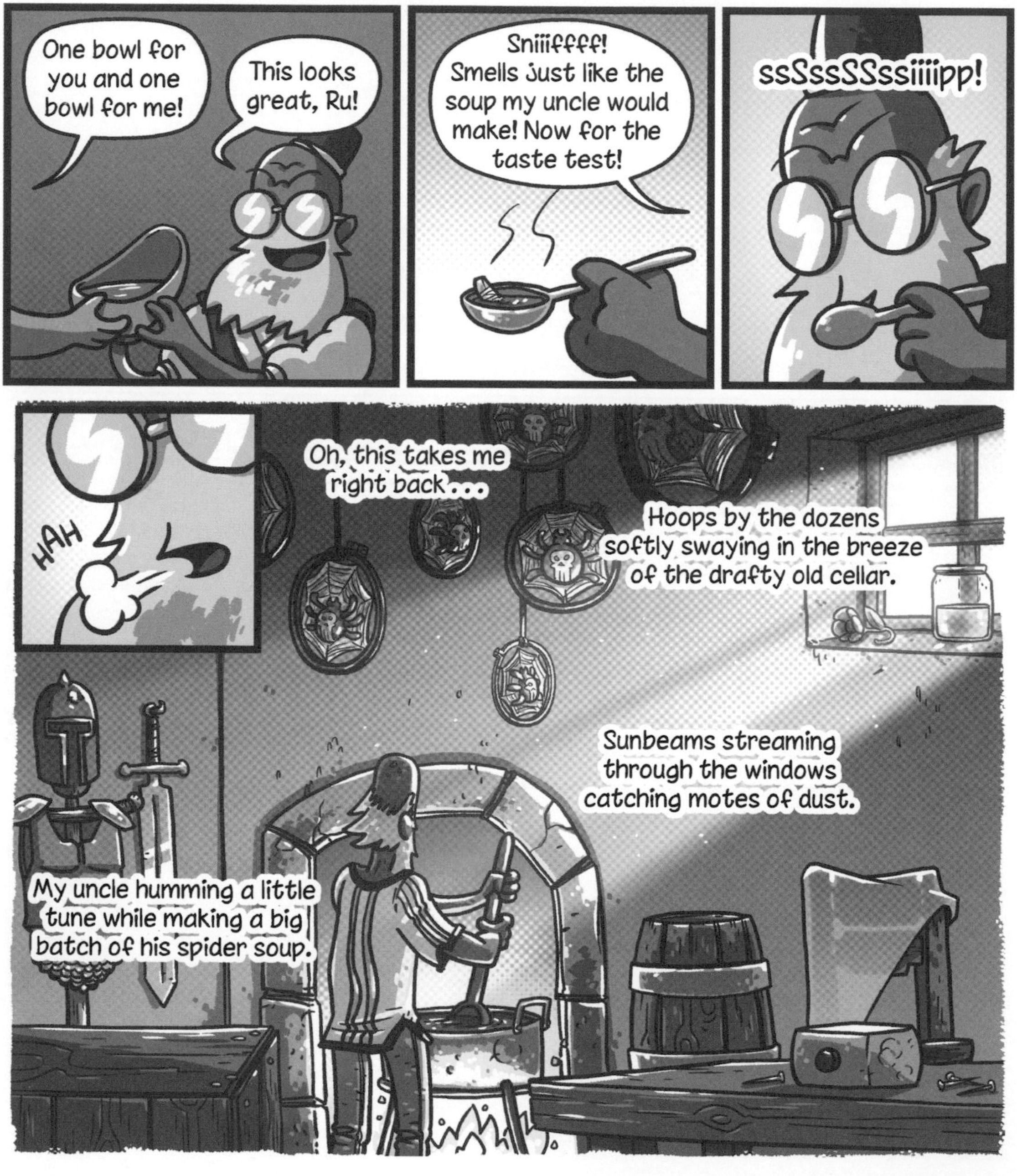
One bowl for you and one bowl for me!
This looks great, Ru!
Sniiiffff! Smells just like the soup my uncle would make! Now for the taste test!
ssSssSSssiiiipp!
HAH
Oh, this takes me right back . . .
Hoops by the dozens softly swaying in the breeze of the drafty old cellar.
Sunbeams streaming through the windows catching motes of dust.
My uncle humming a little tune while making a big batch of his spider soup.

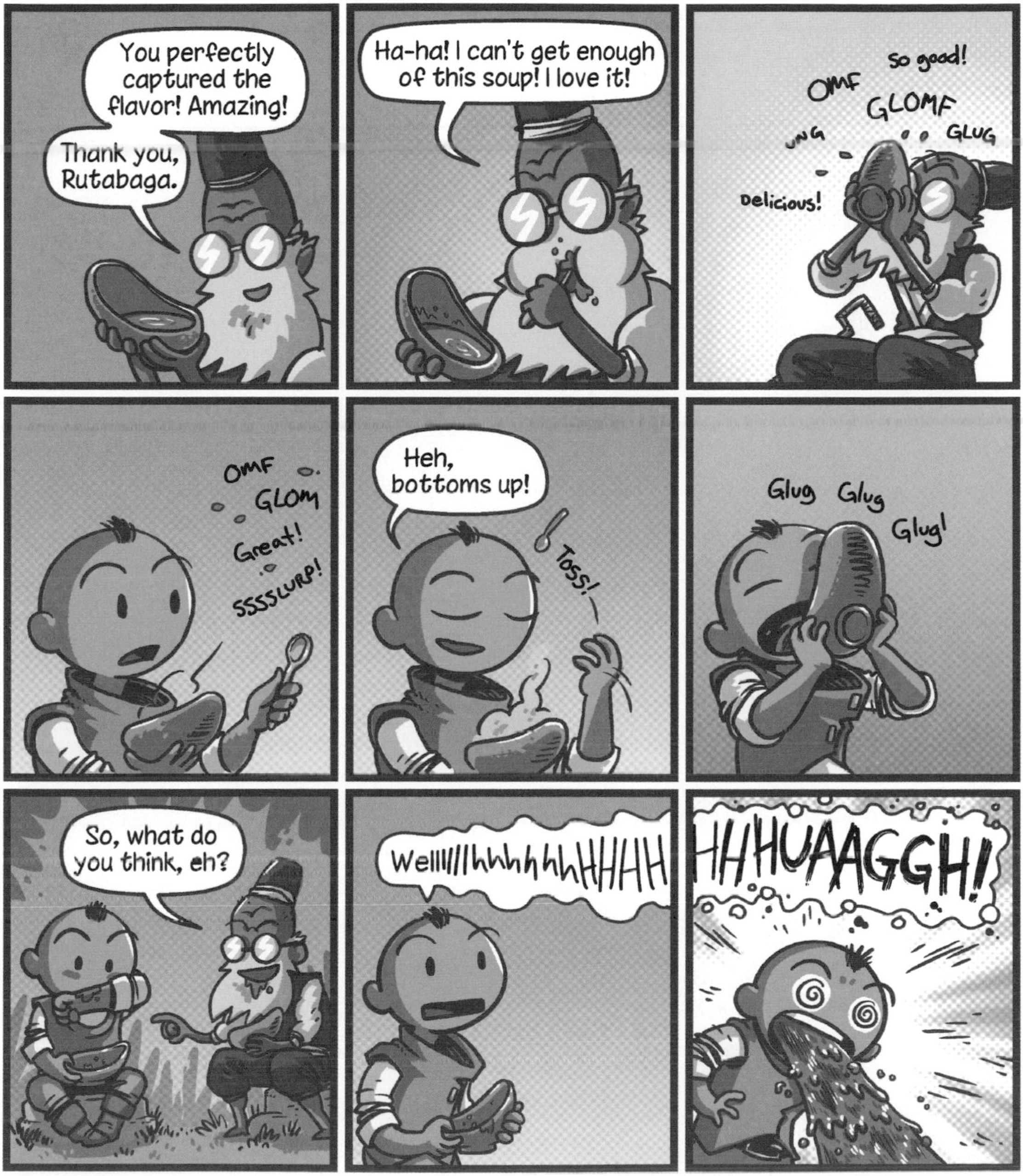
You perfectly captured the flavor! Amazing!
Thank you, Rutabaga.
Ha-ha! I can't get enough of this soup! I love it!
So good!
OMF
GLOMF
UNG
GLUG
Delicious!
OMF
GLOM
Great!
SSSSLURP!
Heh, bottoms up!
Toss!
Glug Glug
Glug!
So, what do you think, eh?
WellIIlhhhhhhHHHH
HHHUAAGGH!

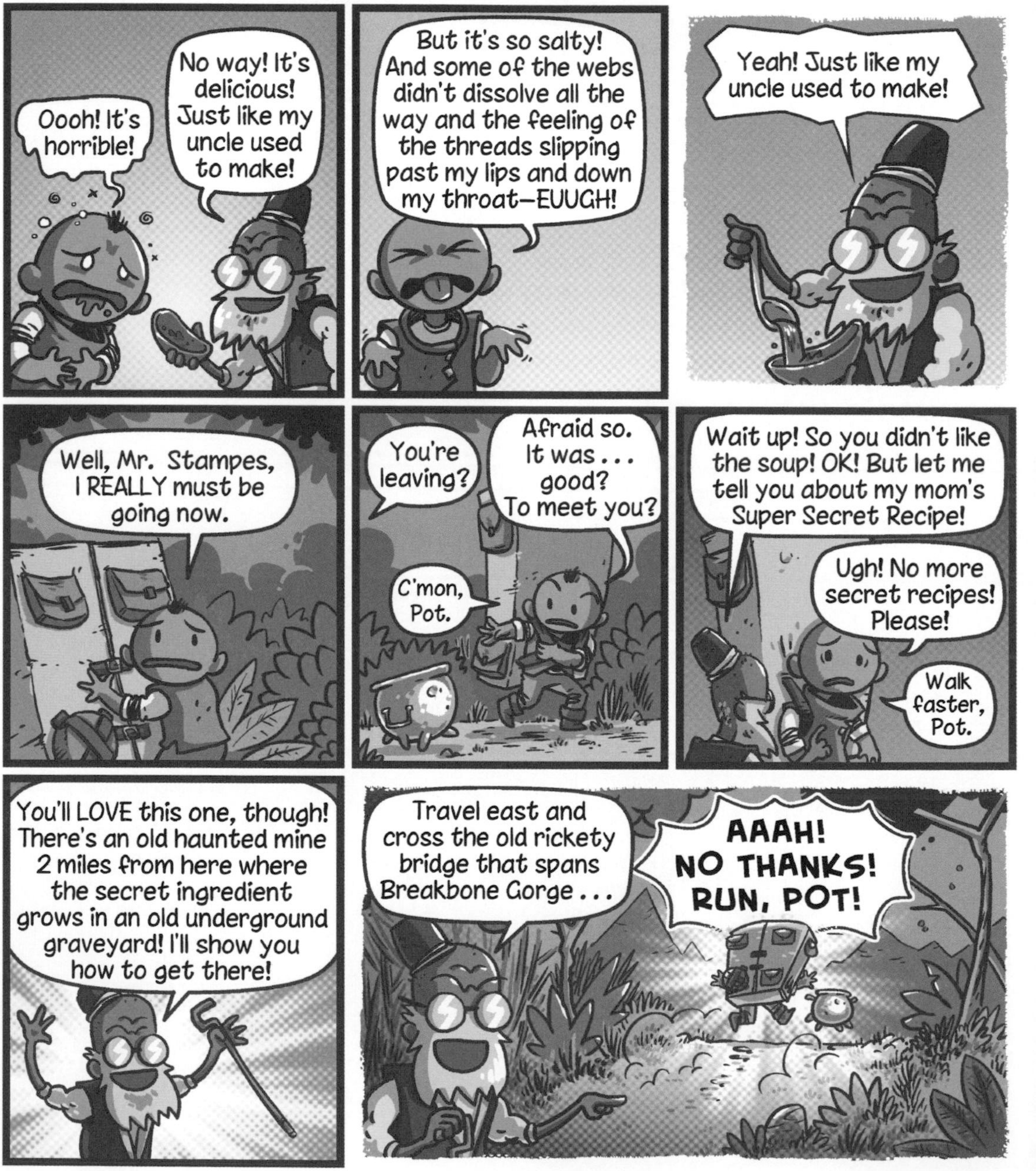
Oooh! It's horrible!
No way! It's delicious! Just like my uncle used to make!
But it's so salty! And some of the webs didn't dissolve all the way and the feeling of the threads slipping past my lips and down my throat—EUUGH!
Yeah! Just like my uncle used to make!
Well, Mr. Stampes, I REALLY must be going now.
You're leaving?
Afraid so. It was . . . good? To meet you?
C'mon, Pot.
Wait up! So you didn't like the soup! OK! But let me tell you about my mom's Super Secret Recipe!
Ugh! No more secret recipes! Please!
Walk faster, Pot.
You'll LOVE this one, though! There's an old haunted mine 2 miles from here where the secret ingredient grows in an old underground graveyard! I'll show you how to get there!
Travel east and cross the old rickety bridge that spans Breakbone Gorge . . .
AAAH! NO THANKS! RUN, POT!

End of Chapter One

RUTABAGA
THE ADVENTURE CHEF

BEWARE! Gubblins!

Where the heck are we?! I can't find us on the map!

Okay, Grimmond Road is around here somewhere. We ran south for maybe 10 minutes and then . . .

I'm lost!

Rrrrr! Why does everything have to be so tiny on maps?!

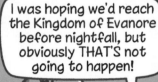

I was hoping we'd reach the Kingdom of Evanore before nightfall, but obviously THAT'S not going to happen!

I wanted to sleep in a nice soft bed tonight. I guess it'll be the cold hard ground again!

Hang on, is that a fire? Let's go see who it is. Maybe they know how to get to Evanore!

C'mon, Pot!

RUSTLE

RUSTLE

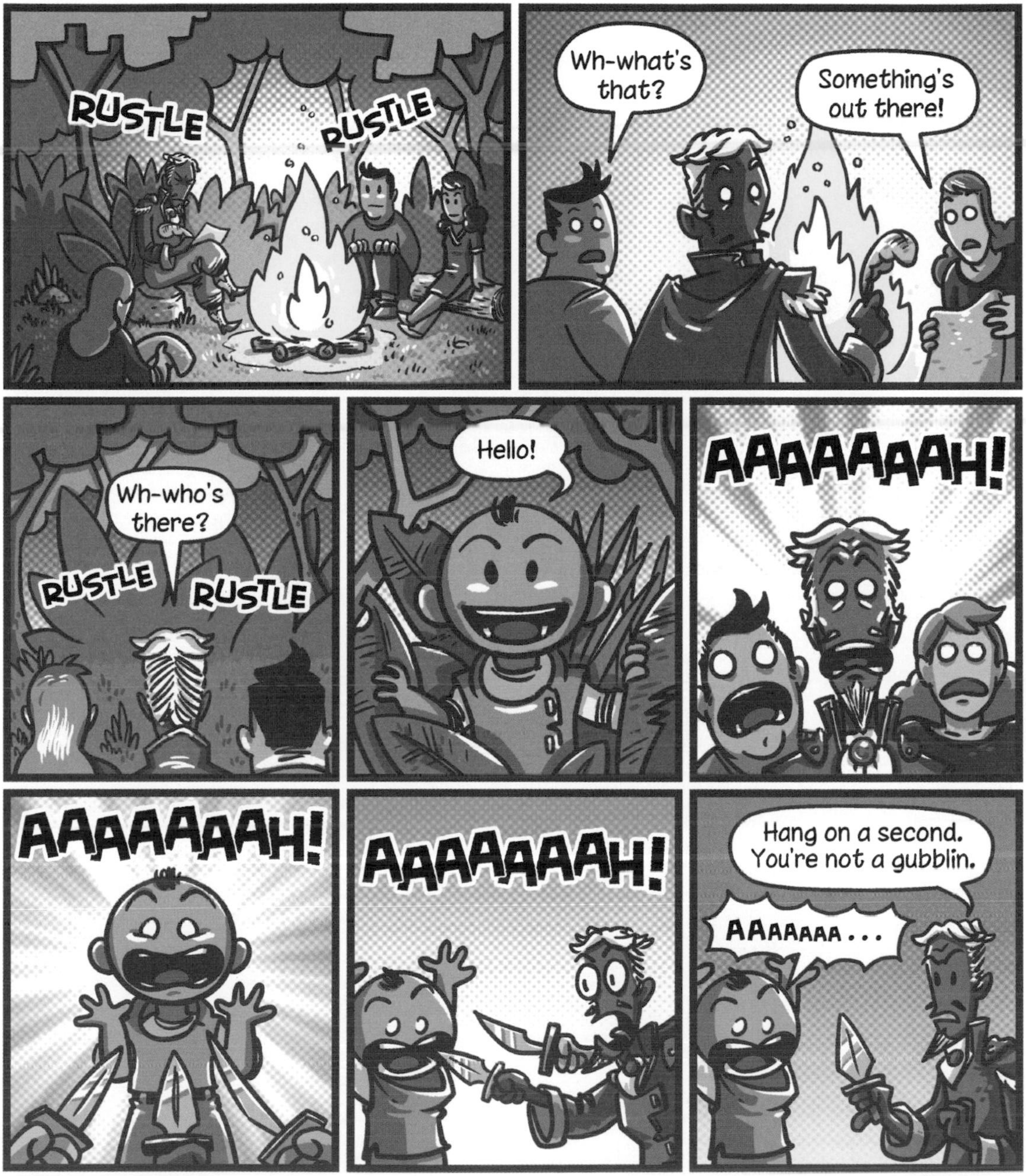
RUSTLE
RUSTLE
Wh-what's that?
Something's out there!
Wh-who's there?
RUSTLE
RUSTLE
Hello!
AAAAAAAAH!
AAAAAAAAH!
AAAAAAAAH!
Hang on a second. You're not a gubblin.
AAAAAAA . . .

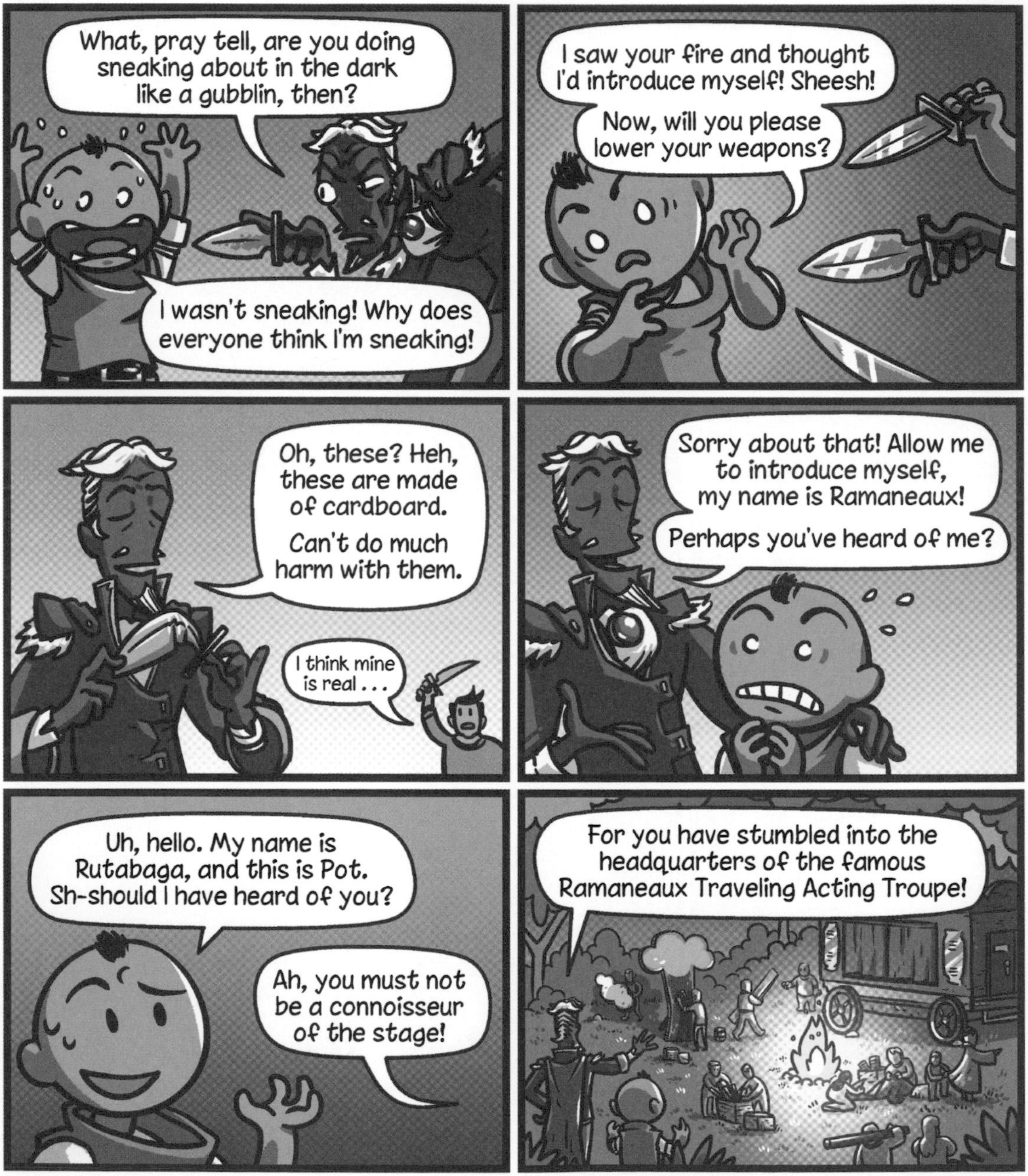
What, pray tell, are you doing sneaking about in the dark like a gubblin, then?
I wasn't sneaking! Why does everyone think I'm sneaking!
I saw your fire and thought I'd introduce myself! Sheesh!
Now, will you please lower your weapons?
Oh, these? Heh, these are made of cardboard.
Can't do much harm with them.
I think mine is real . . .
Sorry about that! Allow me to introduce myself, my name is Ramaneaux!
Perhaps you've heard of me?
Uh, hello. My name is Rutabaga, and this is Pot. Sh-should I have heard of you?
Ah, you must not be a connoisseur of the stage!
For you have stumbled into the headquarters of the famous Ramaneaux Traveling Acting Troupe!

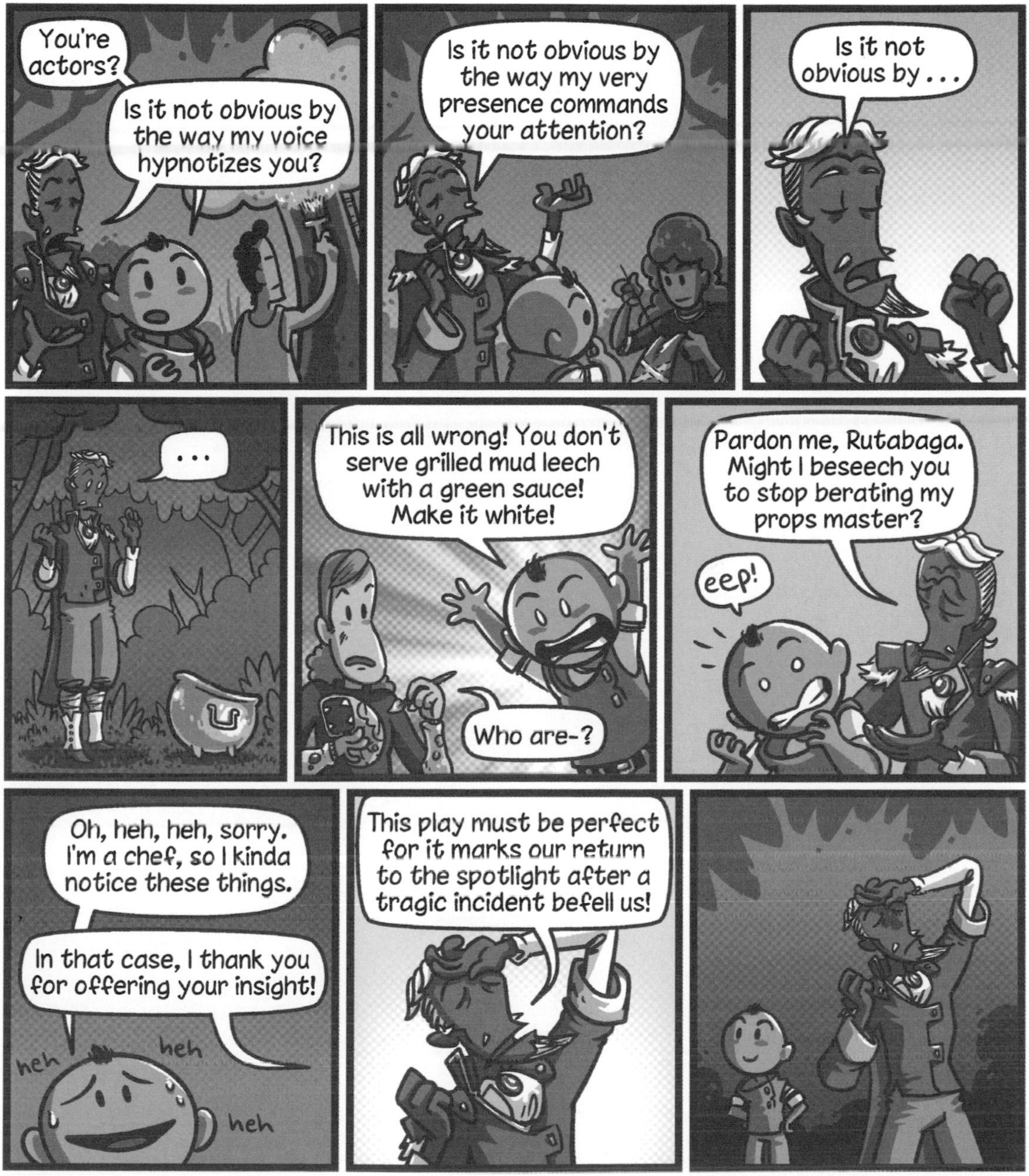
You're actors?
Is it not obvious by the way my voice hypnotizes you?
Is it not obvious by the way my very presence commands your attention?
Is it not obvious by . . .
. . .
This is all wrong! You don't serve grilled mud leech with a green sauce! Make it white!
Who are-?
Pardon me, Rutabaga. Might I beseech you to stop berating my props master?
eep!
Oh, heh, heh, sorry. I'm a chef, so I kinda notice these things.
In that case, I thank you for offering your insight!
heh
heh
heh
This play must be perfect for it marks our return to the spotlight after a tragic incident befell us!

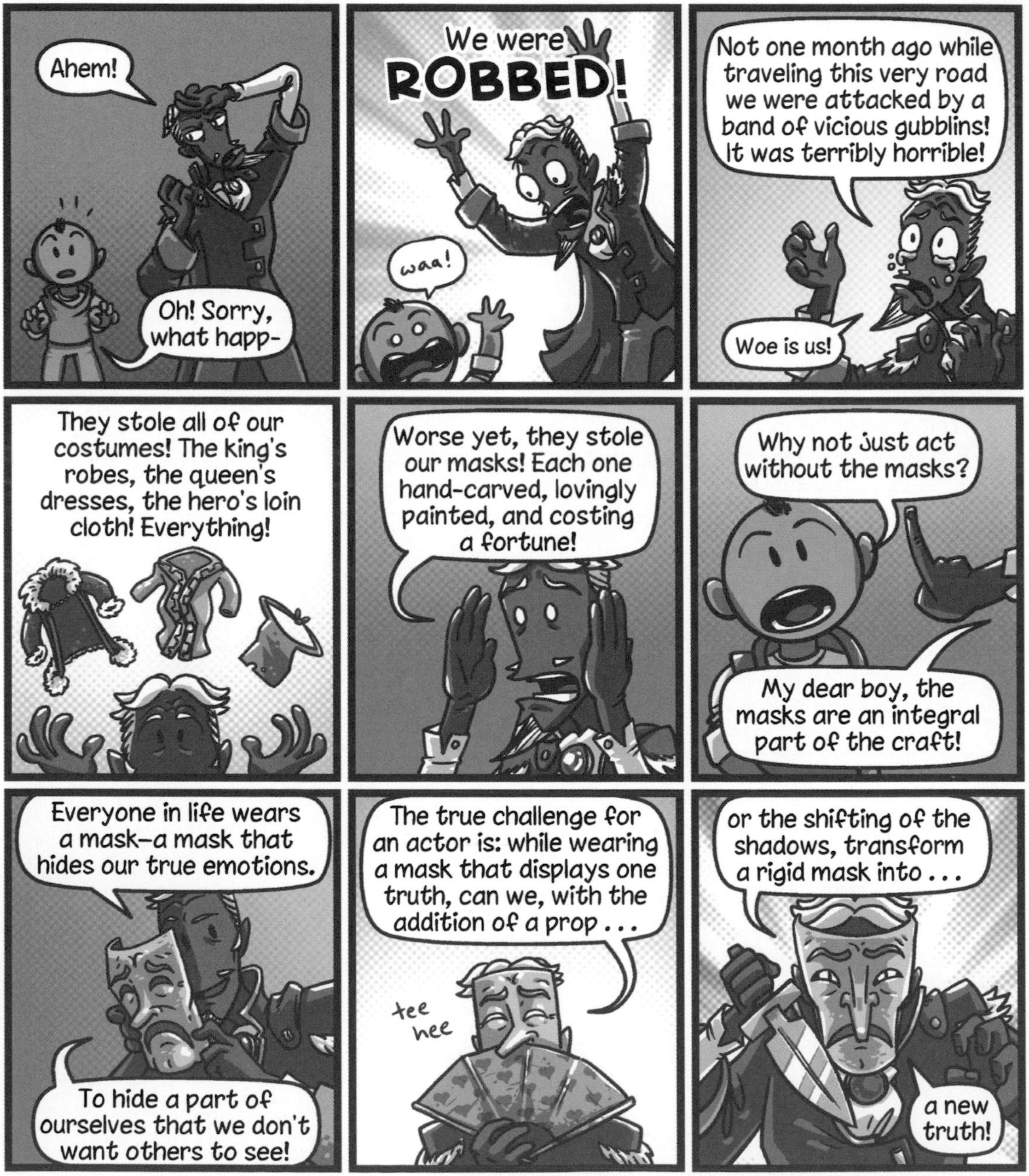
Ahem!
Oh! Sorry, what happ-
We were ROBBED!
waa!
Not one month ago while traveling this very road we were attacked by a band of vicious gubblins! It was terribly horrible!
Woe is us!
They stole all of our costumes! The king's robes, the queen's dresses, the hero's loin cloth! Everything!
Worse yet, they stole our masks! Each one hand-carved, lovingly painted, and costing a fortune!
Why not just act without the masks?
My dear boy, the masks are an integral part of the craft!
Everyone in life wears a mask—a mask that hides our true emotions.
To hide a part of ourselves that we don't want others to see!
The true challenge for an actor is: while wearing a mask that displays one truth, can we, with the addition of a prop . . .
tee hee
or the shifting of the shadows, transform a rigid mask into . . .
a new truth!

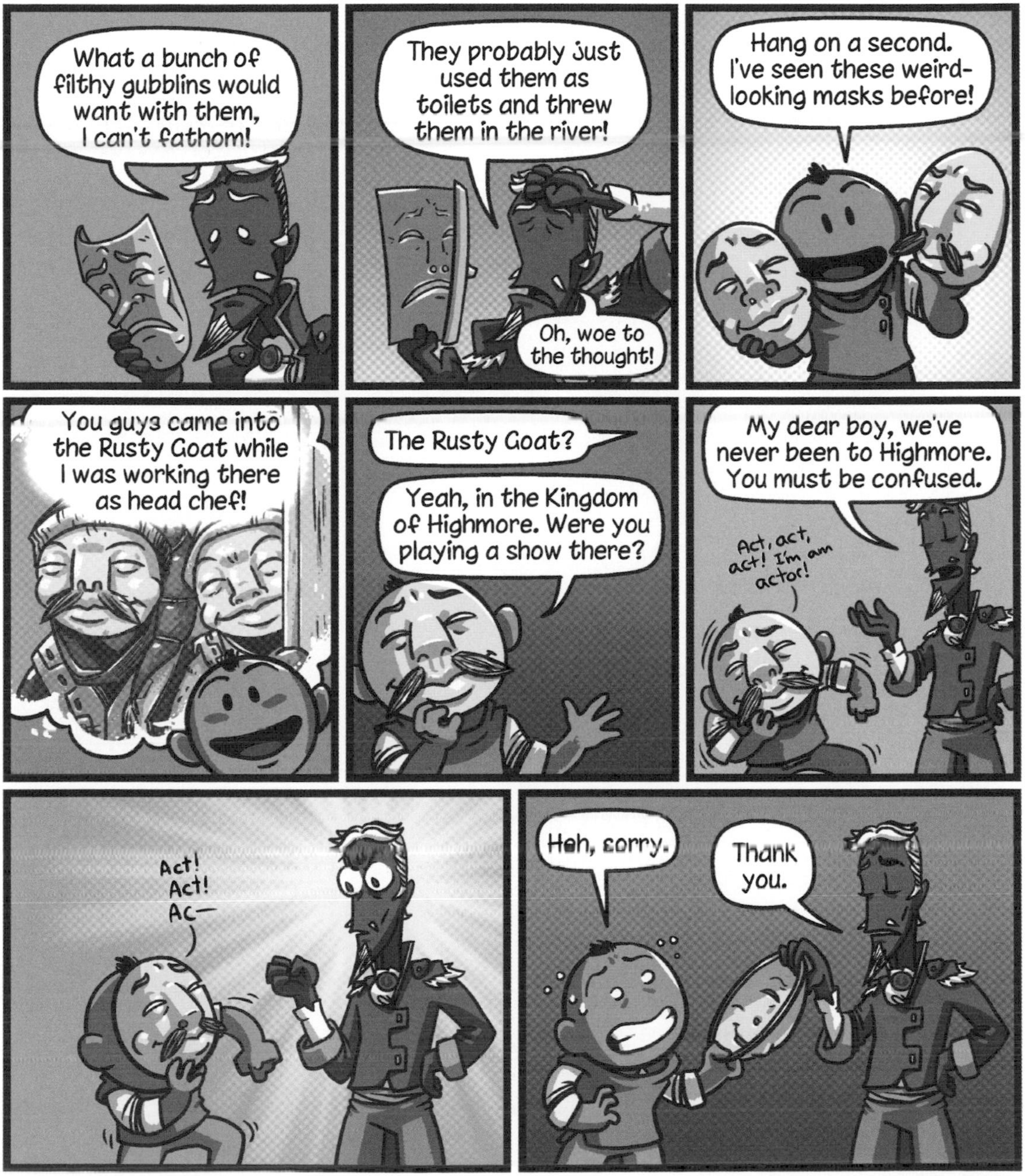
What a bunch of filthy gubblins would want with them, I can't fathom!
They probably just used them as toilets and threw them in the river!
Oh, woe to the thought!
Hang on a second. I've seen these weird-looking masks before!
You guys came into the Rusty Goat while I was working there as head chef!
The Rusty Goat?
Yeah, in the Kingdom of Highmore. Were you playing a show there?
My dear boy, we've never been to Highmore. You must be confused.
Act, act, act! I'm am actor!
Act! Act! Ac—
Heh, sorry.
Thank you.

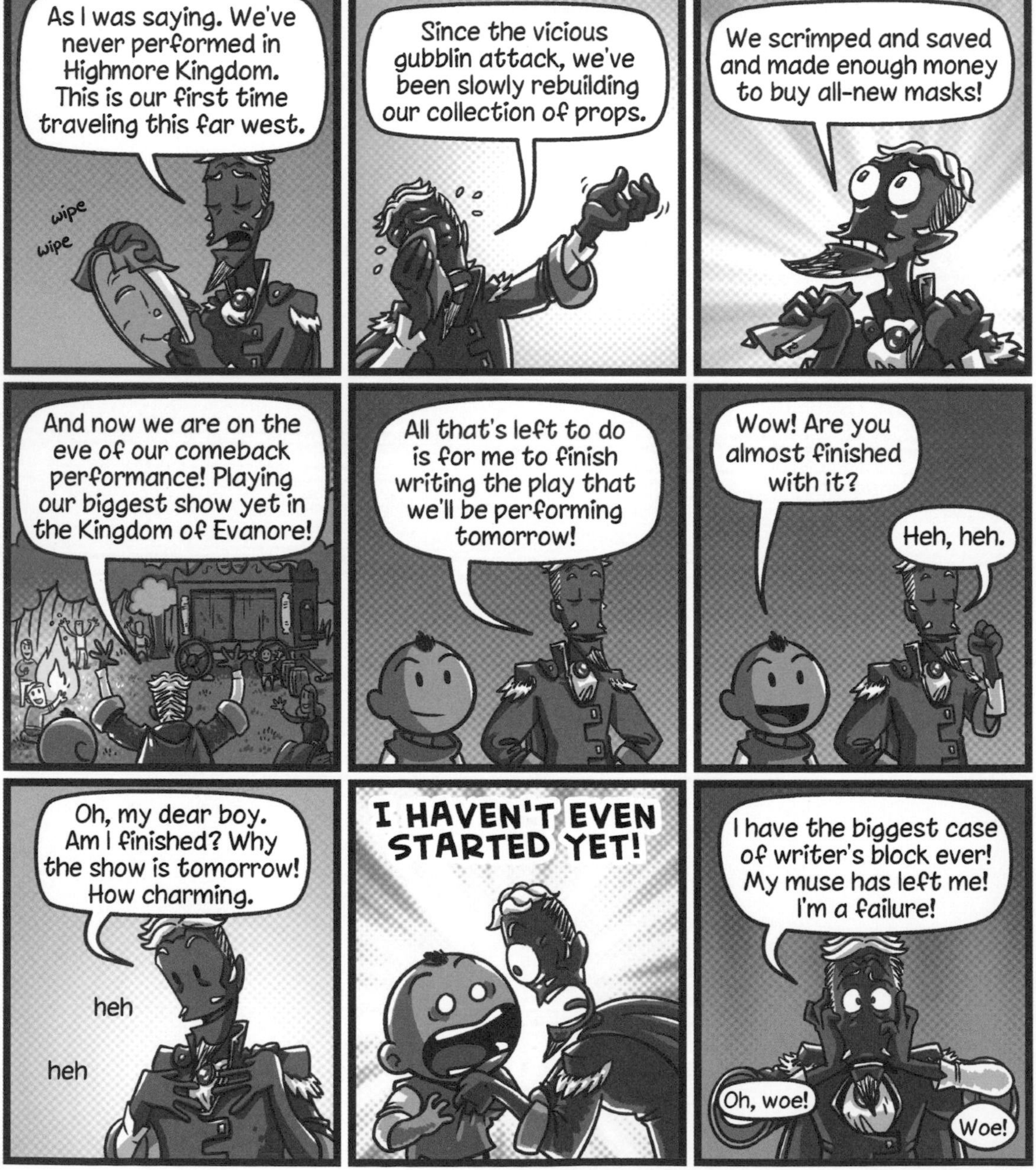
As I was saying. We've never performed in Highmore Kingdom. This is our first time traveling this far west.
wipe
wipe
Since the vicious gubblin attack, we've been slowly rebuilding our collection of props.
We scrimped and saved and made enough money to buy all-new masks!
And now we are on the eve of our comeback performance! Playing our biggest show yet in the Kingdom of Evanore!
All that's left to do is for me to finish writing the play that we'll be performing tomorrow!
Wow! Are you almost finished with it?
Heh, heh.
Oh, my dear boy. Am I finished? Why the show is tomorrow! How charming.
heh
heh
I HAVEN'T EVEN STARTED YET!
I have the biggest case of writer's block ever! My muse has left me! I'm a failure!
Oh, woe!
Woe!

It's horrible! I haven't slept! I haven't eaten!

Well, you gotta eat! Eating gives the mind energy!

Why don't you sit down right here and I'll cook you a nice meal.

R-really?

SNIFF SNIFF

I'd love to!

Let's Get COOKING!

1. Gather shredded turkey, veggies, ghost mushrooms, chicken stock, and a single lime-green bean.

2. Soften the onion in a pan and add a whole heap of butter, flour, and the stock. Stir constantly until the sauce has thickened.

3. Add the rest of the ingredients and pour into individual bowls.

4. Make some biscuit dough and stretch it over the bowls.

5. Choose one bowl and secretly drop the bean into it! Bake them all in an oven until the tops are golden brown!

You have made a
POISONED POT PIE

Dinner is served!

Uhh...

hmm

What's wrong?

W-why do you call them poisoned?

Ha-ha! Remember that bean I put in one of the bowls?

uh-huh

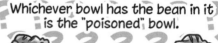

Whichever bowl has the bean in it is the "poisoned" bowl.

Whoever gets the bowl with the bean in it gets "poisoned"!

It's a game we used to play in cooking school.

How delightfully creative, Rutabaga!

I trust you aren't trying to poison us, so I shall be the first to try this delicious-looking meal!

HOMF!

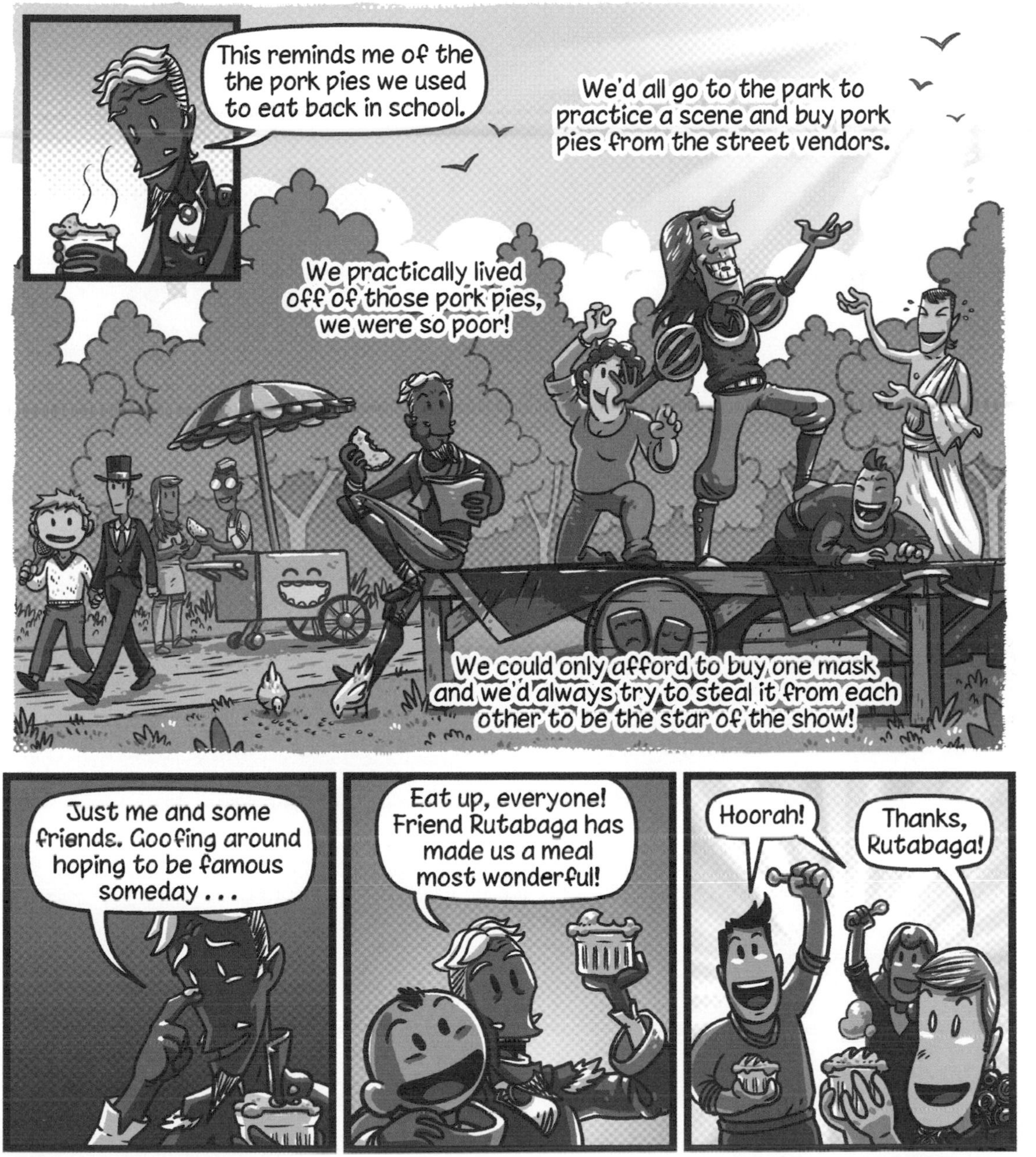
This reminds me of the the pork pies we used to eat back in school.
We'd all go to the park to practice a scene and buy pork pies from the street vendors.
We practically lived off of those pork pies, we were so poor!
We could only afford to buy one mask and we'd always try to steal it from each other to be the star of the show!
Just me and some friends. Goofing around hoping to be famous someday . . .
Eat up, everyone! Friend Rutabaga has made us a meal most wonderful!
Hoorah!
Thanks, Rutabaga!

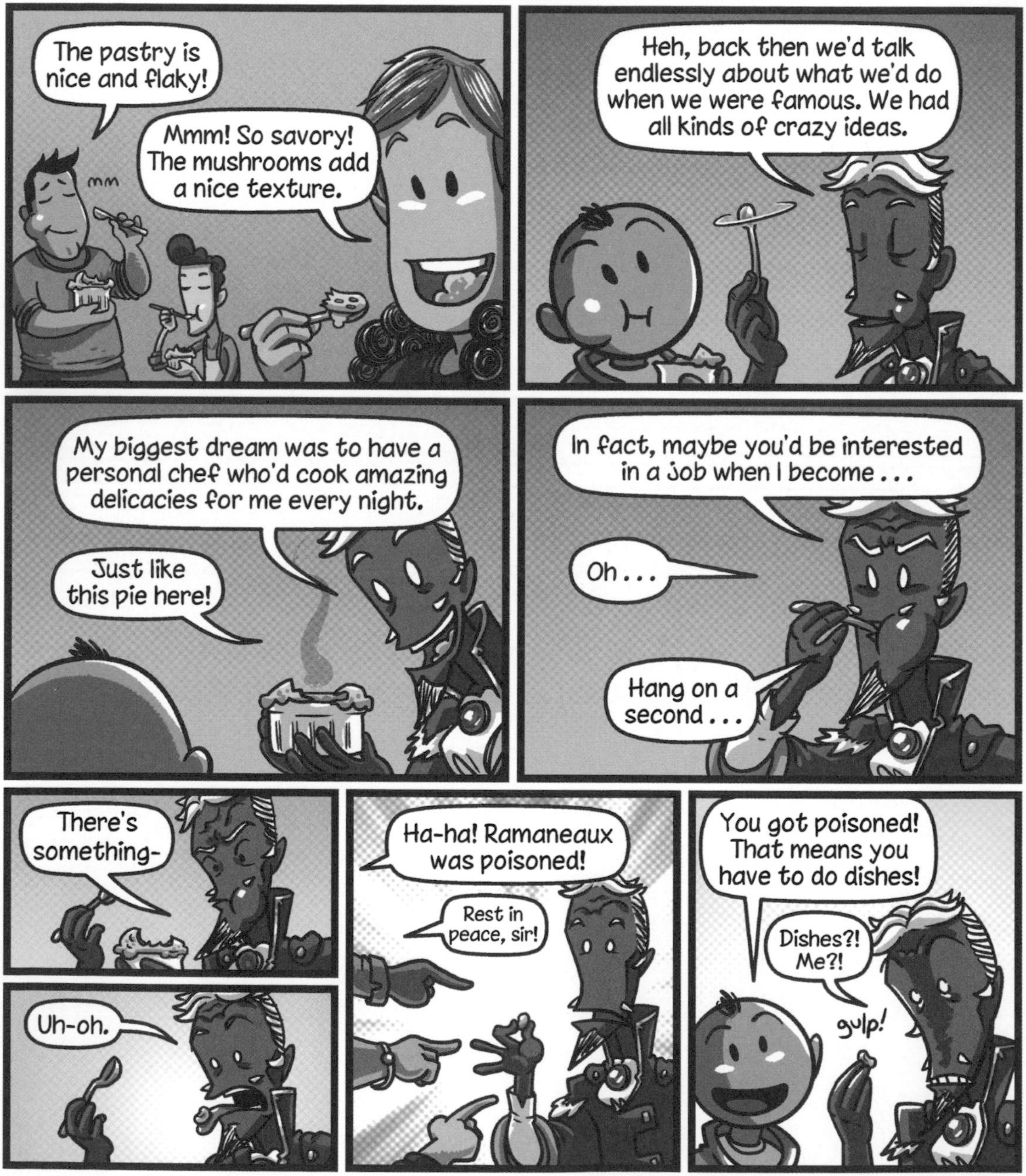
The pastry is nice and flaky!
mm
Mmm! So savory! The mushrooms add a nice texture.
Heh, back then we'd talk endlessly about what we'd do when we were famous. We had all kinds of crazy ideas.
My biggest dream was to have a personal chef who'd cook amazing delicacies for me every night.
Just like this pie here!
In fact, maybe you'd be interested in a job when I become . . .
Oh . . .
Hang on a second . . .
There's something-
Uh-oh.
Ha-ha! Ramaneaux was poisoned!
Rest in peace, sir!
You got poisoned! That means you have to do dishes!
Dishes?! Me?!
gulp!

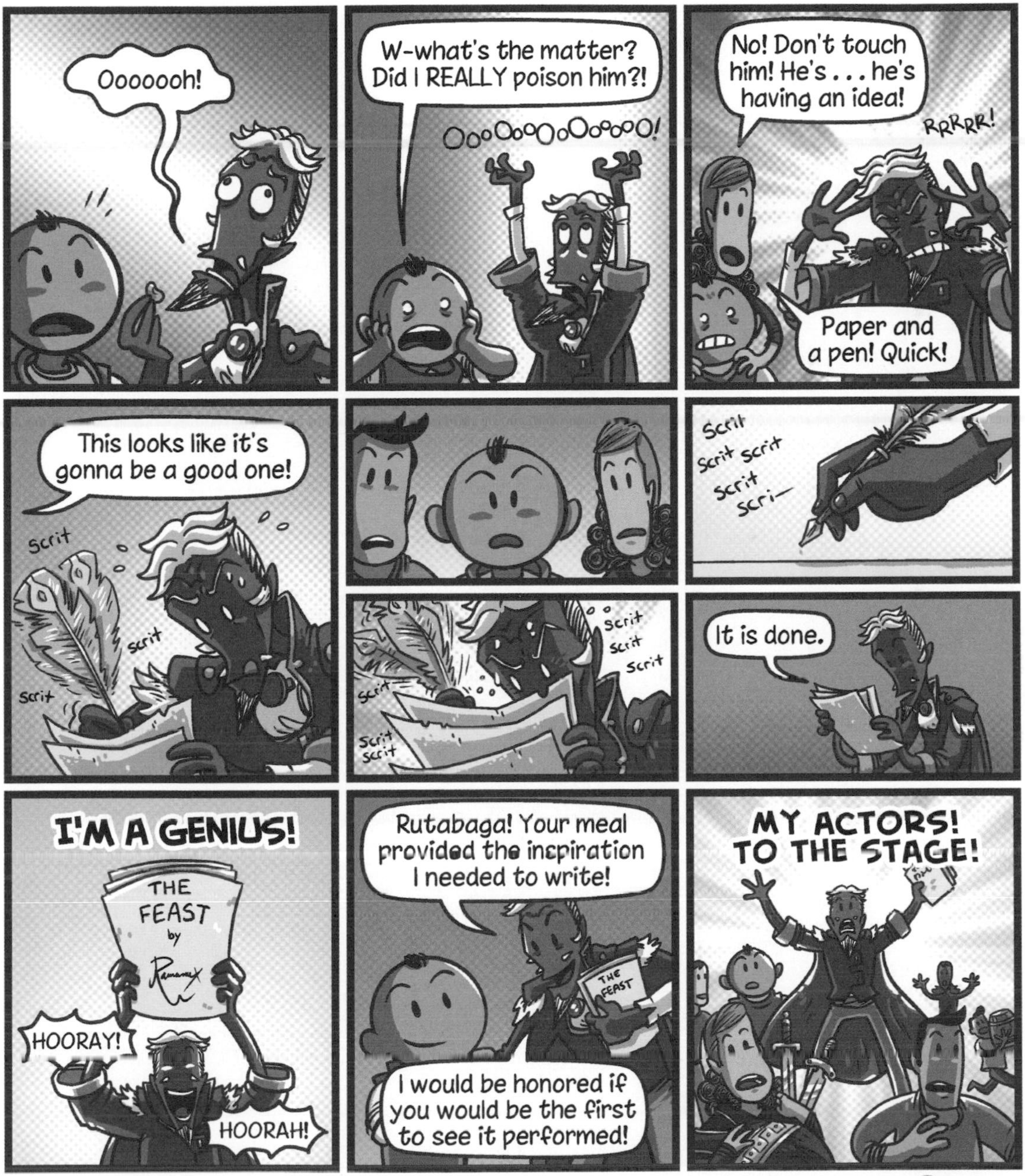
Ooooooh!
W-what's the matter? Did I REALLY poison him?!
OooOooOoOoOooO!
No! Don't touch him! He's . . . he's having an idea!
RRRRR!
Paper and a pen! Quick!
This looks like it's gonna be a good one!
scrit
scrit
scrit
Scrit
Scrit scrit
scrit
scri—
scrit
scrit
scrit
scrit
Scrit
scrit
It is done.
I'M A GENIUS!
THE FEAST by
HOORAY!
HOORAH!
Rutabaga! Your meal provided the inspiration I needed to write!
THE FEAST
I would be honored if you would be the first to see it performed!
MY ACTORS! TO THE STAGE!

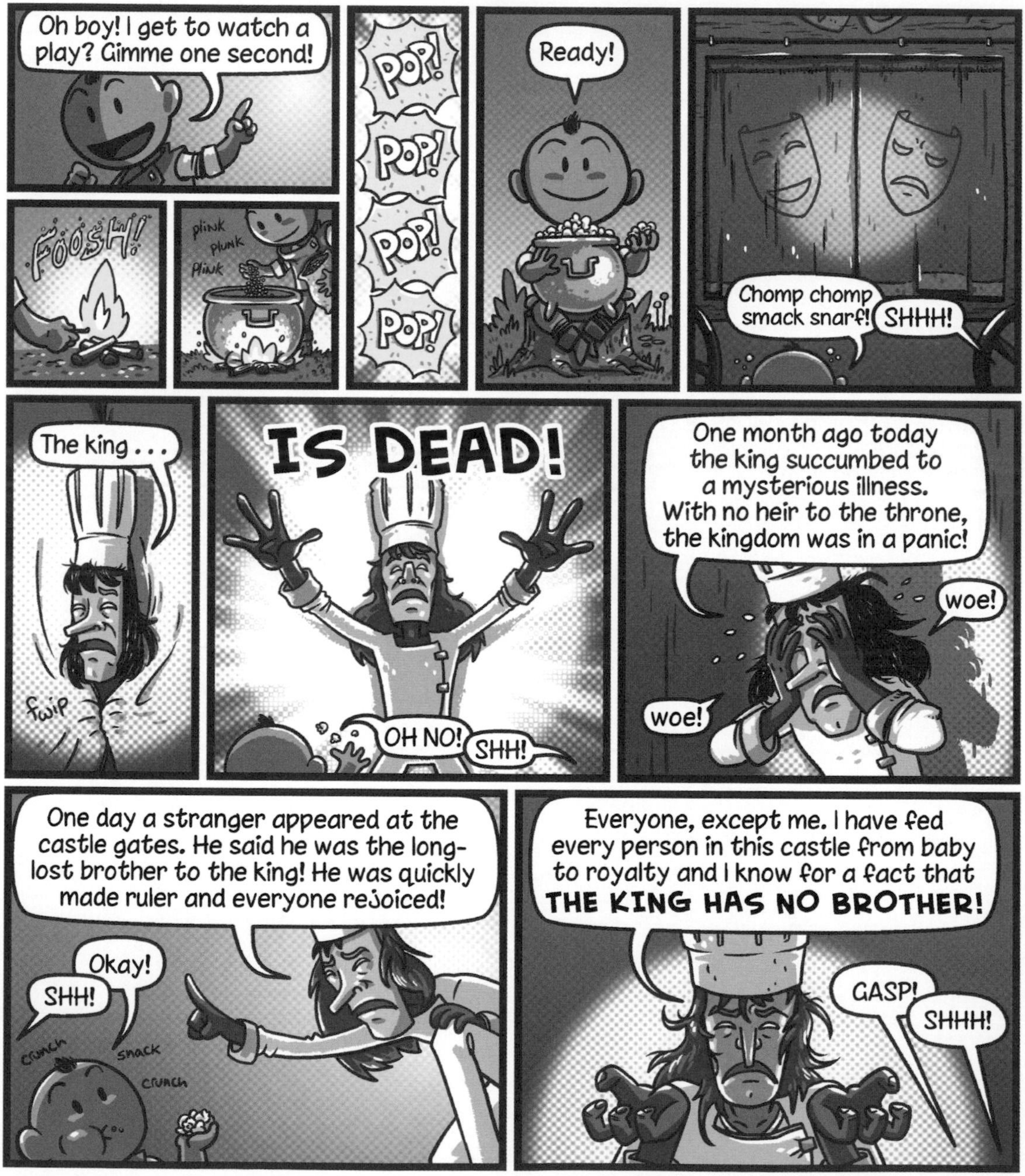

Oh boy! I get to watch a play? Gimme one second!
FOOSH!
plink
plunk
plink
POP!
POP!
POP!
POP!
Ready!
Chomp chomp smack snarf!
SHHH!
The king . . .
fwip
IS DEAD!
OH NO!
SHH!
One month ago today the king succumbed to a mysterious illness. With no heir to the throne, the kingdom was in a panic!
woe!
woe!
One day a stranger appeared at the castle gates. He said he was the long-lost brother to the king! He was quickly made ruler and everyone rejoiced!
Okay!
SHH!
crunch
snack
crunch
Everyone, except me. I have fed every person in this castle from baby to royalty and I know for a fact that THE KING HAS NO BROTHER!
GASP!
SHHH!

This fake king has done nothing but gamble away huge amounts of money! The kingdom is in ruins!

I tried to bring my evidence to the Captain of the Guard, but he's too busy attending parties thrown by the fake king.

SNARF
SNARF
CRUNCH
SMAK

I also approached the Duke and Duchess, but they refuse to listen. Too concerned with their newfound riches, won by beating the king at poker!

woe!
woe!
woe!
woe!

I can't sit by and watch as this impostor ruins my beloved home.

That is why I must . . .

POISON THE KING!

woe!
woe!

Tonight's banquet will be his last!

Gods forgive me!

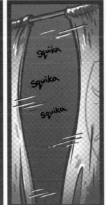

squika
squika
squika

WOW!
SHHH!

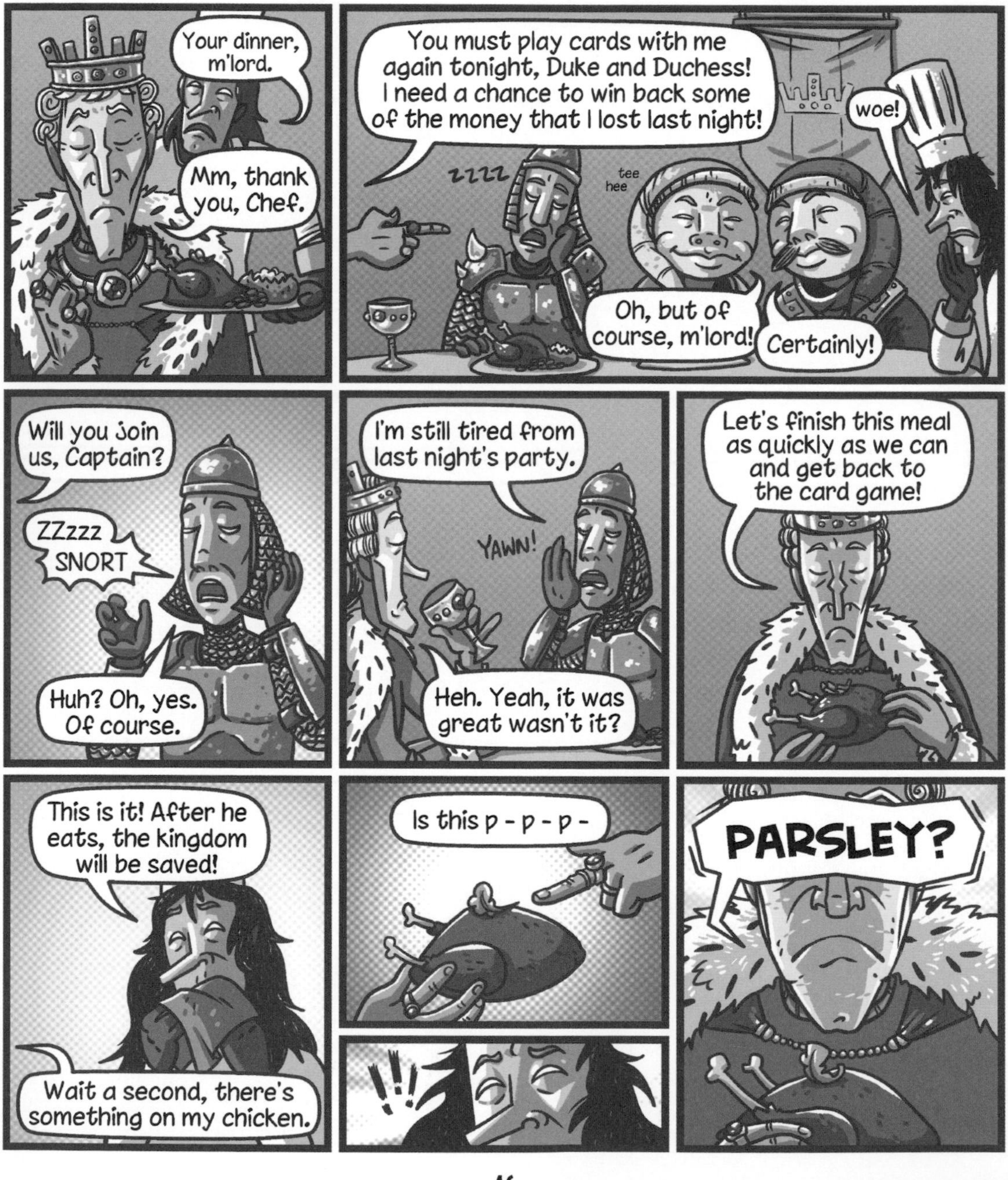
Your dinner, m'lord.
Mm, thank you, Chef.
You must play cards with me again tonight, Duke and Duchess! I need a chance to win back some of the money that I lost last night!
zzzz
tee hee
woe!
Oh, but of course, m'lord!
Certainly!
Will you join us, Captain?
ZZzzz SNORT
Huh? Oh, yes. Of course.
I'm still tired from last night's party.
YAWN!
Heh. Yeah, it was great wasn't it?
Let's finish this meal as quickly as we can and get back to the card game!
This is it! After he eats, the kingdom will be saved!
Wait a second, there's something on my chicken.
Is this p - p - p -
!!
PARSLEY?

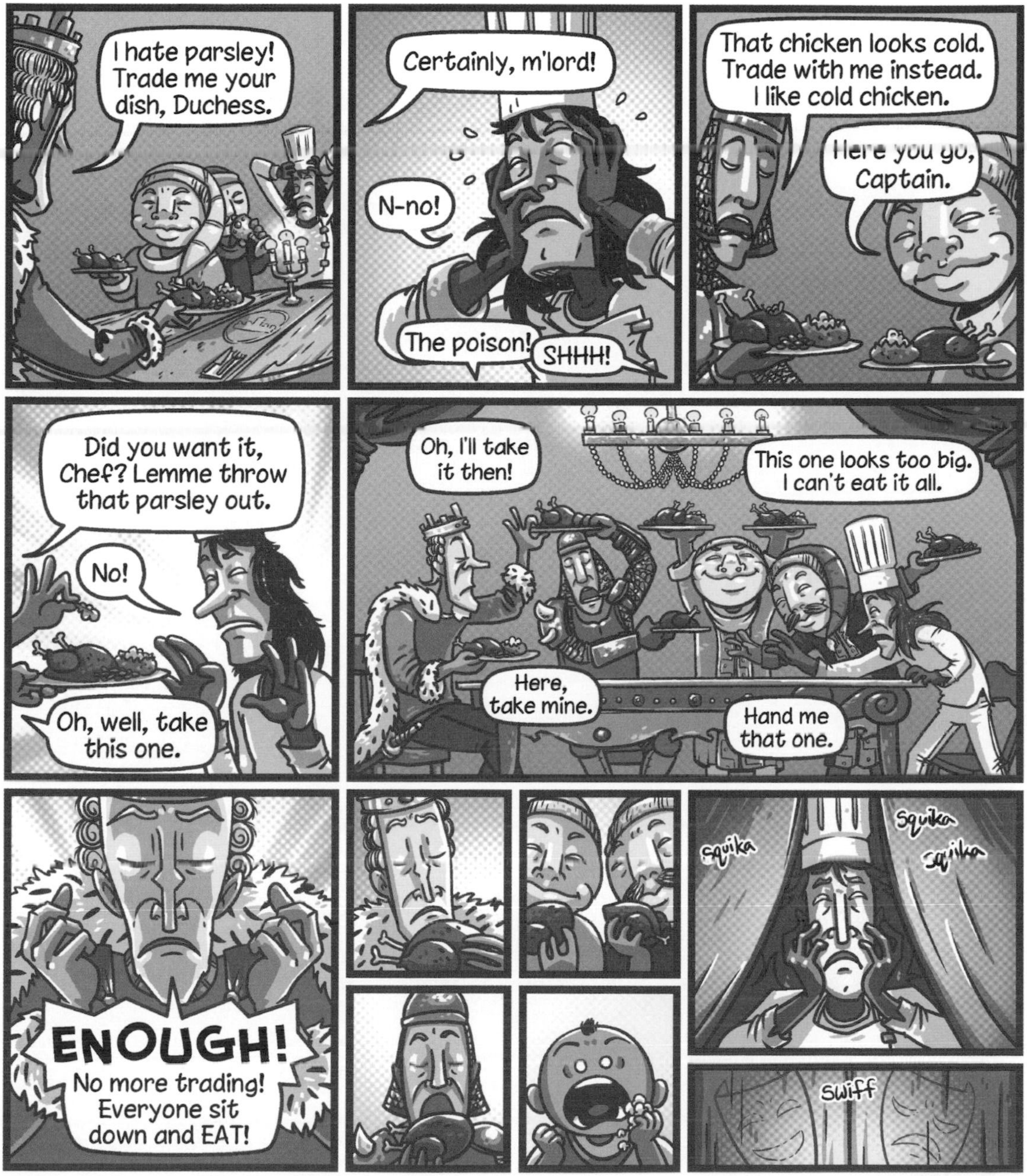
I hate parsley! Trade me your dish, Duchess.
Certainly, m'lord!
N-no!
The poison!
SHHH!
That chicken looks cold. Trade with me instead. I like cold chicken.
Here you go, Captain.
Did you want it, Chef? Lemme throw that parsley out.
No!
Oh, well, take this one.
Oh, I'll take it then!
This one looks too big. I can't eat it all.
Here, take mine.
Hand me that one.
ENOUGH! No more trading! Everyone sit down and EAT!
Squika
Squika
Squika
Swiff

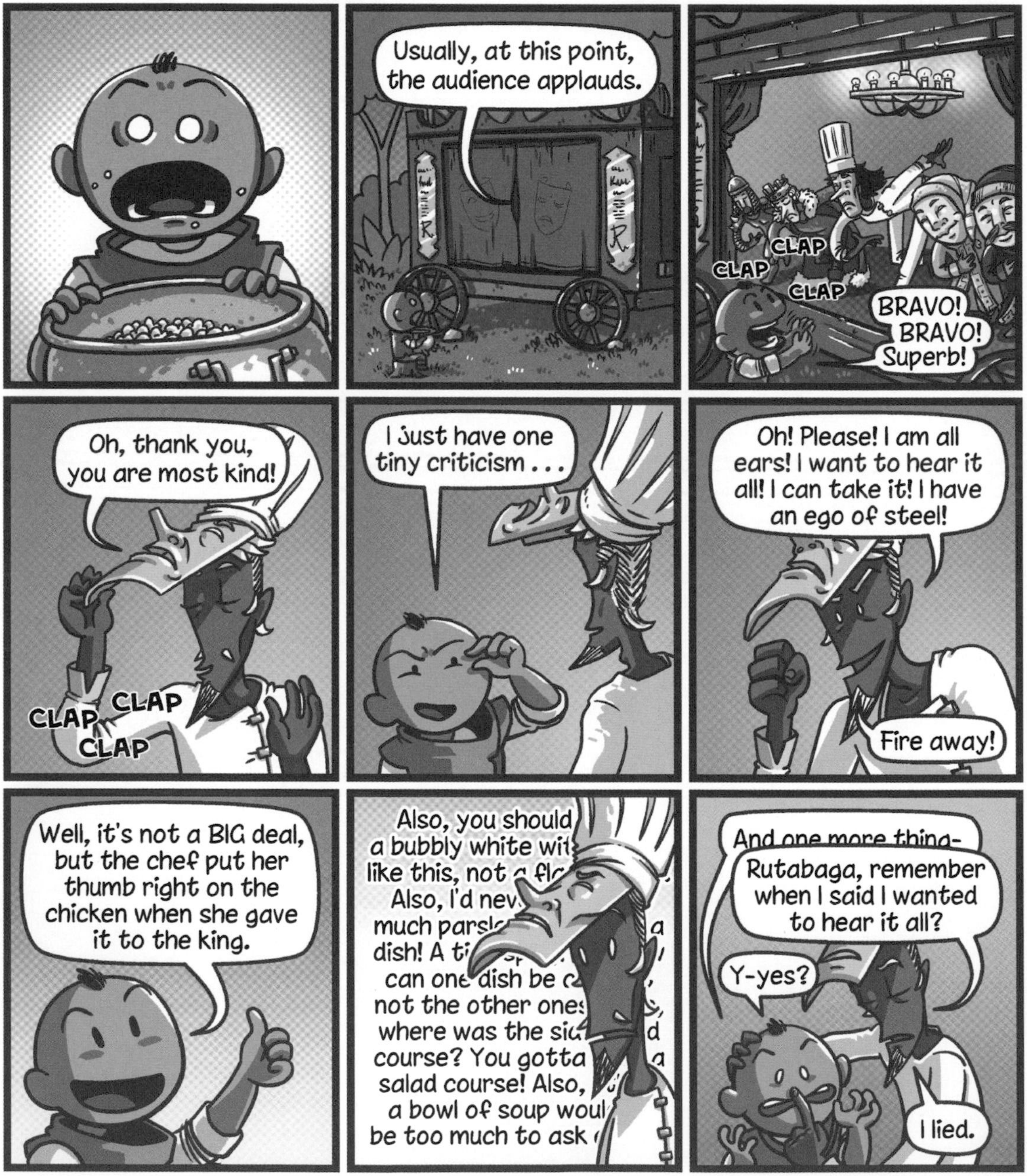
Usually, at this point, the audience applauds.
CLAP
CLAP
CLAP
BRAVO! BRAVO! Superb!
Oh, thank you, you are most kind!
CLAP
CLAP
CLAP
I just have one tiny criticism . . .
Oh! Please! I am all ears! I want to hear it all! I can take it! I have an ego of steel!
Fire away!
Well, it's not a BIG deal, but the chef put her thumb right on the chicken when she gave it to the king.
Also, you should a bubbly white wit like this, not a fl Also, I'd nev much pars a dish! A ti can one dish be not the other ones where was the si d course? You gotta a salad course! Also, a bowl of soup woul be too much to ask
And one more thing-
Rutabaga, remember when I said I wanted to hear it all?
Y-yes?
I lied.

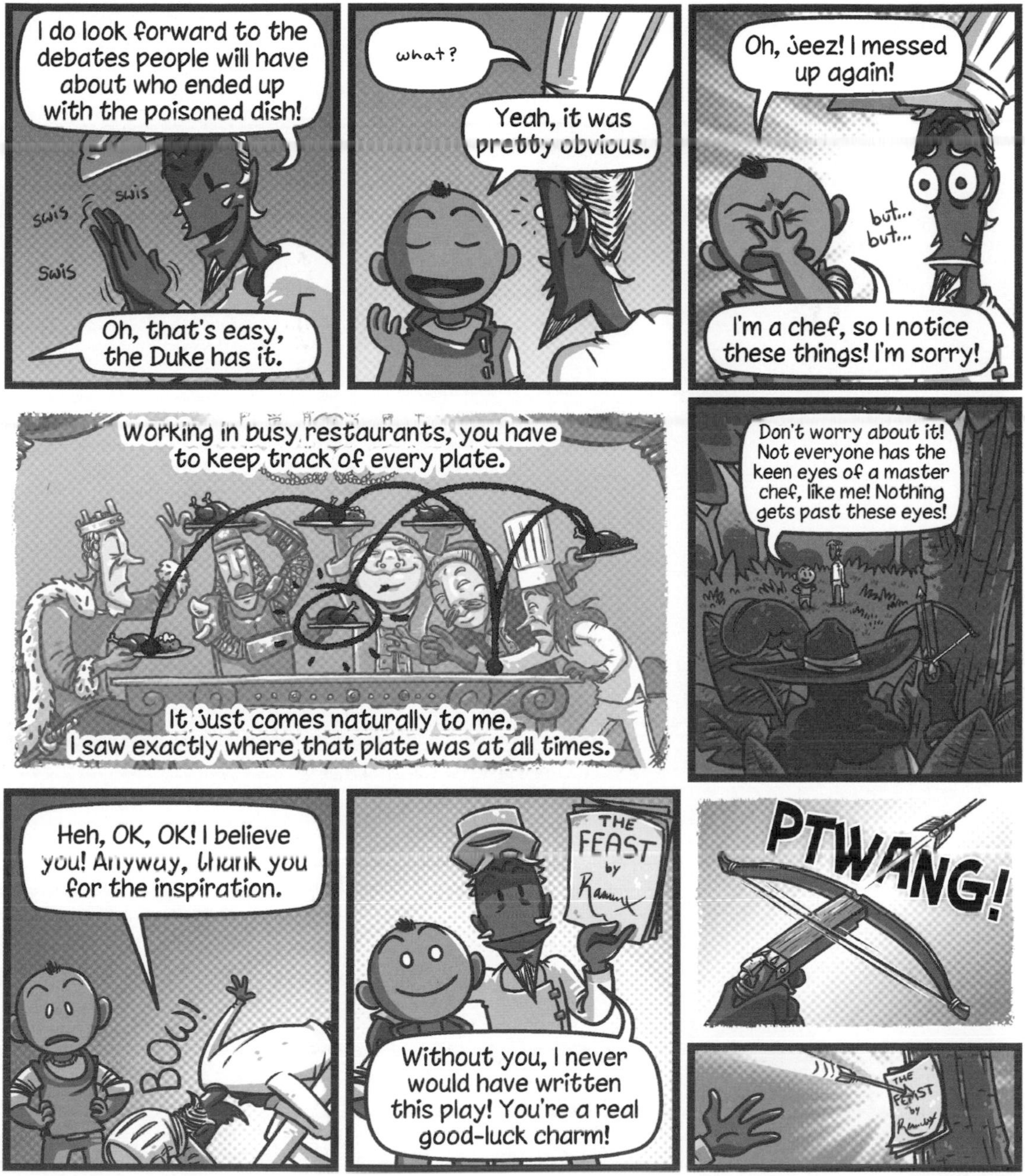
I do look forward to the debates people will have about who ended up with the poisoned dish!
swis
swis
swis
Oh, that's easy, the Duke has it.
what?
Yeah, it was pretty obvious.
Oh, jeez! I messed up again!
but... but...
I'm a chef, so I notice these things! I'm sorry!
Working in busy restaurants, you have to keep track of every plate.
It just comes naturally to me. I saw exactly where that plate was at all times.
Don't worry about it! Not everyone has the keen eyes of a master chef, like me! Nothing gets past these eyes!
Heh, OK, OK! I believe you! Anyway, thank you for the inspiration.
BOW!
THE FEAST by
Without you, I never would have written this play! You're a real good-luck charm!
PTWANG!
THE FEAST by

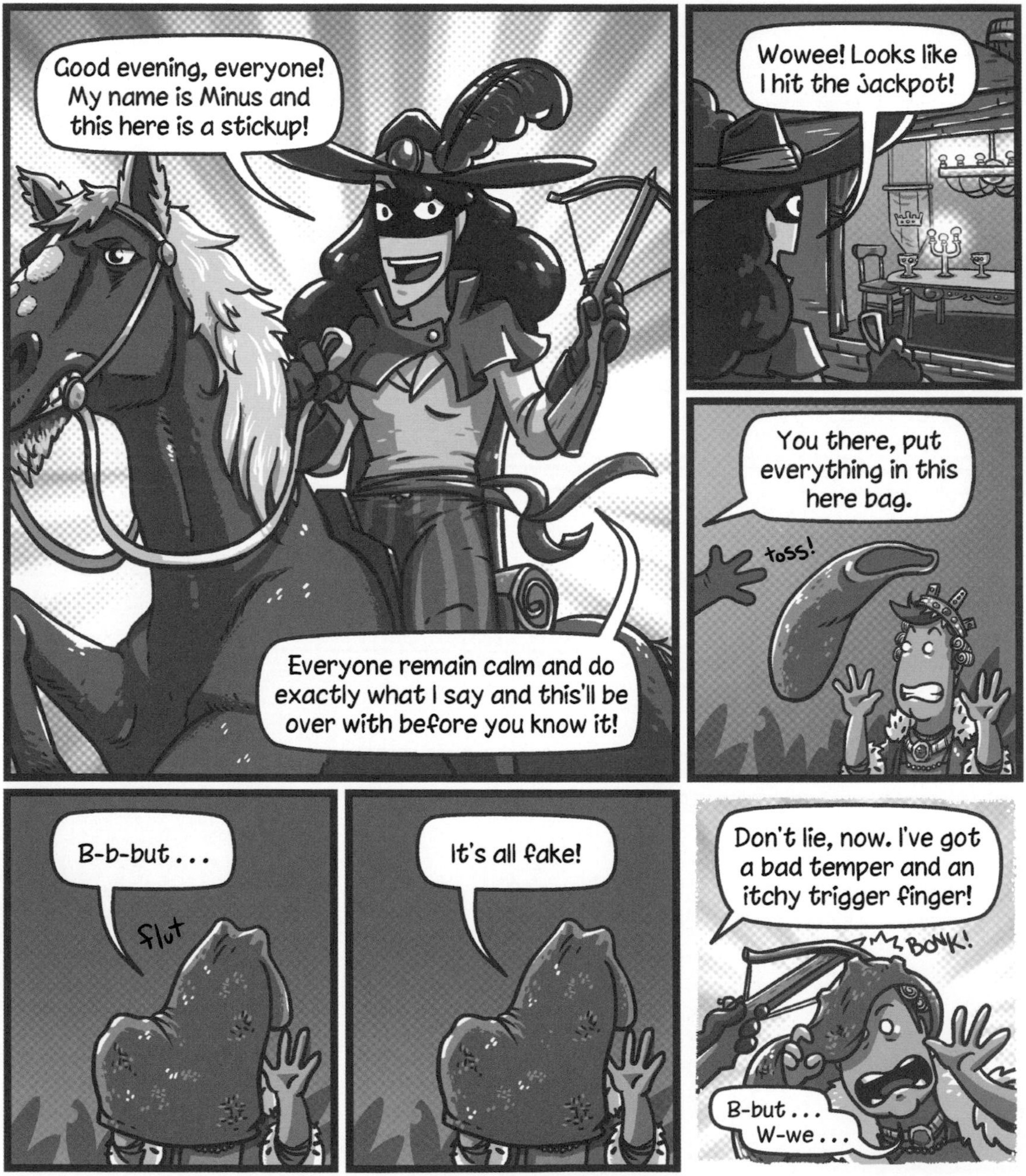
Good evening, everyone! My name is Minus and this here is a stickup!
Everyone remain calm and do exactly what I say and this'll be over with before you know it!
Wowee! Looks like I hit the jackpot!
You there, put everything in this here bag.
toss!
B-b-but . . .
flut
It's all fake!
Don't lie, now. I've got a bad temper and an itchy trigger finger!
BONK!
B-but . . . W-we . . .

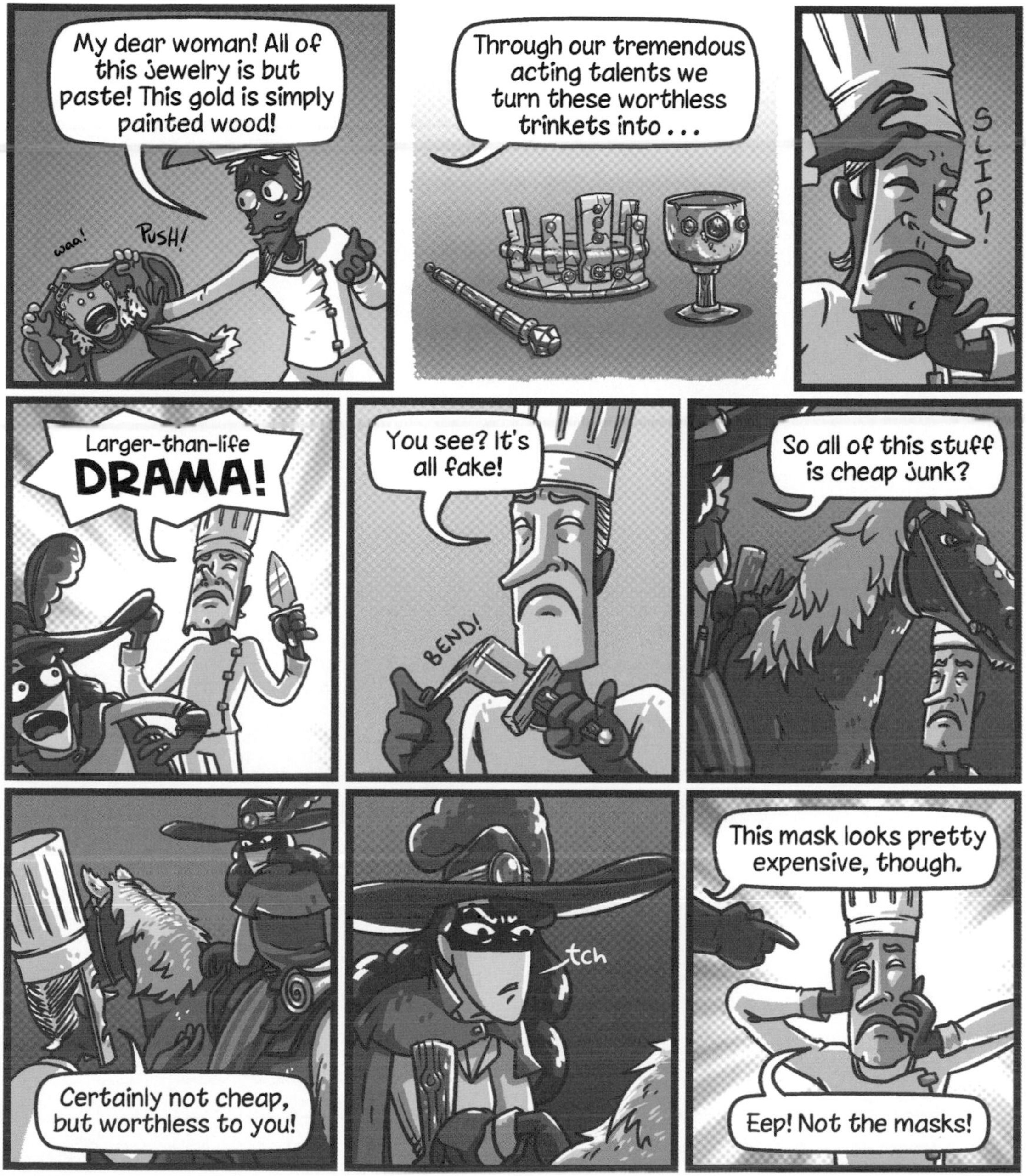
My dear woman! All of this jewelry is but paste! This gold is simply painted wood!
waa!
PUSH!
Through our tremendous acting talents we turn these worthless trinkets into . . .
SLIP!
Larger-than-life DRAMA!
You see? It's all fake!
BEND!
So all of this stuff is cheap junk?
Certainly not cheap, but worthless to you!
tch
This mask looks pretty expensive, though.
Eep! Not the masks!

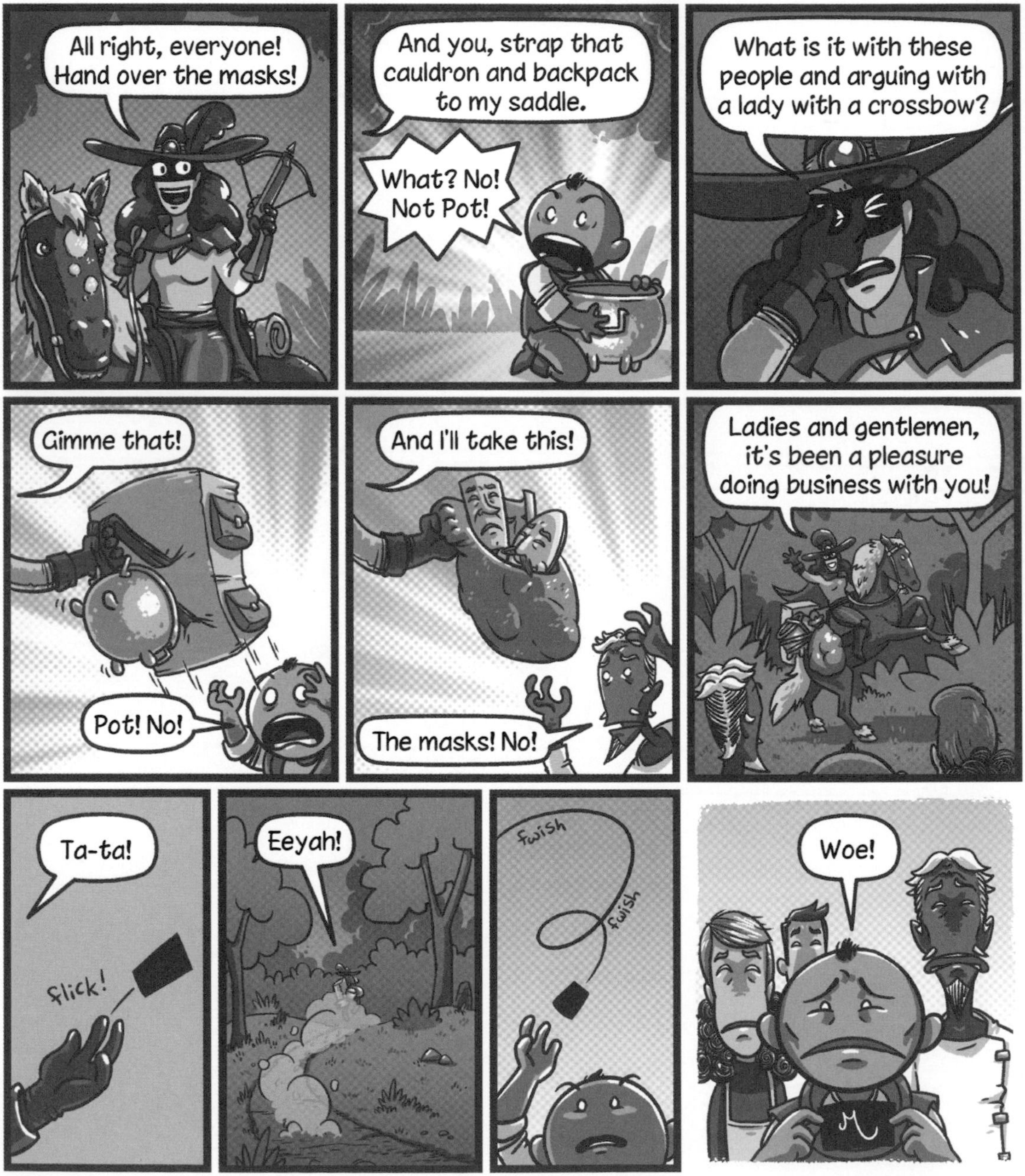
All right, everyone! Hand over the masks!
And you, strap that cauldron and backpack to my saddle.
What? No! Not Pot!
What is it with these people and arguing with a lady with a crossbow?
Gimme that!
Pot! No!
And I'll take this!
The masks! No!
Ladies and gentlemen, it's been a pleasure doing business with you!
Ta-ta!
flick!
Eeyah!
fwish
fwish
Woe!

END OF CHAPTER TWO

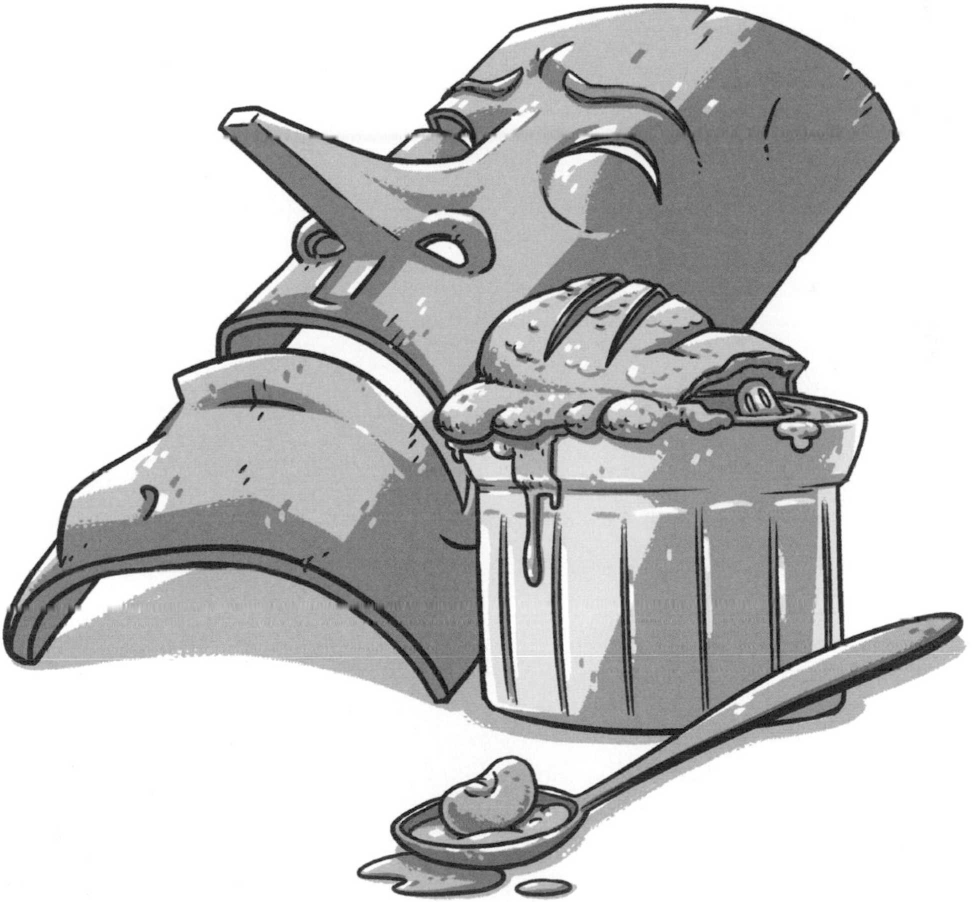

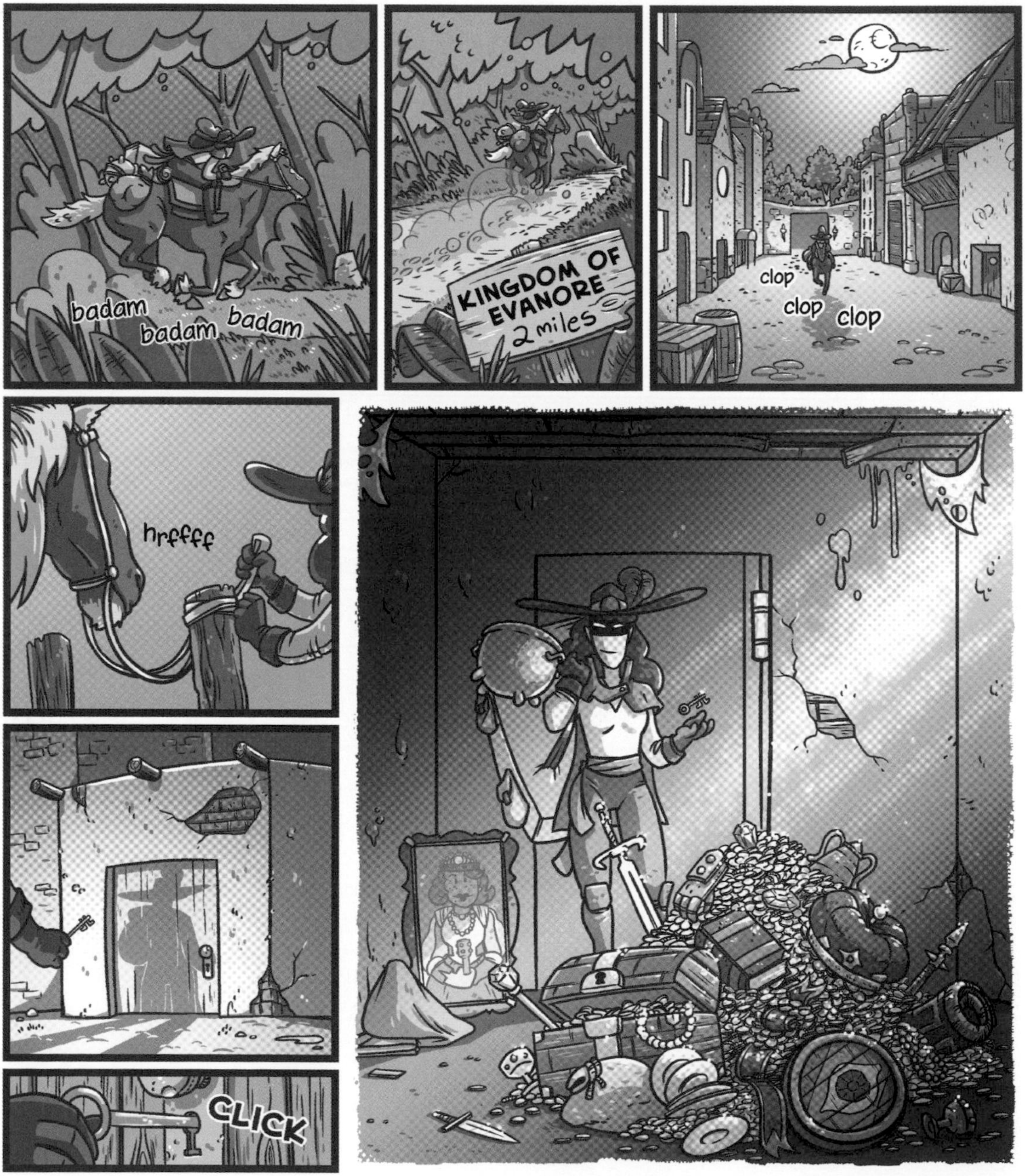
badam
badam
badam
KINGDOM OF
EVANORE
2 miles
clop
clop
clop
hrffff
CLICK

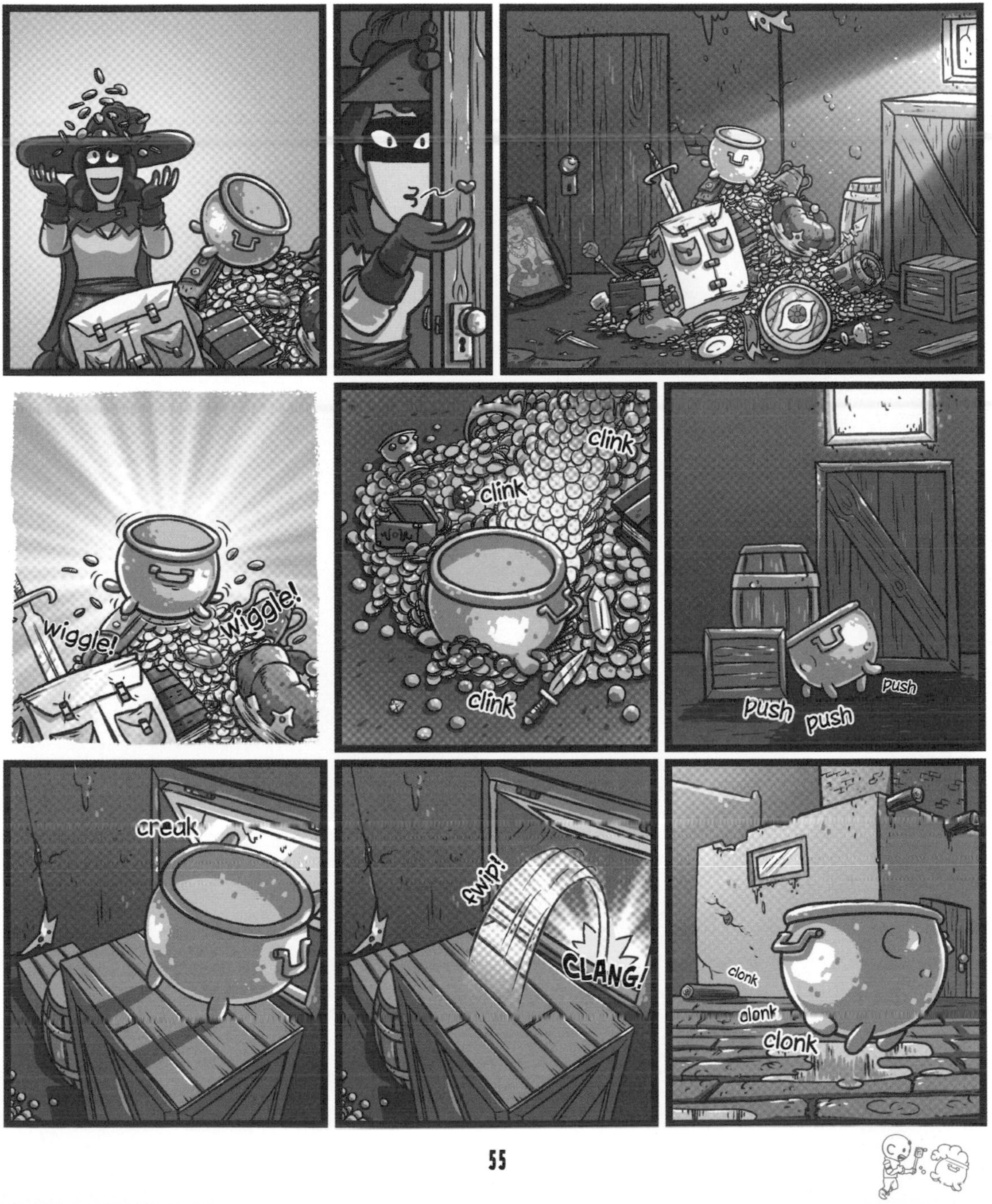
wiggle!
wiggle!
clink
clink
clink
push
push
push
creak
fwip!
CLANG!
clonk
clonk
clonk

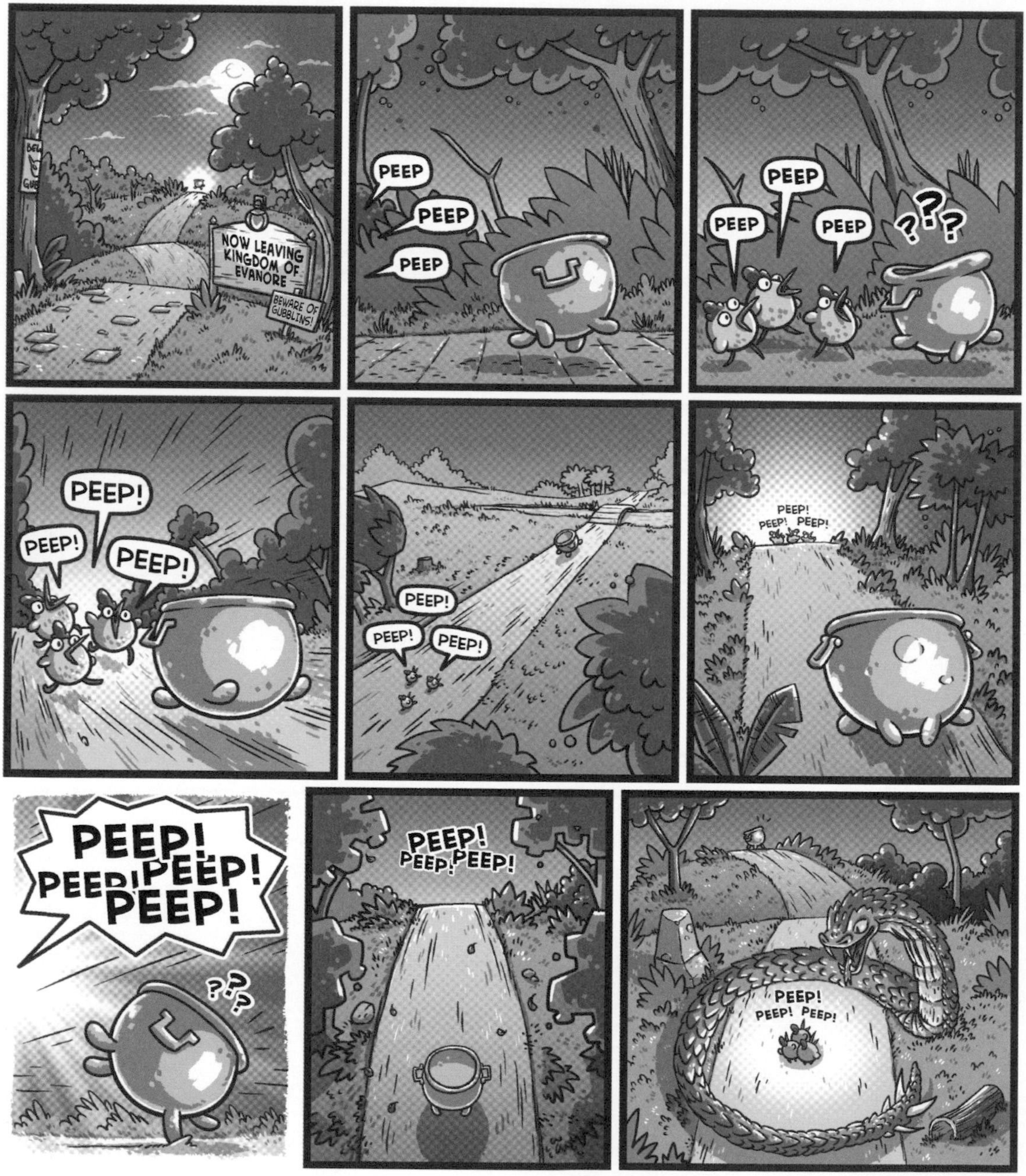
NOW LEAVING KINGDOM OF EVANORE
BEWARE OF GUBBLINS!
PEEP
PEEP
PEEP
PEEP
PEEP
PEEP
???
PEEP!
PEEP!
PEEP!
PEEP!
PEEP!
PEEP!
PEEP!
PEEP! PEEP!
PEEP!
PEEP!
PEEP!
PEEP!
??
PEEP!
PEEP! PEEP!
PEEP!
PEEP! PEEP!

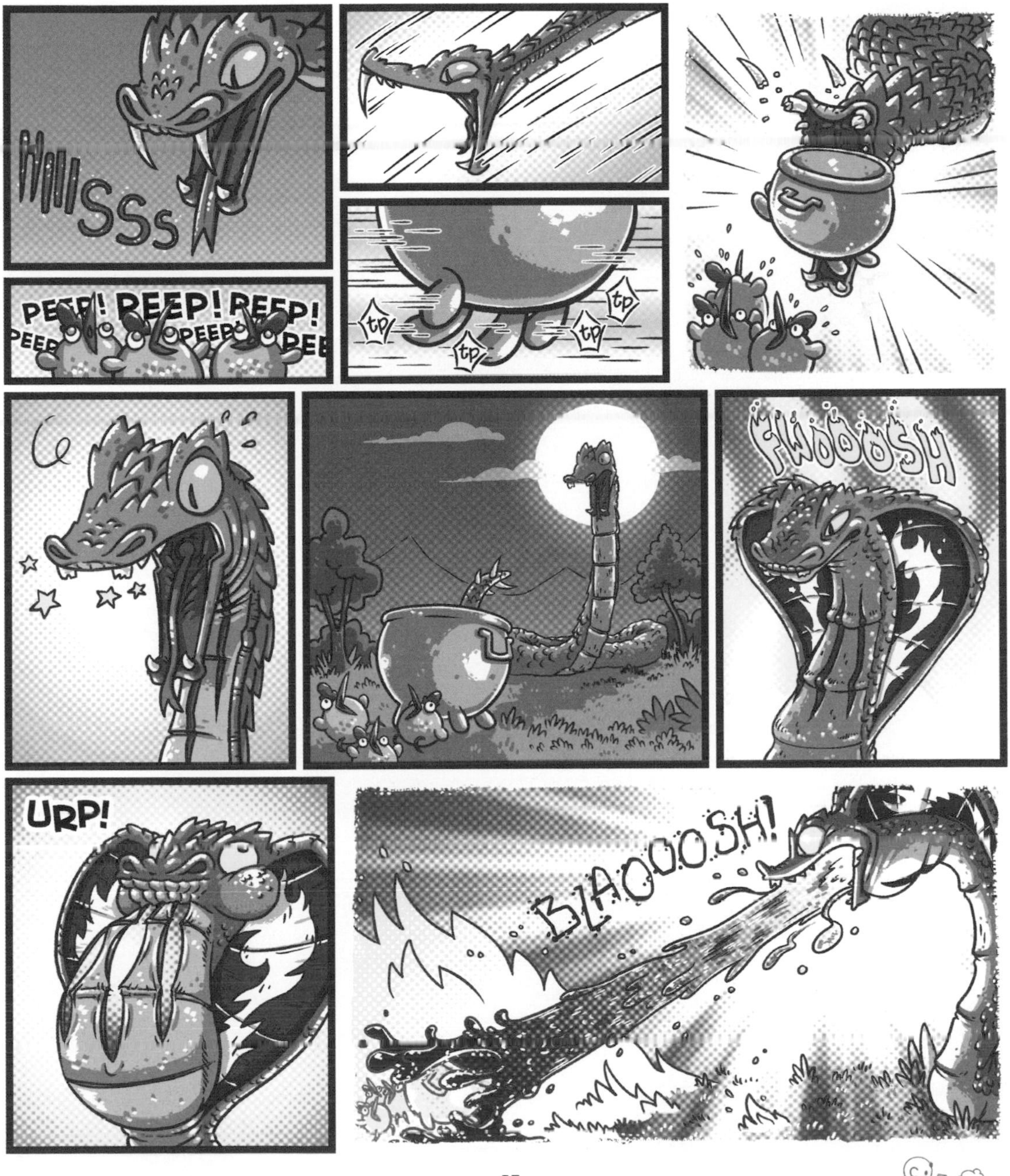
HIIISSs
PEEP! PEEP! PEEP!
PEEP!
tp tp tp tp
FWOOOSH
URP!
BLAOOOSH!

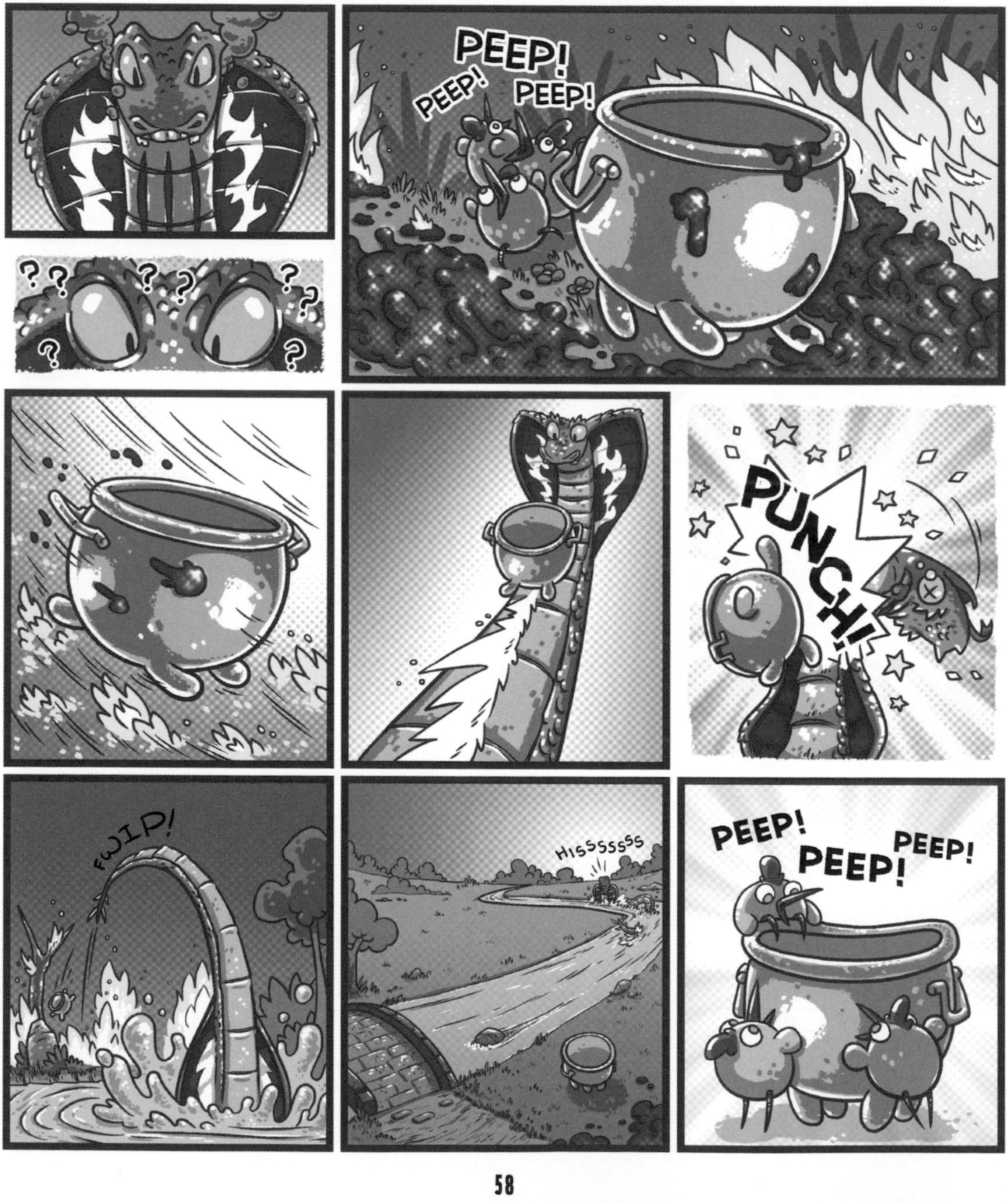
PEEP!
PEEP!
PEEP!
PUNCH!
FWIP!
HISSSSSSS
PEEP!
PEEP!
PEEP!

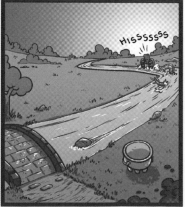

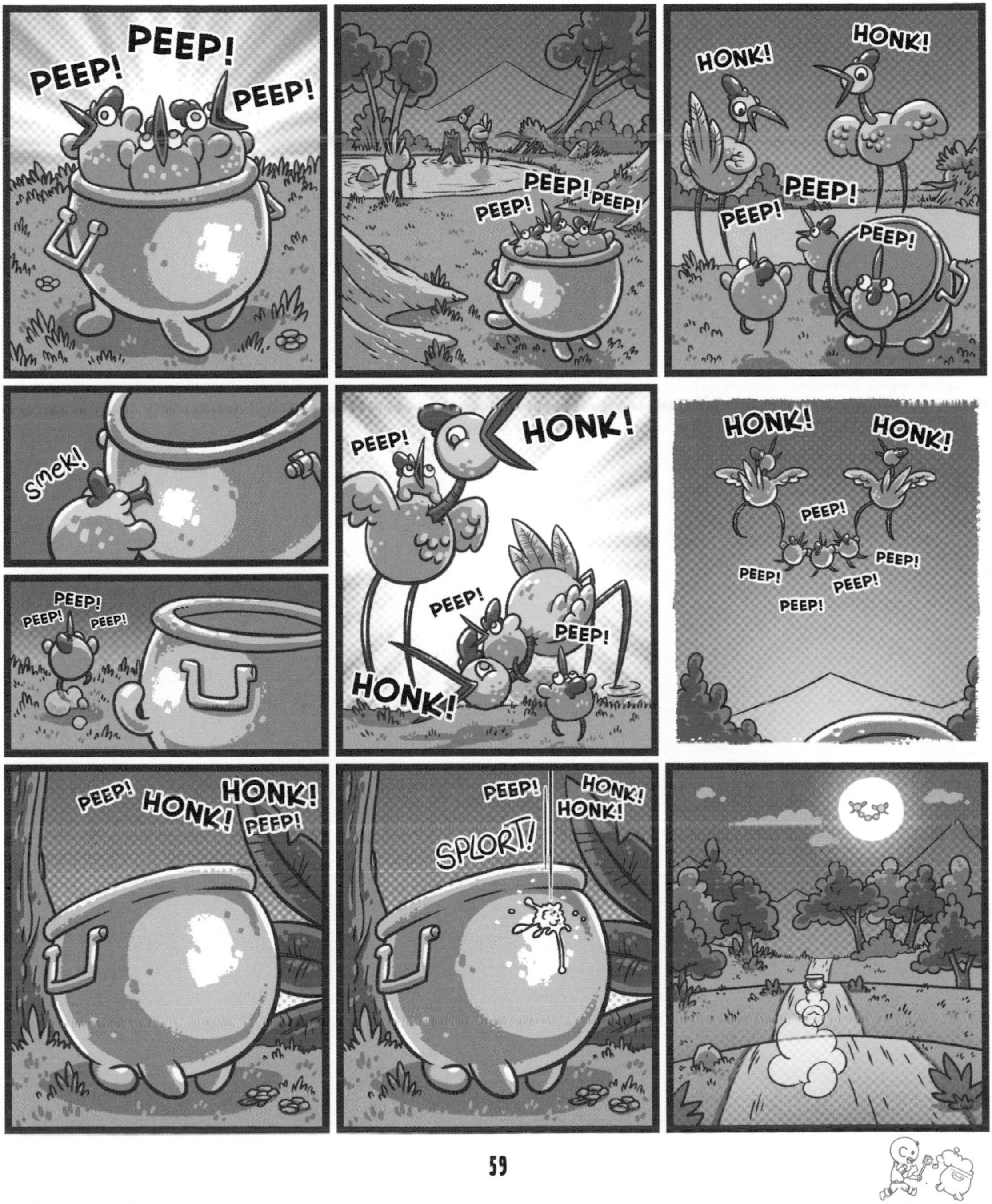
PEEP!
PEEP!
PEEP!
PEEP!
PEEP!
PEEP!
HONK!
HONK!
PEEP!
PEEP!
PEEP!
SMEK!
PEEP!
PEEP!
PEEP!
PEEP!
HONK!
PEEP!
PEEP!
HONK!
HONK!
HONK!
PEEP!
PEEP!
PEEP!
PEEP!
PEEP!
PEEP!
PEEP!
HONK!
HONK!
PEEP!
PEEP!
HONK!
HONK!
SPLORT!

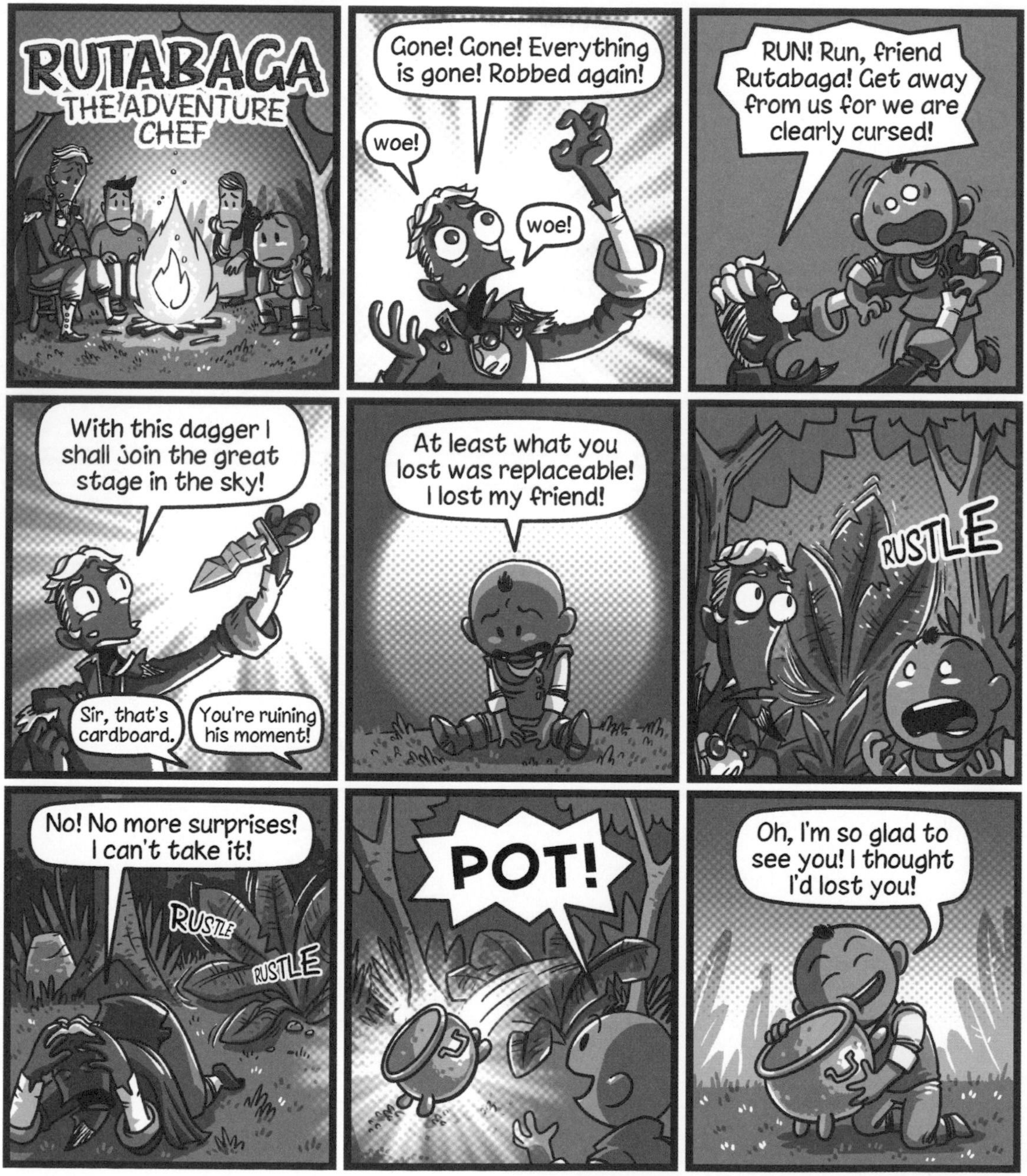
RUTABAGA
THE ADVENTURE CHEF
Gone! Gone! Everything is gone! Robbed again!
woe!
woe!
RUN! Run, friend Rutabaga! Get away from us for we are clearly cursed!
With this dagger I shall join the great stage in the sky!
Sir, that's cardboard.
You're ruining his moment!
At least what you lost was replaceable! I lost my friend!
RUSTLE
No! No more surprises! I can't take it!
RUSTLE
RUSTLE
POT!
Oh, I'm so glad to see you! I thought I'd lost you!

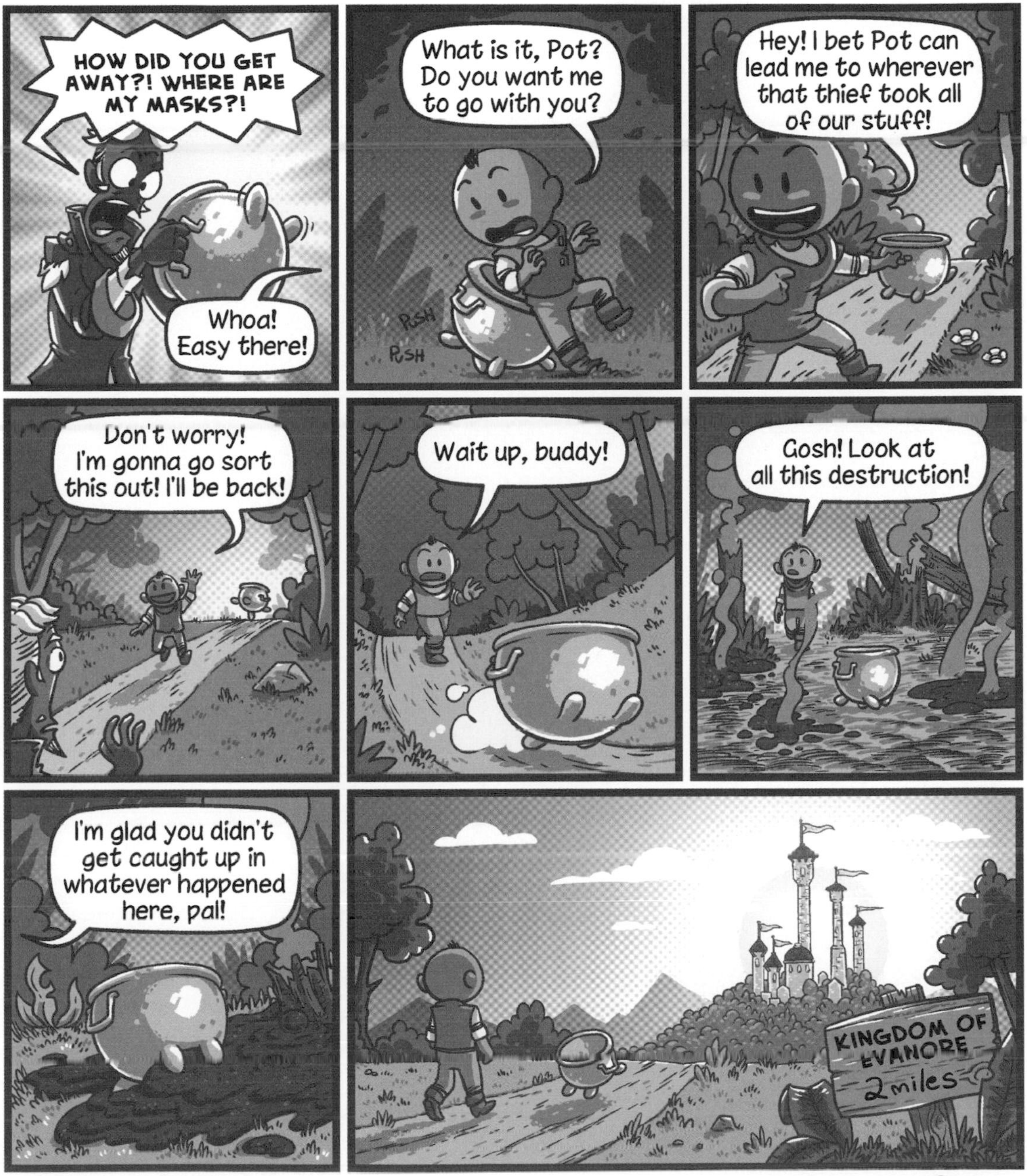
HOW DID YOU GET AWAY?! WHERE ARE MY MASKS?!
Whoa! Easy there!
What is it, Pot? Do you want me to go with you?
PUSH
PUSH
Hey! I bet Pot can lead me to wherever that thief took all of our stuff!
Don't worry! I'm gonna go sort this out! I'll be back!
Wait up, buddy!
Gosh! Look at all this destruction!
I'm glad you didn't get caught up in whatever happened here, pal!
KINGDOM OF EVANORE
2 miles

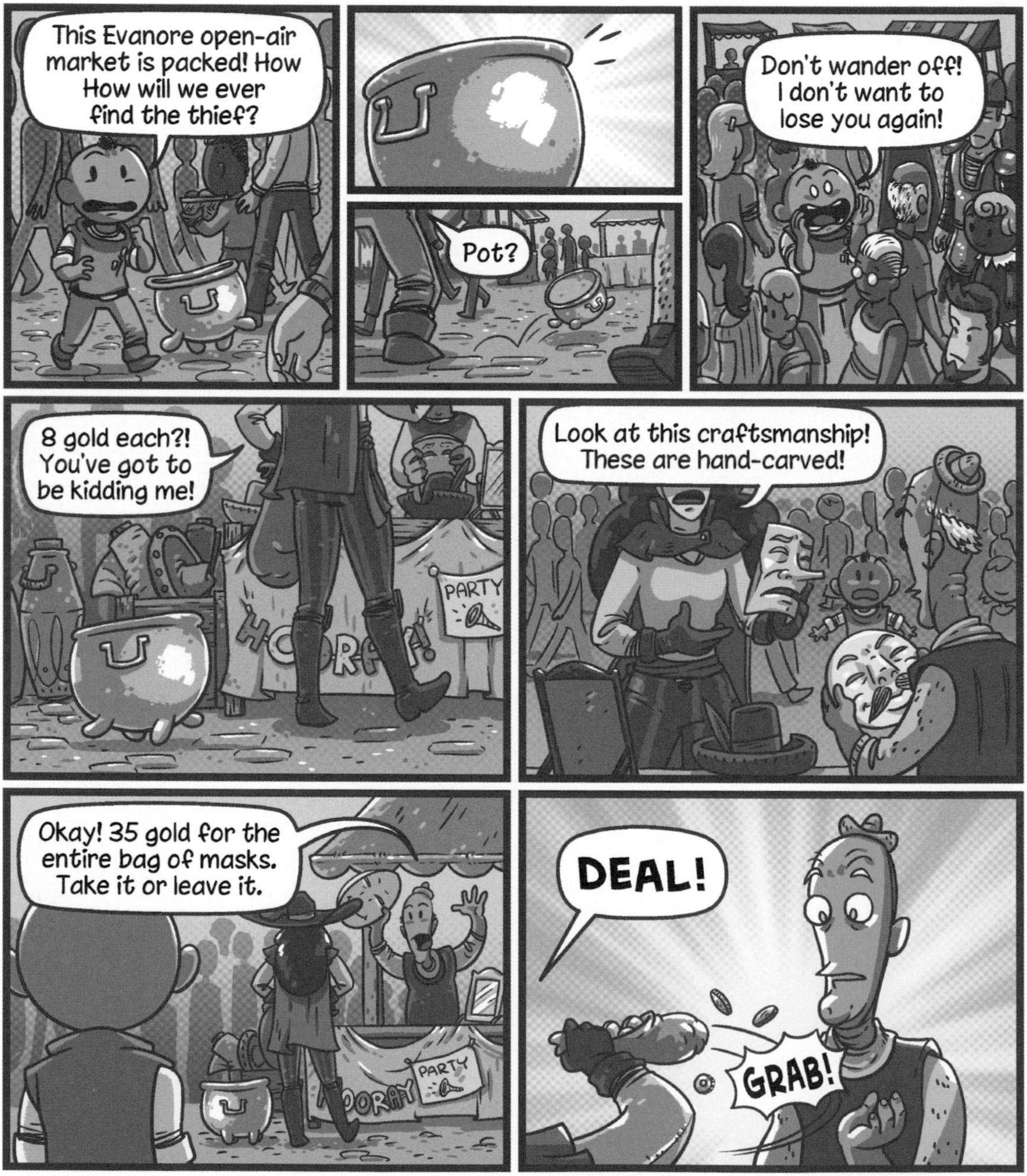
This Evanore open-air market is packed! How How will we ever find the thief?
Pot?
Don't wander off! I don't want to lose you again!
8 gold each?! You've got to be kidding me!
PARTY
HOORAY!
Look at this craftsmanship! These are hand-carved!
Okay! 35 gold for the entire bag of masks. Take it or leave it.
PARTY
HOORAY
DEAL!
GRAB!

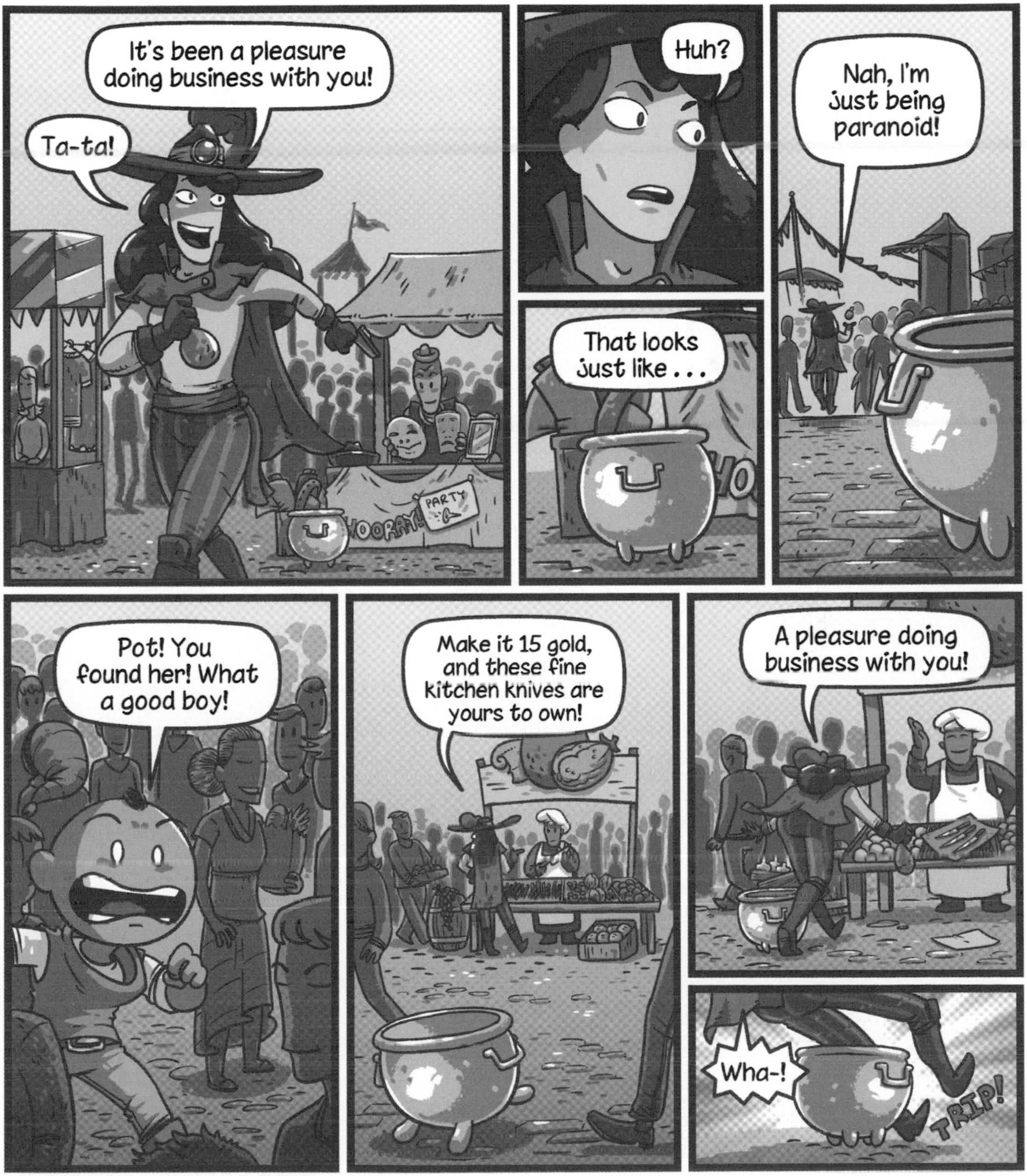
It's been a pleasure doing business with you!
Ta-ta!
PARTY
Huh?
That looks just like . . .
Nah, I'm just being paranoid!
Pot! You found her! What a good boy!
Make it 15 gold, and these fine kitchen knives are yours to own!
A pleasure doing business with you!
Wha-!
TRIP!

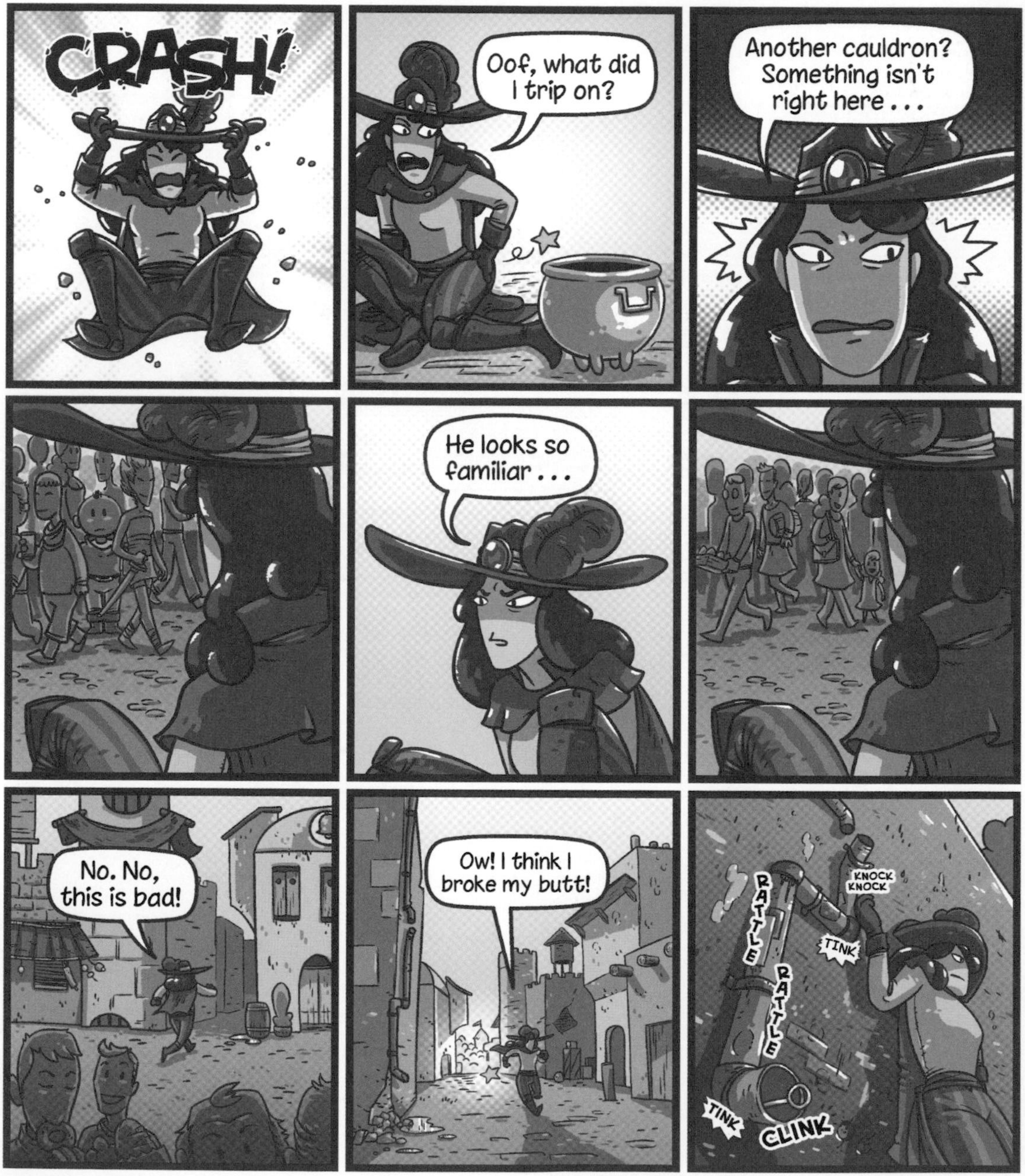
CRASH!
Oof, what did I trip on?
Another cauldron? Something isn't right here . . .
He looks so familiar . . .
No. No, this is bad!
Ow! I think I broke my butt!
RATTLE
KNOCK KNOCK
TINK
RATTLE
TINK
CLINK

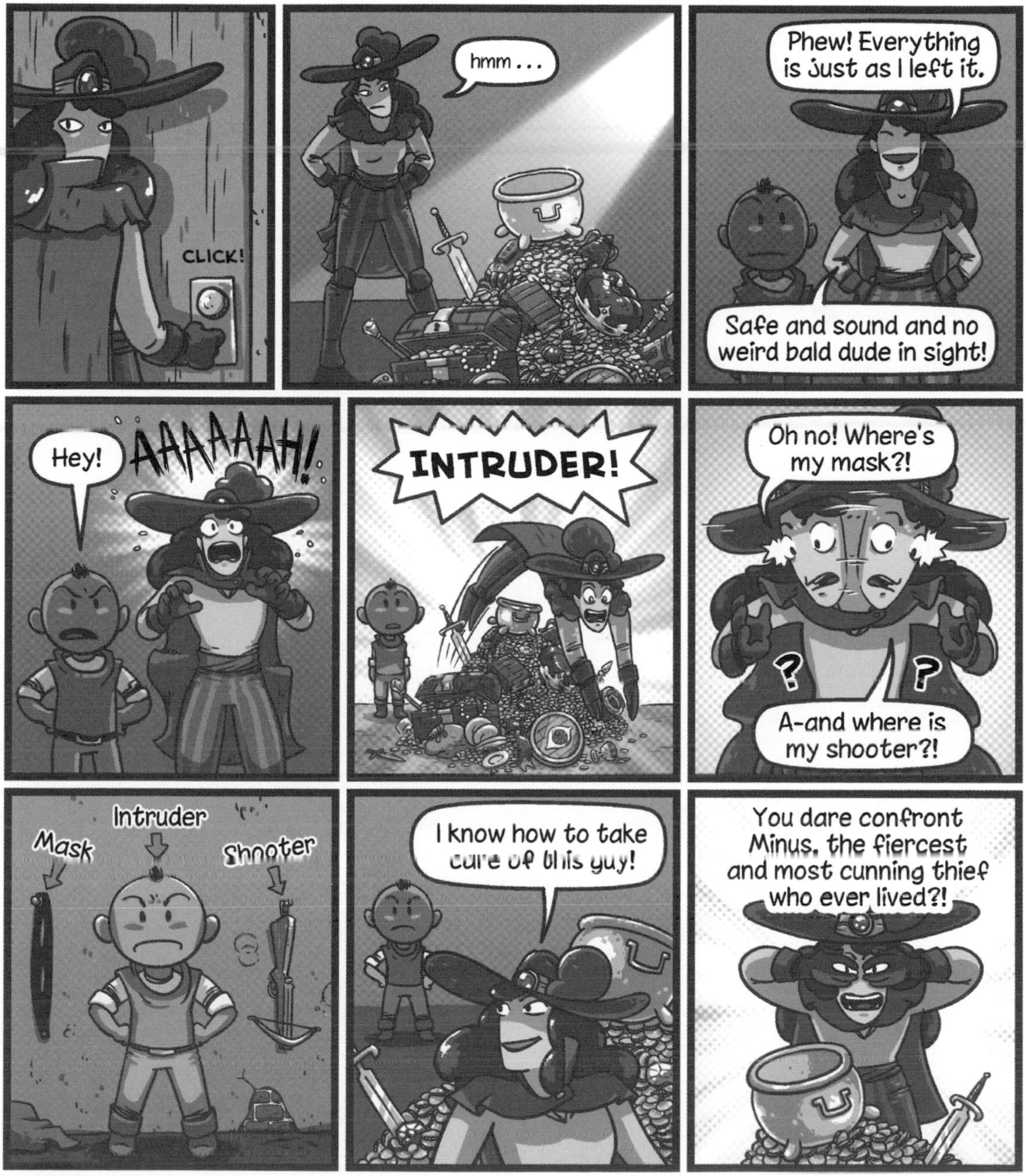
CLICK!
hmm . . .
Phew! Everything is just as I left it.
Safe and sound and no weird bald dude in sight!
Hey!
AAAAAAH!
INTRUDER!
Oh no! Where's my mask?!
?
?
A-and where is my shooter?!
Intruder
Mask
Shooter
I know how to take care of this guy!
You dare confront Minus, the fiercest and most cunning thief who ever lived?!

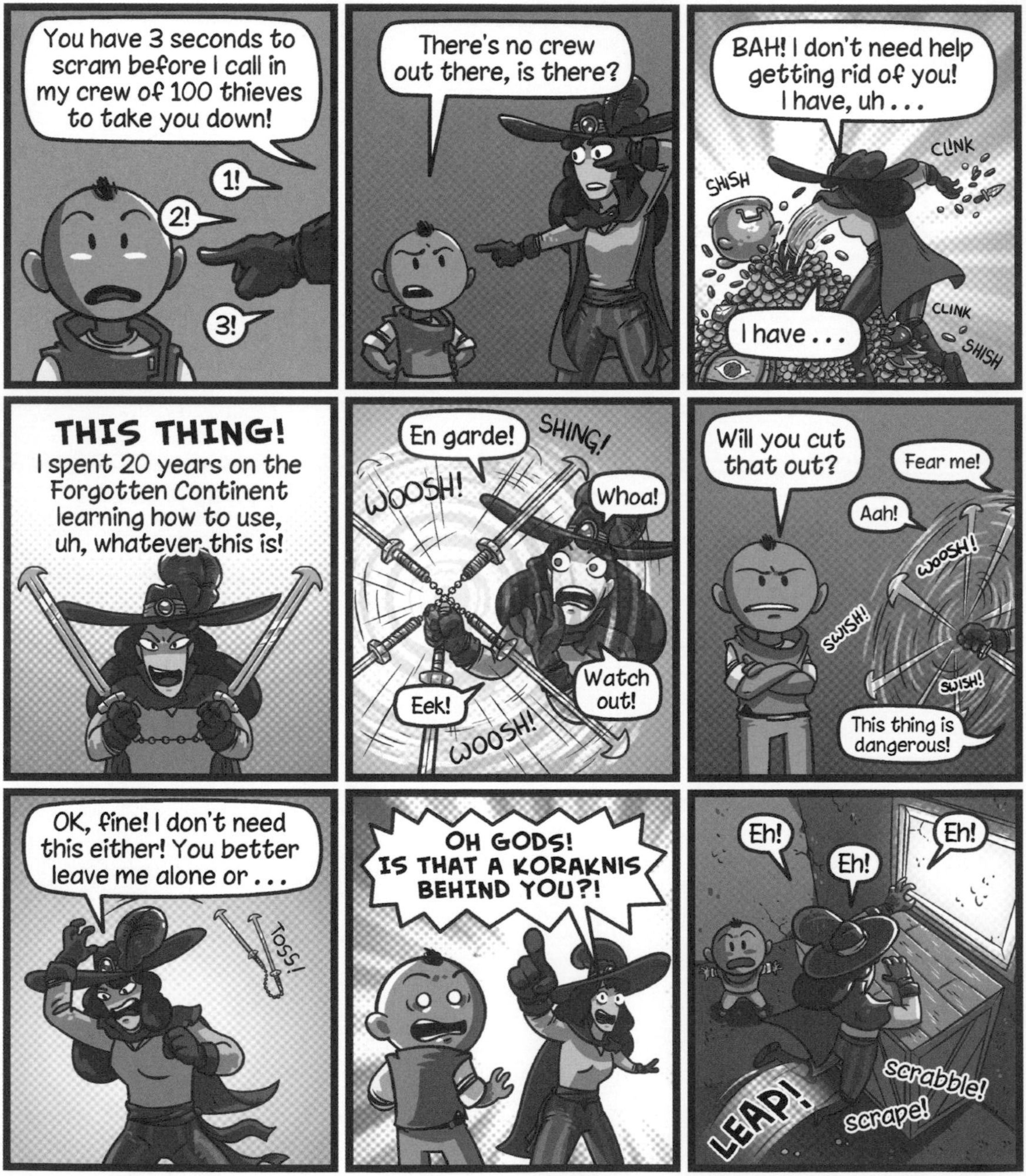
You have 3 seconds to scram before I call in my crew of 100 thieves to take you down!
1!
2!
3!
There's no crew out there, is there?
BAH! I don't need help getting rid of you! I have, uh . . .
CLINK
SHISH
CLINK
SHISH
I have . . .
THIS THING!
I spent 20 years on the Forgotten Continent learning how to use, uh, whatever this is!
En garde!
SHING!
WOOSH!
Whoa!
Watch out!
Eek!
WOOSH!
Will you cut that out?
Fear me!
Aah!
WOOSH!
SWISH!
SWISH!
This thing is dangerous!
OK, fine! I don't need this either! You better leave me alone or . . .
TOSS!
OH GODS! IS THAT A KORAKNIS BEHIND YOU?!
Eh!
Eh!
Eh!
scrabble!
scrape!
LEAP!

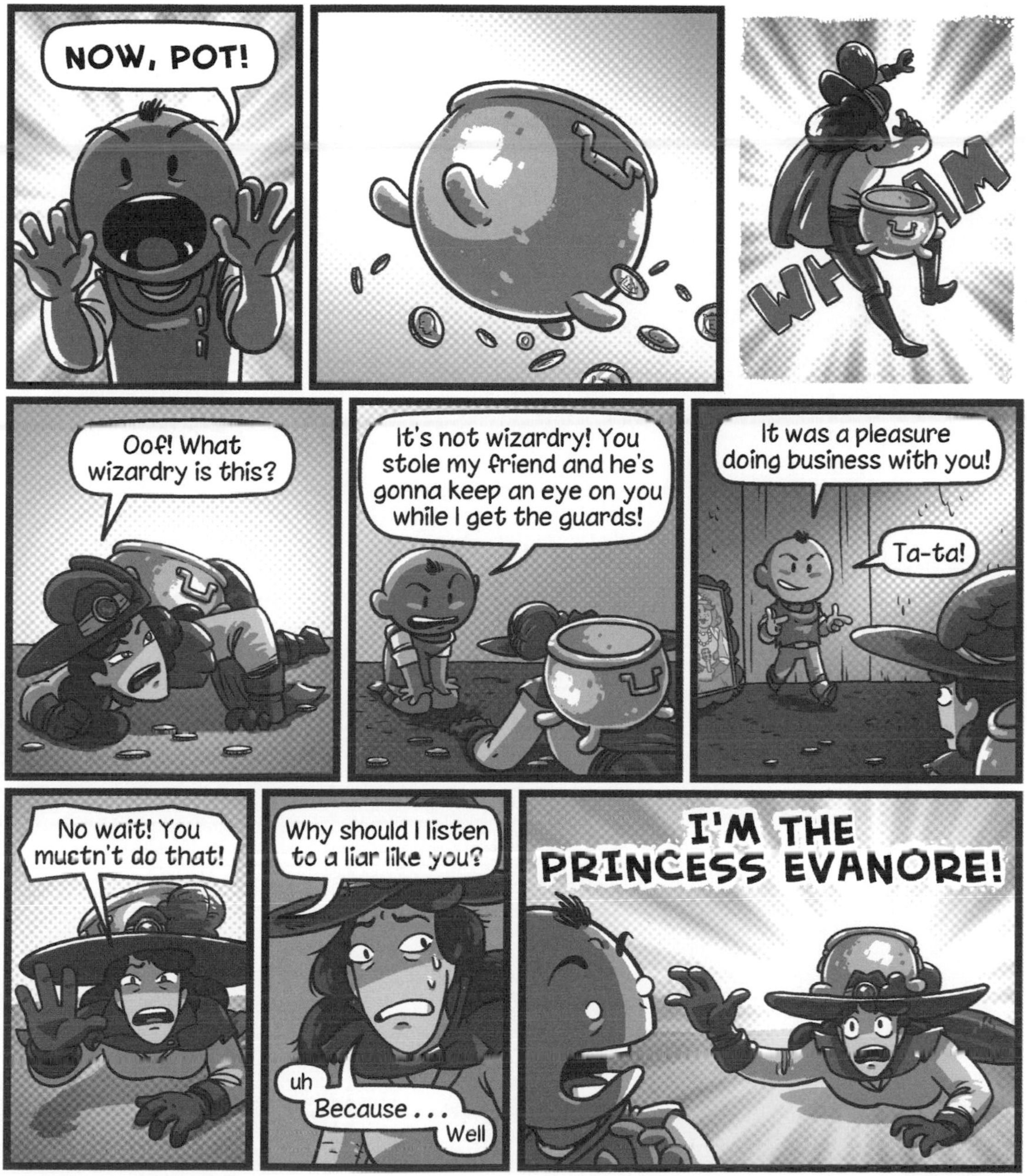
NOW, POT!
WHAM
Oof! What wizardry is this?
It's not wizardry! You stole my friend and he's gonna keep an eye on you while I get the guards!
It was a pleasure doing business with you!
Ta-ta!
No wait! You muctn't do that!
Why should I listen to a liar like you?
uh
Because . . .
Well
I'M THE PRINCESS EVANORE!

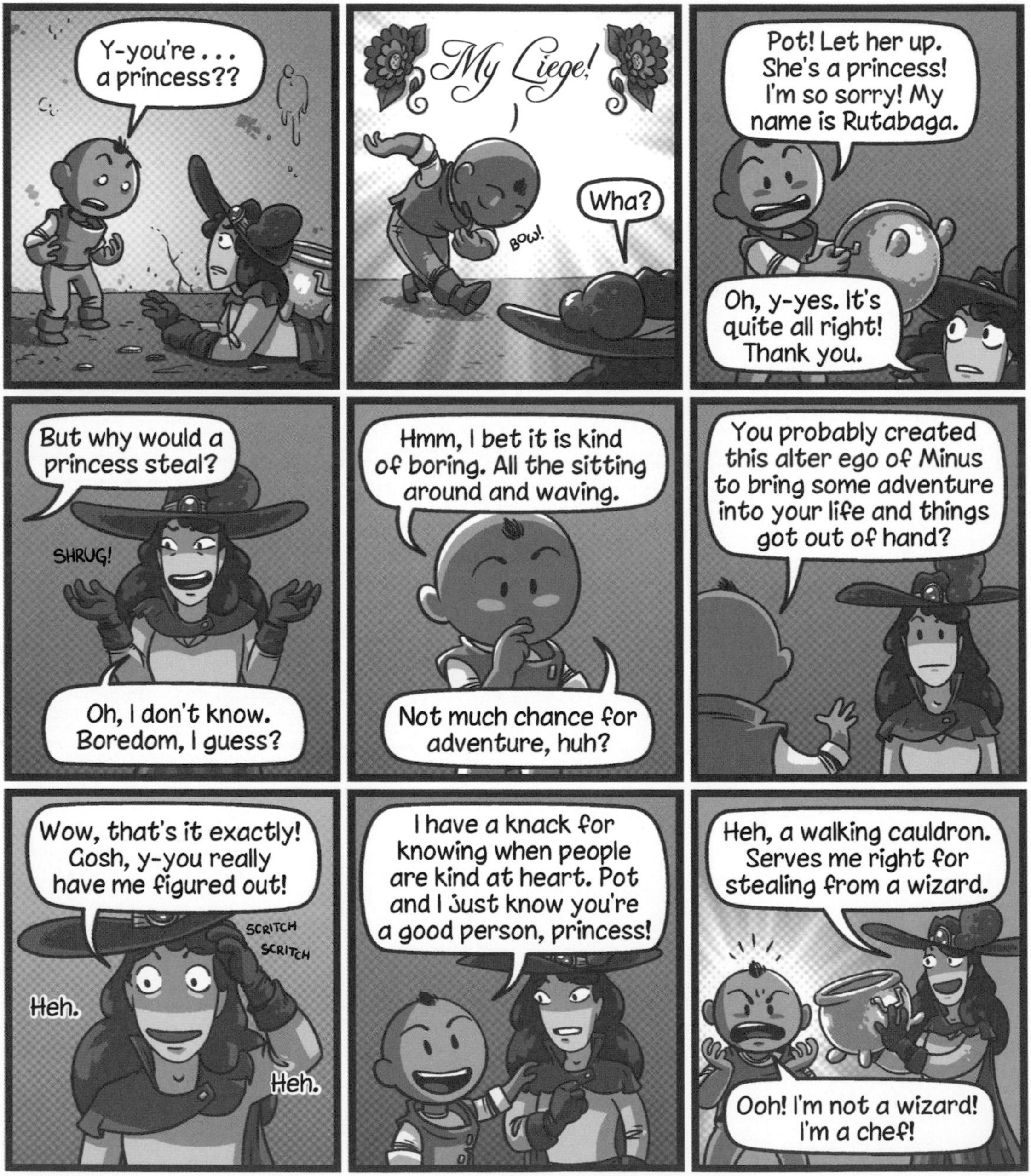
Y-you're . . . a princess??
My Liege!
BOW!
Wha?
Pot! Let her up. She's a princess! I'm so sorry! My name is Rutabaga.
Oh, y-yes. It's quite all right! Thank you.
But why would a princess steal?
SHRUG!
Oh, I don't know. Boredom, I guess?
Hmm, I bet it is kind of boring. All the sitting around and waving.
Not much chance for adventure, huh?
You probably created this alter ego of Minus to bring some adventure into your life and things got out of hand?
Wow, that's it exactly! Gosh, y-you really have me figured out!
SCRITCH SCRITCH
Heh.
Heh.
I have a knack for knowing when people are kind at heart. Pot and I just know you're a good person, princess!
Heh, a walking cauldron. Serves me right for stealing from a wizard.
Ooh! I'm not a wizard! I'm a chef!

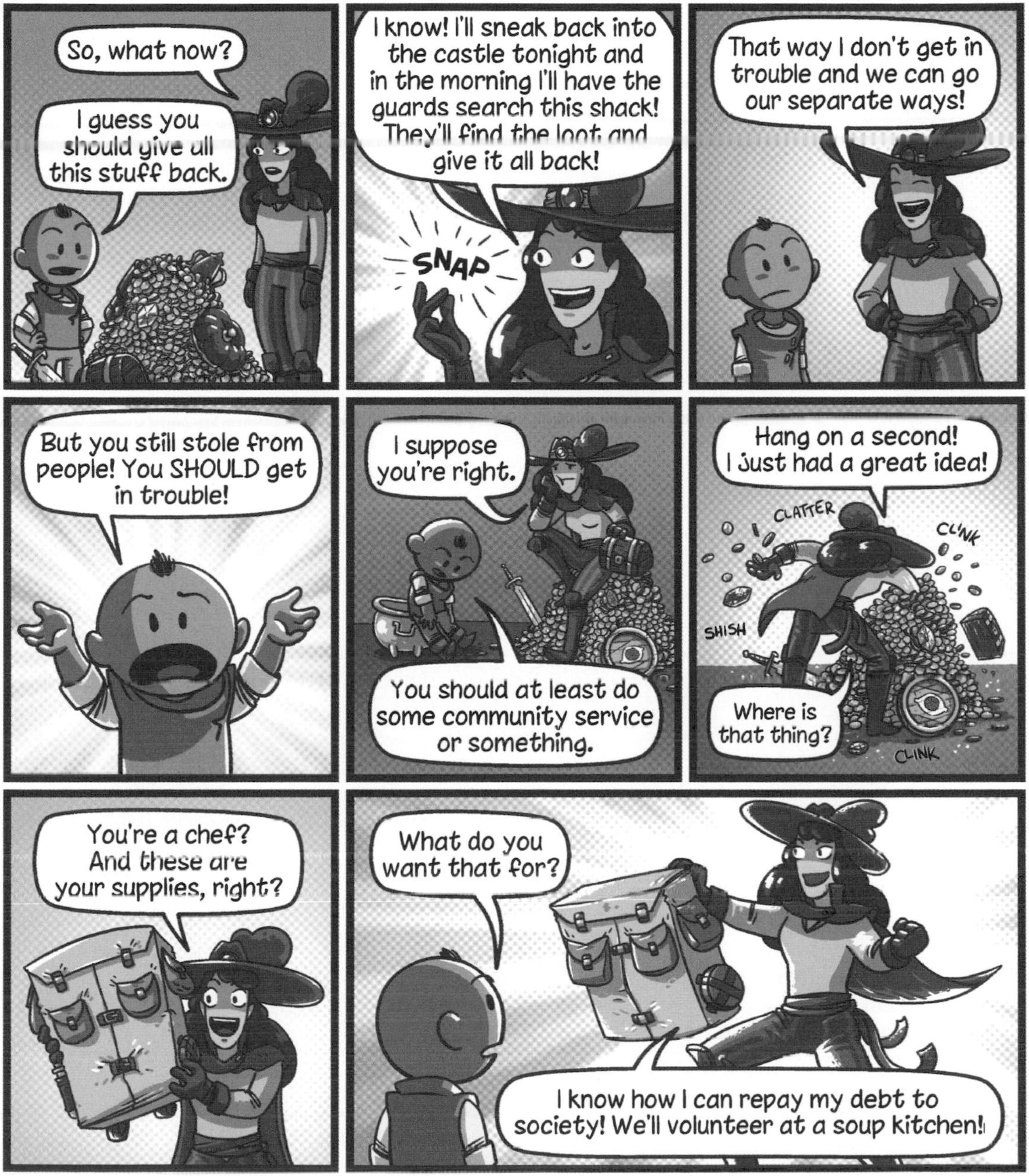
So, what now?
I guess you should give all this stuff back.
I know! I'll sneak back into the castle tonight and in the morning I'll have the guards search this shack! They'll find the loot and give it all back!
SNAP
That way I don't get in trouble and we can go our separate ways!
But you still stole from people! You SHOULD get in trouble!
I suppose you're right.
You should at least do some community service or something.
Hang on a second! I just had a great idea!
CLATTER
CLINK
SHISH
Where is that thing?
CLINK
You're a chef? And these are your supplies, right?
What do you want that for?
I know how I can repay my debt to society! We'll volunteer at a soup kitchen!

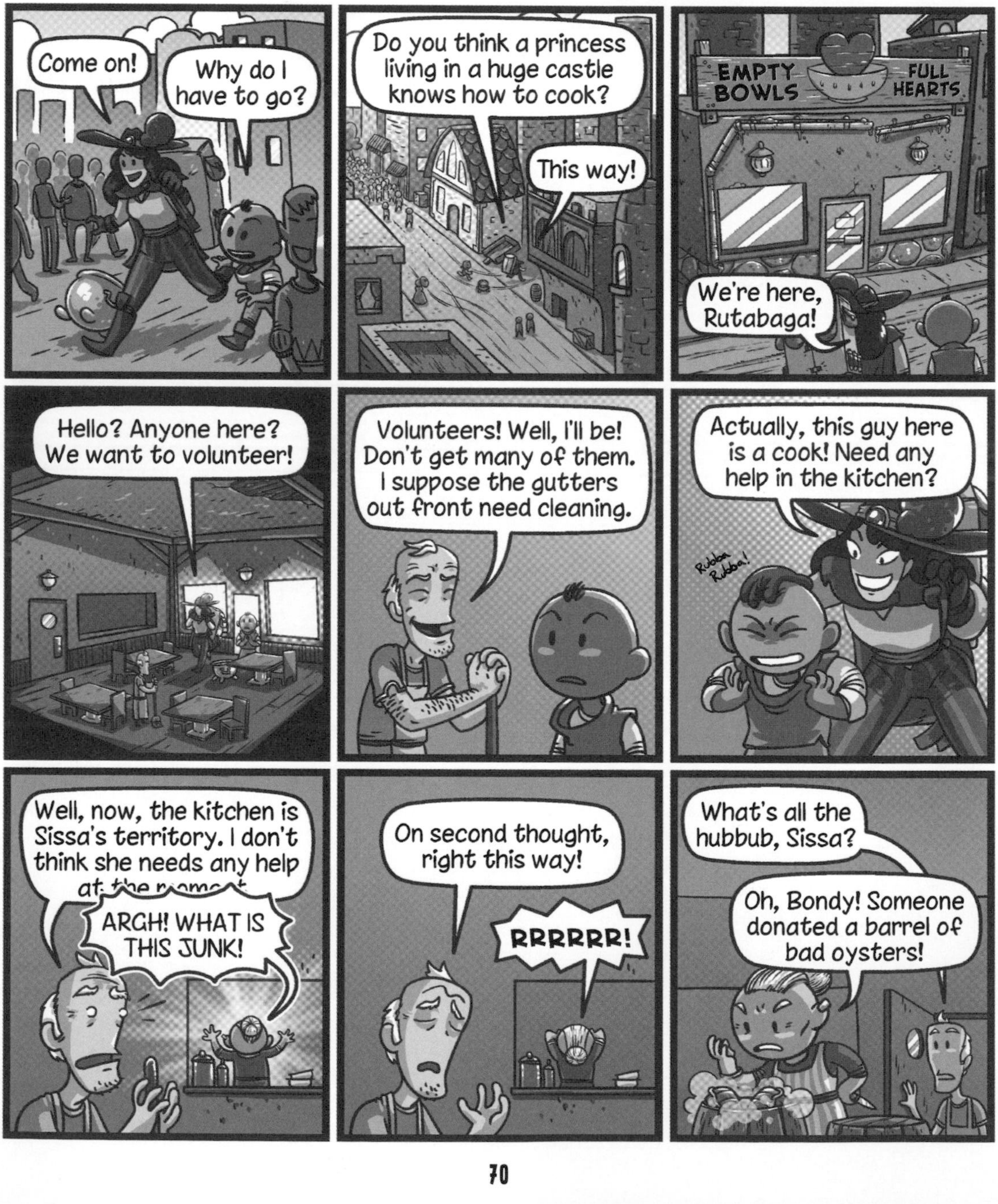
Come on!
Why do I have to go?
Do you think a princess living in a huge castle knows how to cook?
This way!
EMPTY BOWLS
FULL HEARTS
We're here, Rutabaga!
Hello? Anyone here? We want to volunteer!
Volunteers! Well, I'll be! Don't get many of them. I suppose the gutters out front need cleaning.
Actually, this guy here is a cook! Need any help in the kitchen?
Rubba Rubba!
Well, now, the kitchen is Sissa's territory. I don't think she needs any help
ARGH! WHAT IS THIS JUNK!
On second thought, right this way!
RRRRRR!
What's all the hubbub, Sissa?
Oh, Bondy! Someone donated a barrel of bad oysters!

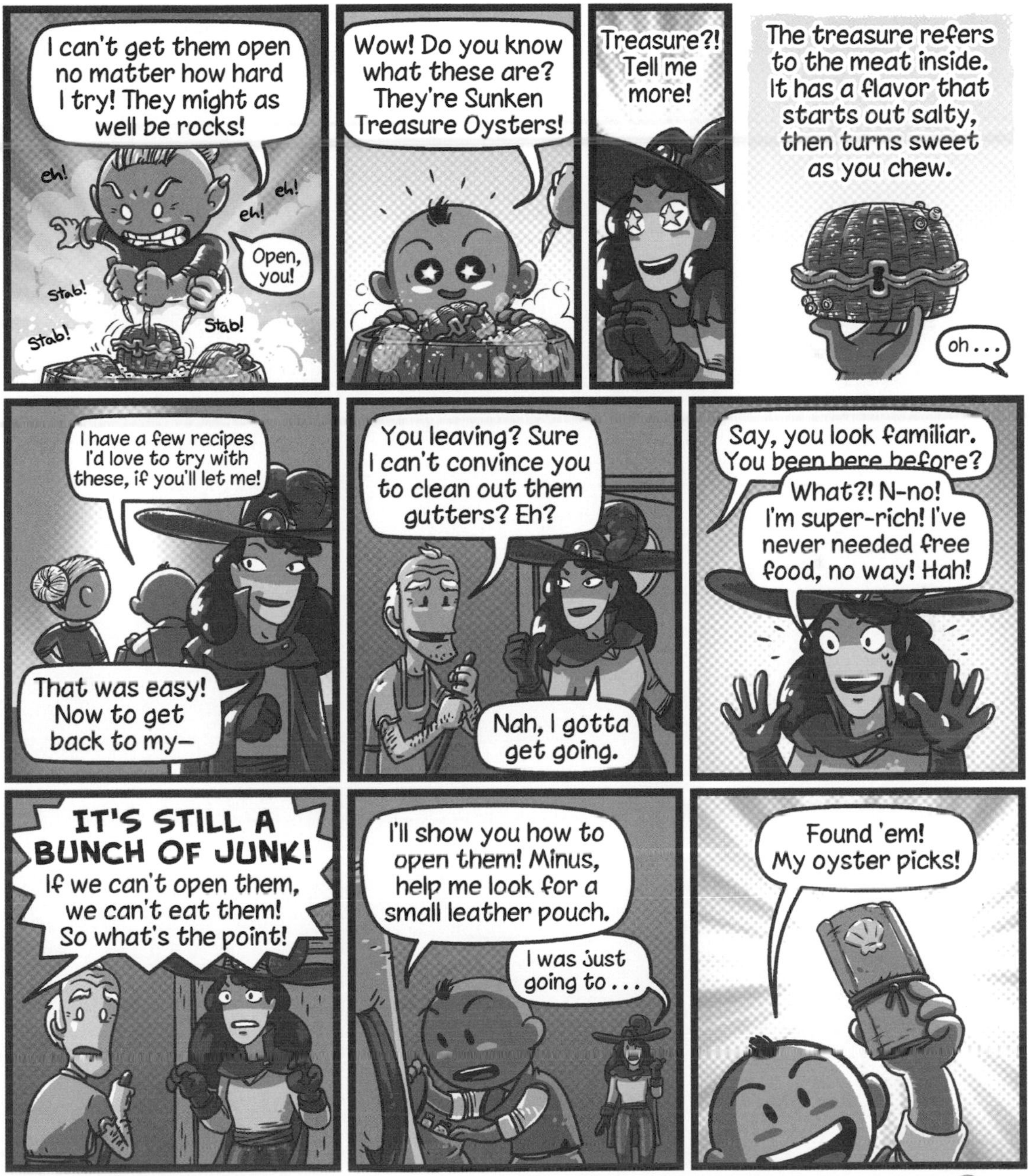

I can't get them open no matter how hard I try! They might as well be rocks!
eh!
eh!
eh!
Open, you!
Stab!
Stab!
Stab!
Wow! Do you know what these are? They're Sunken Treasure Oysters!
Treasure?! Tell me more!
The treasure refers to the meat inside. It has a flavor that starts out salty, then turns sweet as you chew.
oh . . .
I have a few recipes I'd love to try with these, if you'll let me!
That was easy! Now to get back to my—
You leaving? Sure I can't convince you to clean out them gutters? Eh?
Nah, I gotta get going.
Say, you look familiar. You been here before?
What?! N-no! I'm super-rich! I've never needed free food, no way! Hah!
IT'S STILL A BUNCH OF JUNK!
If we can't open them, we can't eat them! So what's the point!
I'll show you how to open them! Minus, help me look for a small leather pouch.
I was just going to . . .
Found 'em! My oyster picks!

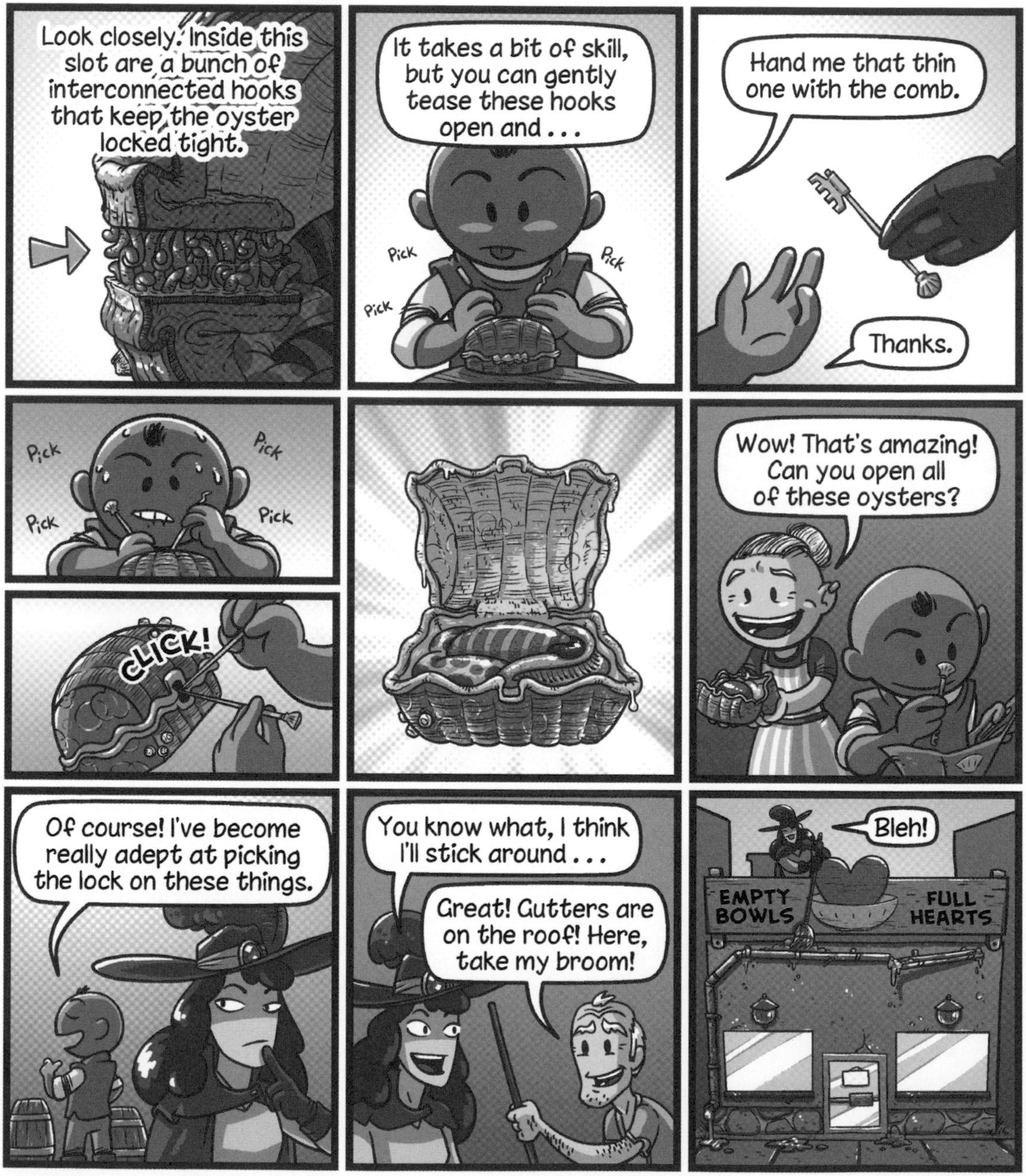
Look closely. Inside this slot are a bunch of interconnected hooks that keep the oyster locked tight.
It takes a bit of skill, but you can gently tease these hooks open and . . .
Pick
Pick
Pick
Hand me that thin one with the comb.
Thanks.
Pick
Pick
Pick
Pick
CLICK!
Wow! That's amazing! Can you open all of these oysters?
Of course! I've become really adept at picking the lock on these things.
You know what, I think I'll stick around . . .
Great! Gutters are on the roof! Here, take my broom!
Bleh!
EMPTY BOWLS
FULL HEARTS

Hello, hello! Welcome to Empty Bowls. Have a seat, we'll be serving dinner shortly.

Oh, look, customers! We'll serve them soup and salad as the first course and then oysters as a main dish!

Let's Get Cooking!

1. Combine oil, spinach, bread crumbs, parsley, salt, and hot sauce.

BUB   BUB   BUB   BLB

2. Boil the oysters!

3. Pick the locks and place oysters on a bed of sea salt. Don't spill those juices!

4. Spoon spinach mixture onto the oysters and bake for 10 minutes.

5. Add cheese and bacon. Broil until it's all melty!

6. Finally, add a single pickled pearl onion to the top and serve!

You have made
A SUNKEN TREASURE OYSTER!

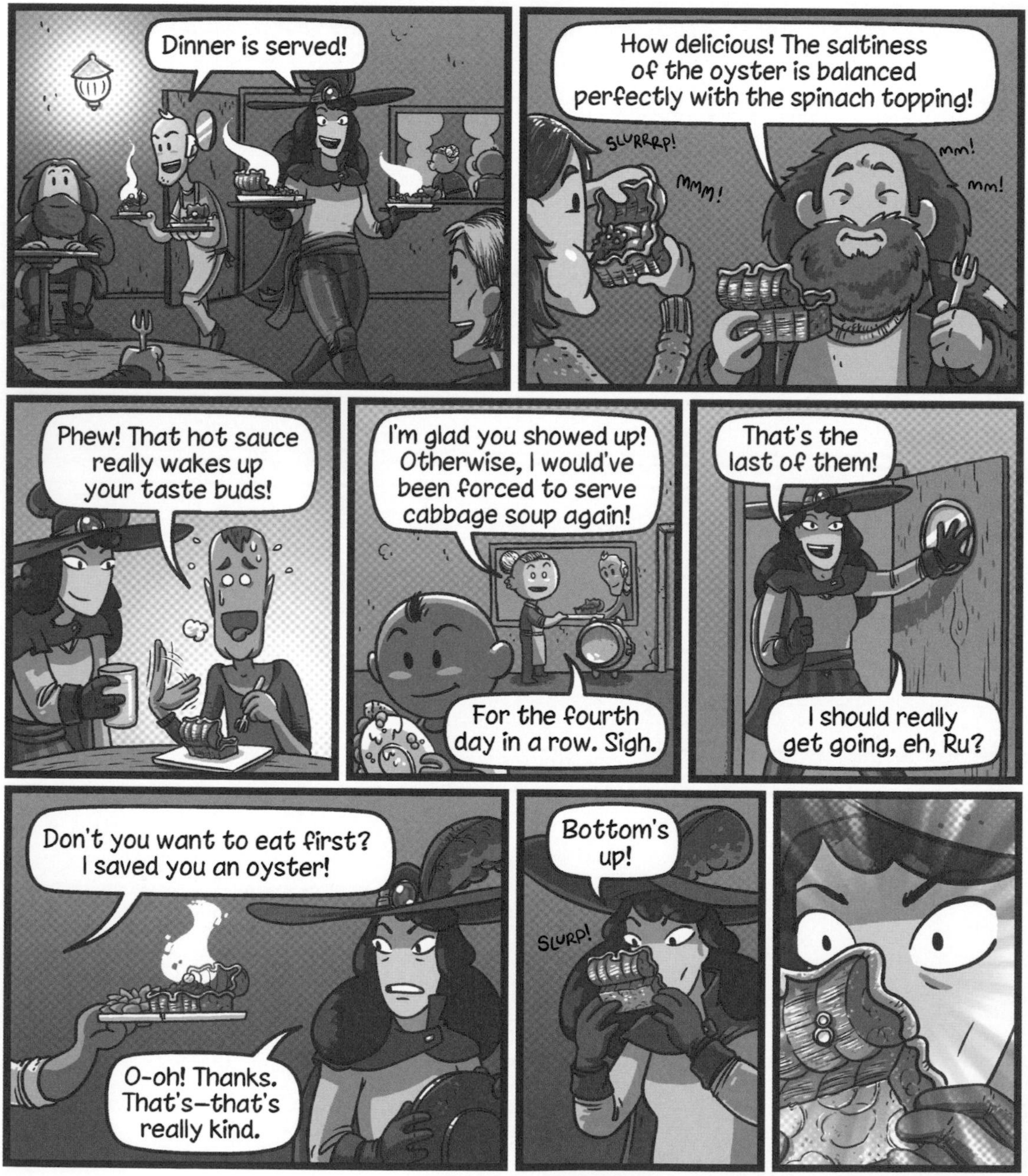
Dinner is served!
How delicious! The saltiness of the oyster is balanced perfectly with the spinach topping!
SLURRRP!
MMM!
mm!
mm!
Phew! That hot sauce really wakes up your taste buds!
I'm glad you showed up! Otherwise, I would've been forced to serve cabbage soup again!
For the fourth day in a row. Sigh.
That's the last of them!
I should really get going, eh, Ru?
Don't you want to eat first? I saved you an oyster!
O-oh! Thanks. That's—that's really kind.
Bottom's up!
SLURP!

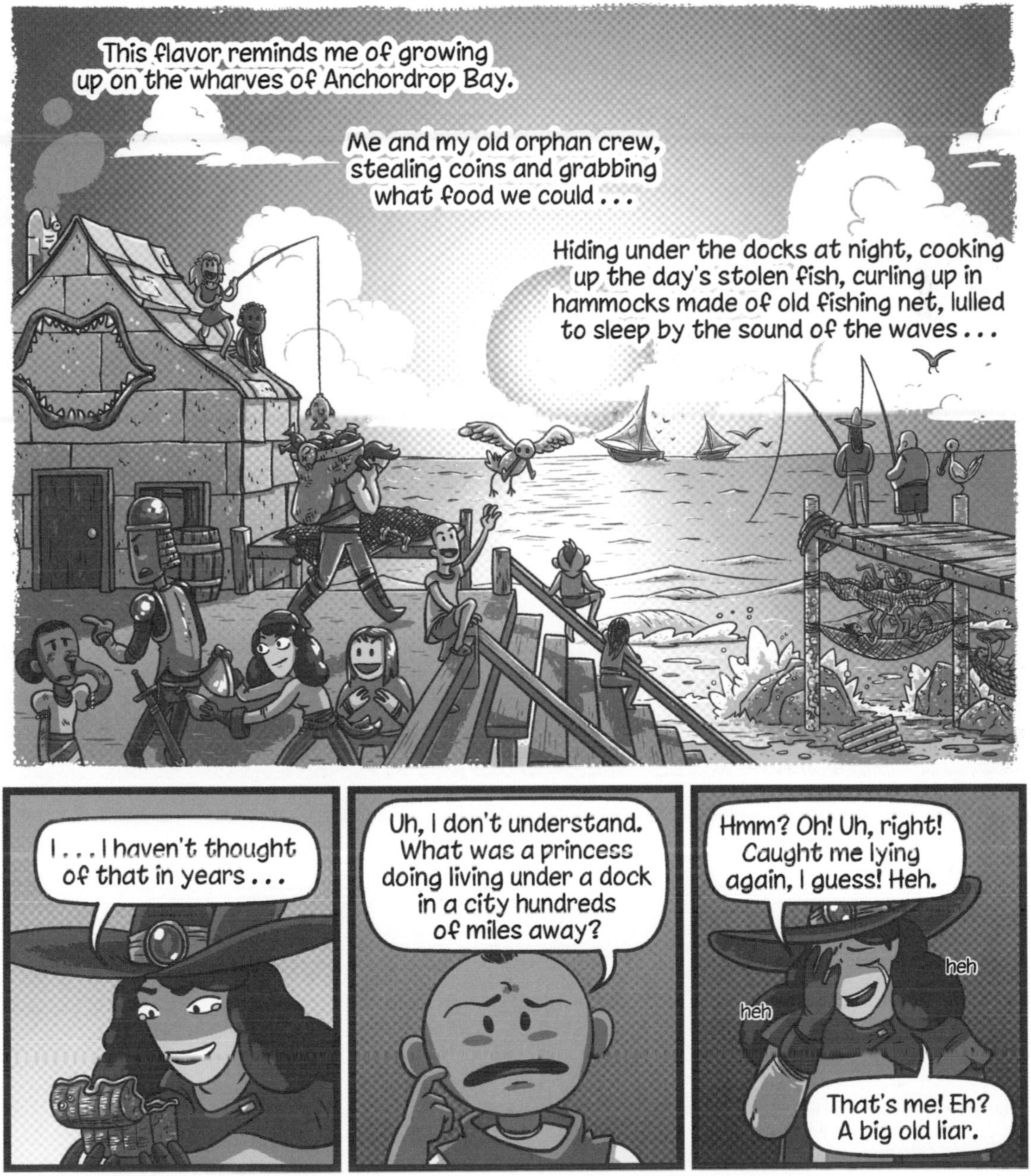
This flavor reminds me of growing up on the wharves of Anchordrop Bay.
Me and my old orphan crew, stealing coins and grabbing what food we could . . .
Hiding under the docks at night, cooking up the day's stolen fish, curling up in hammocks made of old fishing net, lulled to sleep by the sound of the waves . . .
I . . . I haven't thought of that in years . . .
Uh, I don't understand. What was a princess doing living under a dock in a city hundreds of miles away?
Hmm? Oh! Uh, right! Caught me lying again, I guess! Heh.
heh
heh
That's me! Eh? A big old liar.

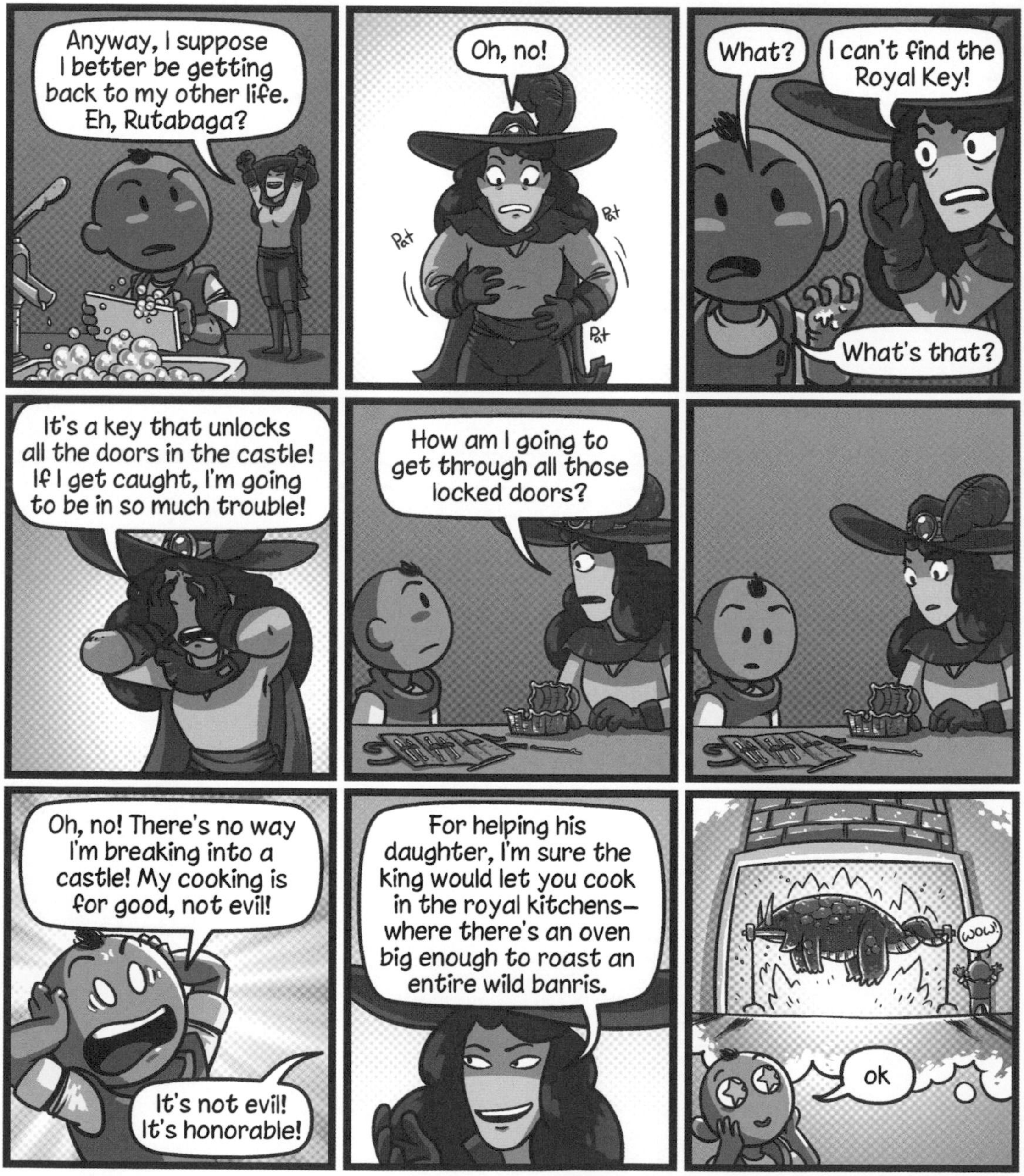
Anyway, I suppose I better be getting back to my other life. Eh, Rutabaga?
Oh, no!
Pat
Pat
Pat
What?
I can't find the Royal Key!
What's that?
It's a key that unlocks all the doors in the castle! If I get caught, I'm going to be in so much trouble!
How am I going to get through all those locked doors?
Oh, no! There's no way I'm breaking into a castle! My cooking is for good, not evil!
It's not evil! It's honorable!
For helping his daughter, I'm sure the king would let you cook in the royal kitchens— where there's an oven big enough to roast an entire wild banris.
WOW!
ok

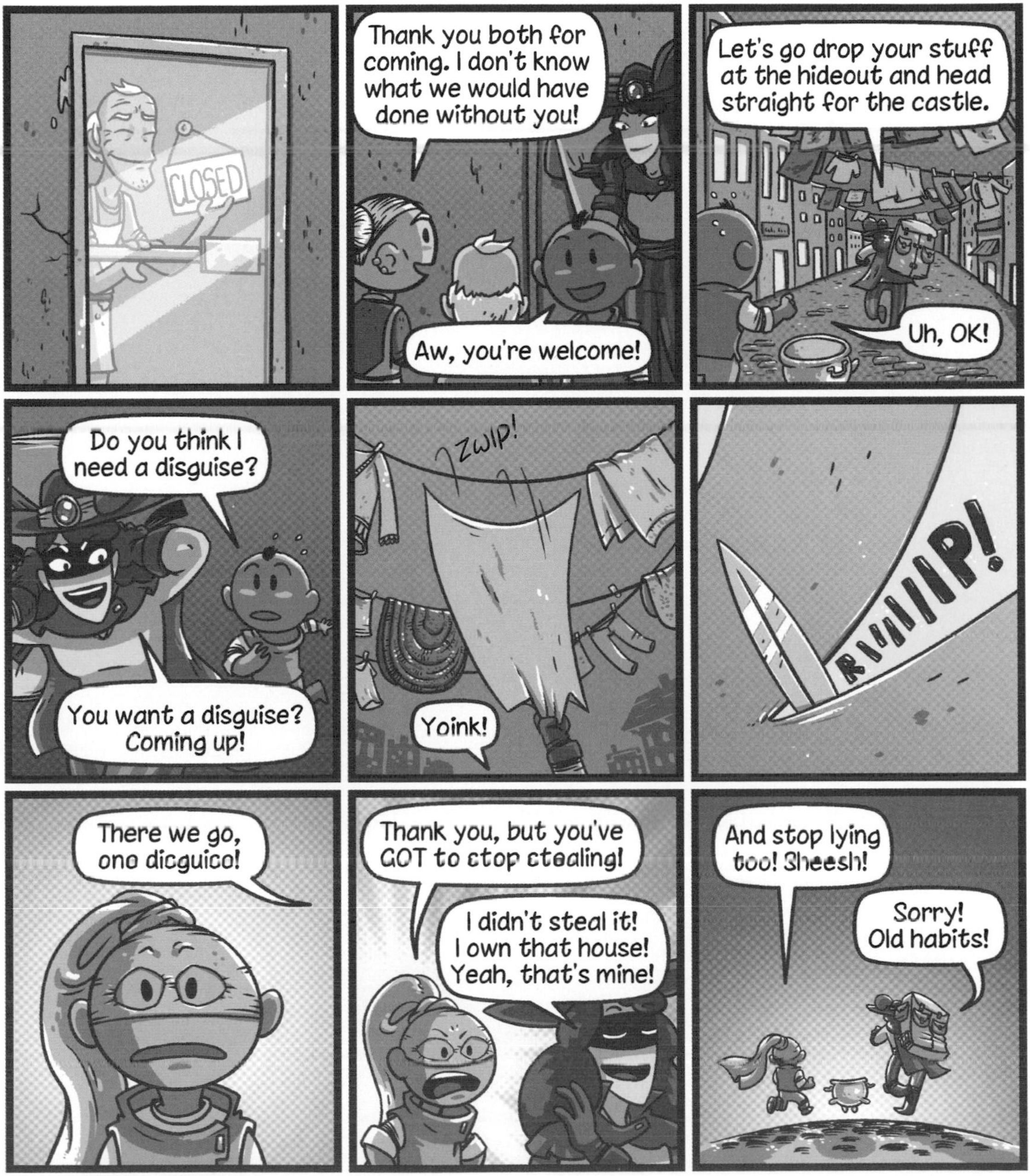
CLOSED
Thank you both for coming. I don't know what we would have done without you!
Aw, you're welcome!
Let's go drop your stuff at the hideout and head straight for the castle.
Uh, OK!
Do you think I need a disguise?
You want a disguise? Coming up!
ZWIP!
Yoink!
RIIIIIIIP!
There we go, one disguise!
Thank you, but you've GOT to stop stealing!
I didn't steal it! I own that house! Yeah, that's mine!
And stop lying too! Sheesh!
Sorry! Old habits!

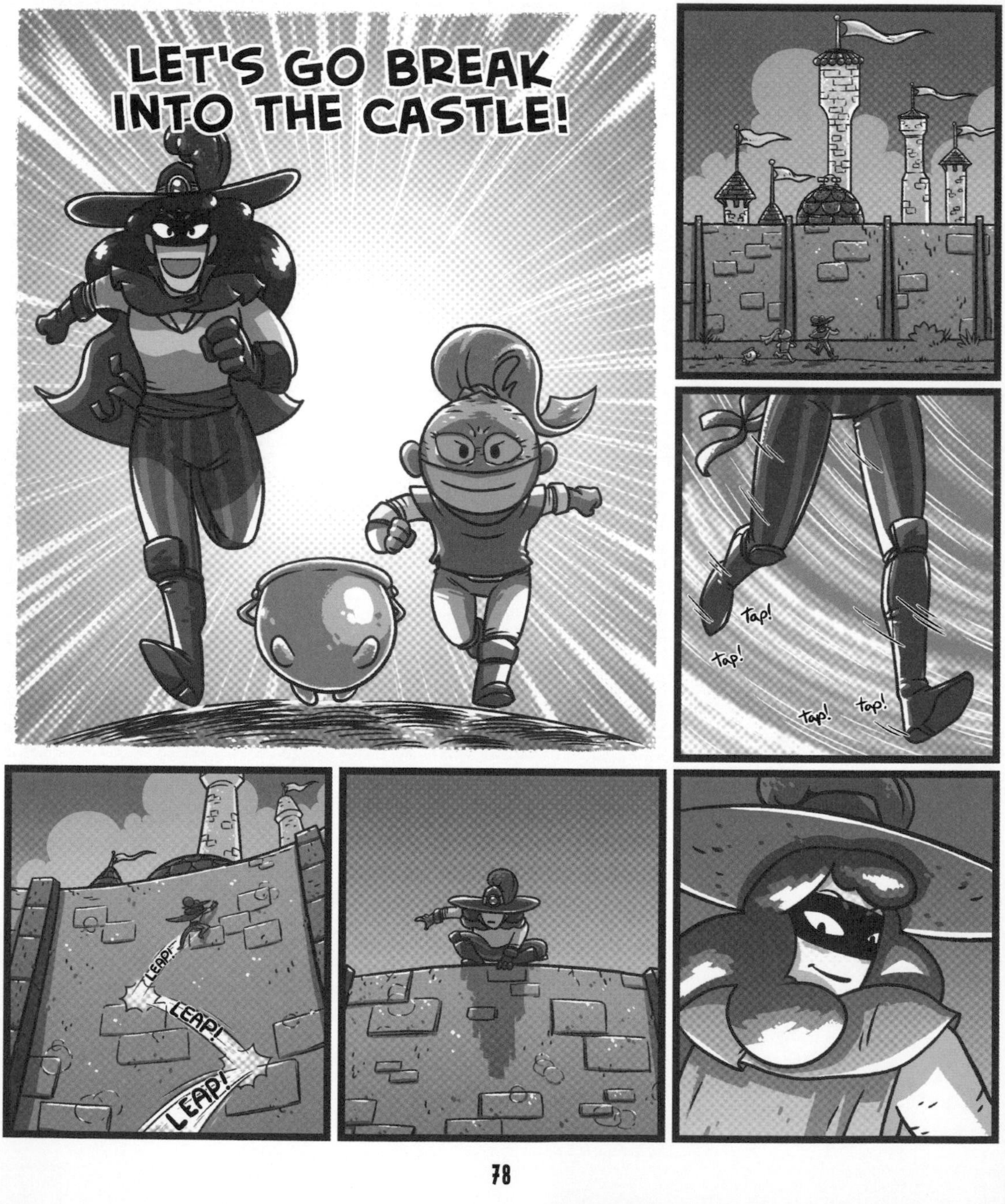
LET'S GO BREAK INTO THE CASTLE!
Tap!
tap!
tap!
tap!
LEAP!
LEAP!
LEAP!

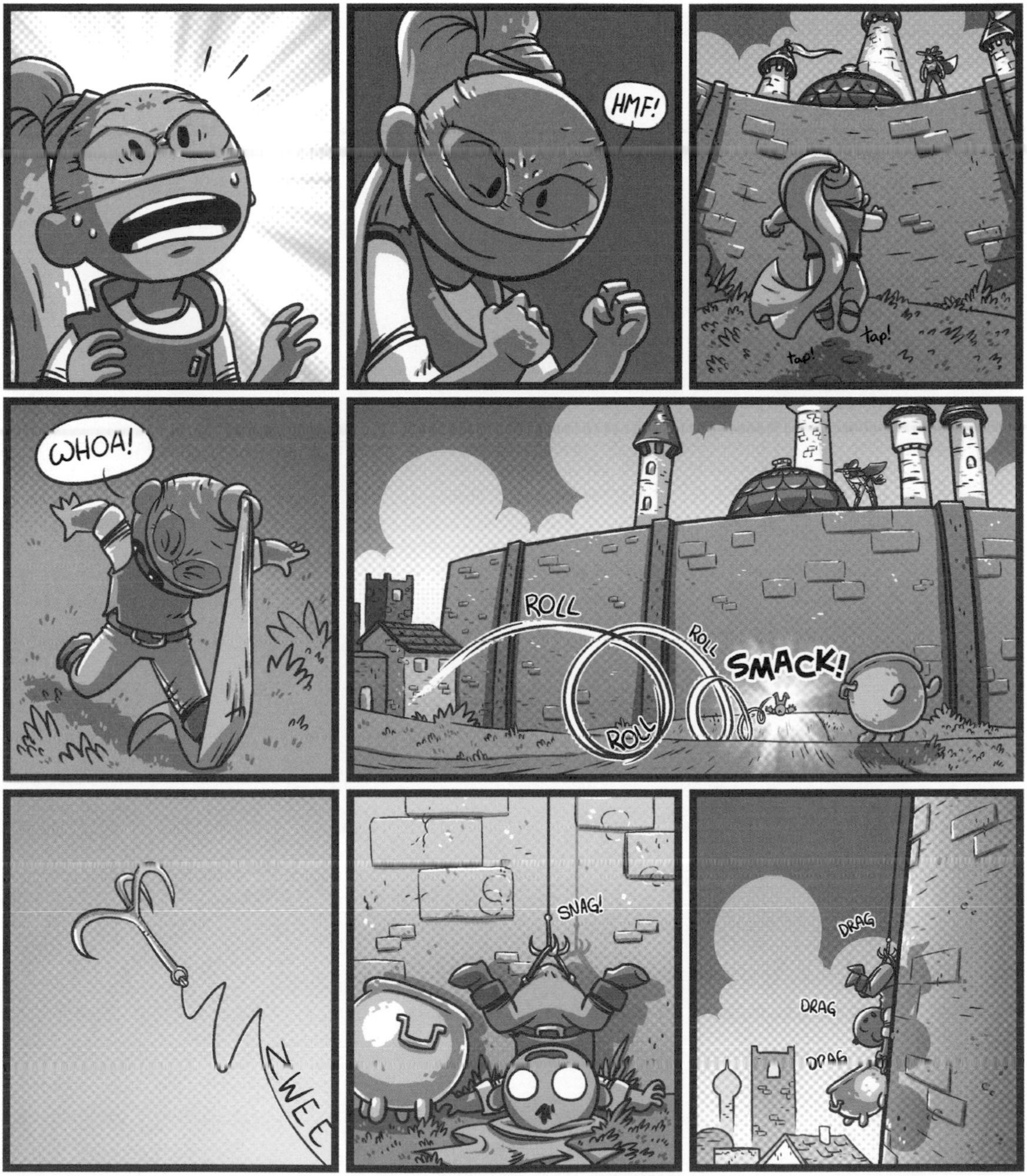
HMF!
tap!
tap!
WHOA!
ROLL
ROLL
ROLL
SMACK!
ZWEE
SNAG!
DRAG
DRAG
DRAG

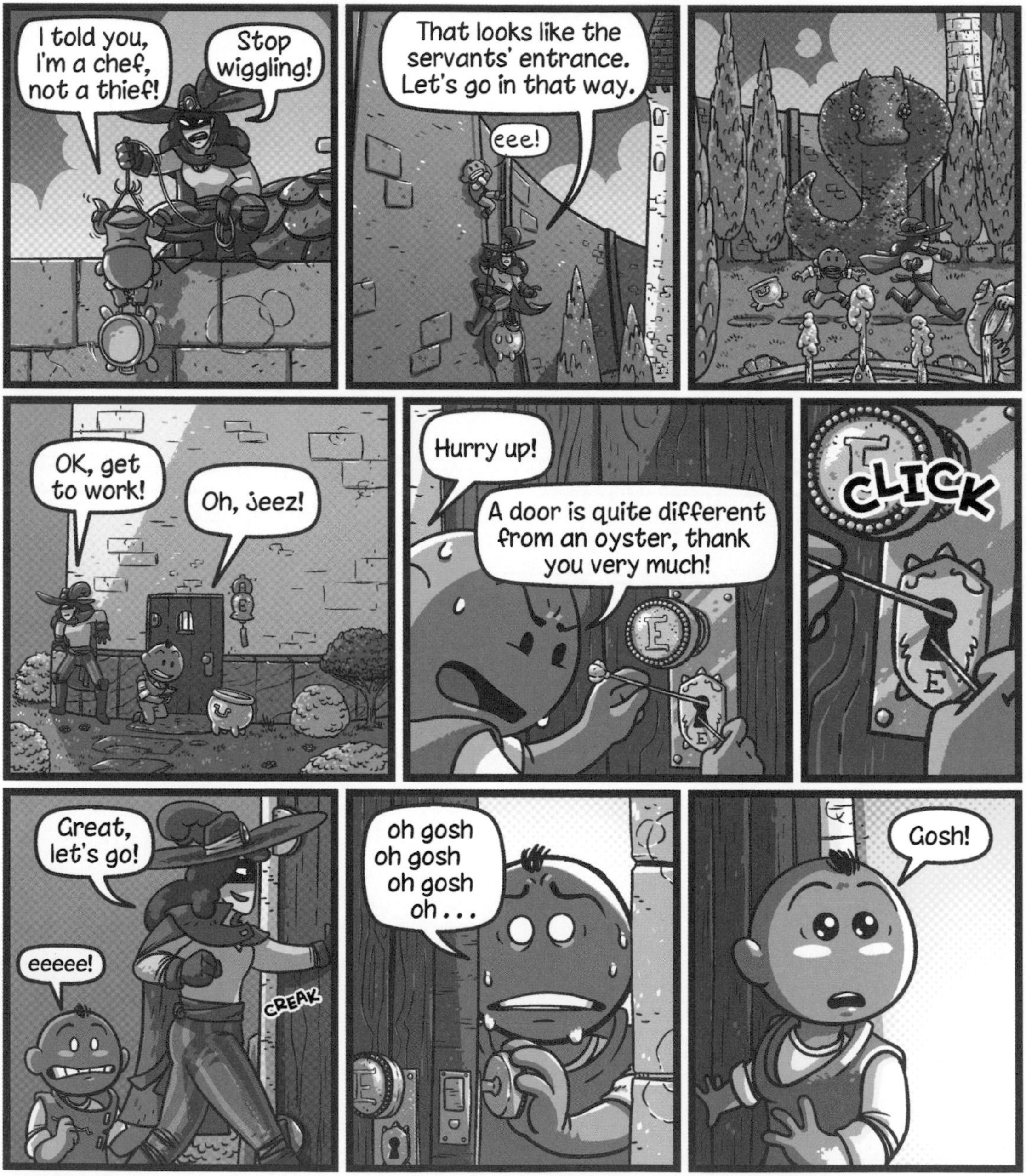
I told you, I'm a chef, not a thief!
Stop wiggling!
That looks like the servants' entrance. Let's go in that way.
eee!
OK, get to work!
Oh, jeez!
Hurry up!
A door is quite different from an oyster, thank you very much!
CLICK
Great, let's go!
eeeee!
CREAK
oh gosh
oh gosh
oh gosh
oh . . .
Gosh!

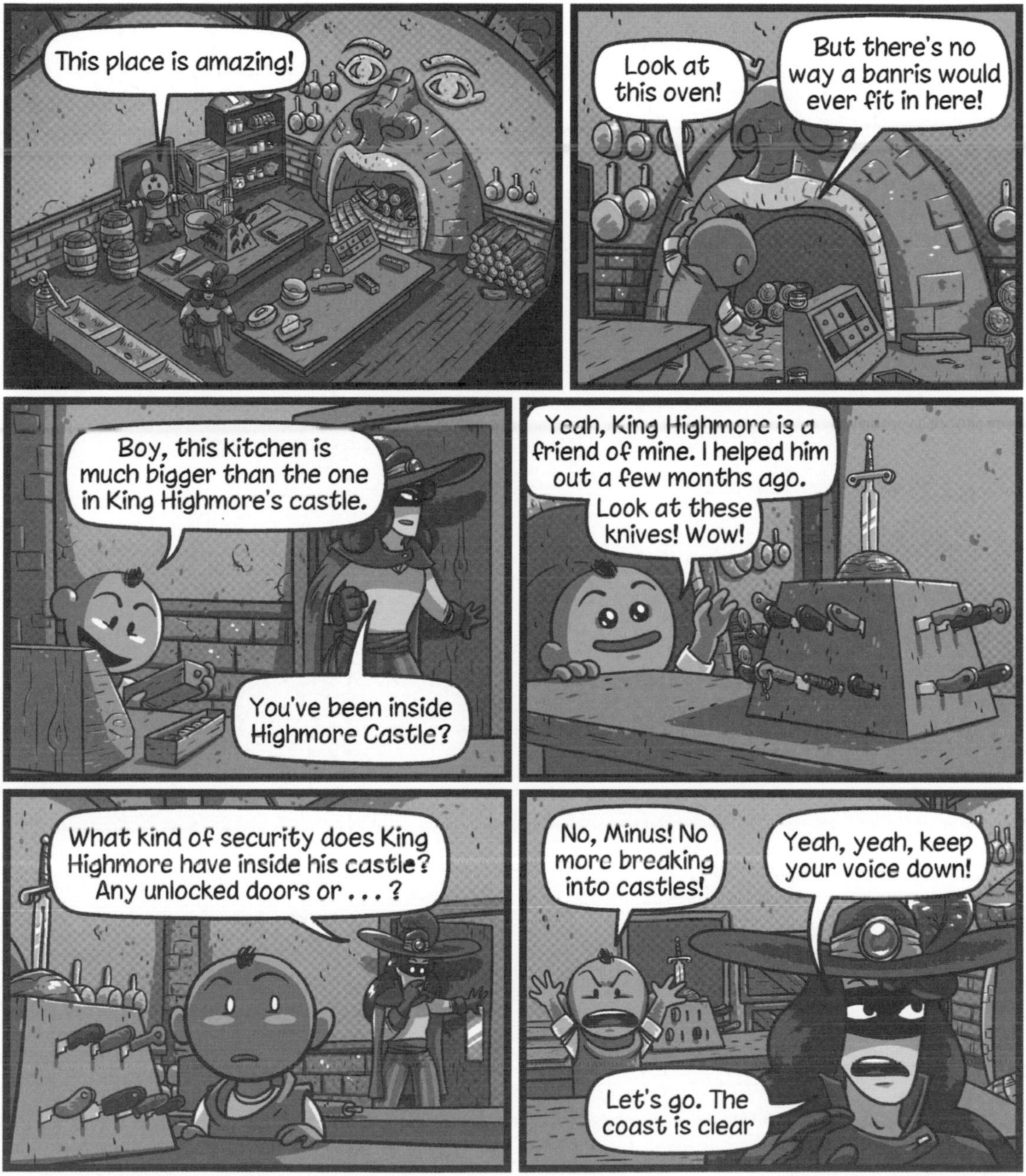
This place is amazing!
Look at this oven!
But there's no way a banris would ever fit in here!
Boy, this kitchen is much bigger than the one in King Highmore's castle.
You've been inside Highmore Castle?
Yeah, King Highmore is a friend of mine. I helped him out a few months ago.
Look at these knives! Wow!
What kind of security does King Highmore have inside his castle? Any unlocked doors or . . . ?
No, Minus! No more breaking into castles!
Yeah, yeah, keep your voice down!
Let's go. The coast is clear

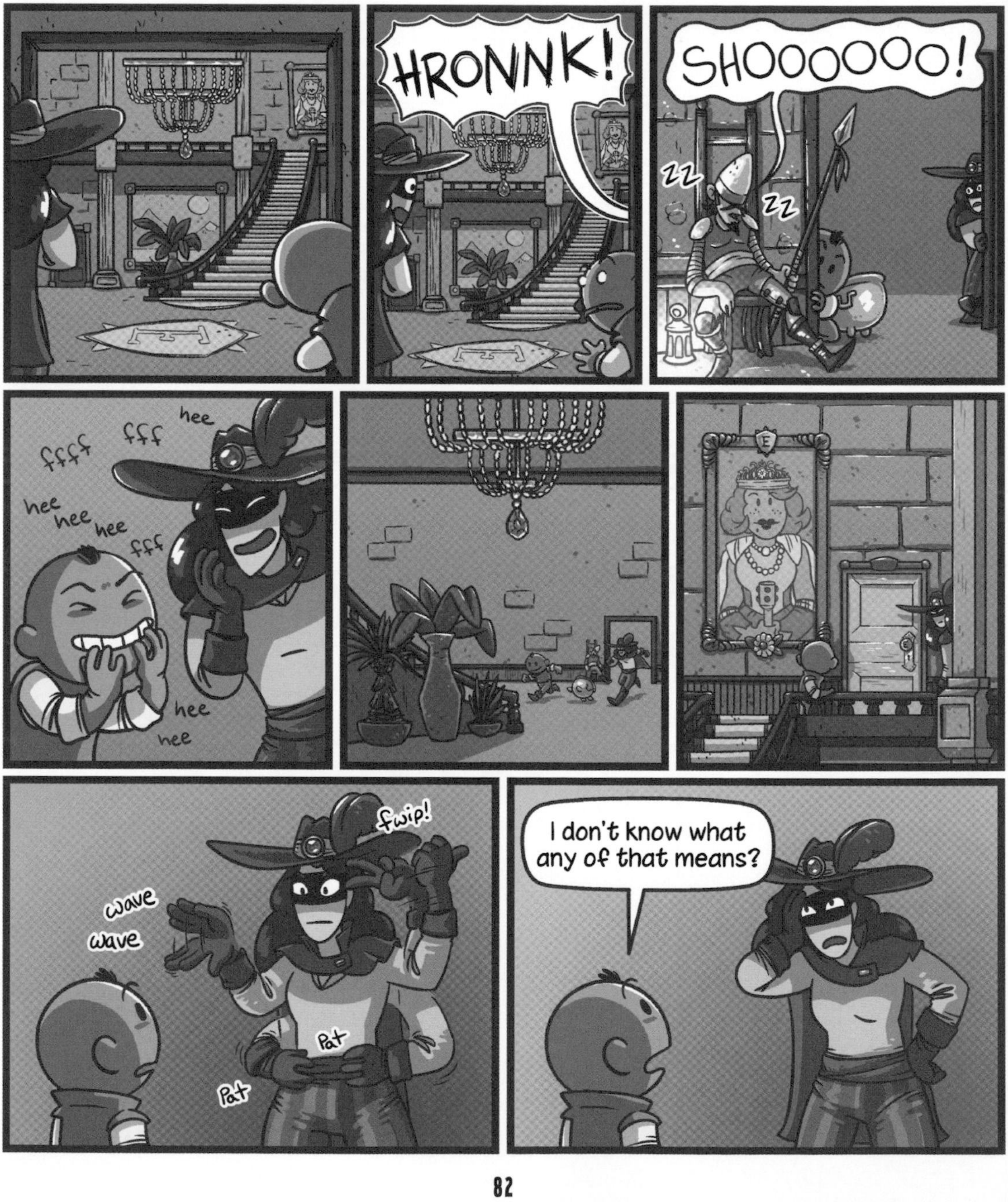
HRONNK!
SHOOOOOO!
ZZ
ZZ
ffff
fff
hee
hee
hee
hee
fff
hee
hee
fwip!
wave
wave
Pat
Pat
I don't know what any of that means?

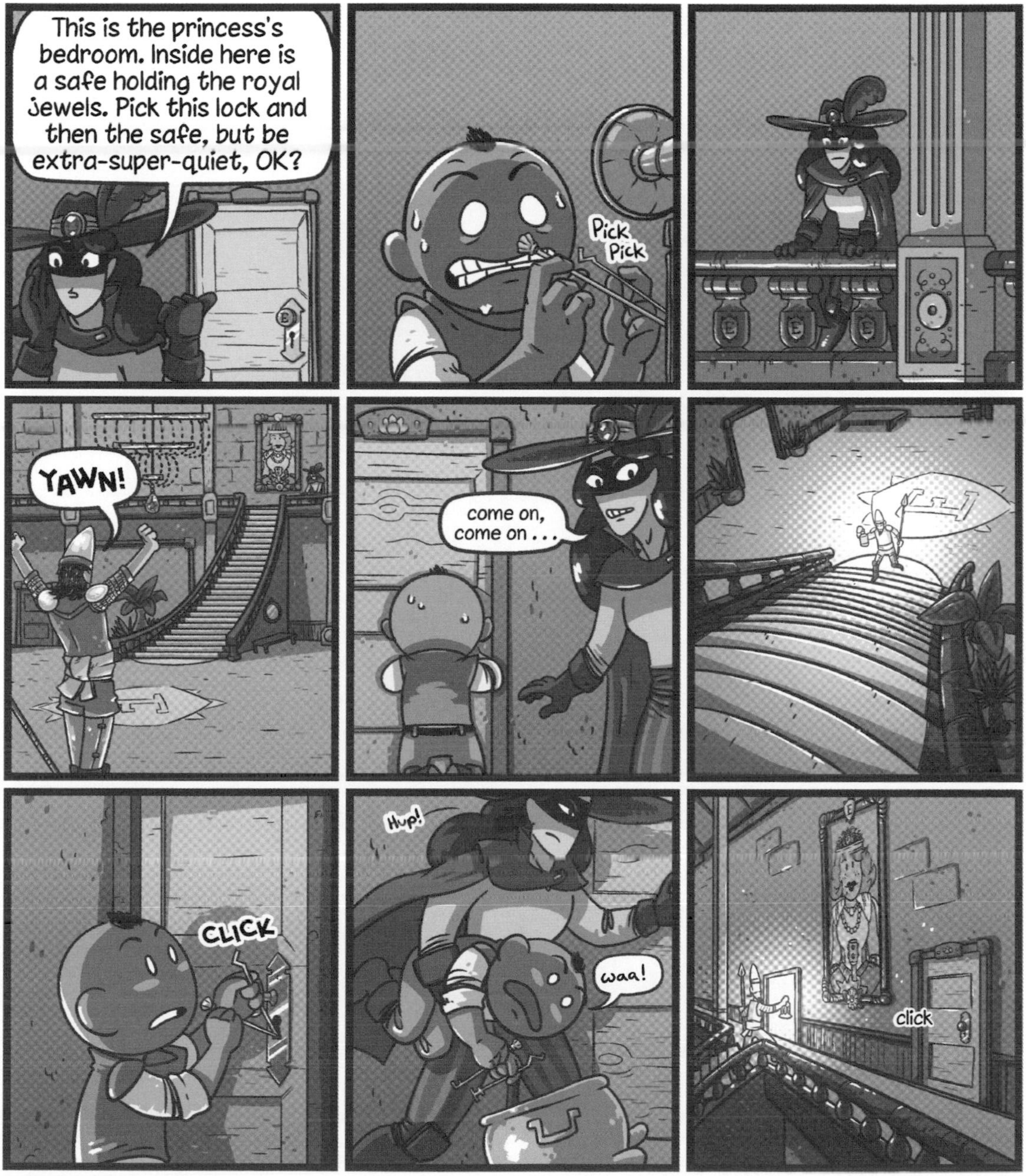

This is the princess's bedroom. Inside here is a safe holding the royal jewels. Pick this lock and then the safe, but be extra-super-quiet, OK?
Pick
Pick
YAWN!
come on, come on . . .
CLICK
Hup!
waa!
click

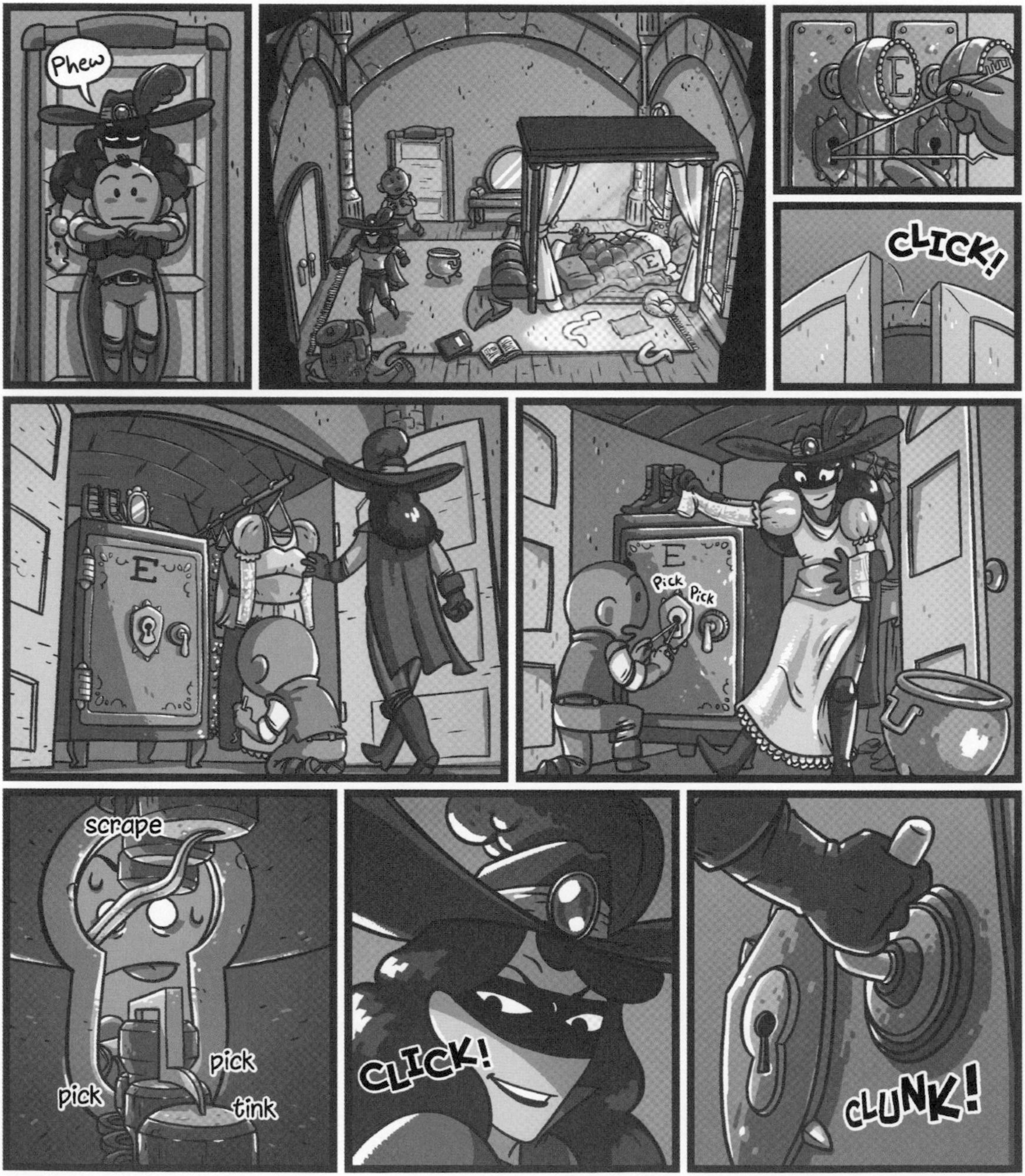
Phew
CLICK!
Pick
Pick
scrape
pick
pick
tink
CLICK!
CLUNK!

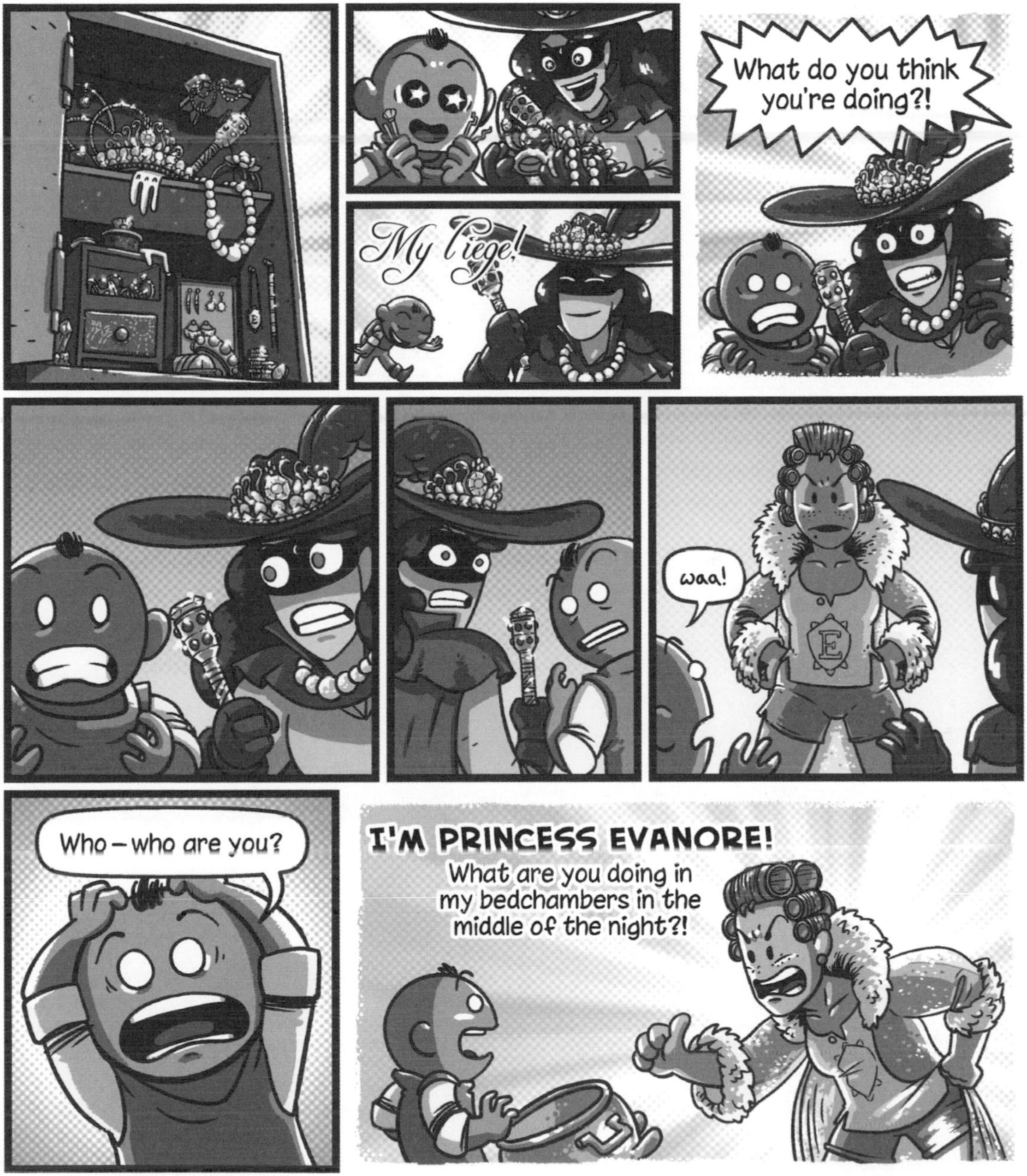
My liege!
What do you think you're doing?!
waa!
Who—who are you?
I'M PRINCESS EVANORE!
What are you doing in my bedchambers in the middle of the night?!

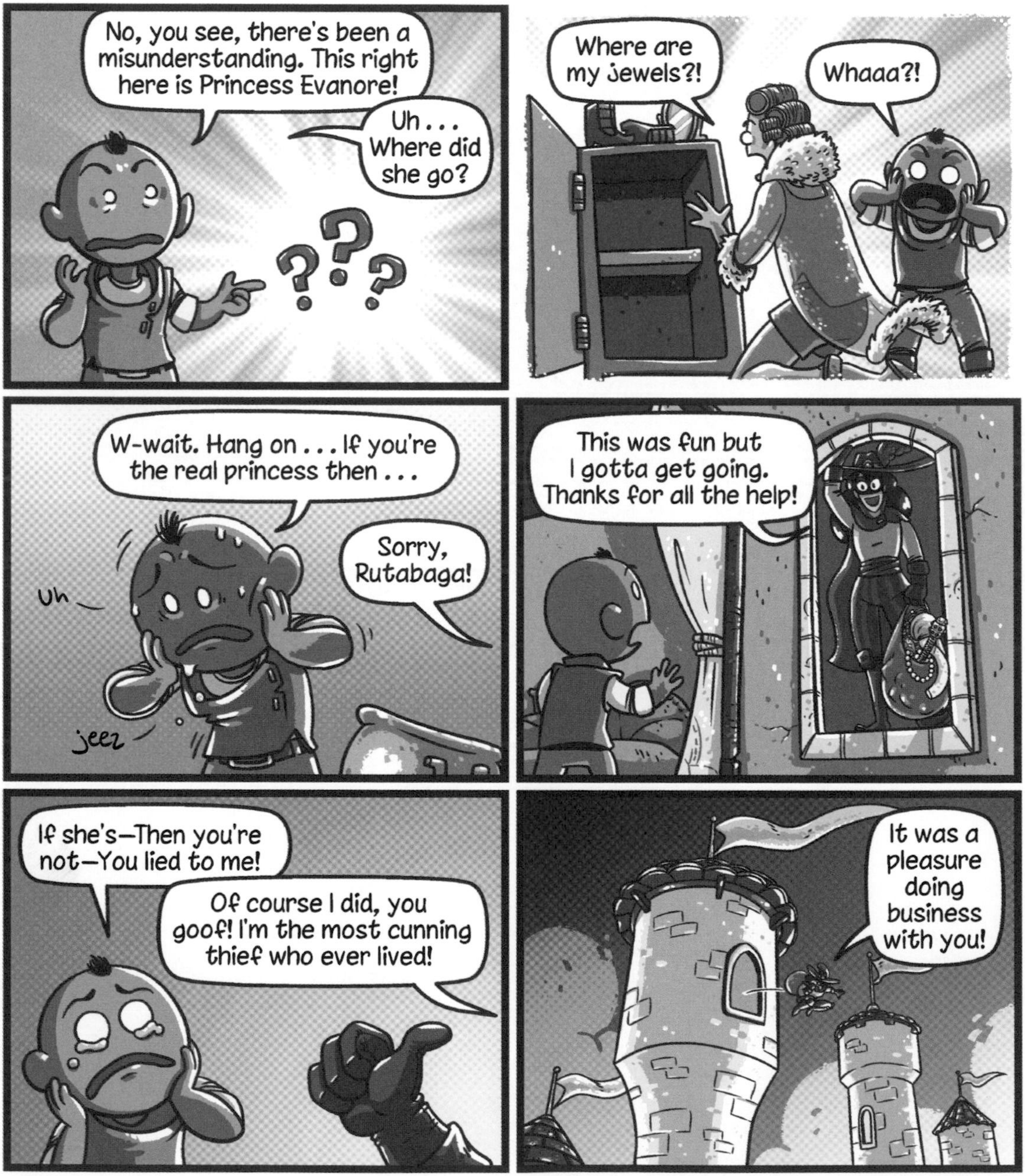
No, you see, there's been a misunderstanding. This right here is Princess Evanore!
Uh . . . Where did she go?
Where are my jewels?!
Whaaa?!
W-wait. Hang on . . . If you're the real princess then . . .
Sorry, Rutabaga!
Uh
jeez
This was fun but I gotta get going. Thanks for all the help!
If she's—Then you're not—You lied to me!
Of course I did, you goof! I'm the most cunning thief who ever lived!
It was a pleasure doing business with you!

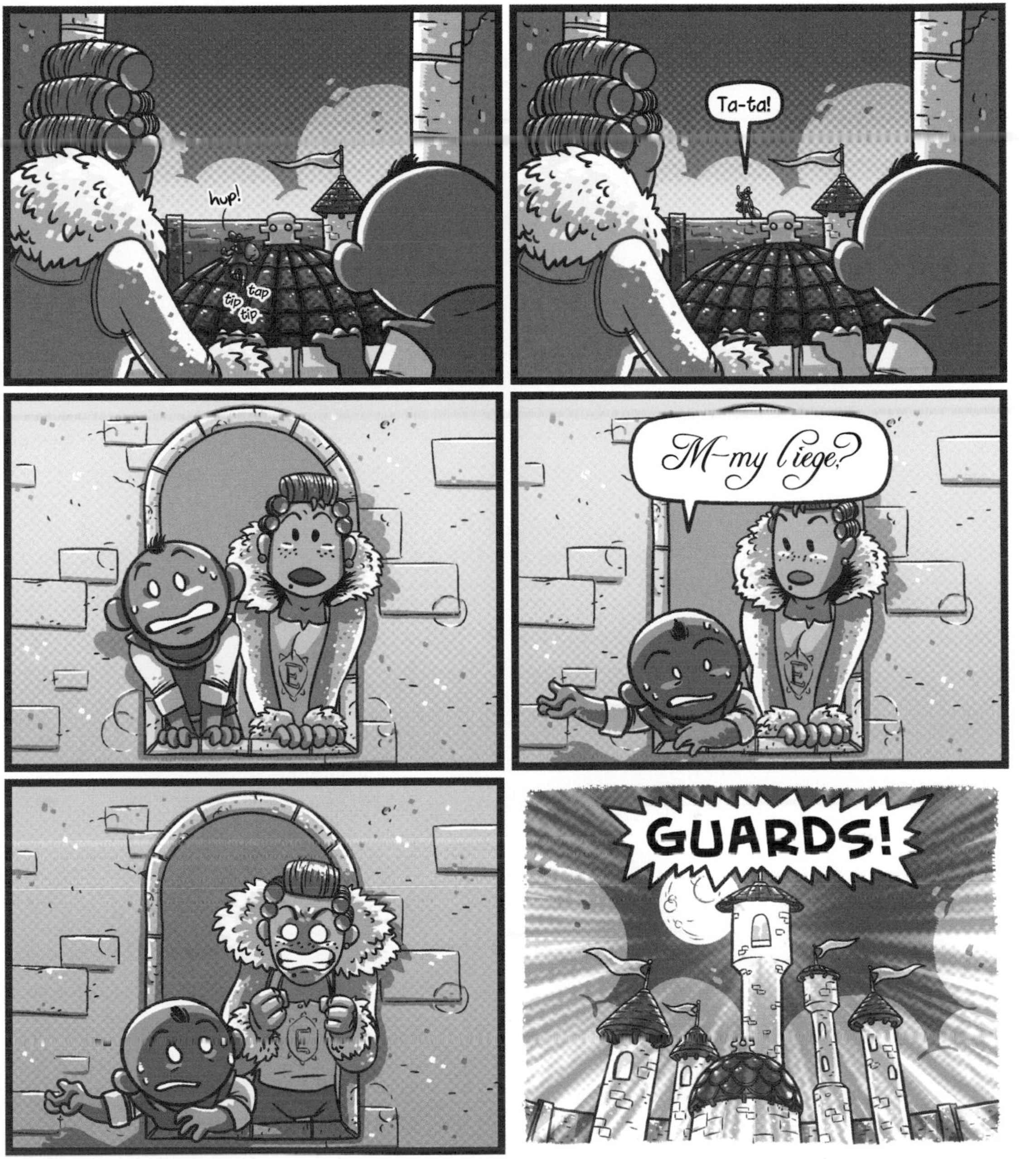

hup!
tap
tip
tip
Ta-ta!
M-my liege?
GUARDS!

End of Chapter Three

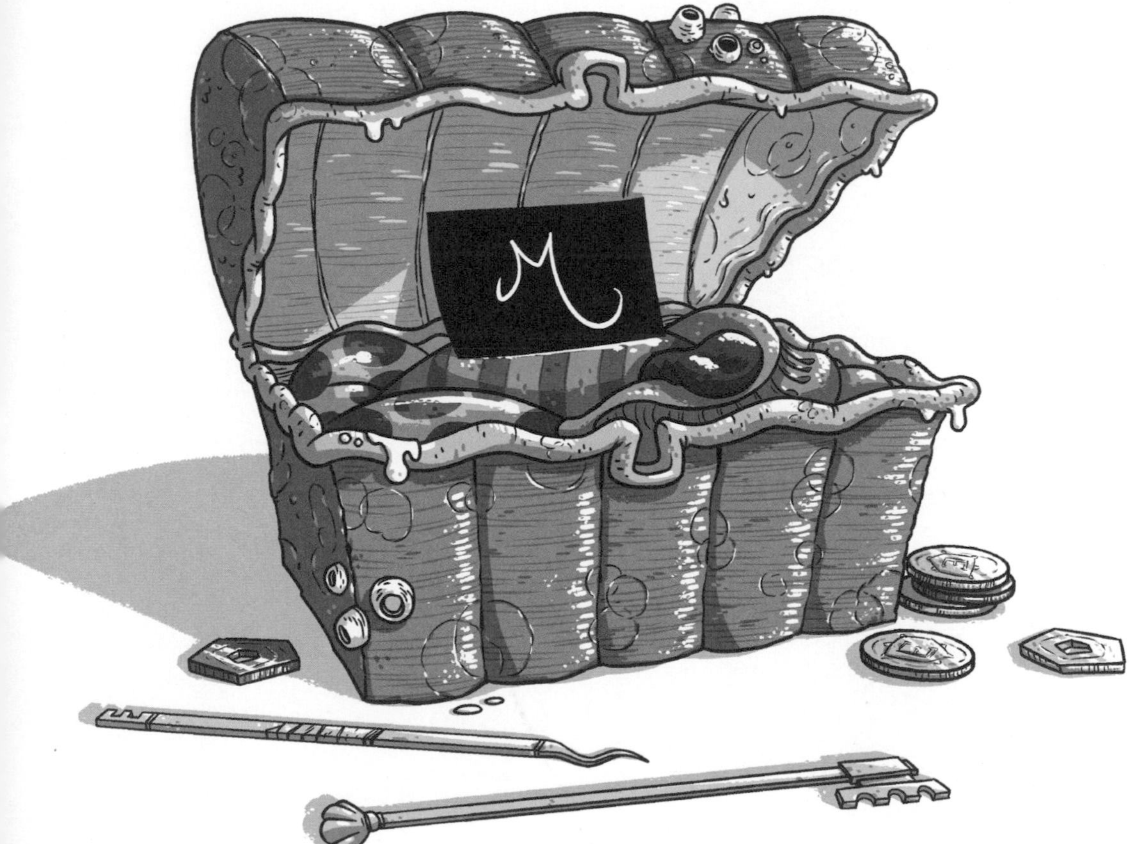

M

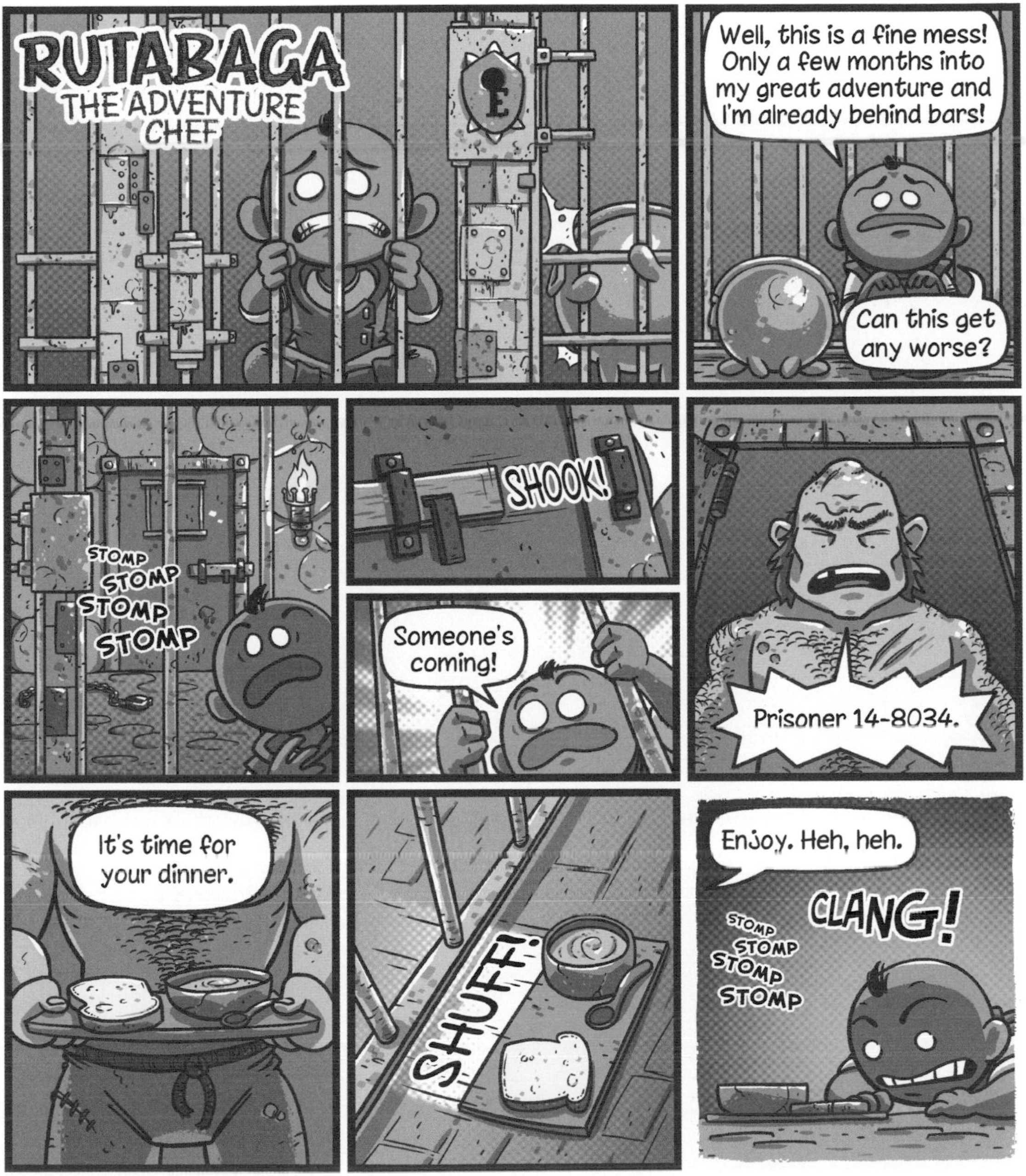
RUTABAGA
THE ADVENTURE CHEF
Well, this is a fine mess! Only a few months into my great adventure and I'm already behind bars!
Can this get any worse?
STOMP STOMP STOMP STOMP
SHOOK!
Someone's coming!
Prisoner 14-8034.
It's time for your dinner.
SHUFF!
Enjoy. Heh, heh.
CLANG!
STOMP STOMP STOMP STOMP

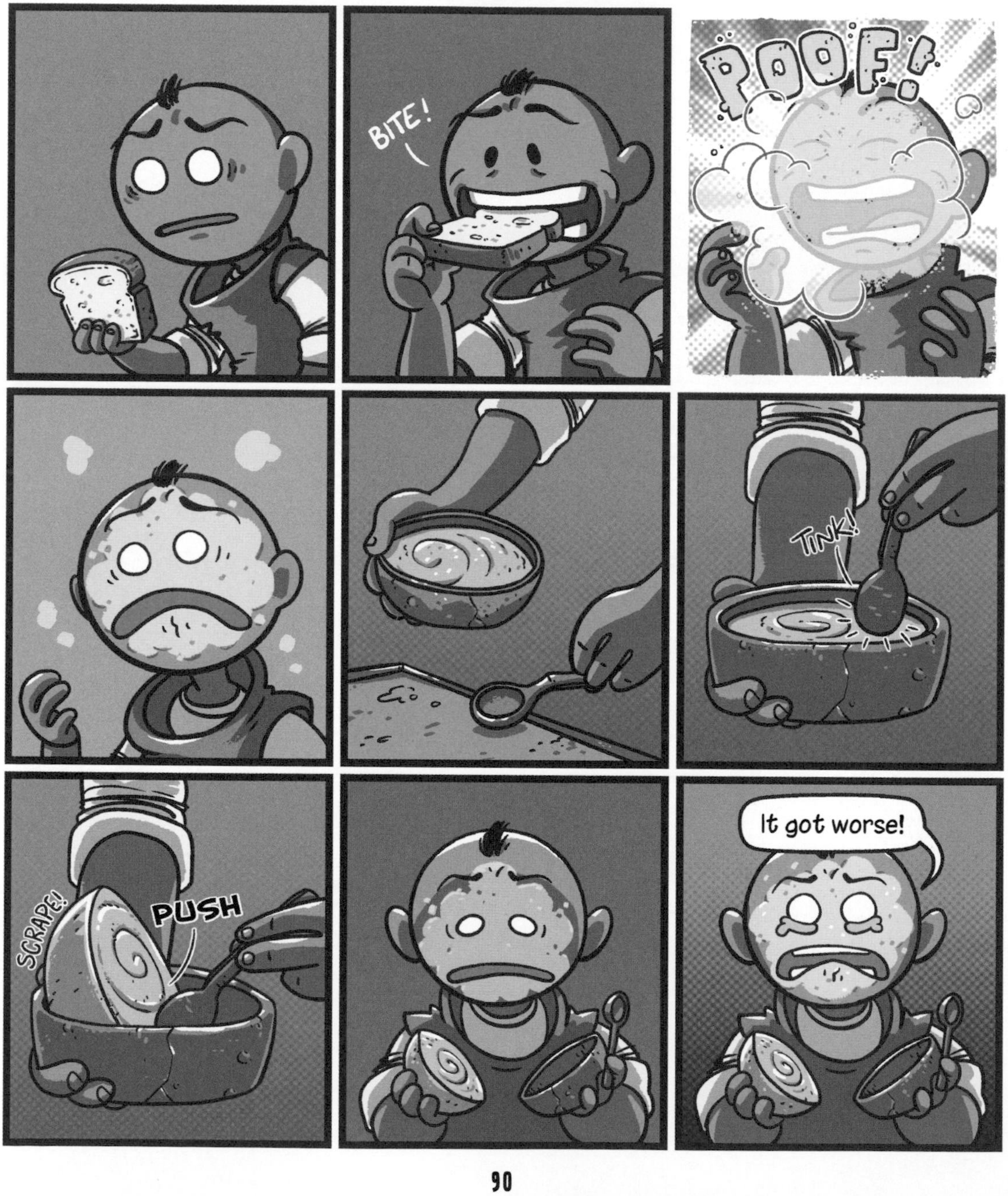
BITE!
POOF!
TINK!
SCRAPE!
PUSH
It got worse!

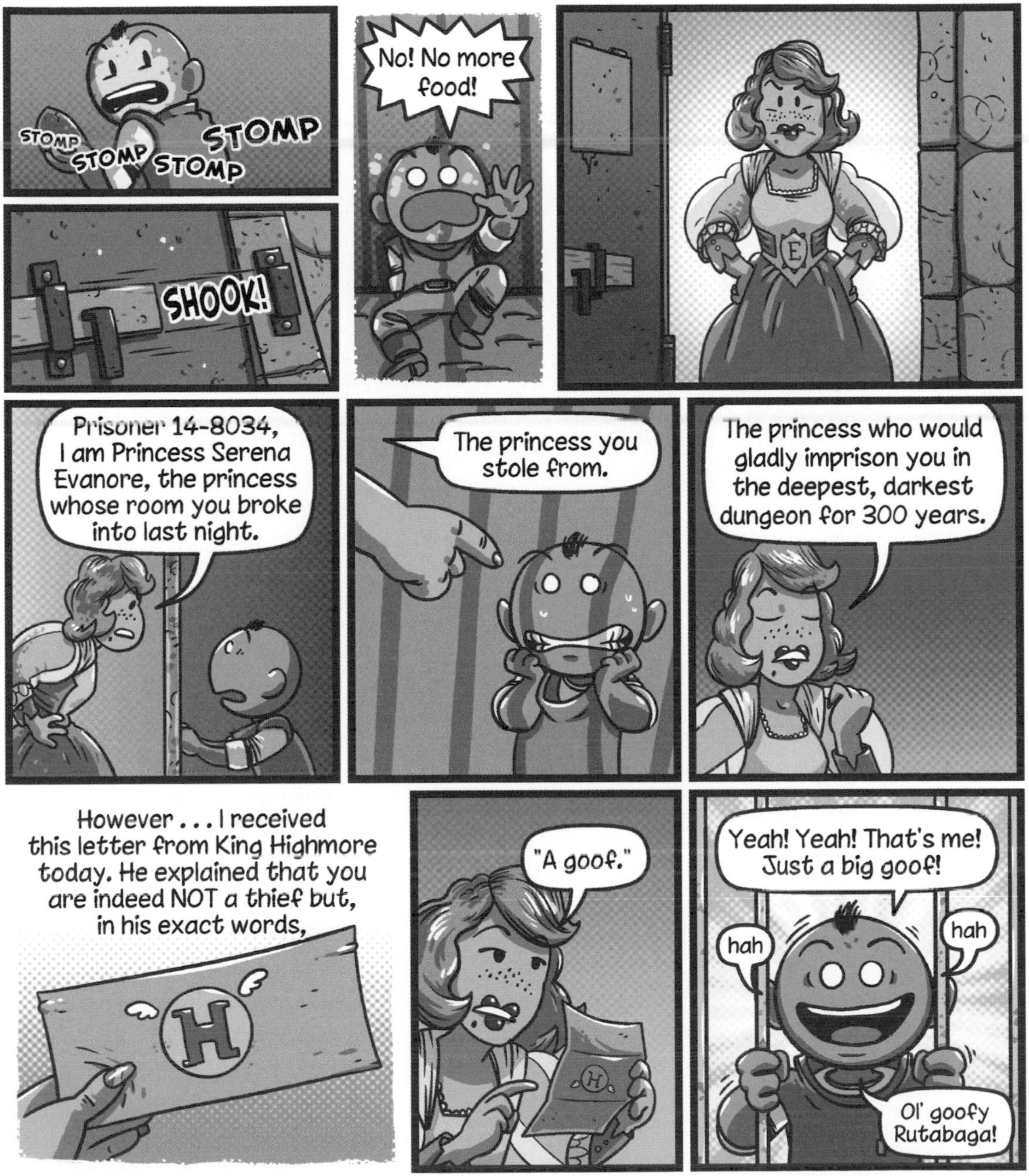
STOMP
STOMP
STOMP
STOMP
SHOOK!
No! No more food!
Prisoner 14-8034, I am Princess Serena Evanore, the princess whose room you broke into last night.
The princess you stole from.
The princess who would gladly imprison you in the deepest, darkest dungeon for 300 years.
However . . . I received this letter from King Highmore today. He explained that you are indeed NOT a thief but, in his exact words,
"A goof."
Yeah! Yeah! That's me! Just a big goof!
hah
hah
Ol' goofy Rutabaga!

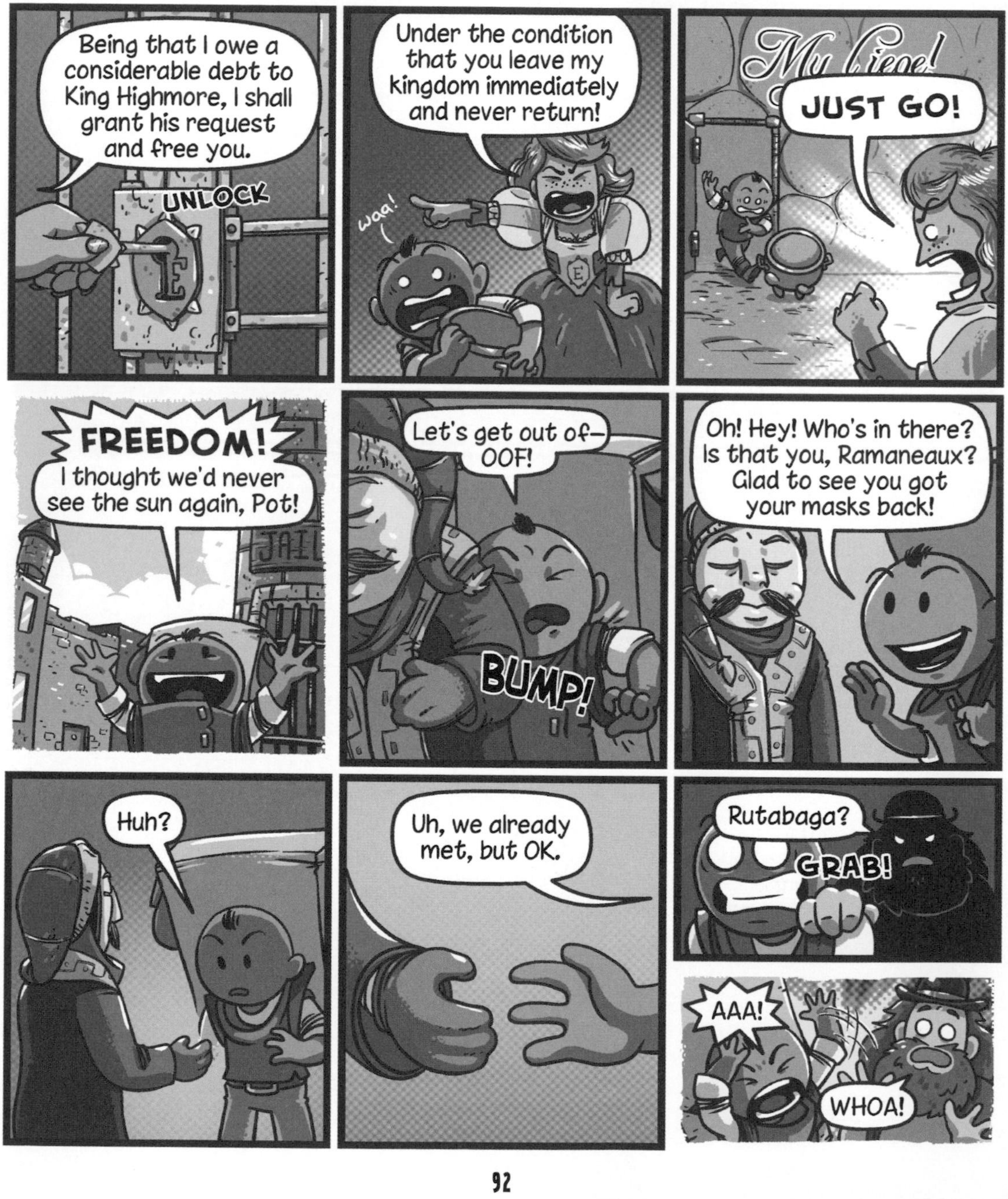

Being that I owe a considerable debt to King Highmore, I shall grant his request and free you.
UNLOCK
Under the condition that you leave my kingdom immediately and never return!
waa!
My Liege!
JUST GO!
FREEDOM!
I thought we'd never see the sun again, Pot!
JAIL
Let's get out of— OOF!
BUMP!
Oh! Hey! Who's in there? Is that you, Ramaneaux? Glad to see you got your masks back!
Huh?
Uh, we already met, but OK.
Rutabaga?
GRAB!
AAA!
WHOA!

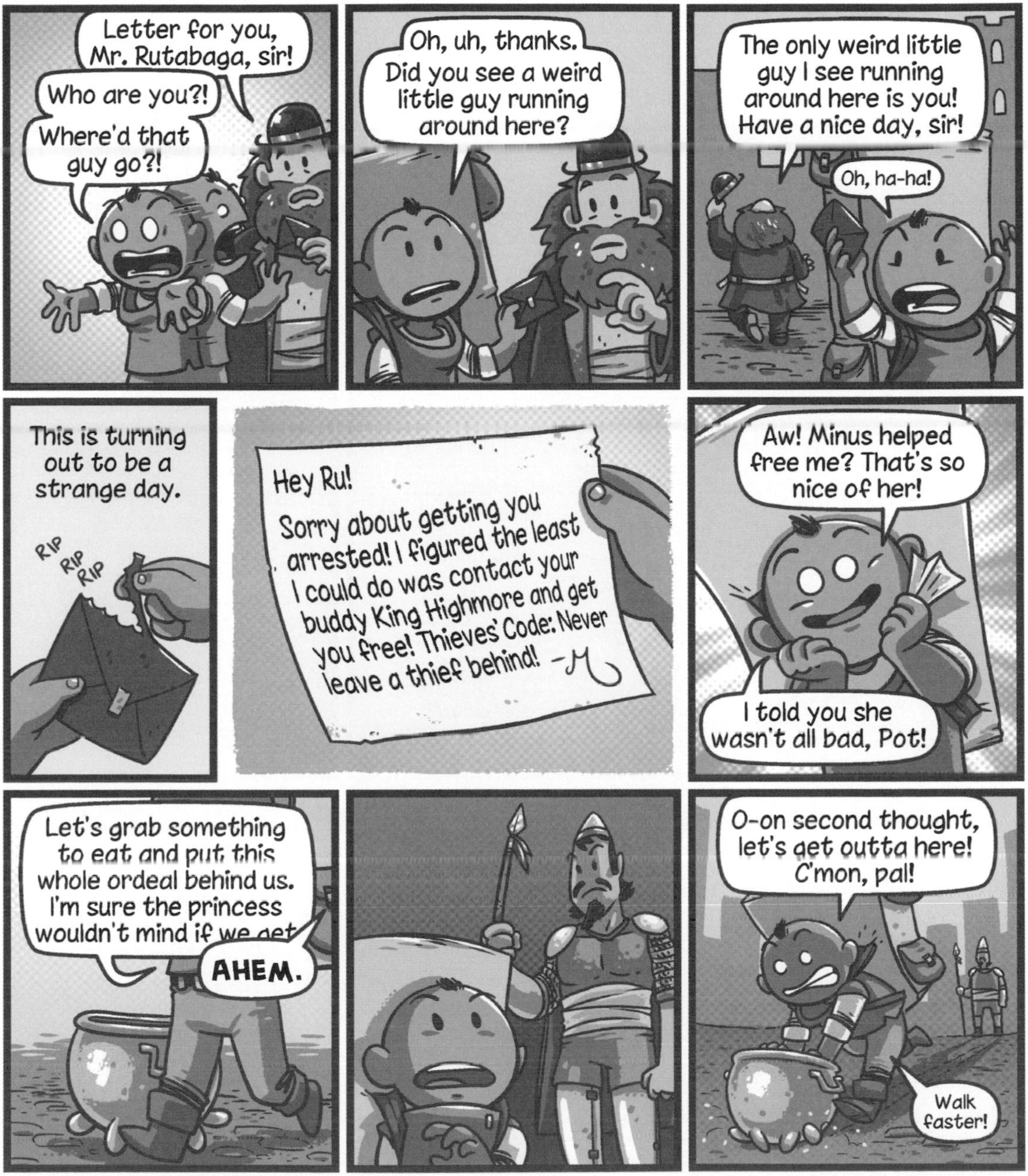
Letter for you, Mr. Rutabaga, sir!
Who are you?!
Where'd that guy go?!
Oh, uh, thanks. Did you see a weird little guy running around here?
The only weird little guy I see running around here is you! Have a nice day, sir!
Oh, ha-ha!
This is turning out to be a strange day.
RIP RIP RIP
Hey Ru!
Sorry about getting you arrested! I figured the least I could do was contact your buddy King Highmore and get you free! Thieves' Code: Never leave a thief behind! -M
Aw! Minus helped free me? That's so nice of her!
I told you she wasn't all bad, Pot!
Let's grab something to eat and put this whole ordeal behind us. I'm sure the princess wouldn't mind if we get
AHEM.
O-on second thought, let's get outta here! C'mon, pal!
Walk faster!

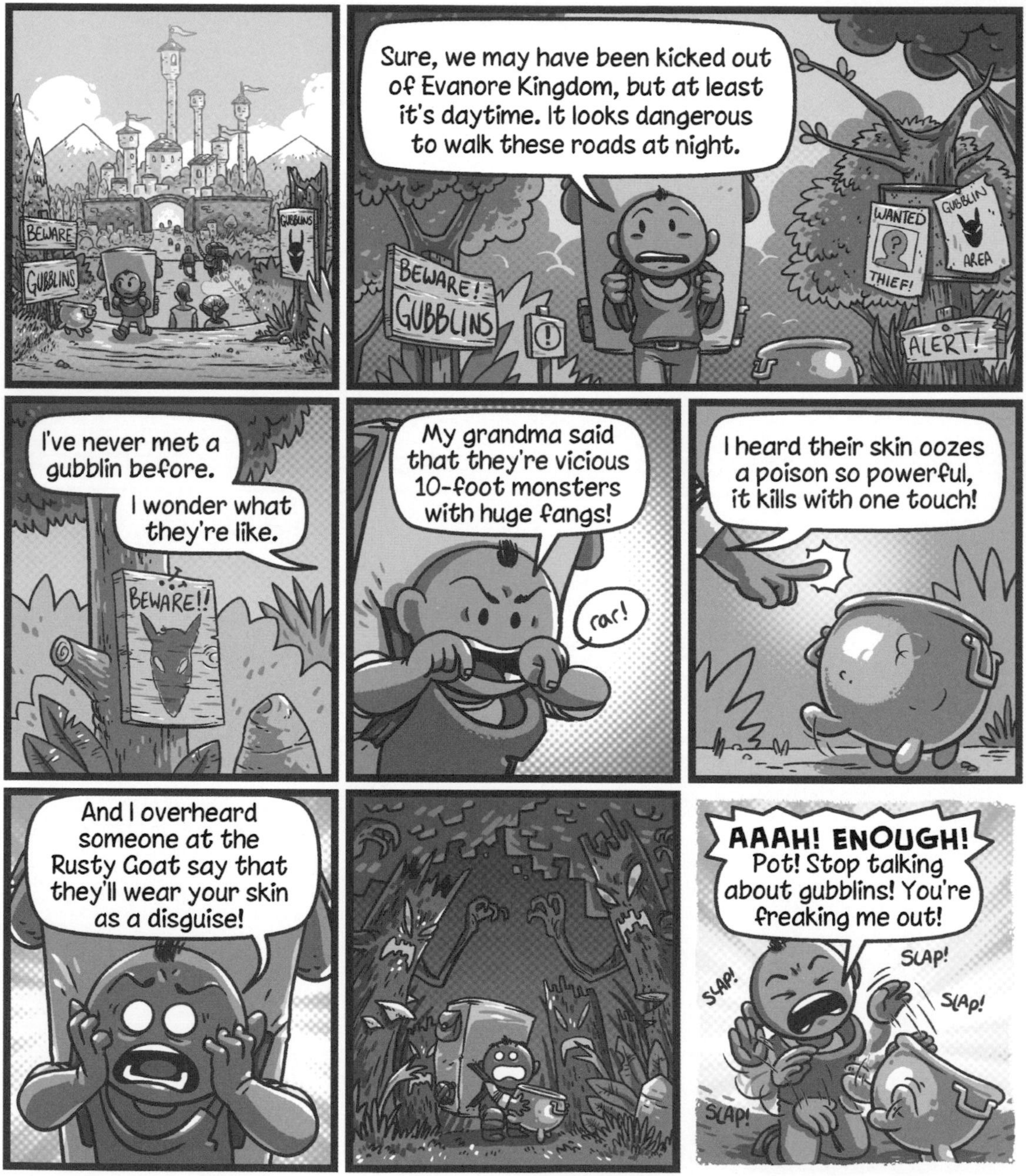
BEWARE
GUBBLINS
GUBBLINS
Sure, we may have been kicked out of Evanore Kingdom, but at least it's daytime. It looks dangerous to walk these roads at night.
BEWARE! GUBBLINS
WANTED
THIEF!
GUBBLIN AREA
ALERT!
I've never met a gubblin before.
I wonder what they're like.
BEWARE!!
My grandma said that they're vicious 10-foot monsters with huge fangs!
rar!
I heard their skin oozes a poison so powerful, it kills with one touch!
And I overheard someone at the Rusty Goat say that they'll wear your skin as a disguise!
AAAH! ENOUGH! Pot! Stop talking about gubblins! You're freaking me out!
SLAP!
SLAP!
SLAP!
SLAP!

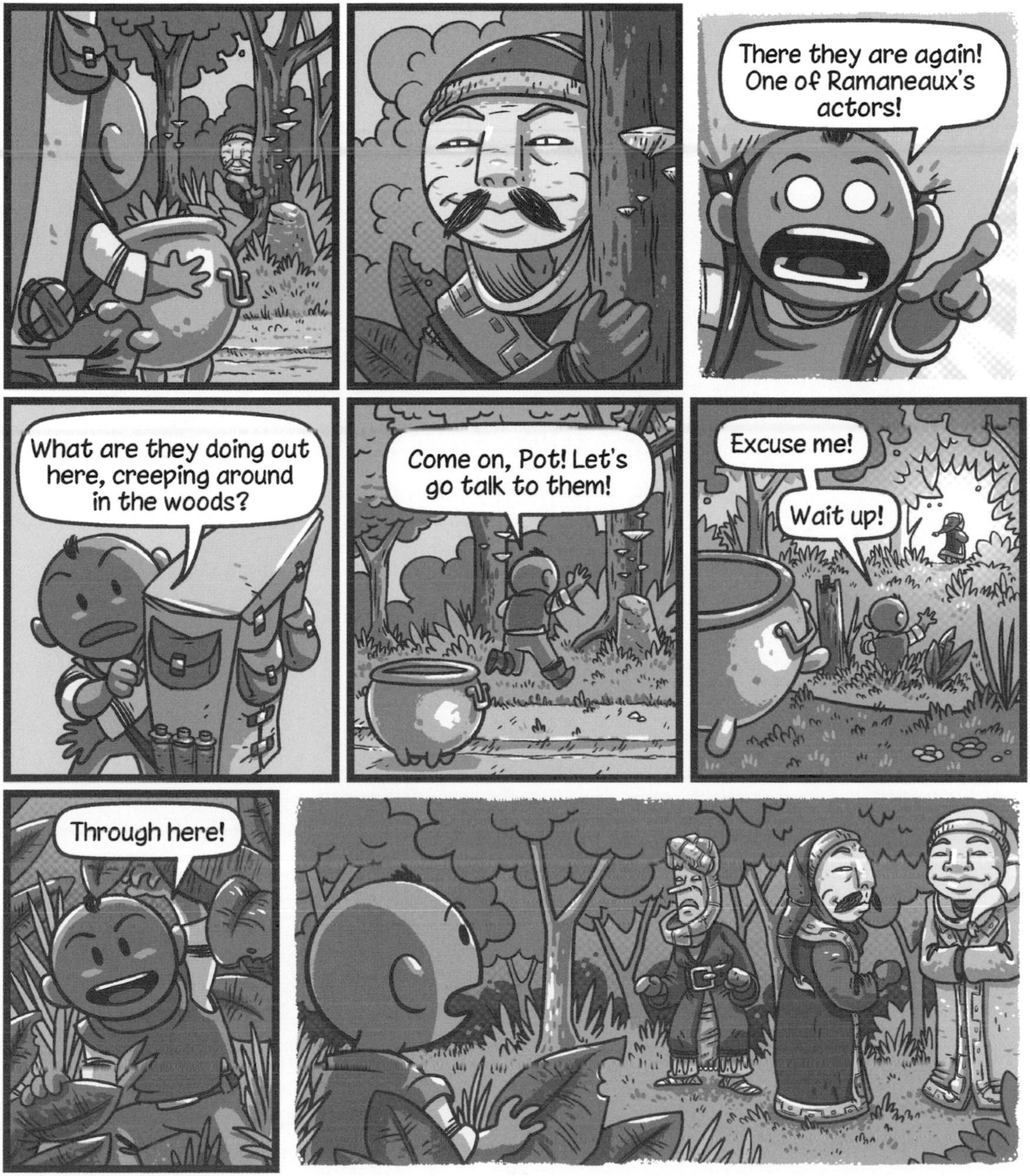
There they are again! One of Ramaneaux's actors!
What are they doing out here, creeping around in the woods?
Come on, Pot! Let's go talk to them!
Excuse me!
Wait up!
Through here!

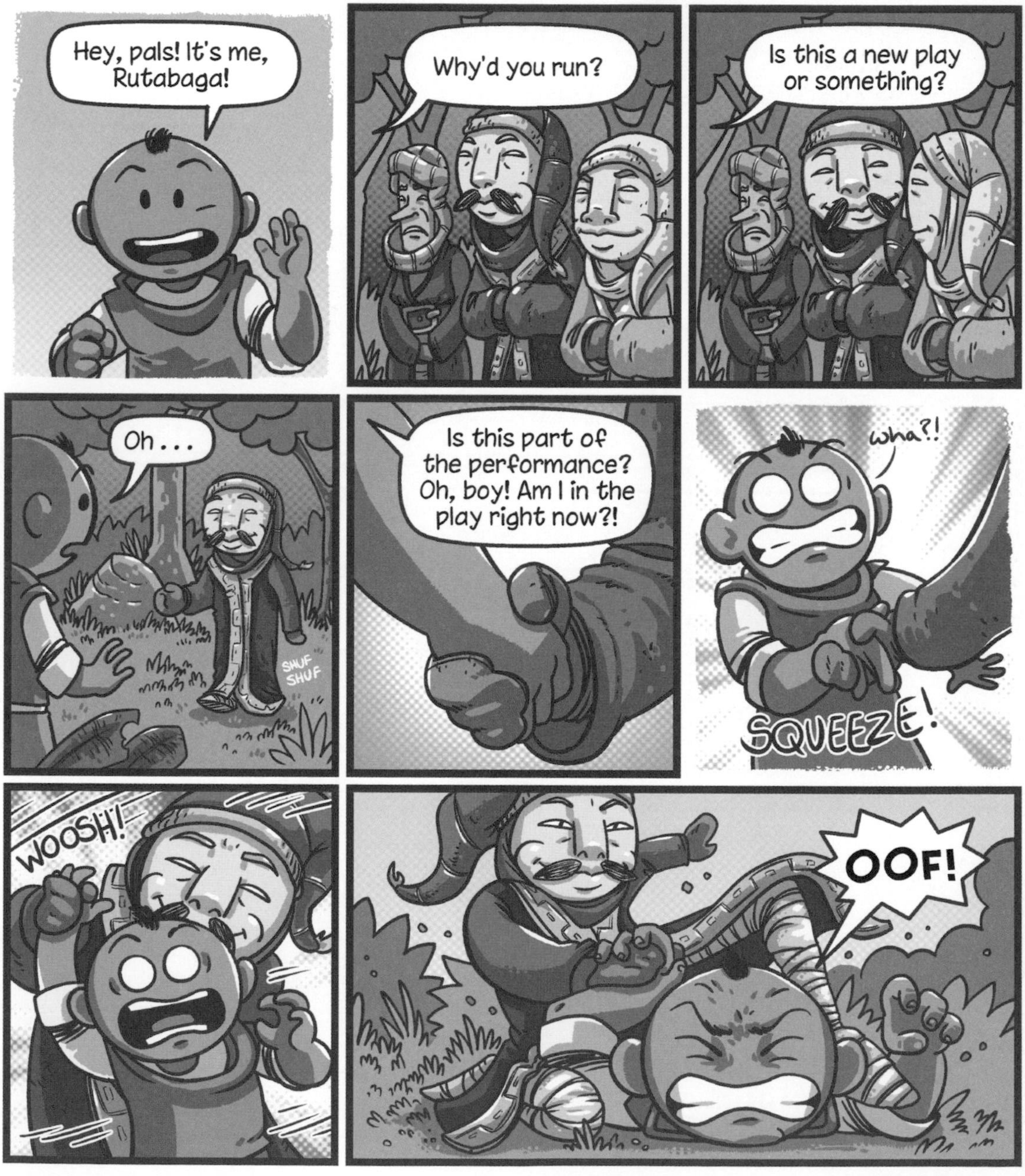
Hey, pals! It's me, Rutabaga!
Why'd you run?
Is this a new play or something?
Oh . . .
SHUF SHUF
Is this part of the performance? Oh, boy! Am I in the play right now?!
wha?!
SQUEEZE!
WOOSH!
OOF!

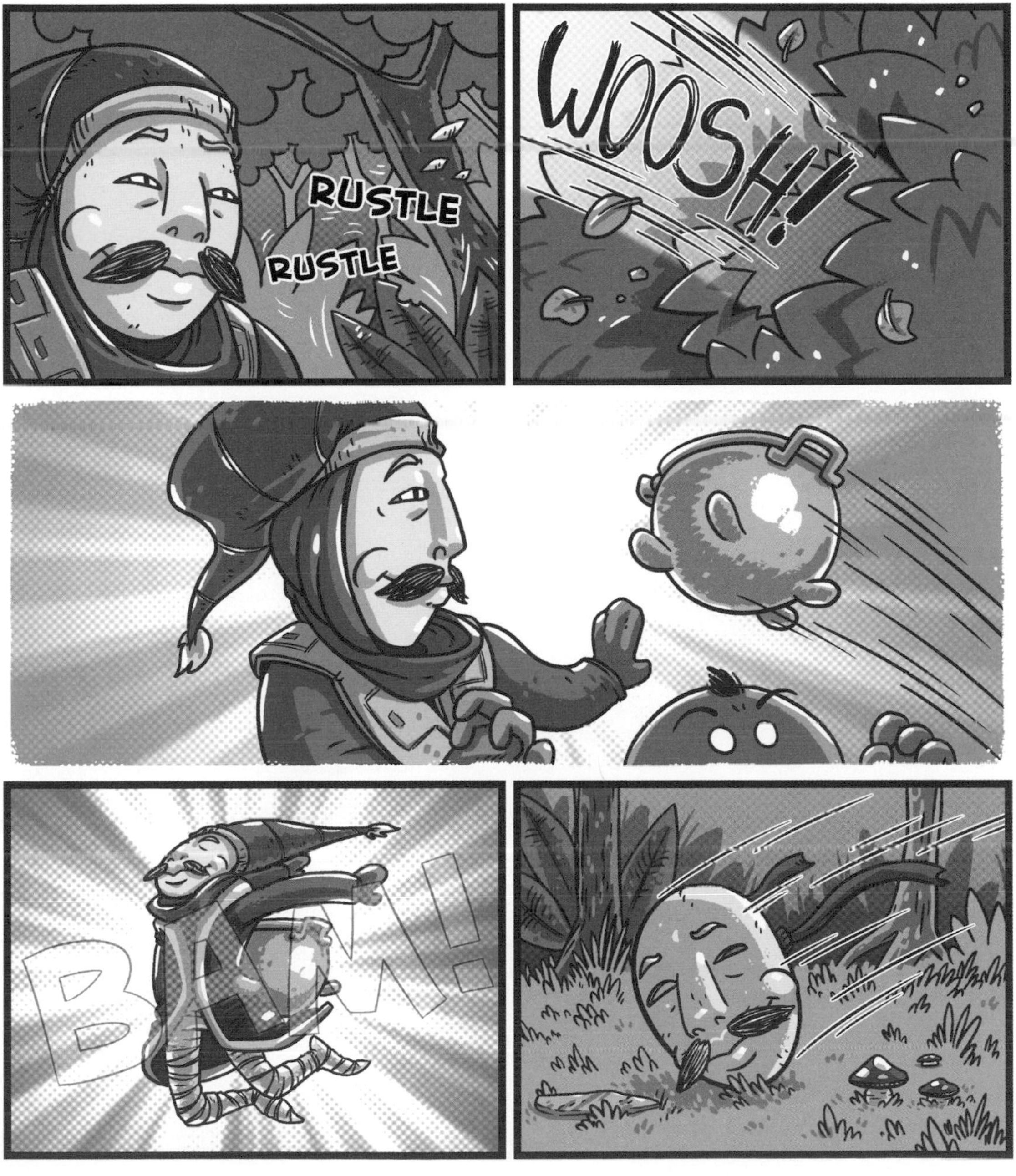
RUSTLE
RUSTLE
WOOSH!
BAM!

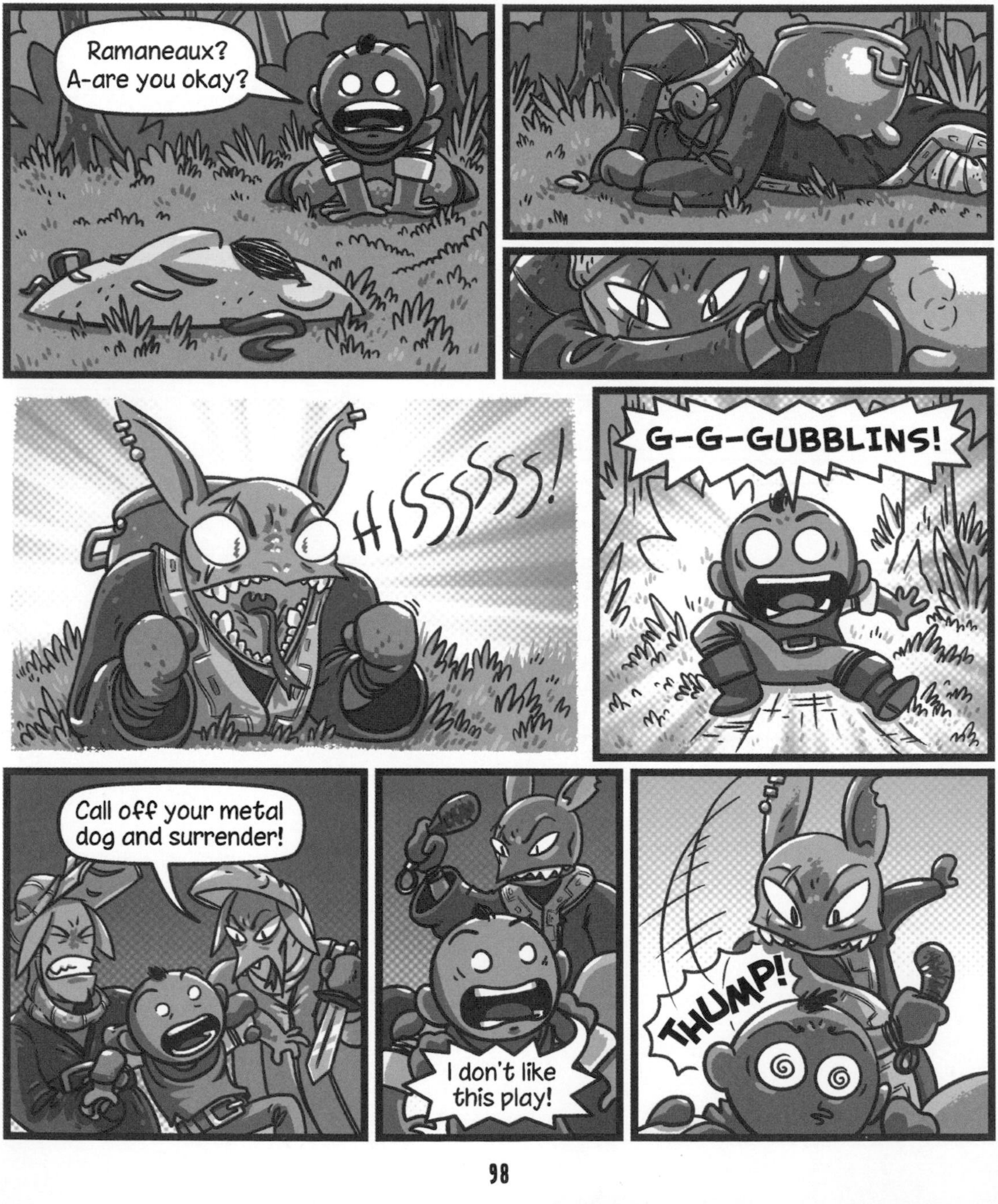
Ramaneaux?
A-are you okay?
HISSSSSS!
G-G-GUBBLINS!
Call off your metal dog and surrender!
I don't like this play!
THUMP!

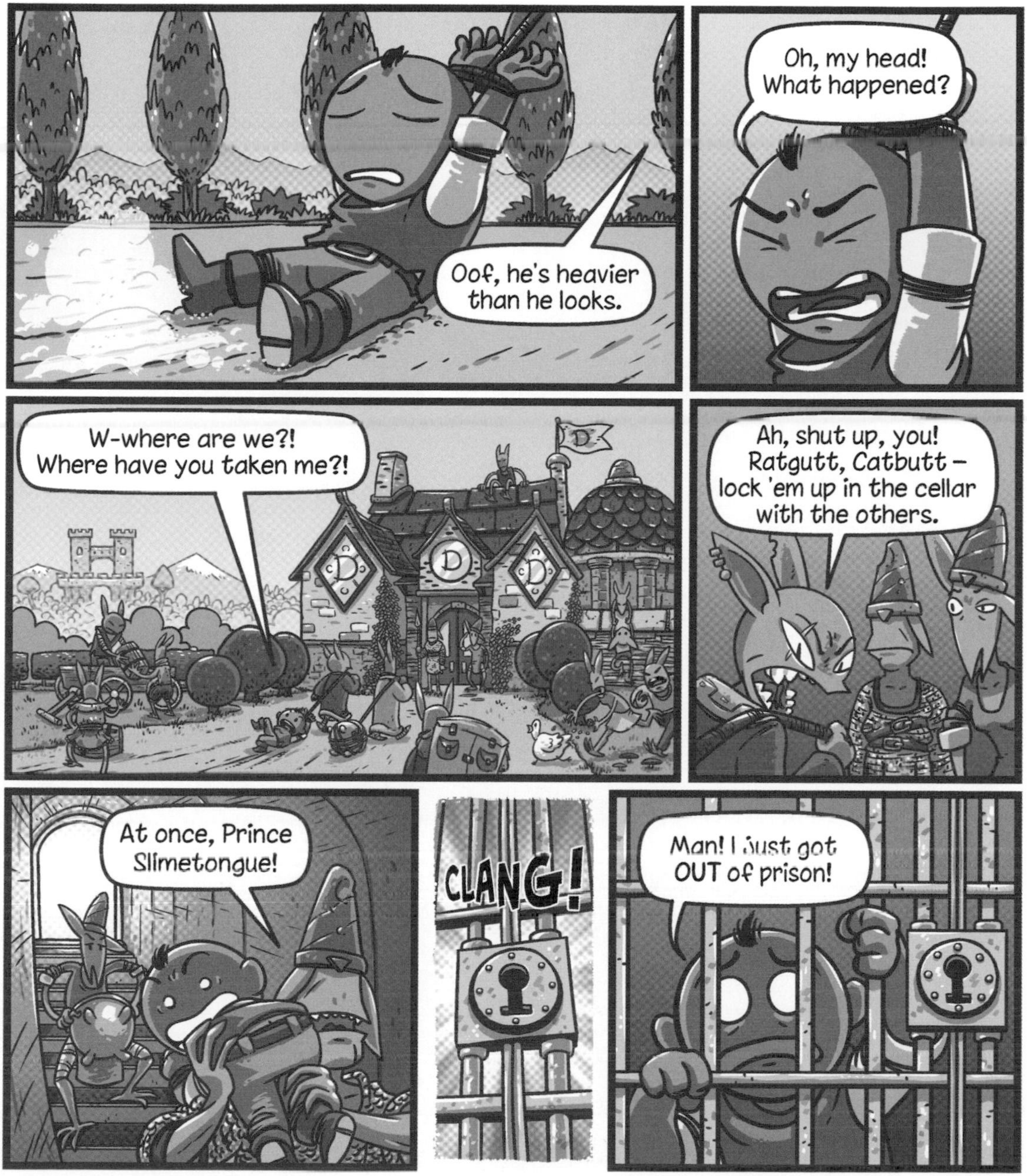
Oof, he's heavier than he looks.
Oh, my head! What happened?
W-where are we?! Where have you taken me?!
Ah, shut up, you! Ratgutt, Catbutt – lock 'em up in the cellar with the others.
At once, Prince Slimetongue!
CLANG!
Man! I Just got OUT of prison!

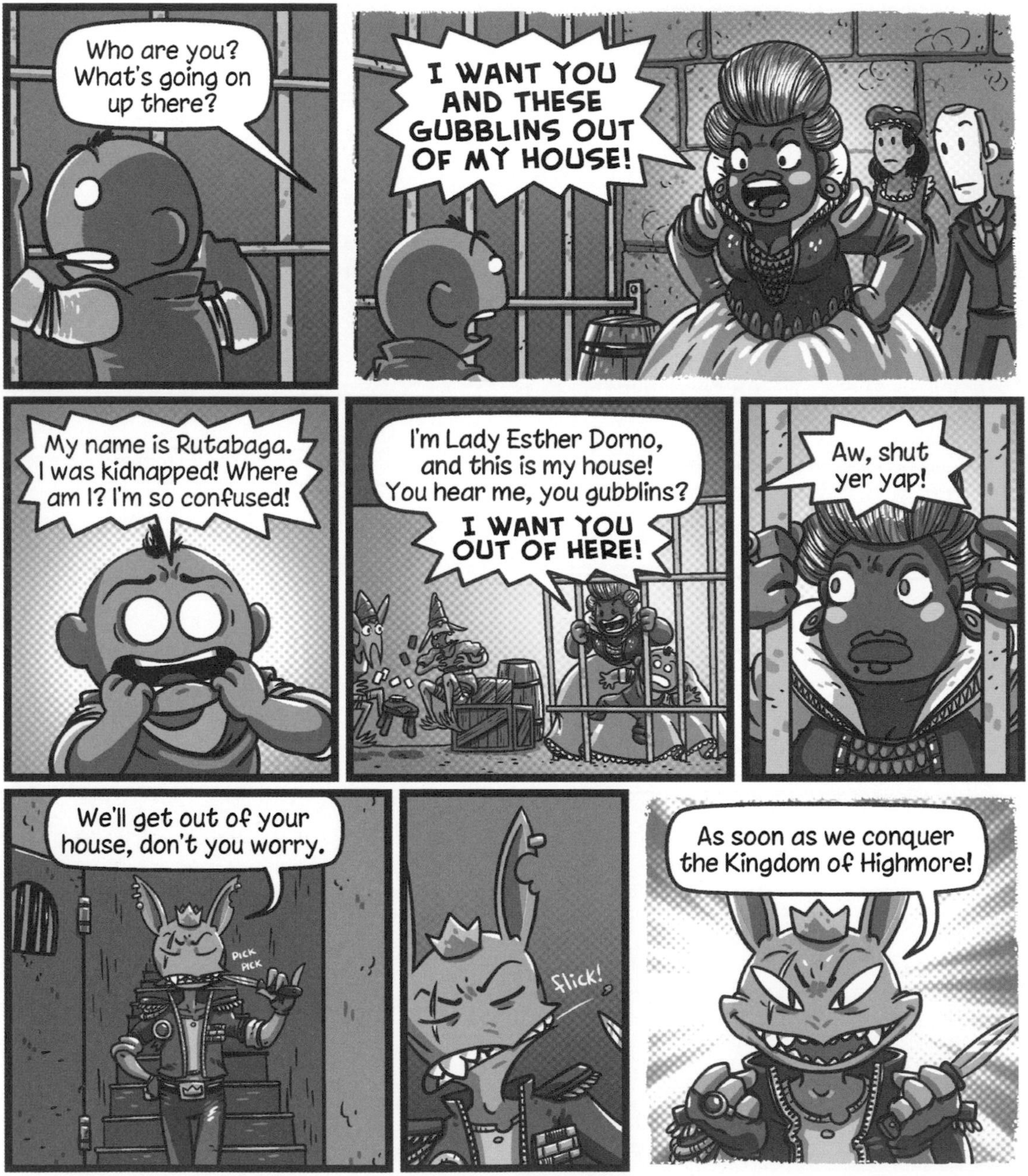
Who are you? What's going on up there?
I WANT YOU AND THESE GUBBLINS OUT OF MY HOUSE!
My name is Rutabaga. I was kidnapped! Where am I? I'm so confused!
I'm Lady Esther Dorno, and this is my house! You hear me, you gubblins?
I WANT YOU OUT OF HERE!
Aw, shut yer yap!
We'll get out of your house, don't you worry.
PICK PICK
flick!
As soon as we conquer the Kingdom of Highmore!

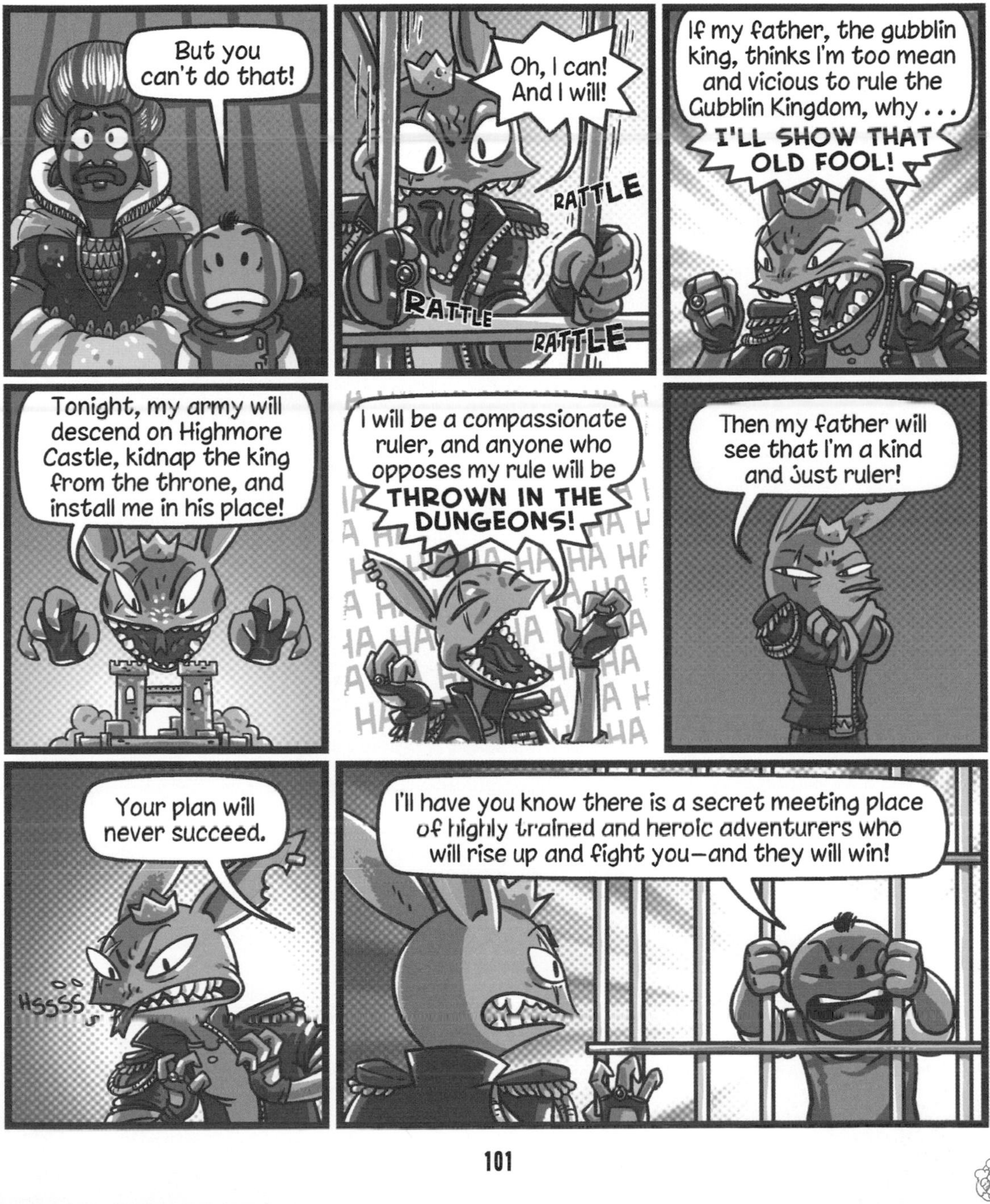
But you can't do that!
Oh, I can! And I will!
RATTLE
RATTLE
RATTLE
If my father, the gubblin king, thinks I'm too mean and vicious to rule the Gubblin Kingdom, why . . .
I'LL SHOW THAT OLD FOOL!
Tonight, my army will descend on Highmore Castle, kidnap the king from the throne, and install me in his place!
I will be a compassionate ruler, and anyone who opposes my rule will be
THROWN IN THE DUNGEONS!
HA HA HA HA
Then my father will see that I'm a kind and just ruler!
Your plan will never succeed.
HSSSS
I'll have you know there is a secret meeting place of highly trained and heroic adventurers who will rise up and fight you—and they will win!

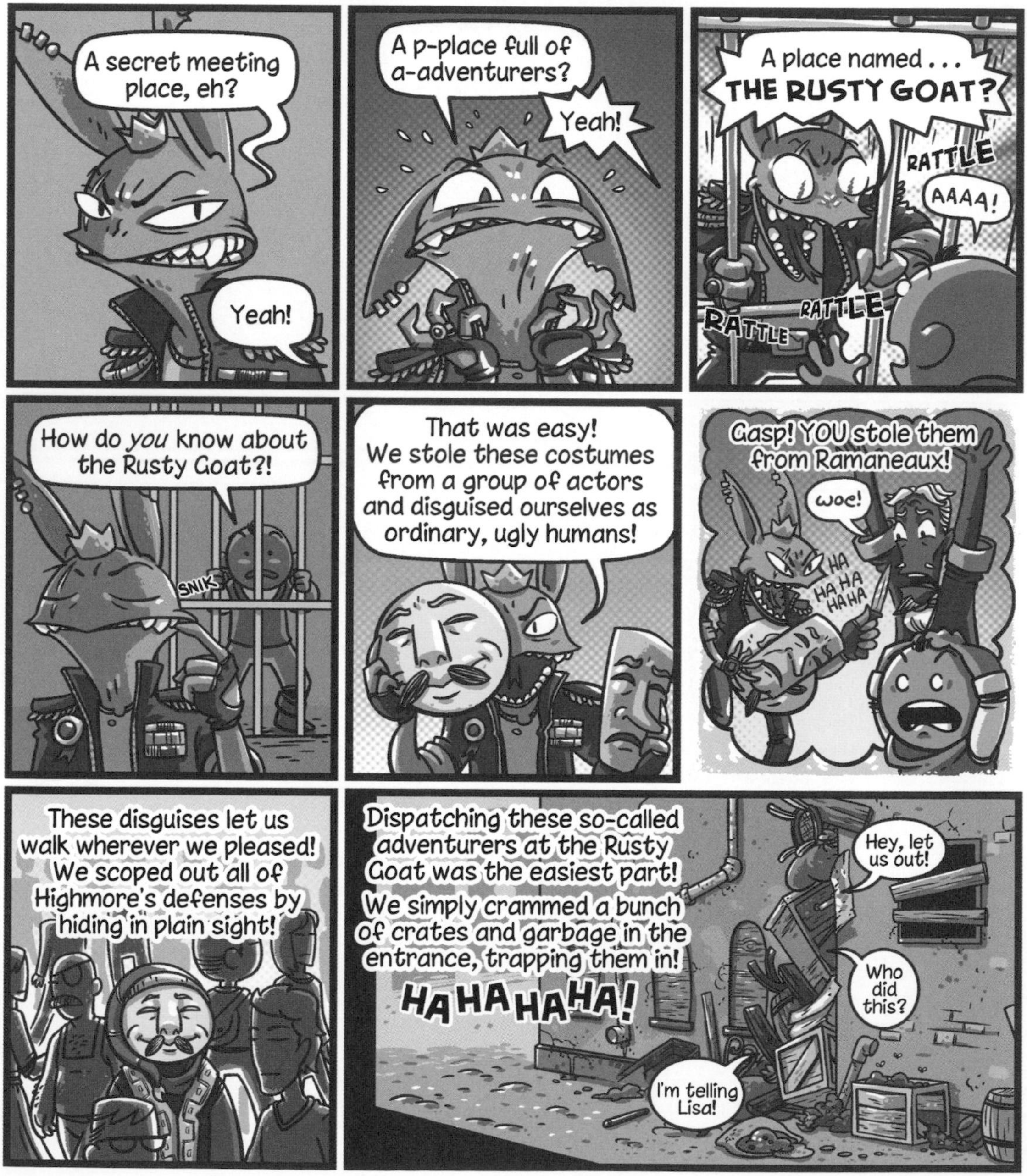
A secret meeting place, eh?
Yeah!
A p-place full of a-adventurers?
Yeah!
A place named . . . THE RUSTY GOAT?
RATTLE
AAAA!
RATTLE
RATTLE
How do *you* know about the Rusty Goat?!
SNIK
That was easy! We stole these costumes from a group of actors and disguised ourselves as ordinary, ugly humans!
Gasp! YOU stole them from Ramaneaux!
woe!
HA HA HA HA HA
These disguises let us walk wherever we pleased! We scoped out all of Highmore's defenses by hiding in plain sight!
Dispatching these so-called adventurers at the Rusty Goat was the easiest part!
We simply crammed a bunch of crates and garbage in the entrance, trapping them in!
HA HA HA HA!
Hey, let us out!
Who did this?
I'm telling Lisa!

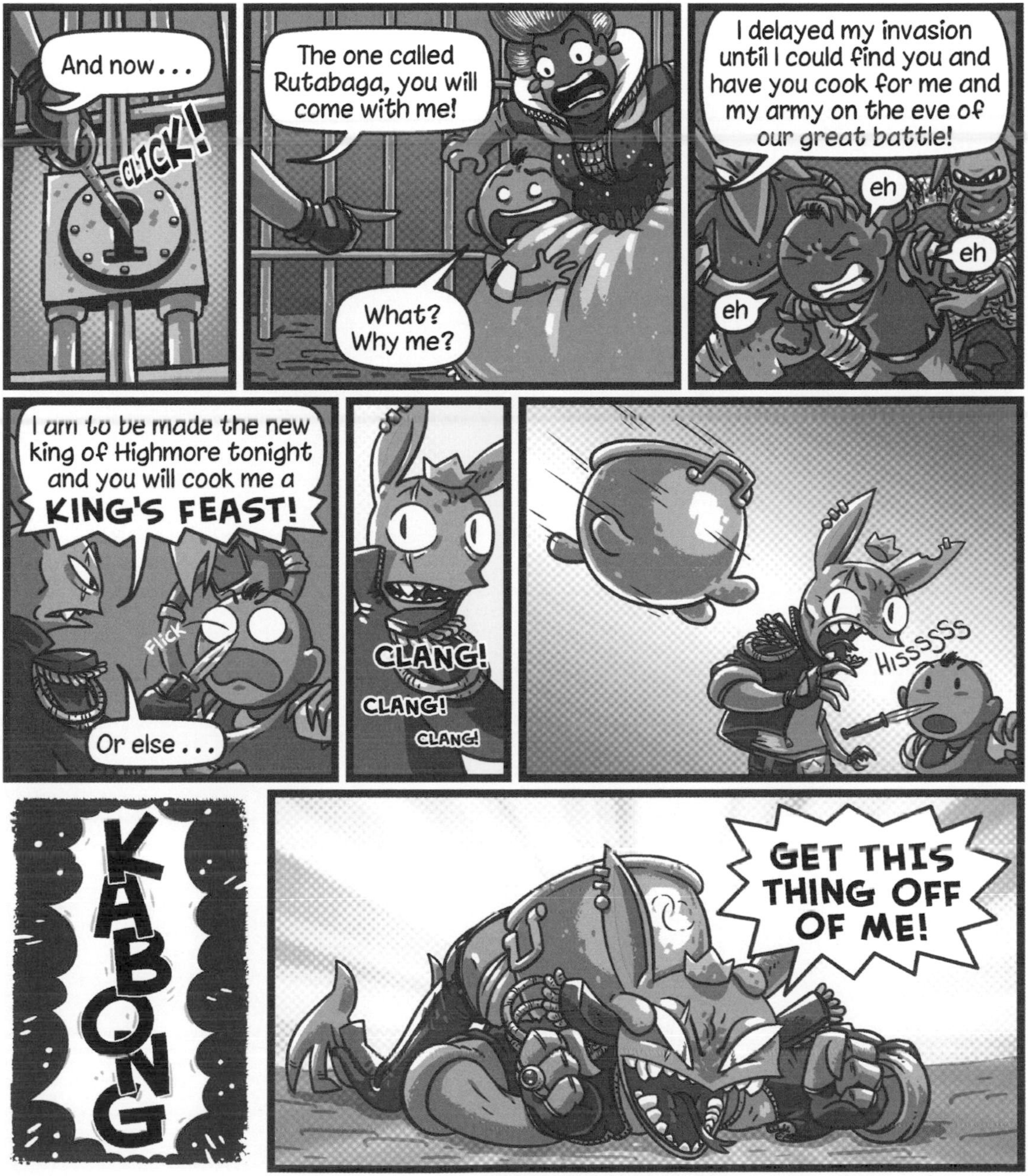
And now . . .
CLICK!
The one called Rutabaga, you will come with me!
What? Why me?
I delayed my invasion until I could find you and have you cook for me and my army on the eve of our great battle!
eh
eh
eh
I am to be made the new king of Highmore tonight and you will cook me a KING'S FEAST!
Flick
Or else . . .
CLANG!
CLANG!
CLANG!
HISSSSSS
KABONG
GET THIS THING OFF OF ME!

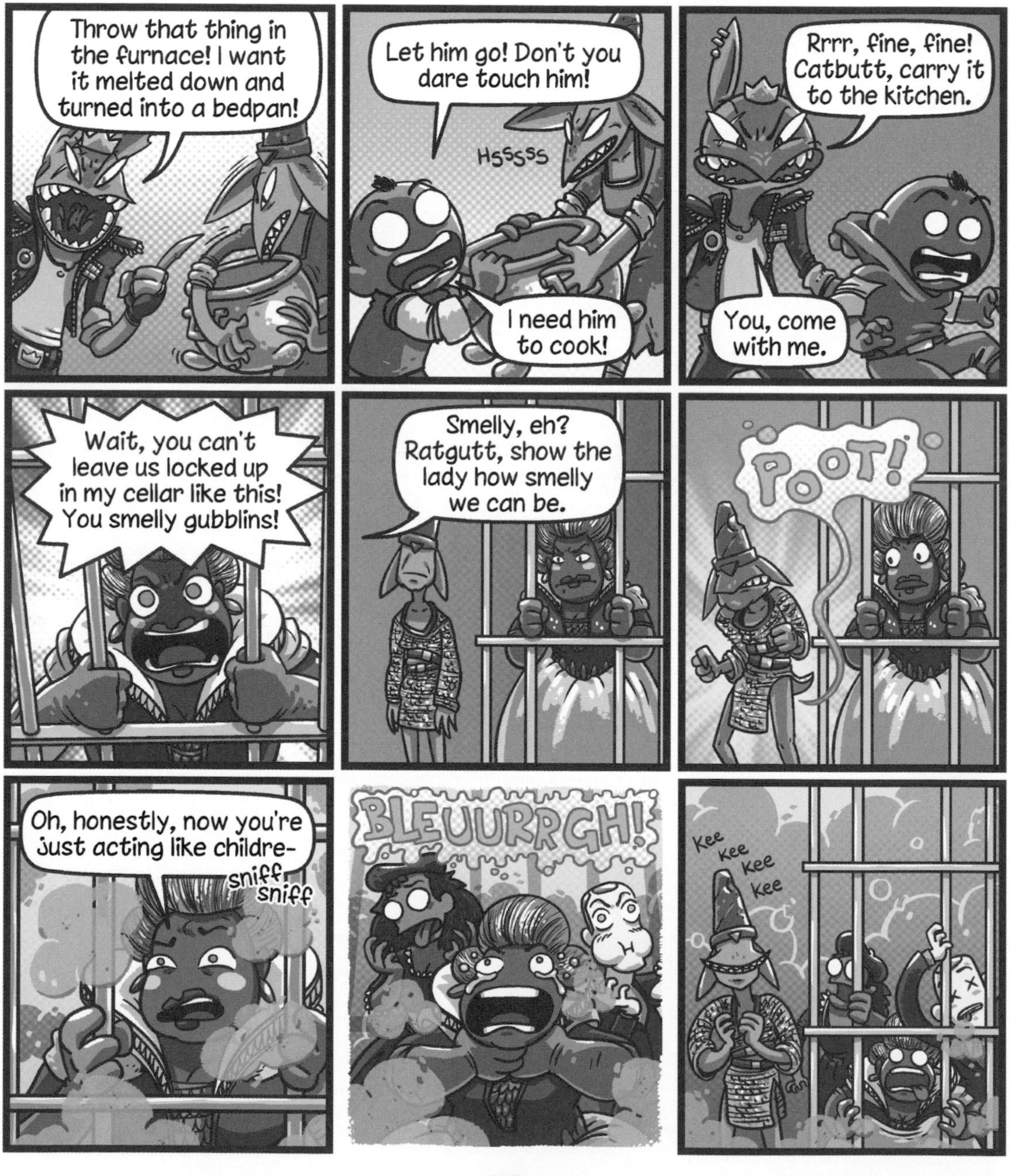
Throw that thing in the furnace! I want it melted down and turned into a bedpan!
Let him go! Don't you dare touch him!
HSSSSS
I need him to cook!
Rrrr, fine, fine! Catbutt, carry it to the kitchen.
You, come with me.
Wait, you can't leave us locked up in my cellar like this! You smelly gubblins!
Smelly, eh? Ratgutt, show the lady how smelly we can be.
POOT!
Oh, honestly, now you're just acting like childre-
sniff sniff
BLEUURRGH!
Kee Kee Kee Kee

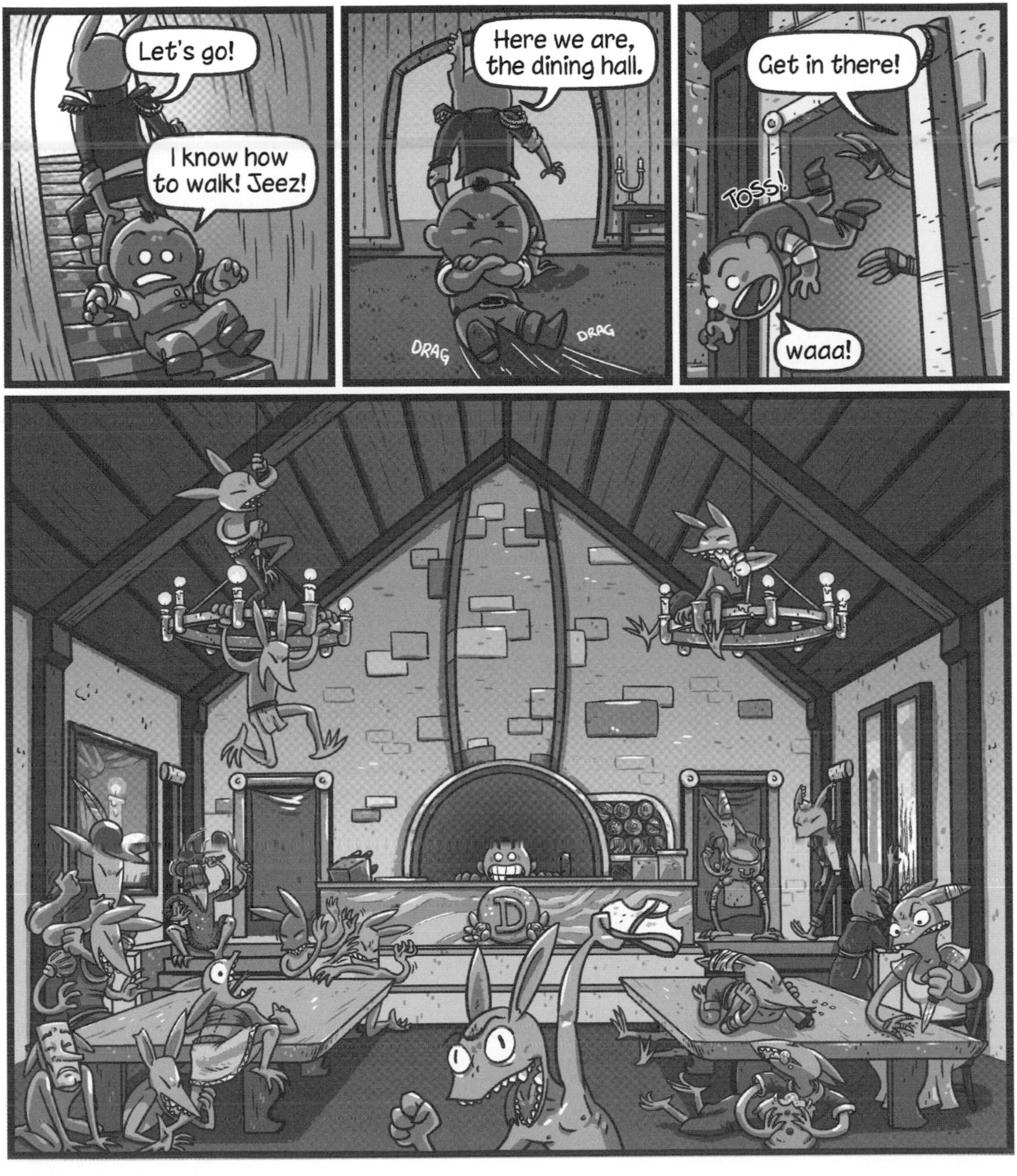
Let's go!
I know how to walk! Jeez!
Here we are, the dining hall.
DRAG
DRAG
Get in there!
TOSS!
waaa!

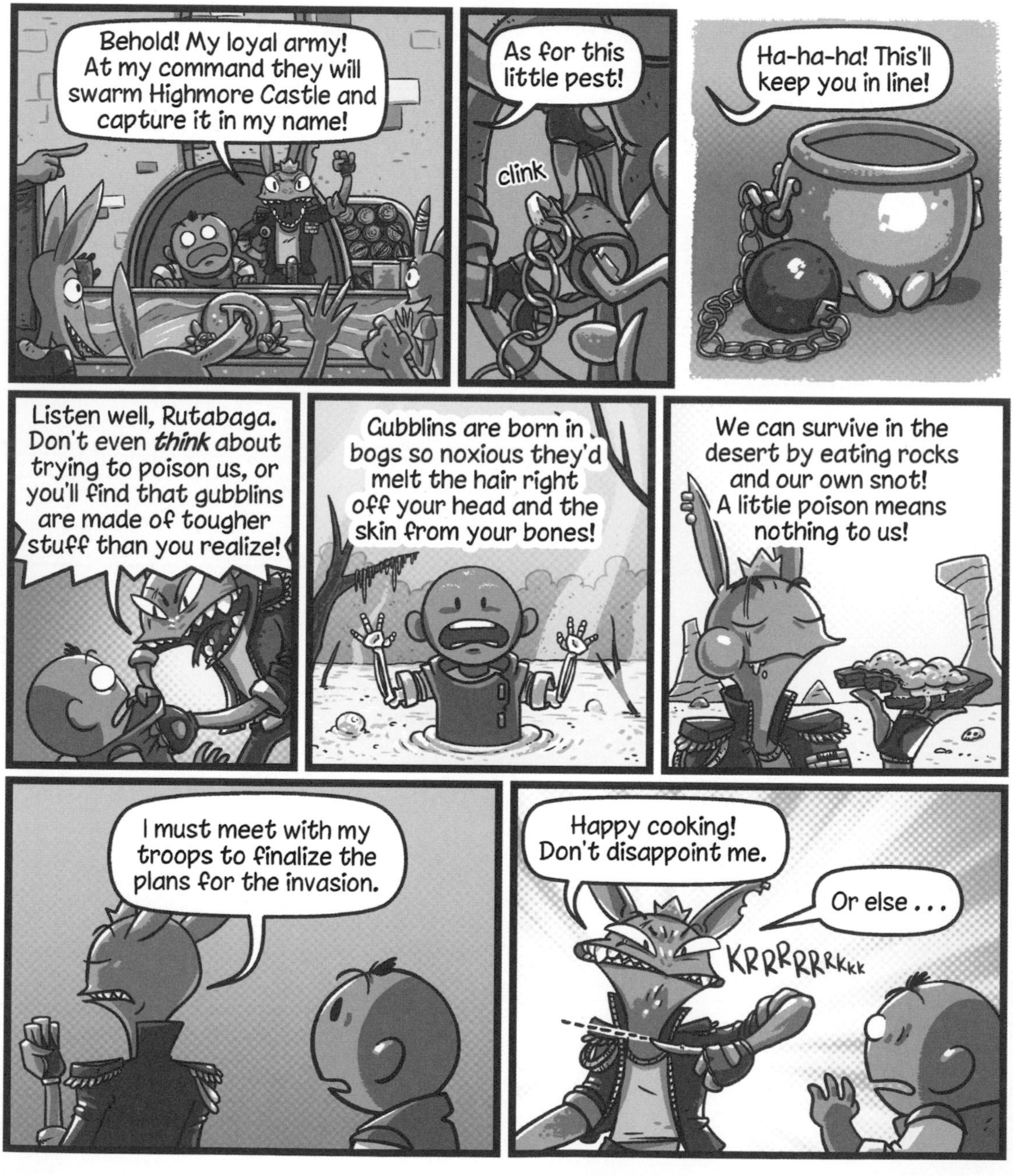
Behold! My loyal army! At my command they will swarm Highmore Castle and capture it in my name!
As for this little pest!
clink
Ha-ha-ha! This'll keep you in line!
Listen well, Rutabaga. Don't even *think* about trying to poison us, or you'll find that gubblins are made of tougher stuff than you realize!
Gubblins are born in bogs so noxious they'd melt the hair right off your head and the skin from your bones!
We can survive in the desert by eating rocks and our own snot! A little poison means nothing to us!
I must meet with my troops to finalize the plans for the invasion.
Happy cooking! Don't disappoint me.
Or else . . .
KRRRRRRkkk

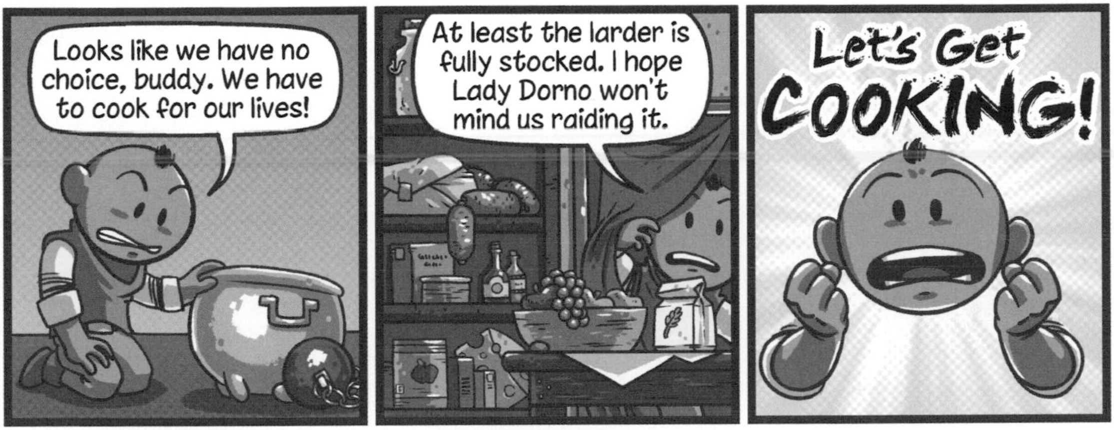
Looks like we have no choice, buddy. We have to cook for our lives!
At least the larder is fully stocked. I hope Lady Dorno won't mind us raiding it.
Let's Get COOKING!

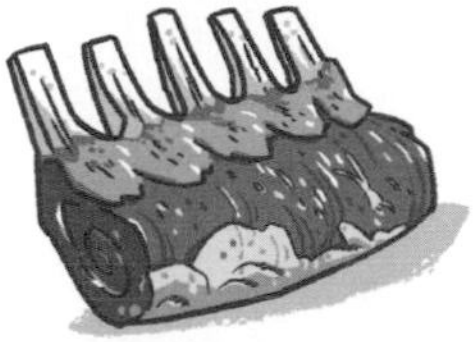

1. Get a nice cut of pork loin with the ribs still intact.

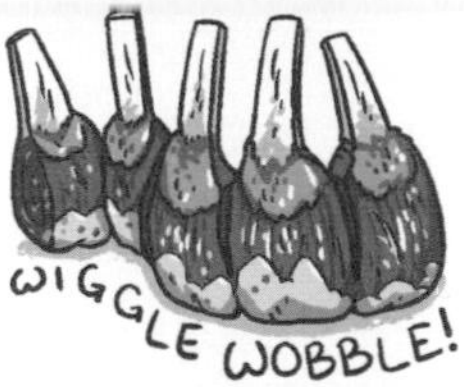
WIGGLE WOBBLE!

2. Cut between the ribs to allow the meat to bend.

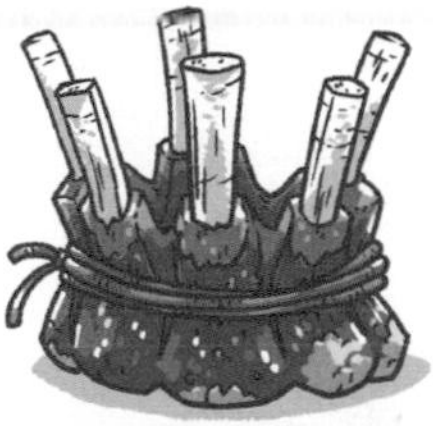

3. Shape the pork loin into a ring and tie it together.

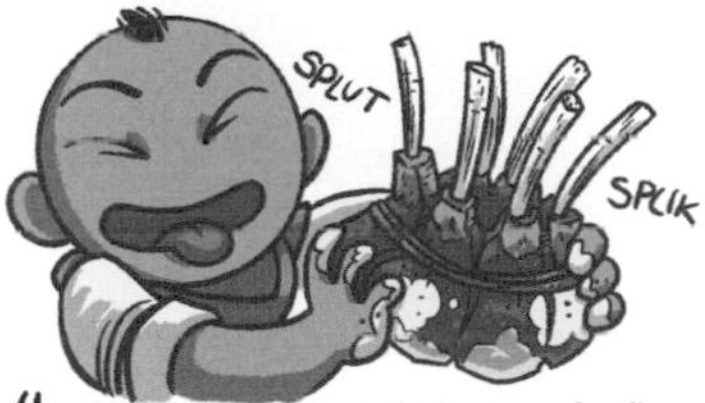
SPLUT
SPLIK

4. Slather on a mixture of oil, salt, pepper, garlic, and spices. Get real messy!

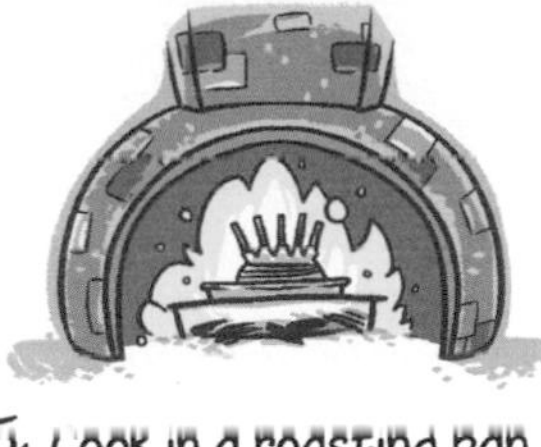

5. Cook in a roasting pan with a bunch of cherries and peeled pears.

You've made a . . .

KING'S CROWN with FRUIT JEWELS

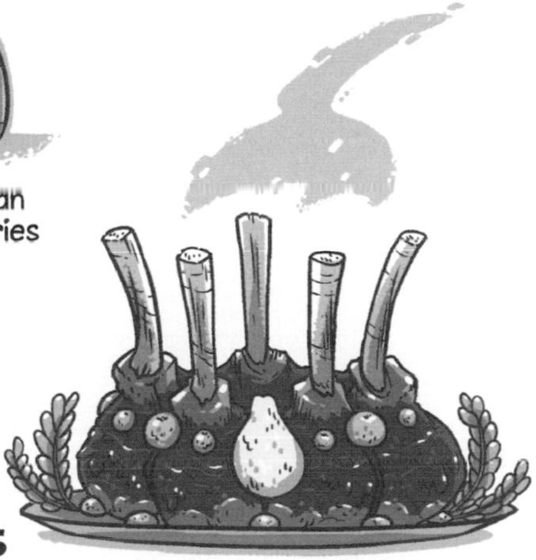

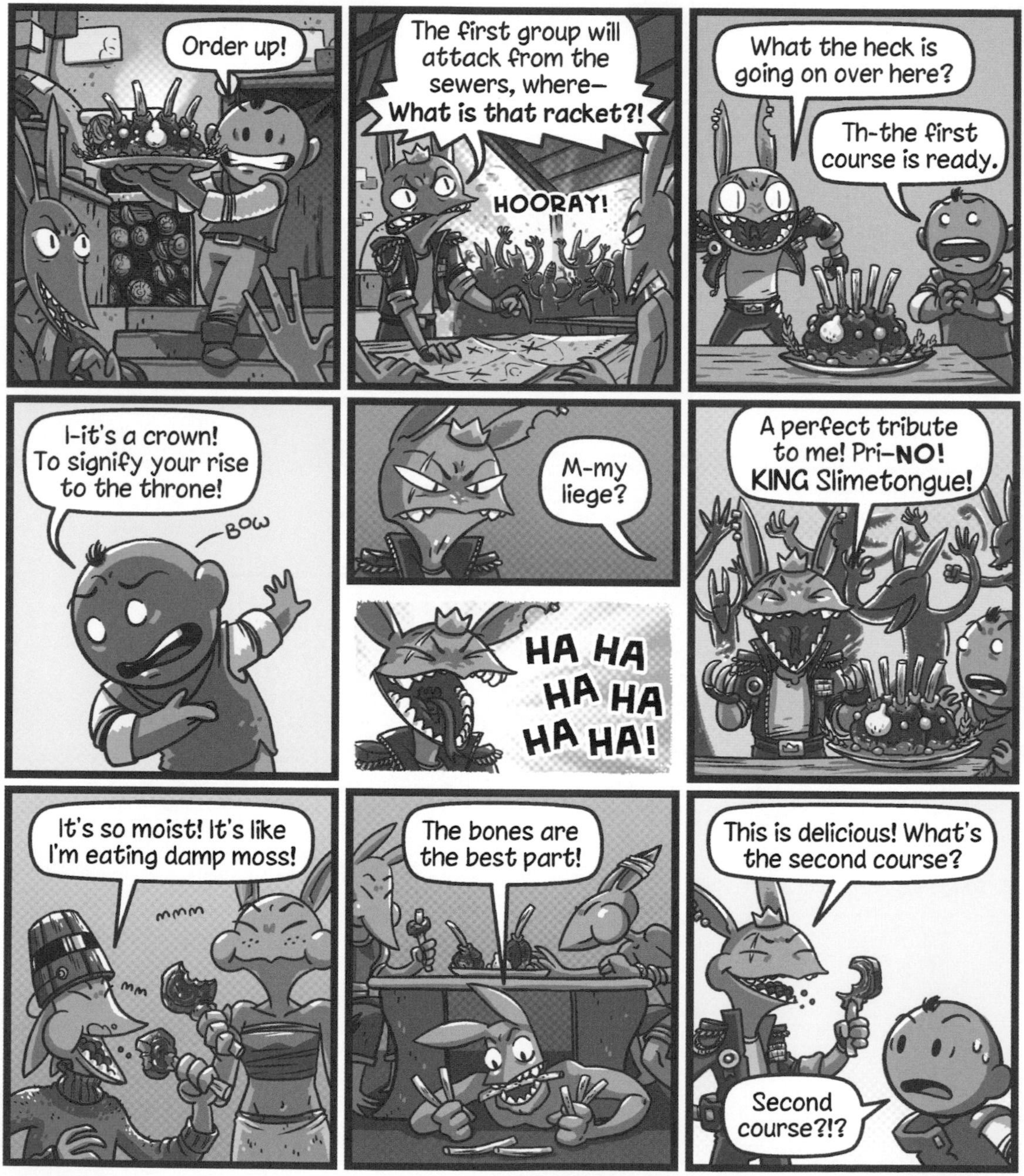
Order up!
The first group will attack from the sewers, where— What is that racket?!
HOORAY!
What the heck is going on over here?
Th-the first course is ready.
I-it's a crown! To signify your rise to the throne!
BOW
M-my liege?
HA HA HA HA HA HA!
A perfect tribute to me! Pri—NO! KING Slimetongue!
It's so moist! It's like I'm eating damp moss!
mmm
mm
The bones are the best part!
This is delicious! What's the second course?
Second course?!?

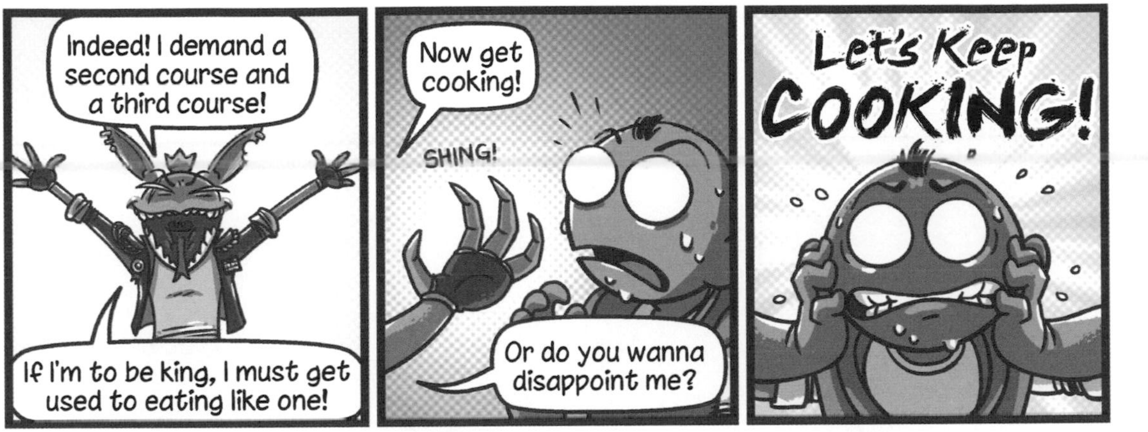

Indeed! I demand a second course and a third course!
If I'm to be king, I must get used to eating like one!
Now get cooking!
SHING!
Or do you wanna disappoint me?
Let's Keep COOKING!

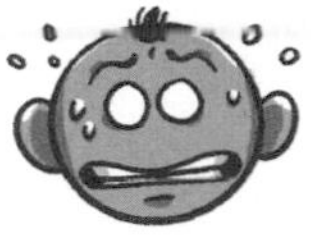

He wants to eat like royalty? Maybe he'd like fondue??

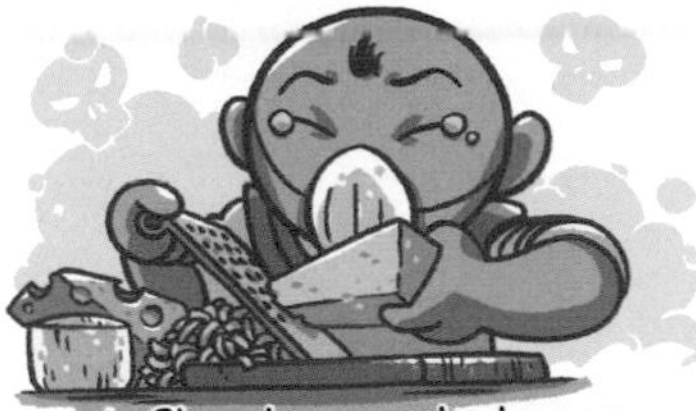

1. Shred as much cheese as you can find! The stinkier the better!

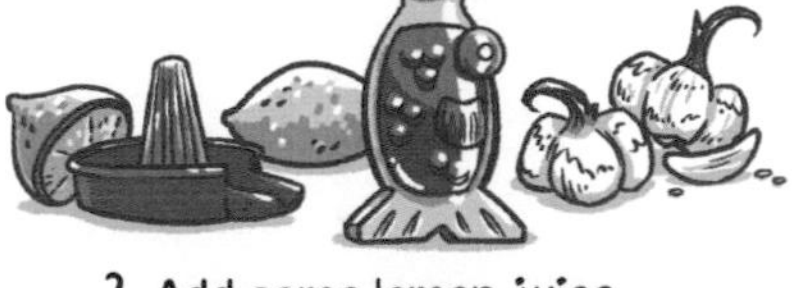

2. Add some lemon juice, fish sauce, and a ton of garlic to the pot.

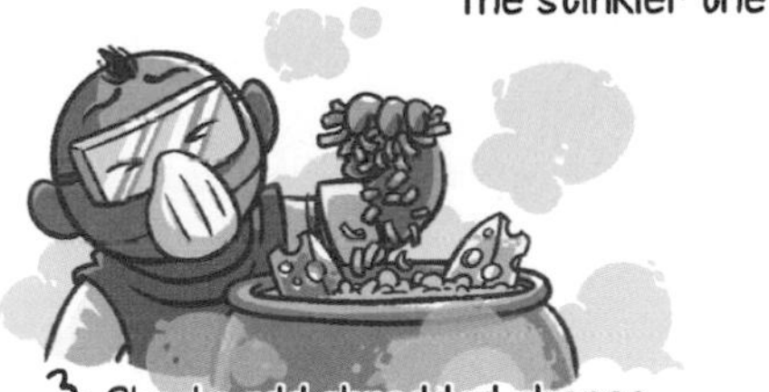

3. Slowly add shredded cheese, stirring constantly until it's all melted.

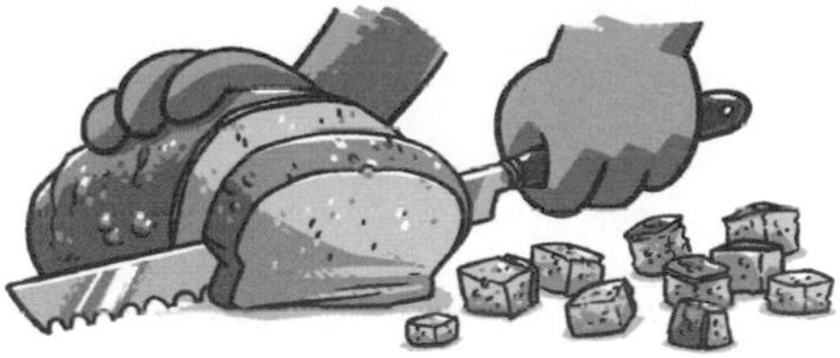

4. Slice a loaf of crusty bread into cubes and serve!

You've made
BUBBLING BOG FONDUE!

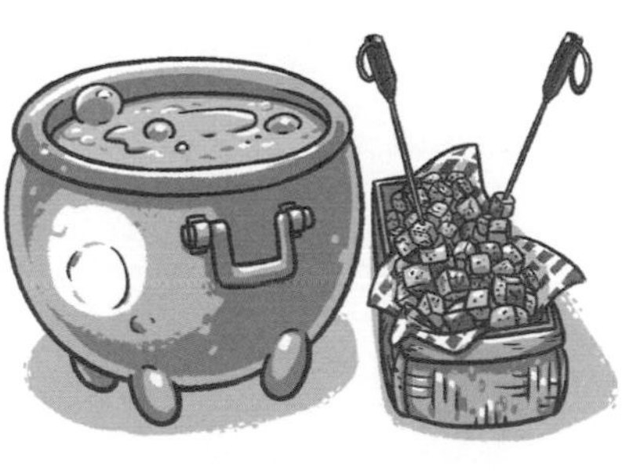

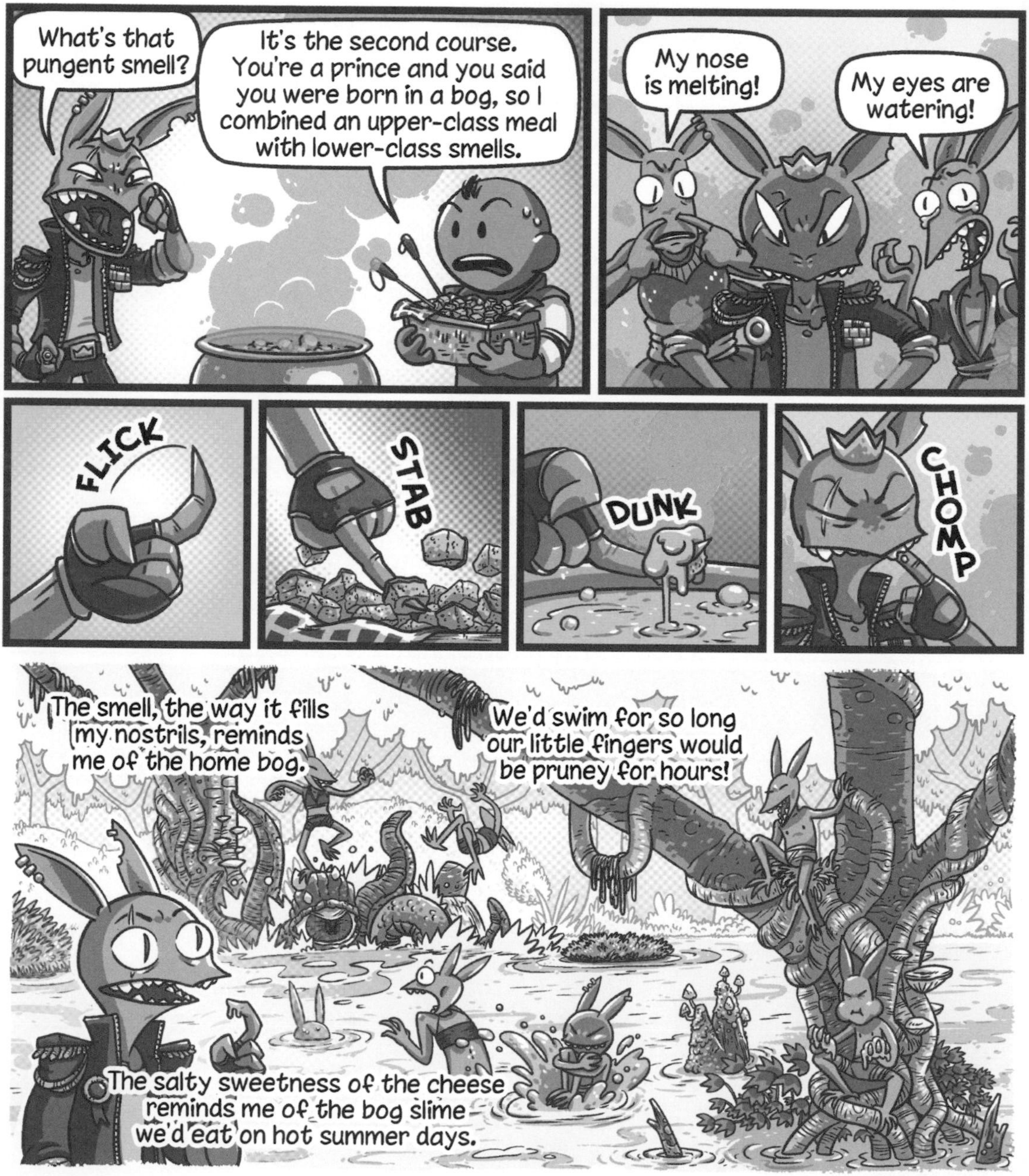
What's that pungent smell?
It's the second course. You're a prince and you said you were born in a bog, so I combined an upper-class meal with lower-class smells.
My nose is melting!
My eyes are watering!
FLICK
STAB
DUNK
CHOMP
The smell, the way it fills my nostrils, reminds me of the home bog.
We'd swim for so long our little fingers would be pruney for hours!
The salty sweetness of the cheese reminds me of the bog slime we'd eat on hot summer days.

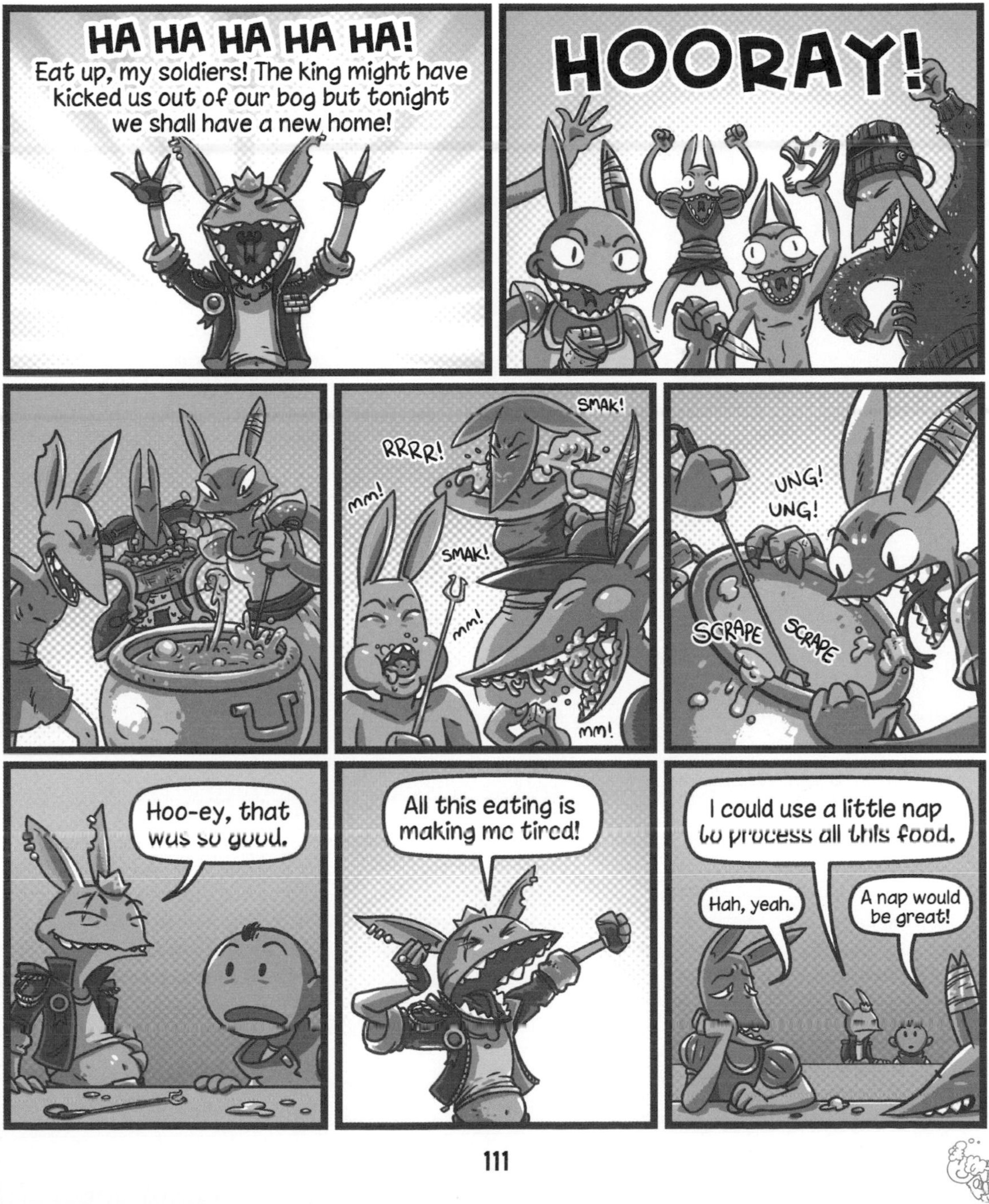
HA HA HA HA HA!
Eat up, my soldiers! The king might have kicked us out of our bog but tonight we shall have a new home!
HOORAY!
SMAK!
RRRR!
mm!
SMAK!
mm!
mm!
UNG! UNG!
SCRAPE
SCRAPE
Hoo-ey, that was so good.
All this eating is making me tired!
I could use a little nap to process all this food.
Hah, yeah.
A nap would be great!

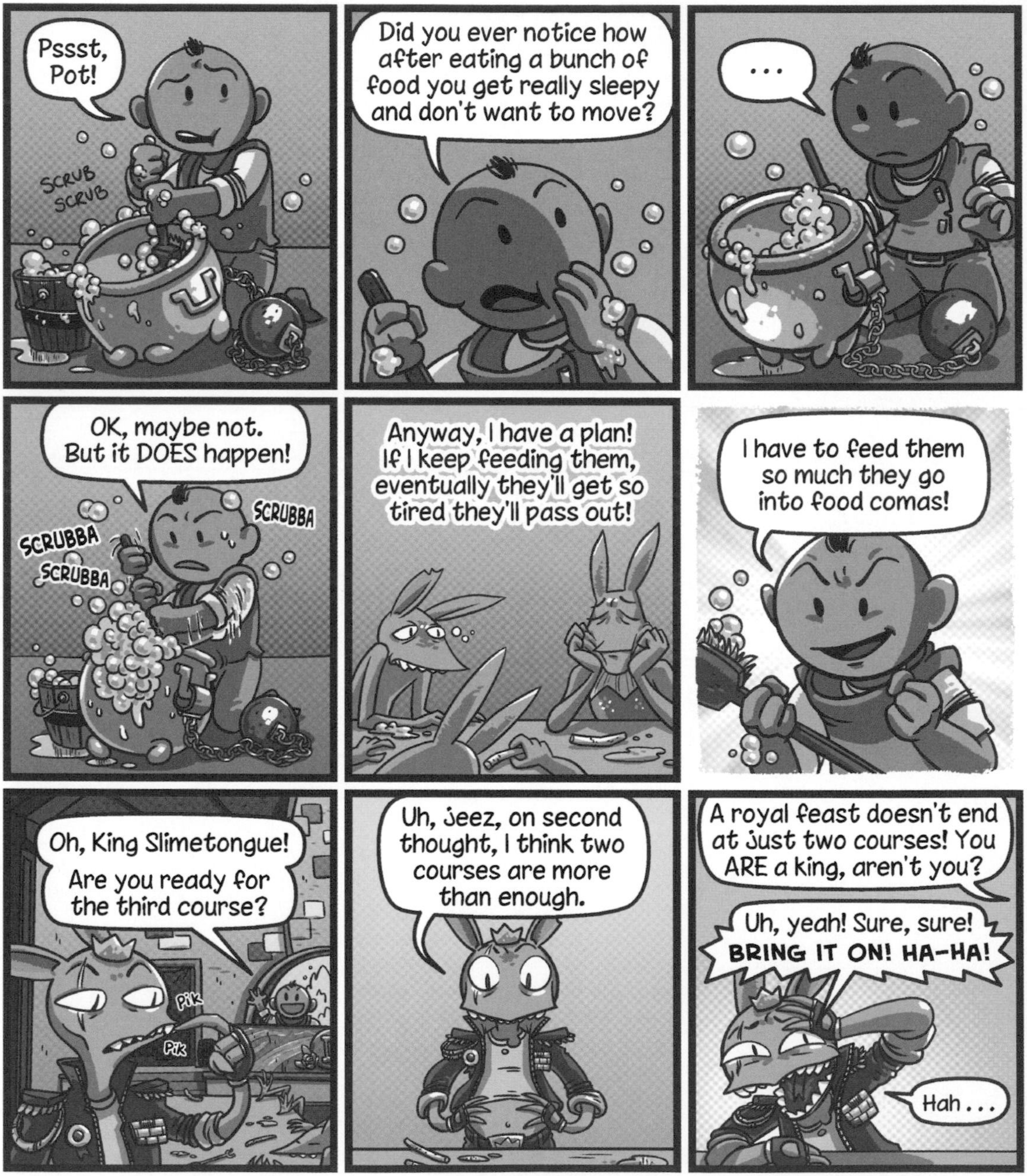

Pssst, Pot!
SCRUB SCRUB
Did you ever notice how after eating a bunch of food you get really sleepy and don't want to move?
...
OK, maybe not. But it DOES happen!
SCRUBBA
SCRUBBA
SCRUBBA
Anyway, I have a plan! If I keep feeding them, eventually they'll get so tired they'll pass out!
I have to feed them so much they go into food comas!
Oh, King Slimetongue!
Are you ready for the third course?
PiK
PiK
Uh, Jeez, on second thought, I think two courses are more than enough.
A royal feast doesn't end at just two courses! You ARE a king, aren't you?
Uh, yeah! Sure, sure! **BRING IT ON! HA-HA!**
Hah...

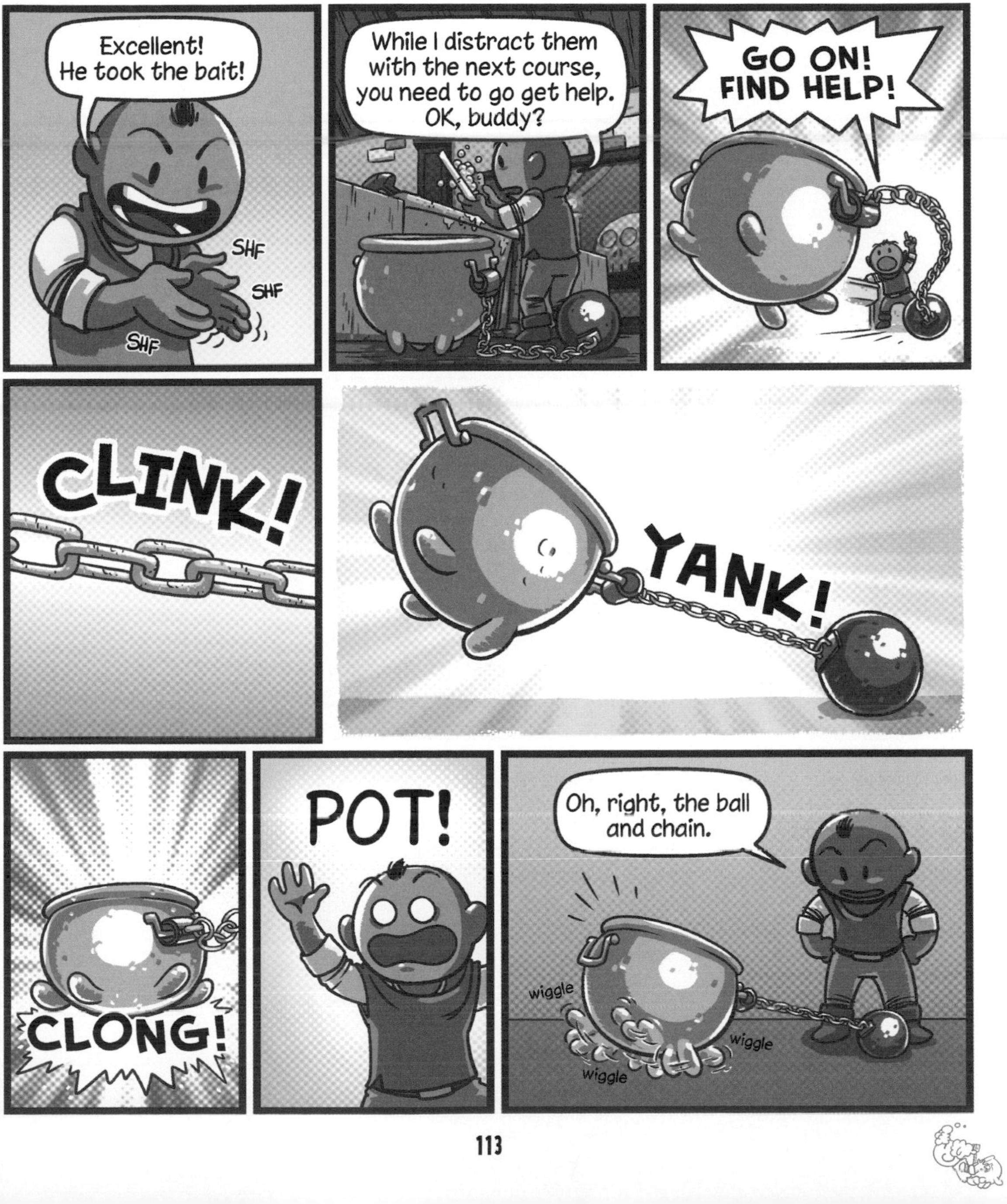
Excellent! He took the bait!
SHF
SHF
SHF
While I distract them with the next course, you need to go get help. OK, buddy?
GO ON! FIND HELP!
CLINK!
YANK!
CLONG!
POT!
Oh, right, the ball and chain.
wiggle
wiggle
wiggle

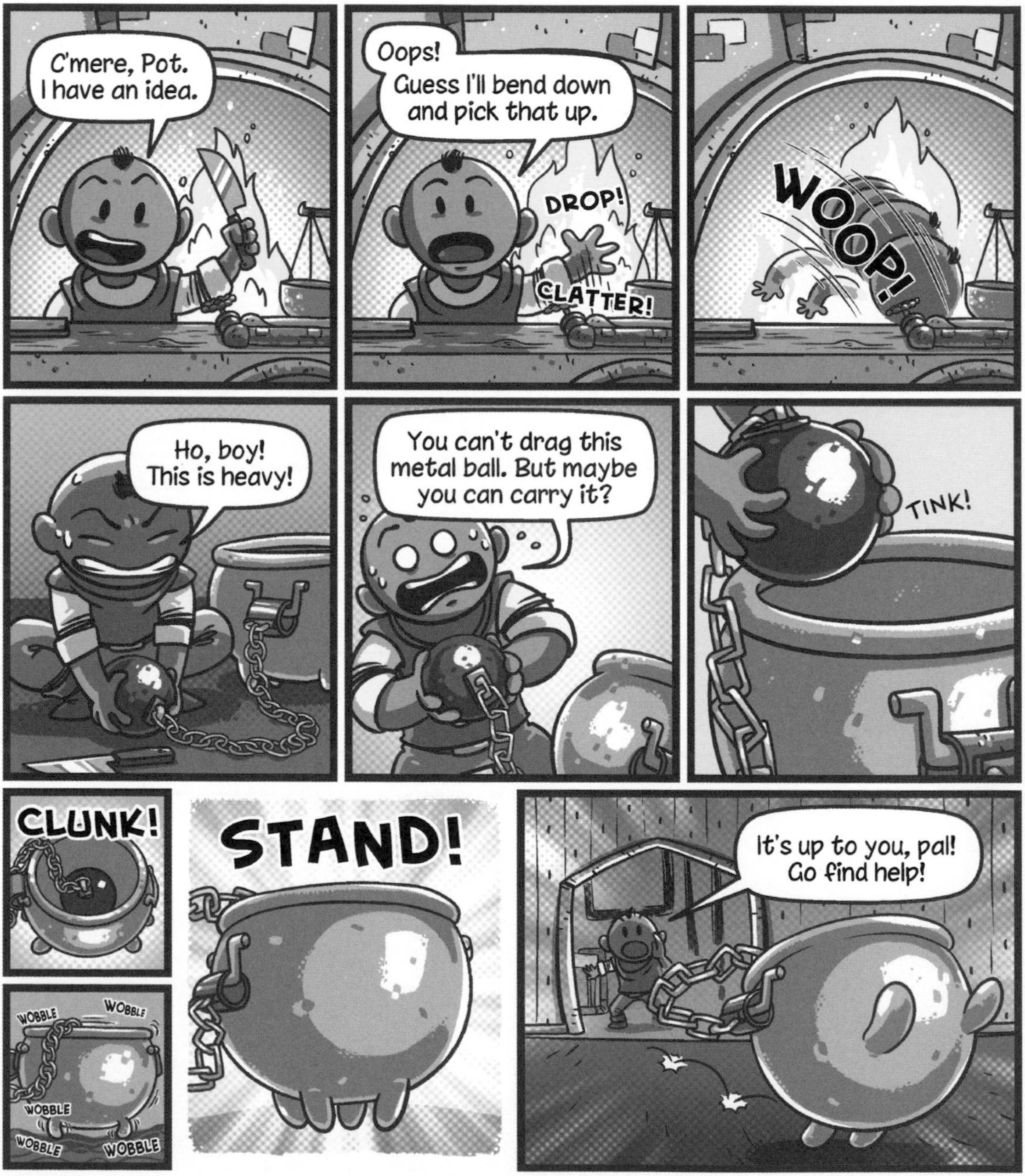
C'mere, Pot.
I have an idea.
Oops!
Guess I'll bend down and pick that up.
DROP!
CLATTER!
WOOP!
Ho, boy!
This is heavy!
You can't drag this metal ball. But maybe you can carry it?
TINK!
CLUNK!
WOBBLE
WOBBLE
WOBBLE
WOBBLE
WOBBLE
STAND!
It's up to you, pal!
Go find help!

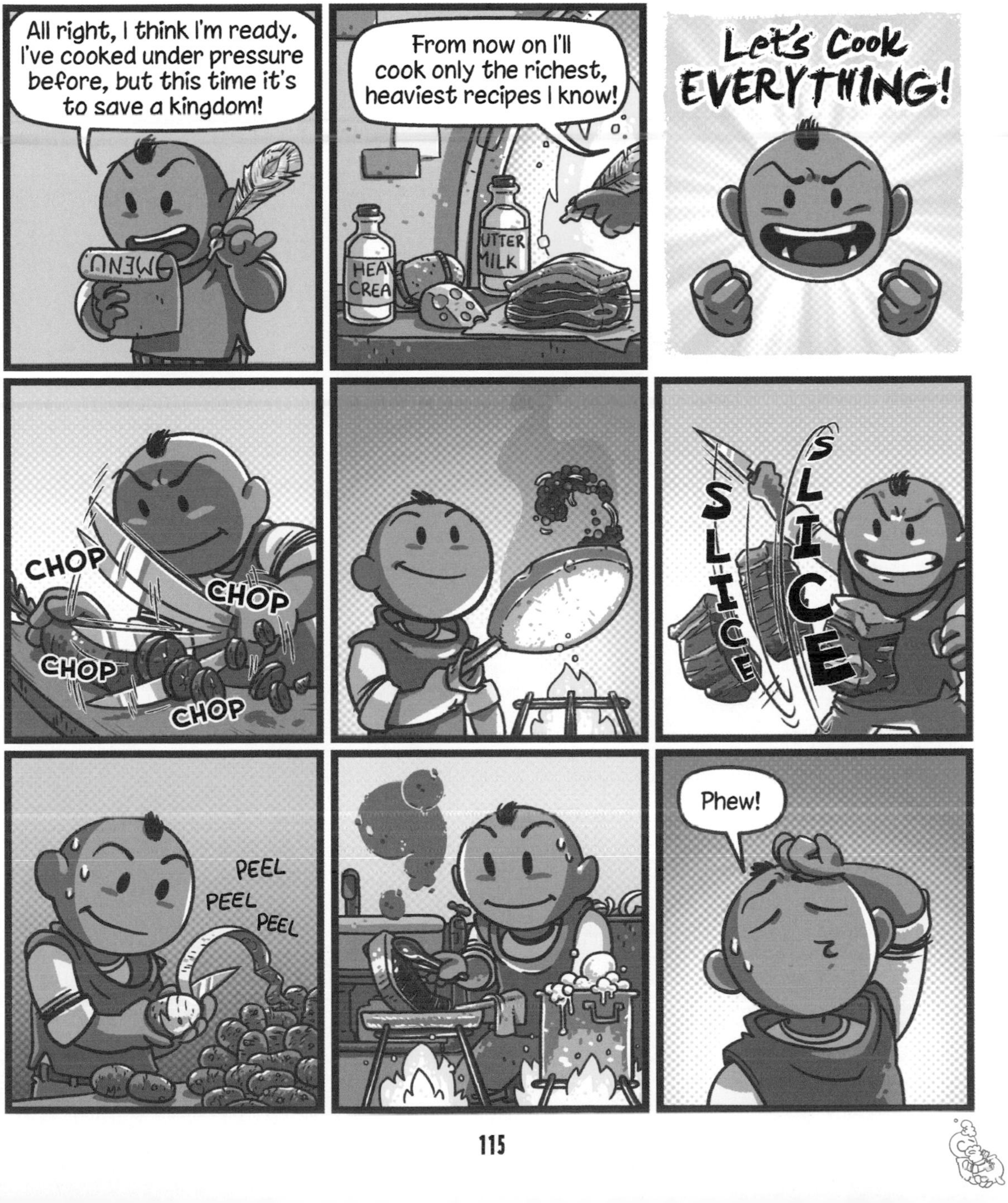
All right, I think I'm ready. I've cooked under pressure before, but this time it's to save a kingdom!
MENU
From now on I'll cook only the richest, heaviest recipes I know!
HEA CREA
UTTER MILK
Let's Cook EVERYTHING!
CHOP
CHOP
CHOP
CHOP
SLICE
SLICE
PEEL
PEEL
PEEL
Phew!

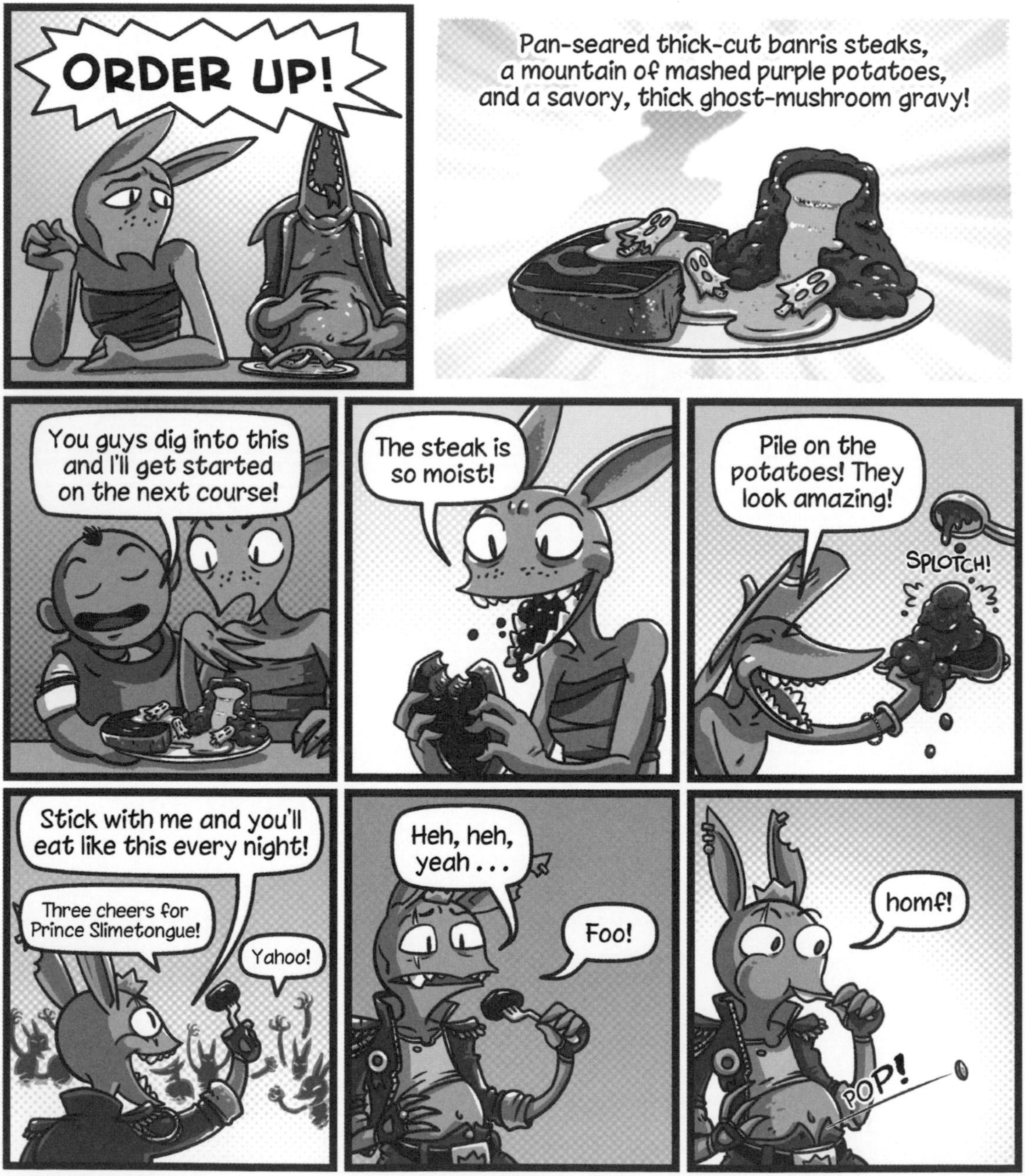
ORDER UP!
Pan-seared thick-cut banris steaks, a mountain of mashed purple potatoes, and a savory, thick ghost-mushroom gravy!
You guys dig into this and I'll get started on the next course!
The steak is so moist!
Pile on the potatoes! They look amazing!
SPLOTCH!
Stick with me and you'll eat like this every night!
Three cheers for Prince Slimetongue!
Yahoo!
Heh, heh, yeah . . .
Foo!
homf!
POP!

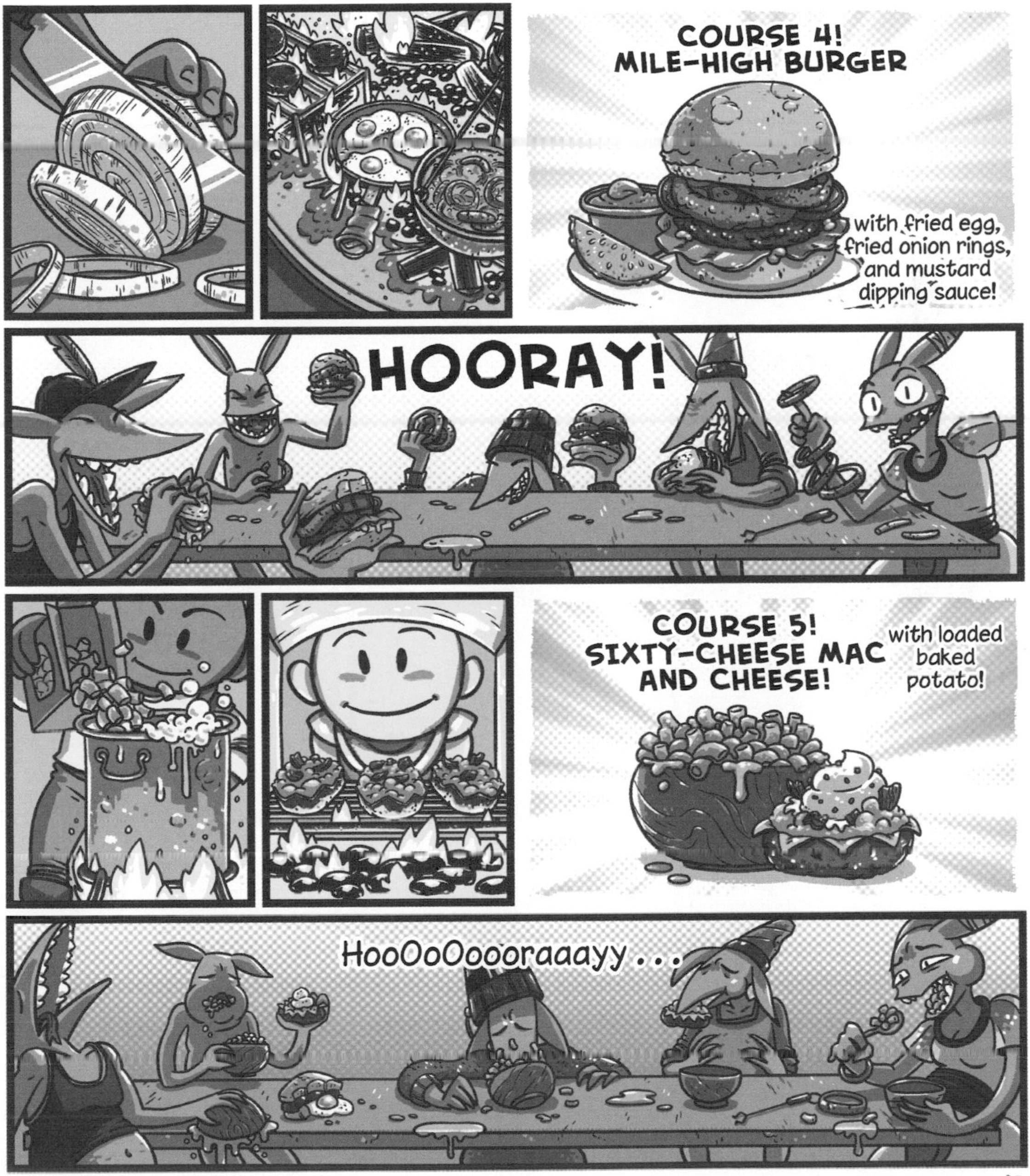
COURSE 4!
MILE-HIGH BURGER
with fried egg, fried onion rings, and mustard dipping sauce!
HOORAY!
COURSE 5!
SIXTY-CHEESE MAC AND CHEESE!
with loaded baked potato!
HooOoOoooraaayy . . .

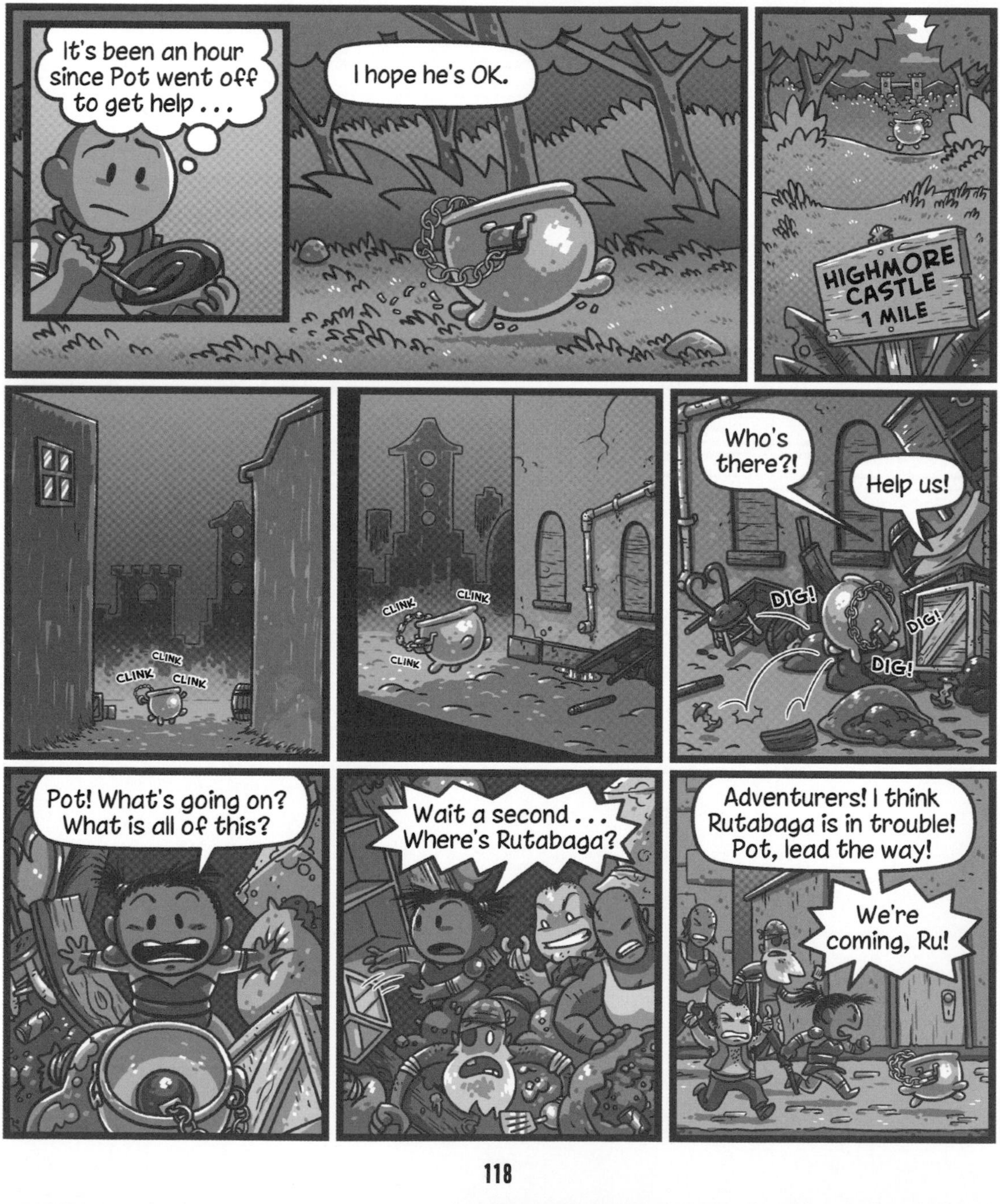
It's been an hour since Pot went off to get help . . .
I hope he's OK.
HIGHMORE CASTLE 1 MILE
CLINK
CLINK
CLINK
CLINK
CLINK
CLINK
Who's there?!
Help us!
DIG!
DIG!
DIG!
Pot! What's going on? What is all of this?
Wait a second . . . Where's Rutabaga?
Adventurers! I think Rutabaga is in trouble! Pot, lead the way!
We're coming, Ru!

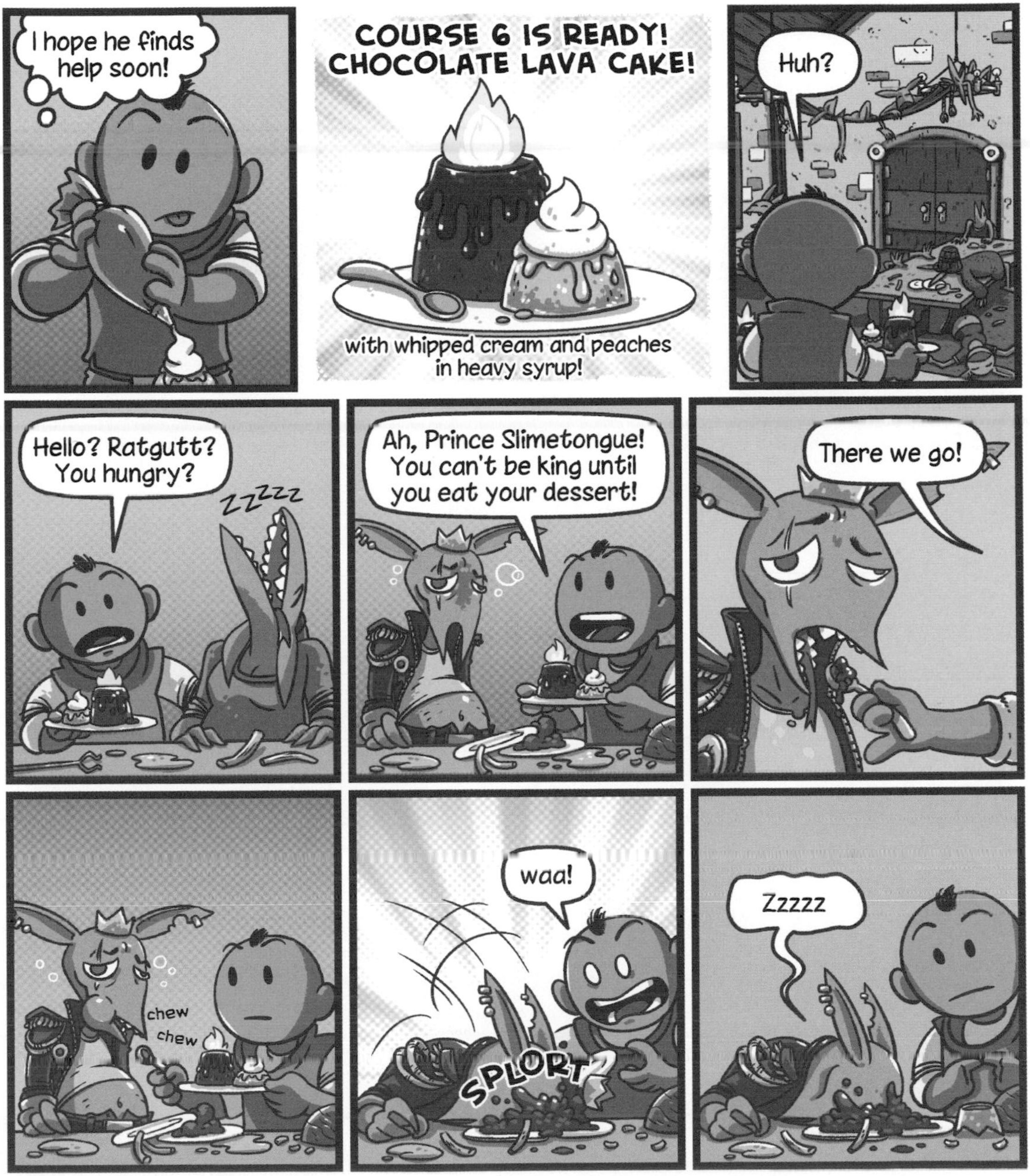

I hope he finds help soon!
COURSE 6 IS READY! CHOCOLATE LAVA CAKE!
with whipped cream and peaches in heavy syrup!
Huh?
Hello? Ratgutt? You hungry?
ZZZZZ
Ah, Prince Slimetongue! You can't be king until you eat your dessert!
There we go!
chew
chew
waa!
SPLORT
Zzzzz

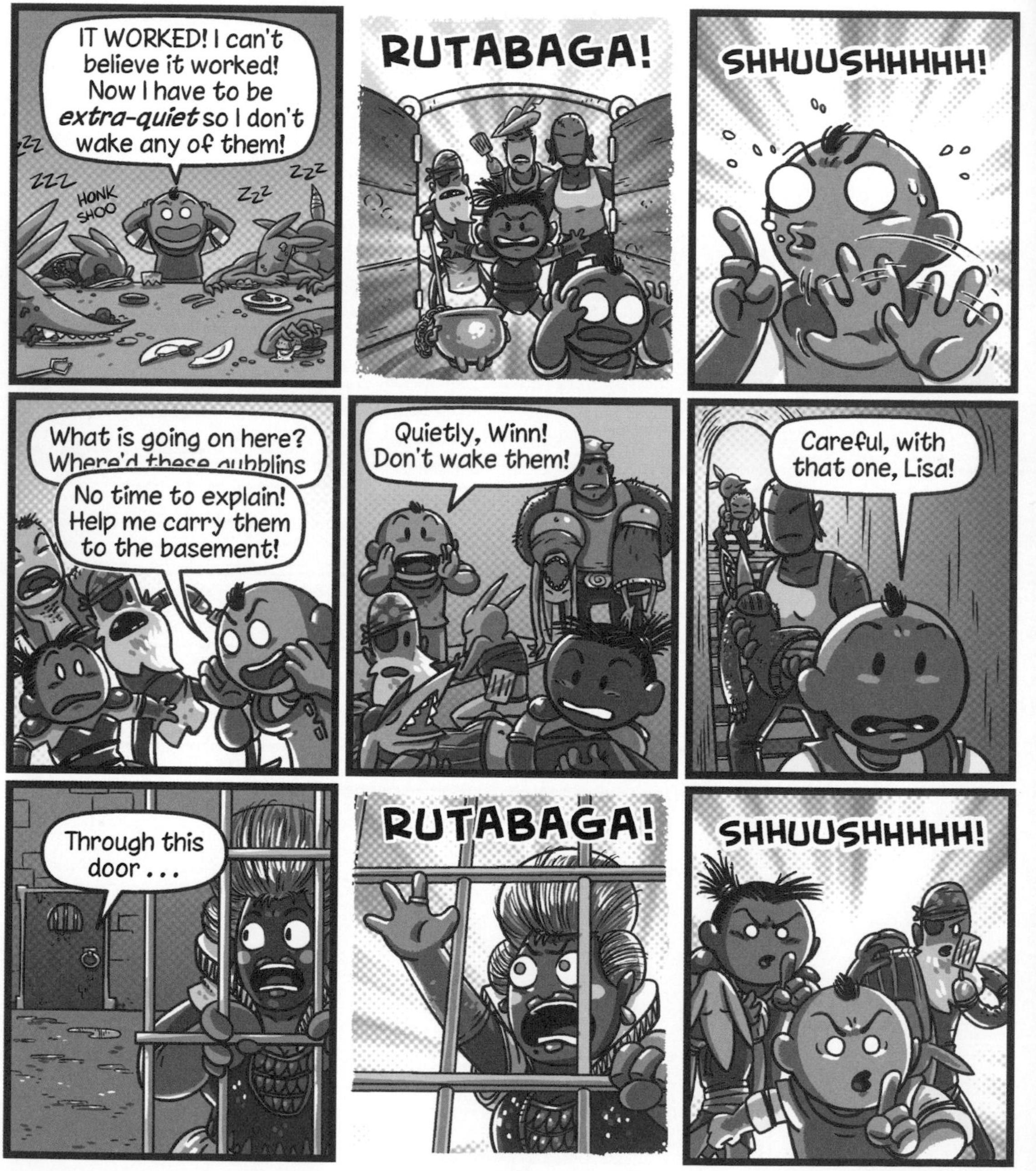
IT WORKED! I can't believe it worked! Now I have to be *extra-quiet* so I don't wake any of them!
ZZZ
HONK SHOO
ZZZ
ZZZ
RUTABAGA!
SHHUUSHHHHH!
What is going on here? Where'd these gubblins
No time to explain! Help me carry them to the basement!
Quietly, Winn! Don't wake them!
Careful, with that one, Lisa!
Through this door . . .
RUTABAGA!
SHHUUSHHHHH!

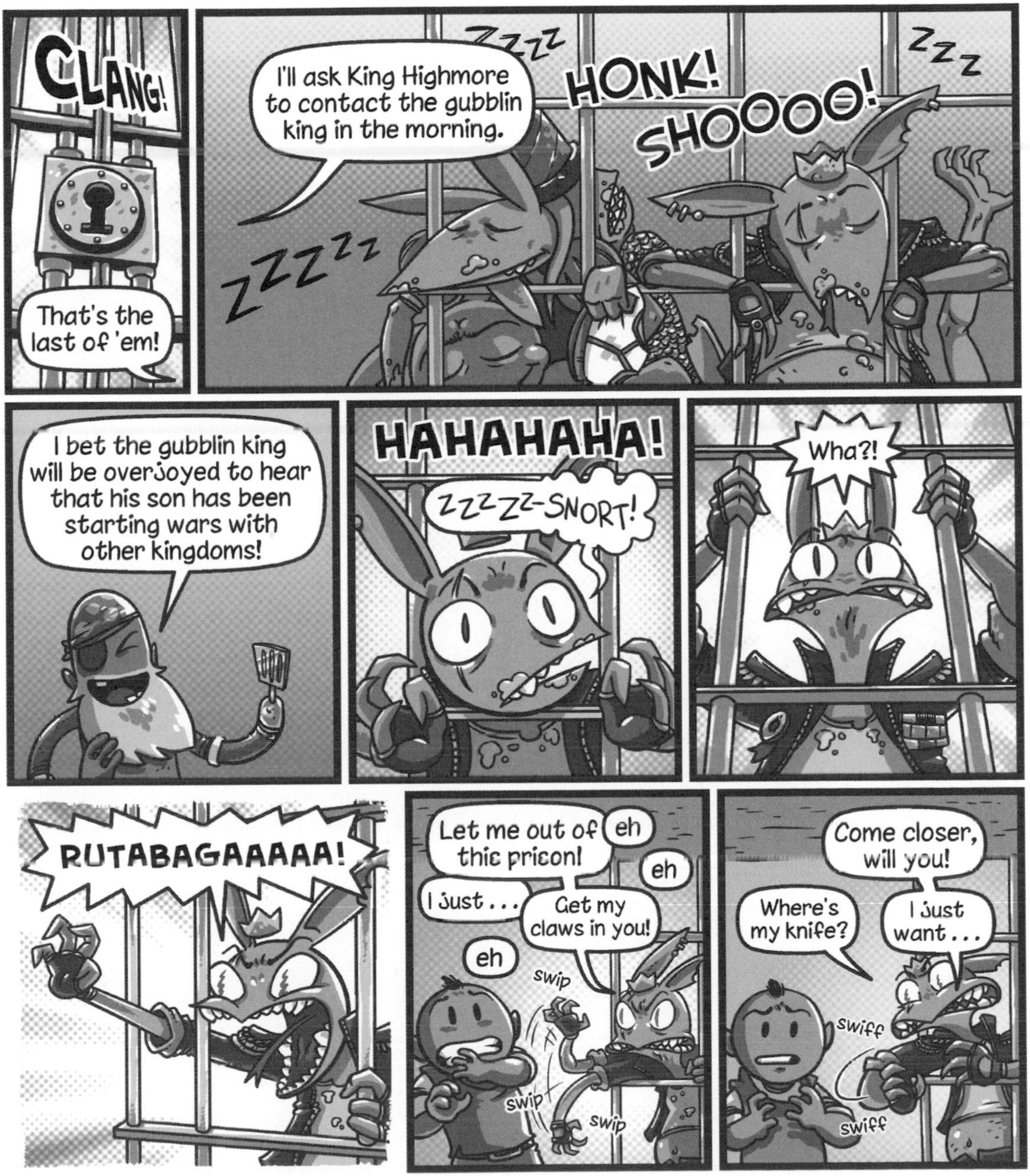
CLANG!
That's the last of 'em!
I'll ask King Highmore to contact the gubblin king in the morning.
ZZZZ
HONK!
SHOOOO!
ZZZ
ZZZZZZ
I bet the gubblin king will be overjoyed to hear that his son has been starting wars with other kingdoms!
HAHAHAHA!
ZZZZZ-SNORT!
Wha?!
RUTABAGAAAAA!
Let me out of thic pricon!
eh
eh
I just . . .
Get my claws in you!
eh
swip
swip
swip
Come closer, will you!
Where's my knife?
I just want . . .
swiff
swiff

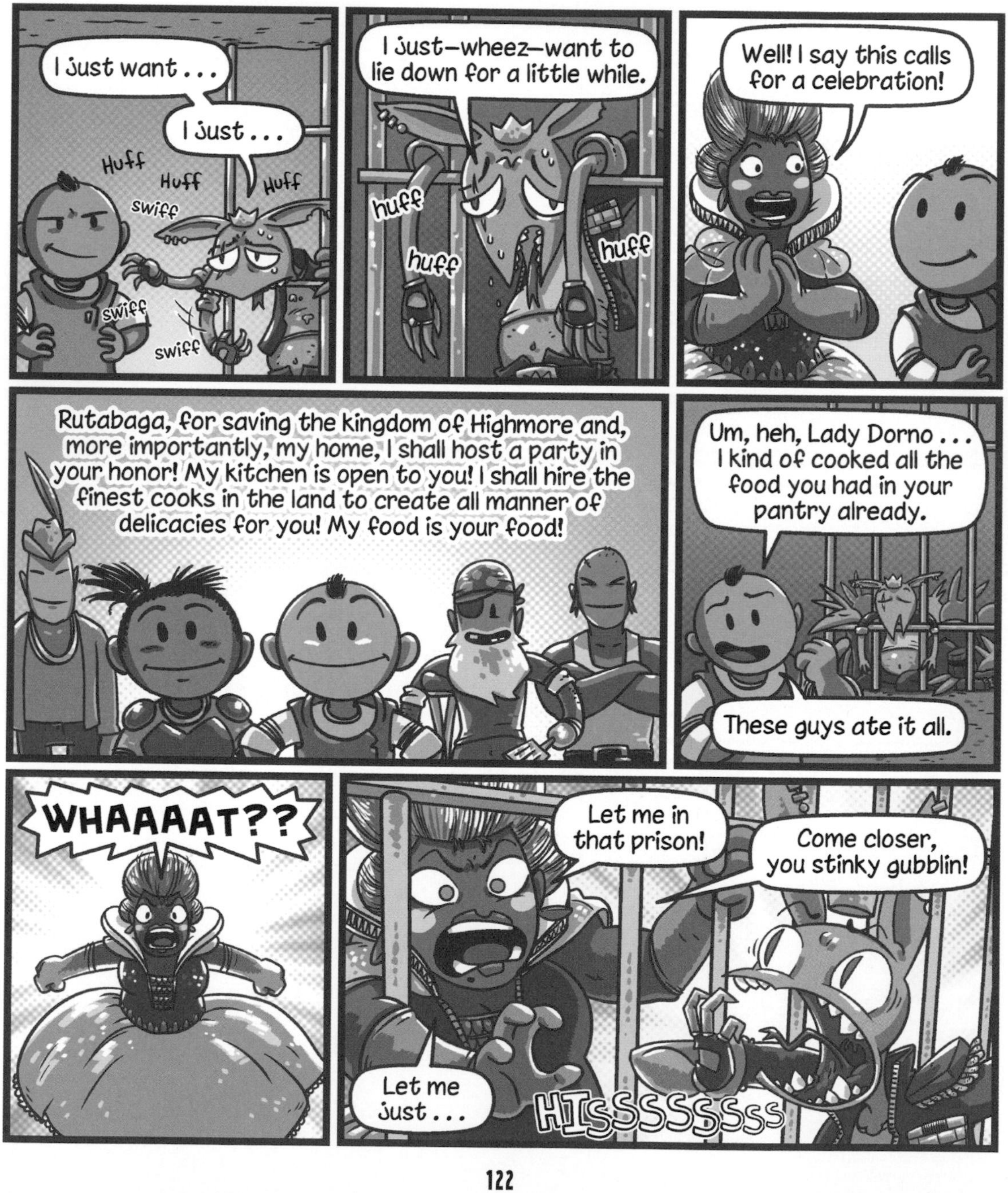
I just want . . .
I just . . .
Huff
Huff
Huff
swiff
swiff
swiff
I just—wheez—want to lie down for a little while.
huff
huff
huff
Well! I say this calls for a celebration!
Rutabaga, for saving the kingdom of Highmore and, more importantly, my home, I shall host a party in your honor! My kitchen is open to you! I shall hire the finest cooks in the land to create all manner of delicacies for you! My food is your food!
Um, heh, Lady Dorno . . . I kind of cooked all the food you had in your pantry already.
These guys ate it all.
WHAAAAT??
Let me in that prison!
Come closer, you stinky gubblin!
Let me just . . .
HISSSSSSSSS

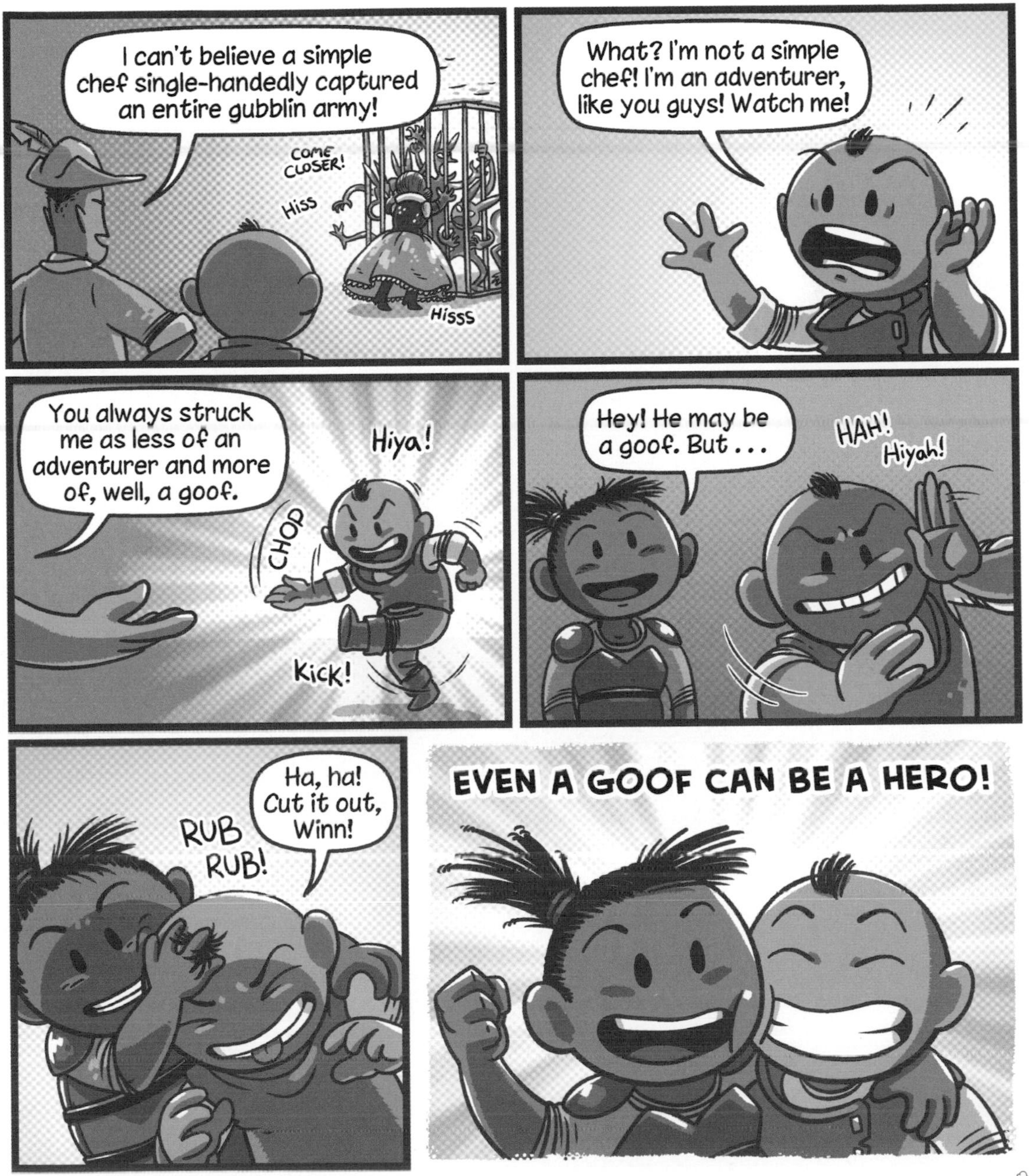
I can't believe a simple chef single-handedly captured an entire gubblin army!
COME CLOSER!
HISS
HISSS
What? I'm not a simple chef! I'm an adventurer, like you guys! Watch me!
You always struck me as less of an adventurer and more of, well, a goof.
Hiya!
CHOP
KICK!
Hey! He may be a goof. But . . .
HAH!
Hiyah!
RUB RUB!
Ha, ha! Cut it out, Winn!
EVEN A GOOF CAN BE A HERO!

End of Chapter Four

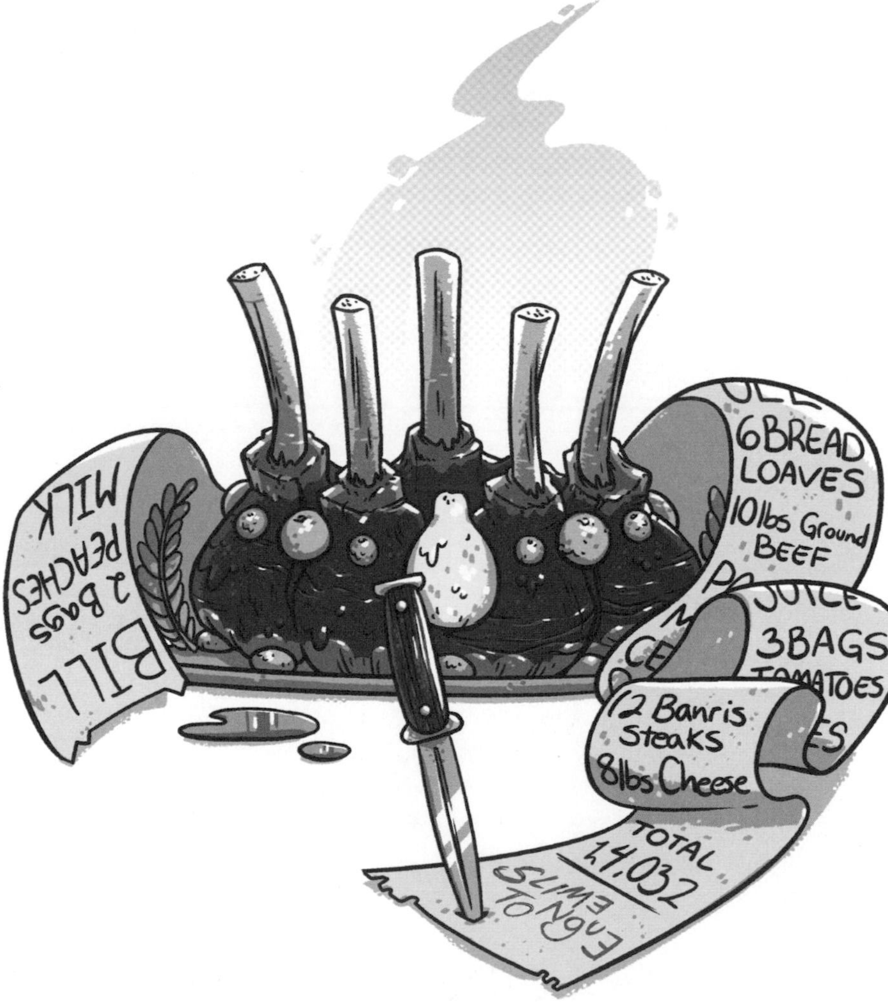

6 BREAD LOAVES
10lbs Ground BEEF
3 BAGS
12 Banris Steaks
8lbs Cheese
TOTAL
14,032
BILL
2 Bags PEACHES
MILK

POPPING CHOCOLATE SPIDERS!

INGREDIENTS

- chocolate melts
- seedless grapes
- plastic sandwich bags
- chocolate sprinkles
- parchment or waxed paper

Wash and FULLY DRY the grapes! Even a tiny drop of water will ruin the chocolate! Let the grapes come to room temperature.

 GET AN ADULT'S HELP WHEN HEATING ANYTHING IN THE MICROWAVE OR ON THE STOVE!

Melt chocolate according to package instructions.

Place a few heaping spoonfuls of chocolate into the corner of a plastic sandwich bag.

Snip off the tip of the plastic bag with a pair of scissors.

Place the parchment paper on a baking pan. With a steady hand, draw spider legs on the paper by squeezing the bag VERY GENTLY and piping the chocolate onto the paper. This will take some practice! Use the design on the right if you need help!

spider design!

After you've drawn a few spider legs, drop a grape in the leftover chocolate and coat it. Use a spoon to swoosh it around in the chocolate and place it on the back end of the spider legs, where the X is in the diagram. Repeat until all the spiders have butts.

Sprinkle chocolate sprinkles all over the spider butts while they're still wet!

Refrigerate for a few minutes and then carefully remove them from the parchment paper!

You have made

POPPING CHOCOLATE SPIDERS!

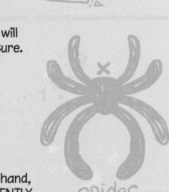

GUBBLIN SNOT!

INGREDIENTS

- 1 ripe kiwi
- 3/4 cup lemon-lime soda
- 3/4 cup pineapple juice
- 1/4 cup coconut milk

Chop the kiwi in half and squeeze the insides of one of the halves into a tall glass. Be careful not to let any of the kiwi skin slip into the drink!

Take a fork and smash the kiwi by pressing it into the sides of the glass. Really smoosh it up! Get it good and goopy!

Pour the pineapple juice and the lemon-lime soda into the glass.

Slowly pour the coconut milk over the mixture.

Take the fork and give it a few quick stirs so the soda fizzes up and makes the coconut milk a little frothy. Don't let it foam up too much and spill!

Finally, drink up!

You have made
GUBBLIN SNOT!

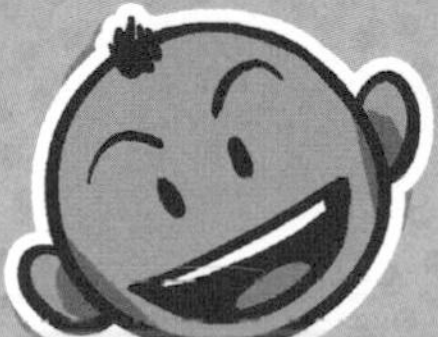

NO-BAKE "POISONED" COOKIES!

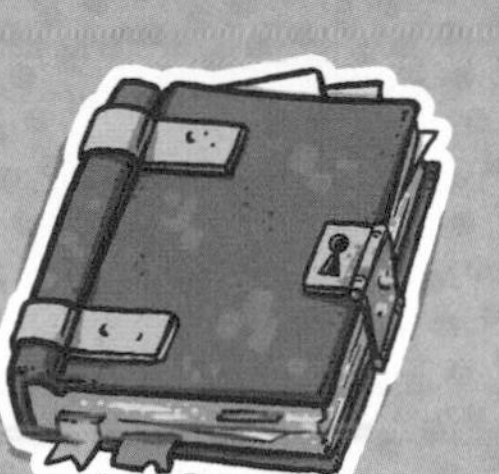

INGREDIENTS

- 1 3/4 cups granulated sugar
- 1/2 cup milk
- 8 tablespoons butter, cut into large pieces
- 3 tablespoons unsweetened cocoa powder
- 1 teaspoon vanilla extract
- 1/4 teaspoon salt
- 3 cups quick cooking oats
- green jelly beans
- parchment or waxed paper

Add sugar, milk, butter, and cocoa powder to a medium saucepan.

STOP! GET AN ADULT'S HELP WHEN HEATING ANYTHING IN THE MICROWAVE OR ON THE STOVE!

Over medium-high heat, bring to a boil for about three minutes.

Remove from heat and stir in vanilla, salt, and oats.

With a spoon, drop large scoops of the mixture onto parchment paper.

Press them flat with the spoon so they look like little pancakes.

Select a few cookies and place a green jelly bean in the center.

This cookie is now "POISONED"!

Fold each cookie in half, making sure the jelly beans are hidden!

Place the cookies on the counter or in the fridge until firm.

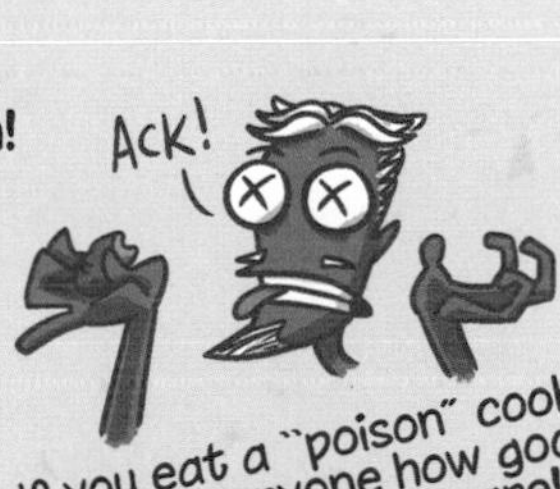
ACK!

If you eat a "poison" cookie, show everyone how good of an actor you are! Really ham it up!

You have made

NO-BAKE "POISONED" COOKIES!

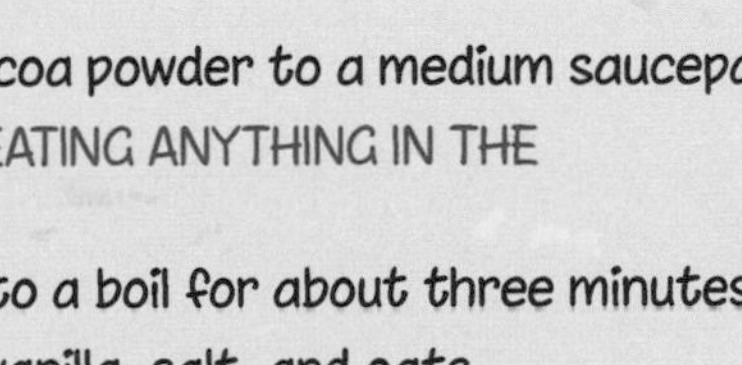

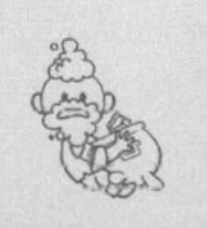

ERIC COLOSSAL is an artist living and working in Upstate New York. His great loves are his cats, Juju and Bear; his lovely girlfriend, Jess; and eating. He is currently looking for a group of brave adventurers who will help him defeat whatever is making that horrible smell in the back of his fridge.